Pat Booth is the London-born bestselling author of such novels as *Palm Beach*, *The Sisters*, *Beverly Hills*, *Marry Me* and *Temptation*. She is also the author of three books on photography and is herself an accomplished photographer. She is married to Garth Wood, an Old Harrovian psychiatrist, and they live with their children Orlando and Camellia in homes in Palm Beach, London and New York.

This book is dedicated to
my husband, Garth, and
my son, Orlando, with all my love.

# *Sparklers*

## PAT BOOTH

**WARNER BOOKS**

A *Warner* Book

First published in Great Britain in 1983
by Futura Publications
Reprinted 1984, 1986, 1990
This edition published by Warner Books in 1992
Reprinted 1993, 1994, 1996, 1999, 2000

ISBN 0 7515 0465 3

Printed in England by Clays Ltd, St Ives plc

Warner Books
A Division of
Little, Brown and Company (UK)
Brettenham House
Lancaster Place
London WC2E 7EN

# Chapter 1

## I

*Saturday, 24th April, Gstaad.*

Like the biblical cloud, at first no bigger than a man's hand, the red speck grew and grew. On the sun-bathed balcony of Gstaad's smart Eagle Club nobody paid it any attention, for it was the magical hour of the cocktail. Blood-red against the white powder snow, the skier hurtled downwards like a flaming meteorite re-entering the earth's atmosphere, trailing its vapour cloud. One or two people on the sun deck had by now become aware of the intruder. The skier was far from any run and was making an alarmingly swift and steep descent. Skiing was not the preoccupation of the majority of the Eagle Club members, most of whom would take the ski lift back to the town after their lunch, but this was after all the Swiss Alps and they could recognize a good skier when they saw one in the same way that they could tell a man's class from forty feet. This skier was good – very good. Two hundred yards away now and the style had changed. The crouch of the downhill racer, legs apart for maximum stability at high speed, had replaced the graceful *wëdeln* of the earlier descent. It seemed that disaster was about to strike the crowded balcony as at this speed it appeared unlikely that the skier would be able to stop, and along the more exposed edges of the group several people attempted surreptitiously to take up more advantageous positions. The combined effect of several people changing their places, with not a little urgency, at the same time caused a small wave in the crowd and at least one dry martini was spilt. By now conversation was flagging and most people had turned to investigate the mysterious gate crasher. The man who had lost his martini

5

and the woman who had received it over her cream silk Dior shirt did not bother to suppress the wish that they might witness a nasty little accident. They were to be disappointed. At the very last minute, when all but congenital optimists feared the worst, the skier's body arched, the skis came together and over thirty yards was demonstrated one of the most daring and effective christie stops that any of that sophisticated audience could remember having seen.

For a split second, both hands on hips, the skier stared back at them through the smoked-black, plastic visor before sweeping off the red crash helmet. Blonde hair cascaded down and the girl shook her head from side to side laughing as she did so. Only those who had met Caroline Montgomery before had seen a girl as beautiful. Blue eyes, shining hair and perfectly proportioned features were not alone the foundation of her unique beauty. She had about her a vibrancy, a liveliness that seemed to give new meaning to what on others would have been described as merely conventional good looks. Her hair, teeth and skin gleamed and glinted and it took no doctor to diagnose a girl in the very peak of physical condition. The bronzed face showed traces of freckles around the upturned nose. She wore no make-up. And then there was her amazing body. From her neck to her bright red, plastic ski boots Caroline was encased in a pillar-box red, soft leather one-piece jump suit fitted tight against her skin. Seemingly endless strong legs met a small upturned bottom. Her back was long but her shoulders were not broad and it seemed to at least one connoisseur of female beauty that the design department in Heaven should have won some sort of prize for their brilliant achievement in reconciling the apparently conflicting requirements of extreme strength and consummate delicacy of form. Nowhere was this more noticeable than in the construction of her breasts. Caroline was hot and had undone the jump suit zip far enough to show the large, firm breasts pushing forwards. There was no white line to disturb the even sun tan and this hinted at the fact that they needed no unnatural support, and received none.

6

With difficulty the crowd regained its poise. Those who already knew Caroline were quick to mention the fact and bask in the momentary increase in popularity that this information seemed to bring.

'For Christ's sake, Egon, who on earth is that incredible bird?' asked a wiry, good-looking Greek with an impeccable English accent.

Egon Von Furstenberg, a tall, open-faced German aristocrat, smiled impishly. 'Caroline Montgomery of the American chemical family. She's the best skier in the States. But why do you ask? I thought you were only interested in English Dukes' daughters!'

'I think I've just been converted,' laughed Taki Theodaracopoulos.

Theodaracopoulos family ships were probably at that moment carrying Montgomery chemicals across the world's waterways. He should meet her. Taki was not only rich he was also a respected athlete, former Greek karate champion and a right-wing journalist whose articles frequently upset liberal *poseurs* in international high society.

'Come on – let's get on with the introductions,' said Taki. It was time to cut the cackle.

'No problem,' said Egon easily. 'That's her mother, Eleanor, sitting over there. She's a great friend. The bad news is they are both leaving for London in the morning.'

Caroline's athletic stride cut a swathe through the conquered crowd. Still smiling slightly at the extraordinary effect that she was having on this mixed bag of assorted continentals, she headed for her mother's table on the corner of the sun deck.

'Caroline, I have fallen in love with you all over again and I only met you yesterday,' shouted a small, neat Frenchman. Caroline recognized Hubert Michel Pelissier who had been best man at the Princess Caroline/Junot wedding. She threw back her head and gave a throaty laugh.

'You said that to three separate girls in the Green-Go last night,' said Caroline mock-accusingly over her shoulder as she continued on.

7

Eleanor Montgomery watched her daughter's approach with a mixture of pride and alarm. It was she who had suggested that Caroline come with her on this short European tour. Caroline's fascination with skiing was now an obsession. She seemed to have no time for, and little interest in, anything else, including men. Eleanor had felt she was missing out, although paradoxically she admired and respected the single-minded determination that had turned her daughter into a potential world champion skier. She was pleased that she had succeeded in prising her away from the training programme in Aspen.

It had not been easy, and it was only when she suggested that a long weekend in Gstaad should follow a couple of days of meetings with Zurich gnomes on the Bahnhofstrasse that she had sold the idea to Caroline. Now Eleanor saw that her plan was working if anything rather too well. Eleanor was an American through and through but her childhood had been spent in European schools. After the years in England she had been to finishing school, in both Paris and Switzerland. She knew the terrific impact that Caroline's beauty, freshness, enthusiasm and skill would have on these jaded Europeans who required periodic doses of these commodities to alleviate the air of semi-permanent boredom and languor that they outwardly affected. Eleanor knew, too, that the moral systems of these men left much to be desired. Mostly they were underworked and over-rich. They did not however do nothing. What they did, and did with considerable skill, was 'play'. They played backgammon, played at sports, played the stock market, played with drugs, and, thought Eleanor, with a frisson of alarm, played with the affections of young, enthusiastic American girls like Caroline. Life was for them a vast nursery filled with toys to be taken up and thrown down. Ferraris and Bagliettos, Augustas and Lear jets had replaced woolly bears in their endless childhoods. They never knew where they were going, so interested were they in where they had come from. When they married it was for dynastic reasons or because they had found somebody who reminded them of their mothers.

Girls were an essential ingredient, part of the backdrop to their lives, and they had elevated to a fine art the skills of seduction. Eleanor was experienced enough to see through the surface charm and sophistication to the little child inside the man. Would Caroline be able to do the same?

'I think this balcony is more dangerous than that mountain,' said Caroline with a huge smile as she sank down into a chair at Eleanor's table. Eleanor was thinking exactly the same thing and she was pleased that Caroline showed such insight.

'How are the muscles?' Caroline had been complaining that she had been stiffening up since leaving the rigorous exercise programme in Aspen.

Now she ran both hands over her exquisite quadriceps and said, 'The powder is really great up there – it's the best work-out you can get.' Early that morning a private helicopter had ferried her to the top of one of the most inaccessible peaks, allowing her to create her own descent, one that could test her skills to the limit.

She slipped her hand into Eleanor's. 'Oh mother, this is really great. I'm so glad you persuaded me to come.'

'No mountains in London I'm afraid,' said Eleanor. 'We'll get a masseur in each day – and I've arranged for you to swim at the RAC. It's a beautiful pool.' She gazed fondly at her daughter. God, she'd played a blinder. How could she have produced such a perfect specimen? It did not, however, require a Professor of Comparative Anatomy to puzzle out how Eleanor's superior genes had constructed Caroline. There was the same magnificent figure, long thighs and tight upturned bottom, proud, thrusting breasts. Eleanor's nose was straighter and longer than Caroline's, but essentially the features were the same. Only the hair was of a different colour. Old Bill Montgomery had not been left out in the genetic mix, Eleanor's hair being a light brown in contrast to her daughter's honey blonde.

Egon Von Furstenberg and Taki Theodaracopoulos made their way towards the table.

'I think I may have to be in London this week,' said

Taki. He made a mental note to telex the Tregunter Road house, and have it opened up for him.

'Eleanor's incredibly sharp. She runs the whole of Montgomery Chemical single handed now the old boy is dead,' said Egon, by way of gentle warning to his friend. 'Oh, and for God's sake don't ask Caroline to go skiing this afternoon – you'd be in hospital for two months and miss the South of France.'

Eleanor watched the two men approach. She had known Egon for many years and she liked him a lot.

'This is obviously the throbbing heart of Gstaad this morning,' he said charmingly. 'May we join you, Eleanor? I am afraid I have brought a rather disreputable Greek who appears to have fallen in love with your daughter,' he joked as he introduced Taki.

'Like Lloyd George, I knew your father,' smiled Eleanor taking Taki's hand. She well remembered the boisterous and talented Greek shipowner and noted that he had passed on his good looks to his son. Out of the corner of her eye she also noticed that a slightly pinker shade had crept into Caroline's cheeks at Egon's conversational sally.

They sat drinking dry martinis in the April sun and a table was booked for lunch. Eleanor was intrigued to know how Caroline would stand up to the sophisticated badinage to which she would now be subjected. It was a battlefield for which her American upbringing and the slopes of Aspen had scarcely equipped her.

Hubert Michel Pelissier was not to be excluded from such a gathering as it was clear that the Eagle Club could provide no more amusing table this luncheon. He swooped down on them and managed to secure the place on the other side of Caroline from Taki.

Caroline turned to the Frenchman. 'And what do you do besides proposing to girls, Hubert? Do you play any games?'

Taki was in there, quick as a flash. 'The only thing Hubert plays is a rather expensive gramophone.'

Hubert joined in the general laughter, not at all unhappy to be so described. 'My God, do people still talk about gramophones in Europe?' wondered Caroline. Later, as Taki offered to fly Caroline down to Bruen Abbey, his country estate, during her stay in England, Hubert had his revenge.

'Beware of Greeks bearing gifts,' he said, a sentiment with which Eleanor heartily concurred as she watched Taki lay serious siege to her daughter. Professionally she noticed that he had abandoned the jokey façade in favour of the intellectual approach and was now holding forth with some erudition on the advantages to America and the rest of the world of the new right-wing Wayne administration.

'Of course,' said Taki, staring deep into Caroline's eyes, 'there's bound to be a complete revision of foreign policy in favour of South Africa. All those blacks had better watch out!'

'I totally disagree,' said Caroline. He was not going to get away with this. The Montgomery family had never been far from the seat of power in America since the phenomenal success of their business had propelled them into the highest ranks of the plutocracy. Politics vied with skiing as most favoured topic of conversation at Montgomery dinner tables and from an early age Caroline had been keenly interested. On this particular point and at this specific time she was more than usually well informed. Charles Cabot Lodge had been made Secretary of State by President Wayne, his nomination recently overwhelmingly confirmed by the Senate, and this distinguished, debonair former Boston lawyer, member of one of the oldest families in America, was hopelessly in love with her mother, Eleanor. 'Uncle Charles,' generally considered the most eligible bachelor in the land, spent many weekends at the vast Aspen chalet or the house in the Hamptons and Caroline's relationship with him was extremely close. He considered her, rightly, his strongest ally in his battle to persuade Eleanor to marry him, an ambition for which he would gladly have sacrificed his political career. Only a few days before, Cabot Lodge had been saying how vitally important it was that the new government should not lose Africa to the Russians and Chinese and that one of their first jobs should be to reassure people that there would be no major foreign policy re-think in this area. Over lunch they had been discussing the best method of achieving this and Eleanor had suggested that the Secretary of State announce a Pan-African tour to demonstrate the administration's good intentions. The Secretary had joked that this was Eleanor's cunning method of getting him out of her hair, but Caroline knew that as a result of the conversation he had commissioned a position paper to be drawn up by 'Foggy Bottom' setting out the pros and cons of such a mission. This was inside information of the very highest sensitivity and Caroline was far too well trained to part with it in this situation. However, she would remind these dazzling Europeans with whom they were dealing.

She appealed across the table to Eleanor who, she had noted, had been following her conversation. 'I can't see Uncle Charles alienating black Africa by climbing into bed with the South Africans can you mother?' It was a statement rather than a question.

'No way,' said Eleanor. 'Rather the opposite,' she added.

Taki pondered the advisability of taking on this formidable duo and decided that it was time for a lower profile. He could well imagine the identity of 'Uncle Charles' and he knew he was outgunned. As a professional journalist Taki knew that one piece of inside information in politics was worth a hundred bits of 'informed' speculation on the part of those pundits who cultivated their reputation for 'brilliance' and erudition. He admired and respected Eleanor and Caroline for being in a position to possess it. A lesser man might have been irritated by Caroline's outspoken disagreement. Taki liked her more because of it.

'Still "Joy through Strength" and the "Horst Wessel" song, eh Taki?' joked Hubert, still reckoning he was owed one for the gramophone crack.

Taki laughed. 'Hubert has heard of Africa, but he doesn't know where it is because he hasn't been there.'

'*Au contraire*,' protested Hubert, feigning hurt feelings.

'I stayed with Talitha in Marrakech once. Rather too many flies although the food was distinctly distinguished.'

'Next time you go, you must get Egon to design you a sweet little safari suit,' replied Taki, anxious that Egon, whose friends always joked about his job as a top designer of men's clothes, should not be left out of the repartee.

Caroline was having fun. She was used to the company of serious people and, moreover, people who were serious about skiing rather than conversation. She revelled in the frothy lightness of the talk. She was no expert in the conversational thrust and counter-thrust but she did not mind that in the least. Her self-confidence, built on the very solid foundations of her amazing athletic success, was inviolate. The others sensed this and loved her for it.

Eleanor was thrilled that her daughter was coping so well. The three young men were eating out of her hand, captivated by her open enthusiasm and stunning good looks. They were drawn too, thought Eleanor, to the fundamental inaccessibility of Caroline, knowing that she would soon return to her first and only love, the mountains of America, leaving them behind to their boats and aeroplanes, forgotten and unmissed. She remembered a remark of Bill's, 'There is nothing more relaxing than the self-confidence of others, nothing more tedious than neurosis and self-doubt.' How proud Bill had always been of his beautiful daughter, how thrilled he would have been to see her now – at the peak of her powers as a woman, as an athlete.

Eleanor was always thinking of Bill despite the fact that he had been dead now for four years. She smiled wryly to herself as she remembered the attitude of her family when she had told them she would marry him. Shocked incredulity had been replaced by wounded soul searching as her parents asked themselves continually where they had gone wrong. 'Devil' Lawrence, her roistering father, had taken it very badly indeed. He had a long list of potentially eligible husbands for Eleanor, drawn exclusively from the sons of the friends with whom he hunted, fished, rode and drank. Every candidate was rich and well born, smooth and ineffectual – some were already alcoholics, few deigned to work. 'Devil' Lawrence, so called because of his saturnine appearance and foul temper, had frequently cast his eye over these young men, estimating their suitability as husband for his spirited daughter. He had noted their courage on the hunting field, the state of their family's financial fortunes, the way they held their drink, the quality of their tailors. No clear-cut front runner was ever selected because the truth of the matter was that Jack Lawrence was a little in love with Eleanor himself and at the end of the day could not bear to lose her to any man. For Eleanor was just about the only person who could control him. Unlike her timid and brow-beaten mother Eleanor would stand up to him and was not afraid to stand eyeball to eyeball with her bullying father, matching insult for insult until he would admit defeat and suddenly, laughing, pick her up in his huge arms and carry her around the room on his shoulders saying, 'At least I'm stronger than you', as Eleanor would shout to be set down. Perhaps Jack Lawrence felt that if Eleanor married one of the insipid sons of his aristocratic drinking partners he would remain basically unrivalled in her affections.

On hearing that she would marry Bill Montgomery this scenario was drastically revised. Bill Montgomery was not a member of the Knickerbocker, the Racquet Club or the Metropolitan. He did not even come from New England or Virginia. Born the son of a Texan drilling rig engineer, he had paid his own way through the University of Texas and had walked away from Austin with one of the best degrees in chemical engineering that the science faculty had ever awarded. Refusing offers of a fellowship and a sheltered and secure life among the 'groves of academe' he had rented a small garage outside Houston and set out to discover ways of manufacturing and processing chemicals that were more efficient than those of DuPont. He had succeeded brilliantly and by the time he had met and fallen in love with Eleanor, at a sailing regatta at Cape Cod, Montgomery Chemical was one of the largest five hundred companies in America, and his reputation as a resourceful innovator and tough businessman had filtered through to the rarefied social atmosphere that surrounded the Lawrences. In anybody's language Bill Montgomery was a rough diamond. His Texan drawl, scuffed boots, and abrasive manner made him a colourful and at once rather formidable figure. When Bill had met her father for the first time Eleanor had been struck by their fundamental similarities rather than their outwardly obvious differences. Both were men used to having their own way, despisers of hypocrisy, blunt talkers, men of action rather than contemplation. The meeting had not been a success.

'So you want to marry my daughter,' Lawrence had said in his most imperious, grandiloquent manner. 'She is used to a way of life rather different to the one that I imagine you lead.'

Bill had looked him in the eye and replied, 'Yup, the way I see it I just about arrived in the nick of time.'

God, she had loved him in those days and later it had changed, but had grown stronger and better. They had never been out of love, never been unfaithful, their lives full of action and excitement as the company had gone from strength to strength. They had become rich and had enjoyed together the benefits of that enormous wealth. And then as a kind of crowning glory had come Caroline. They had both wanted a girl, to the surprise of everyone, and had never been disappointed. From the earliest moments Caroline had been fascinated by skiing and Bill had indulged her passion to the full, buying up half a mountain in Aspen and building the rambling, comfortable chalet in which they spent so much of their time. They had everything and it looked as if they would have even more. There had been no warning signs of Bill's heart attack, no pain, no shortness of breath. One minute he had been talking, laughing with a business associate, the next lying dead on the carpet of his office. Tears filled Eleanor's eyes as she heard a distant voice.

'A penny for your thoughts,' said Egon.

'Oh, I was far away,' said Eleanor.

Caroline leant across the table and touched her mother's hand tenderly. 'I bet I know what you were thinking,' she said kindly. She knew so well that melancholy, distant look that always meant that Eleanor was thinking of her father. Caroline, too, missed him dreadfully; wished so much that he could know of her success; give him the present of seeing the results of his early encouragement and support; discuss with him the difficult career decisions that she had always to make. She looked lovingly at her mother. As far as she was able Eleanor had taken on Bill Montgomery's mantle. Such was the closeness of her parents' relationship that they had grown to be like each other. Eleanor had become imbued with Bill's common sense, his ability to see to the very heart of the matter, his simple Texan beliefs in hard work, fair dealing. She and Caroline had his religion as well and that helped to keep him close to them. There were no secrets between Eleanor and Caroline. They worked as a team. They did not always agree but they discussed everything and their relationship was completely free from the small-minded bickering that characterized so many mother/daughter relationships.

Eleanor squeezed Caroline's hand in gratitude for her sensitivity. 'Well darling,' she said out loud, 'what do you think of Europe's gilded youth?'

'Terrific,' said Caroline with a laugh, 'if you keep off American politics. But I'd better reserve judgement until I've seen the British contingent.'

'More of the same,' joked Eleanor to howls of protest from Frenchman, Greek and German.

'Don't forget we're going to Annabel's tomorrow night to that party of Mark Birley's,' said Caroline to Eleanor.

Eleanor was pleased that Caroline seemed to be looking forward to this. 'You'll love Annabel's. I reckon it's still just about the best night club in the world.'

'I remember Daddy telling me about it,' said Caroline. 'He said the thing to eat is something called Haddock Monte Carlo which is some sort of a fish with a poached egg on top.'

'My God, what a memory,' said Eleanor, touched by Caroline's gentle intimation that she had been in tune with her mother's earlier thoughts. 'Even in those days Bill always used to say he had to telephone the bank to find out if he could afford to go there. It's lucky we're invited tomorrow!'

'I'm sure we would all be happy to chip in if you and Caroline are ever short of the price of a meal,' interposed Egon amid general hilarity. The idea of Bill Montgomery having to telephone the bank for any other reason than to instruct, or possibly to chastise, was indeed as funny as Eleanor had intended it to be.

'Well, there's no time like the present,' said Eleanor with a twinkle in her eye. 'We really should get the check.'

The party broke up with much exchanging of telephone numbers. Caroline was closely questioned as to her future movements, but the news was not encouraging. She was going back to Aspen after the few days in London and would have time for nothing but training.

'I hope the English don't bore you to death,' said Hubert.

'Watch out for Pigott Brown,' advised Egon.

'If you can get away, remember Bruen,' said Taki.

The question then turned to how they should all get down the mountain. At this point a tall, arrogant German who, Caroline had noticed, had been staring fixedly at their table throughout luncheon seized his chance. He swept up to Caroline, bowing low. 'It is indeed an honour,' he said pompously, 'for us to have you as our guest today. Your skill on skis is well known to me and I much enjoyed your earlier descent. My name is Peter of Bavaria and I would be more than happy to show you a particularly interesting way of getting back to Gstaad.'

Egon smiled inwardly. Peter of Bavaria was a well-known bore who fancied himself as a skier and took himself very seriously indeed. There were few members of the Eagle Club who were not snobs, but all agreed that this man went too far.

'You would be well advised to take Peter up on his offer,' said Egon wickedly. 'Taki has pulled a muscle in his leg, I never ski after lunch and poor Hubert never skis at all.'

Taki immediately caught Egon's purpose and added

slyly. 'Yes, you are very lucky, Caroline. Peter is a brilliant skier. He will not hold you up at all.'

Hubert was less diplomatic. 'How clever,' he said. 'By far the best way to spend twenty minutes with Peter. No need for conversation.'

Caroline needed no persuading. She hadn't taken at all to the German, who she could have sworn had actually clicked his heels together as he introduced himself. But if he could ski she was prepared to forgive him anything.

They walked out into the late April sunshine, Peter of Bavaria a stiff marionette beside the graceful Caroline. Slowly she applied the ski wax to the underside of the racing skis. She checked the bindings before clipping them round the red boots and then spent two minutes bending and straightening herself to relax the quadriceps and hamstrings. Now she twisted her shoulders from side to side, at the same time arching and then bending her back. The after-lunch audience, their minds pleasantly hazy, sipped at their cognacs and enjoyed the calisthenics. Caroline's muscles rippled visibly beneath the tight red leather. Hubert thought of ripe luscious tropical fruit and half hoped that the red skin of the jump suit would burst asunder revealing that magnificent body to an appreciative world.

'Follow me,' said Peter with authority.

Caroline pushed down hard on the ski sticks and moved towards the start of the downhill run with a skating motion. She stood for a moment outlined against the skyline before suddenly dipping down out of sight of the Eagle Club. This first part of the descent was steep and veteran skiers approached it with caution, traversing the decline from side to side. Caroline did no such thing. She went at it vertically, ski sticks tucked up beneath her arms. Twice she was airborne as her high ground speed increased her forward momentum, reducing contact with the snow. At the bottom of this incline was a tight right-hand bend. Caroline made the turn with no great difficulty. This was great. She was skiing well and she knew it. The wind howled against the visor and plucked at her clothes. With this form she would be unbeatable this winter. Last year they had called her the Golden Girl, next year she was determined to become a world-beater. Her desire was nothing less than to be skiing champion of the world and she approached that goal with an obsessional determination. She swung right and left into a tricky chicane.

Could she do it? What about the Russians and the fantastic Czech Jana Soltysova? And what of the jealousy of Anne Carpenter? Once again Caroline was in the air. She leant forward, stabilizing herself before hitting the snow, her supple legs bending to absorb the shock. Exhilaration coursed through her – the exquisite physical sensations that always accompanied a flat-out downhill descent. She imagined the howl of the crowd, the unforgiving stop watch, the beady eyes of the competitors as she sped down the mountain. As if pursued by the devil himself Caroline increased her speed, tightening up on the corners, taking the straighter line. Suddenly she remembered that she had a companion, or rather had had one. A quick glance over her shoulder showed that Peter of Bavaria was rather longer on self-confidence than on skiing ability. He was hopelessly behind. Caroline gave him a cheery wave. She would find her own way down the mountain.

'Time for exercise,' thought Caroline, veering off the beaten track and into the virgin powder. This was the stuff for building strength, strength that she would badly need if she was to be the best woman skier in the world. She remembered the rigorous exercises supervised by Ingemar, her trainer, in the gymnasium of the Aspen house, exercises designed to strengthen the muscles of her legs and stomach until they could withstand the fantastic strain of world class competition. She would lie on her back lifting weights with her legs, sometimes squatting for hours on her haunches as if voluntarily undergoing some cunning oriental torture. Then when she was almost in tears with the pain and stiffness there would be the jogging machine, the lengths of the heated pool before the luxury of the shower and the Swedish massage. This, however, was the real thing. Caroline lent into every turn, punishing herself, extracting the maximum resistance from the thick snow as her muscles screamed their defiance. She felt the sweat run down between her breasts, sensed the wet patches beneath her arms and in her crotch. God she wanted it, almost more than life itself. This was for her the only true existence. The lunch party seemed already a million years away – the faces of its cheerful participants but a dim memory. Tall trees guarded her descent now, acting as ghostly spectators to her agony and ecstasy. Otherwise Caroline was alone on the mountain, its silence and inscrutability enveloping her. She loved it like this. Loved the loneliness, the sense of suspended existence, a background against which she could unleash the full force of her unbending will, the will that would carry her to the triumphs for which all of her life so far had been but a preparation.

Far above her Peter of Bavaria, his considerable Germanic pride compromised and trying desperately to catch up with the speeding Caroline, sustained an unpleasant compound fracture to his right femur that was to keep him in plaster and away from the cruel jokes of the amused Eagle Club members for many months.


*Saturday, 24th April, Umpala.*
The ancient ceiling fan struggled to circulate the moist, heavy air, but it was fighting a losing battle. Indeed the almost non-existent draught that it produced was scarcely sufficient to deter the landing of several lazy flies on the exposed skin surfaces of the sweating men who sat around the big boardroom table. Their physical discomfort did little to lessen the discouraging news that they were digesting. The President of the Republic of Umpala, short and squat, over-fed and under-employed, headed the table, but it was to his Finance Minister that everyone was paying close attention.

Sir Seretse Mwamba, Minister for Financial Affairs in the tiny Central African country, was an impressive figure. Natural authority beamed from him like radio waves in

contrast to the noticeable lack of charisma that characterized his superior, the President. Tall, thin and immaculately dressed in a brilliant white linen safari suit he seemed
immune from the heat that so obviously discomforted his
cabinet colleagues. In fact Mwamba did more to cool the
room than the antiquated fan. His jet black face, rather
aquiline nose and thin lips hinted at racial origins from
further north on the African continent. Somalia perhaps,
or Ethiopia. The accent, however, was pure English and of
the sort for which some *nouveau riche* social climber would
have cheerfully traded his golf club subscription and his
cabin cruiser. In the clipped sentences so much admired
by his tutors at the London School of Economics, Seretse
Mwamba was dissecting the problem with deft, surgical
precision.

'And so gentlemen we should face the fact that the
diamond mine of Umpala must close within days in the
absence of new finance.'

The President flicked impatiently at an incoming fly,
missing it by the distance by which he usually missed the
point. 'But surely,' he interrupted with some irritation,
'funds can be found from somewhere. Why don't we
borrow the money? Everybody else does.'

The supplies of the Lafite-Rothschild, to which the
President was partial, had never dried up. Nor for that
matter had the succession of fair-skinned, loose-moraled
girls from the 'madame' in Paris. Why should mining
machinery, engineers and geologists, petrol and generators
be any different?

With infinite patience and not a little condescension Sir
Seretse continued. 'All efforts to tap the international
capital markets have failed. Unfortunately we are considered a poor risk. The fact is the bankers are correct in
their assessment of our creditworthiness, at least on the
information that we have put before them.'

Nobody really wanted to hear that.

'What about the diamonds? We have nearly $300 million
stockpiled. Why don't we sell them to provide working
capital for the mine? Or we could use them as collateral for

a loan.' The speaker sat on Mwamba's right and the tone of his questions implied hostility.

Mwamba turned to look at his neighbour. He did nothing to conceal his scorn. He inhaled gently. From the edge of the Christian Dior Eau Sauvage force-field that enveloped him came the pungent, acrid smell of body odour.

'Because, if you *remember*' – the implication was clear that memory was not his adversary's strongest suit – 'the whole purpose of our actions since the initial discovery of the diamonds seven years ago has been to keep the size and even the existence of our mine a closely guarded secret. To unload large quantities of fine gem stones onto the market at this stage would immediately alert De Beers to the fact that we had substantial diamond reserves. Similarly the advertising of $300 million of diamonds as collateral in a public loan agreement would hardly go unnoticed. De Beers are not fools, you know.'

The tone hinted that many people sitting not a million miles from Sir Seretse would indubitably qualify for that description.

His opponent, however, was not to be so lightly dismissed. 'But don't you Englishmen have a phrase that goes something like "Needs must when the Devil drives"? Perhaps our position now is so precarious that we should bale out of our original scheme while the going is good, as it were. I never much cared for it in the first place.'

This was rude and the rudeness was intentional. By referring to Sir Seretse as an Englishman, a status that his appearance and his passport, if not his clothes and his accent, belied, the speaker was playing shrewdly to the gallery.

The President of Umpala, a figurehead and a fool, had always resented Sir Seretse. His English affectations provided good ammunition for the occasional jibe such as this.

'The Minister for Internal Affairs has a point, Seretse. The original plan, while elegant in its conception, can hardly work if there are no funds to continue mining the diamonds.' The translation of this was: 'The days of dreamers and tight-rope artists are at an end. The time has come for the honest realists to step in and restore the situation.'

Mwamba allowed a long silence to develop.

Swish . . . Swish . . . Swish . . .

With a languid movement he reached out for the glass of lager. Luckily he had acquired a taste for luke-warm beer from his days in London. He sipped at the fizzy, amber liquid. 'One doesn't,' he said at last, 'construct careful plans over a seven-year period only to abandon them at the first sign of trouble. It is not my style, although I am not at all surprised to hear that it is yours,' – and he turned to his neighbour as he said this – 'to capitulate at the first whiff of grape-shot.' The word 'whiff' was a phonetic masterpiece, a work of art.

He continued. 'Surely you will remember that it was generally agreed when first we learned of the vastness of our diamond discovery that we should exploit it fully and in a way that would best serve the interests of our beloved country and those of the whole continent of Africa. We had the option then of going immediately to De Beers, to the white man's cartel, and letting them have the concession to mine and market the stones. It was the obvious thing to do – what all dumb spades do – sell ourselves short to the whites.'

Seretse's voice was hard now – the bantering tone of the earlier remarks a distant memory. Both the President and the Interior Minister were beginning to regret the attitude they had taken. The use of the emotive word 'spades' implied that Mwamba was thoroughly irritated. His neighbouring colleague felt a large bead of moisture run down the centre of his chest, leaving a wet track mark on the sea-island cotton shirt.

'But we believed that we were made of sterner stuff. We decided to play the capitalists at their own game. We would mine our own stones, tell no one of the mine's existence and stockpile the gems. As of now we have $300 million worth in our vaults and the price has gone up every year. Within three or four years we should possess $1 billion in the finest quality diamonds. *That* is the moment for us to reveal ourselves to De Beers. *Then* we will be in a position to threaten their monopoly. They would have to act to preserve it at all costs. We can name our price and they will have to pay it. We would be acting from a position of tremendous strength. It would be a brilliant financial coup at the expense of De Beers and the South Africans, a tonic for our race, a testimony to our intelligence and business acumen.'

Seretse was the born-again preacher, his cabinet colleagues in the role of castigated congregation. Nobody, the President included, dared to attempt to still the flow of words.

'So, for the moment we have no more money. But we must *not* give up our pride, snatch defeat from the jaws of victory, and go cap in hand to the De Beers' mandarins at Kimberley. That is the losers' way.'

He stared defiantly around the table. Would all who wished to be considered losers make themselves known immediately? Nobody said a word.

Encouraged by the lack of any sign of opposition Seretse continued in a less hectoring vein. 'If we try to sell our diamonds now, before our stockpile is big enough to threaten the monopoly, they will eat us for breakfast. They can refuse to buy the stones leaving us with a considerable problem of how to sell them ourselves, and they can keep their own price up by witholding the sales of stones from their reserves. They will know our secret and mobilize the whole power of their organization against us. They have the means and the skill to outmanoeuvre us. It is vital that we stick to our original plan. If we go off half-cock we will lose everything when we are so near to our objective.'

It was stirring stuff, but the fundamental question remained unanswered, had scarcely even been addressed. Everyone at the table knew that, not least Mwamba himself. Without the cash to keep the mine open it was all blowing in the wind.

*Saturday, 24th April, London.*

Miles Parmere was awake, but he wished he wasn't. Waking in this state was no new thing, but it didn't get any easier. He kept his eyes closed. There were three reasons for this. Firstly, he knew from experience that light would not be a help. Secondly, there was always an outside chance that he might get back to sleep, unlikely in his experience. The third reason had to do with the identity, and more important the appearance, of the 'lady' who was undoubtedly sharing his bed. The week before he had received an unpleasant additional insult to his similarly debilitated state on finding himself in close proximity to, and presumably having shared various intimacies with, a person Miles and his friends could only describe as a 'dog'. He had vowed then to be more discerning in future, but alcohol was not a great sharpener of the critical senses where feminine beauty was concerned. Miles was, however, no chauvinist and he wondered, as far as his addled brain would allow him to, if his bed companion might not be experiencing exactly the same thoughts.

A more discerning view of the situation could have been provided by Miles' housekeeper who had looked in on the sleeping couple a little earlier before starting to prepare the huge breakfast that she regarded as first aid in such circumstances. Like many middle-aged servants who looked after fast-living bachelors, Mrs Baker was a little in love with Miles. She could have reassured the sleeping woman that Miles Parmere was a very fine specimen indeed. His long, aristocratic face was without any trace of the weak chin and mouth so characteristic of the species. It was a tough face, but not cruel, and she knew that his eyes sparkled and laughed when he smiled. They could flash dangerously too, when he was angry. The permanently sun-tanned body, hard and fit, and the short, beautifully cut hair all added to the impression of one of the gentleman athletes of the 1920s or 1930s – an amateur who would always have time 'to finish the game and beat the Spaniards too' in the fashion of Sir Francis Drake. As to his companion, Mrs Baker was content merely to think 'better than most' as she gave her full attention to the bacon and eggs, coffee and Alka Seltzer that would be needed shortly.

Hand grenades continued to explode in Miles' head whenever he moved it and so he stayed still. The taste in his mouth was appalling and he began to compile a list of similes to compare it with. A camel's arm-pit? An athlete's foot? He gave up. This was getting him nowhere. What he needed was water – water to drink, water to be showered with, water to enter his brain to drown the insects that seemed to be crawling around in there. But it was a catch-22, a double bind, a no-win situation, for to get water he would have to open his eyes and, worse, he would have to move. A wave of nausea broke coldly over him. There were so many answers, but they were all in the bathroom. Kaolin and morphine for the sickness, aspirin for the headache, water for the dehydration. He had to get across the room first. Of course he should have remembered to drink lots of water before going to bed as everybody always said. However, if you were sober enough to remember that you were not drunk enough to need it.

At this point Miles felt a hand on his tummy. Slowly it strayed down and the unknown and unseen girl began gently to play with him. The delicious feeling of arousal spread through him, giving welcome relief from his dreadful hangover. He was glad that he had kept his eyes closed and determined to do so for a bit longer. If there was to be disappointment, it could wait. He felt the girl change position – sensed her head dipping below the sheets. Things were getting better. Her mouth enclosed him, sending the familiar warm thrill of anticipation through his body. She was in no hurry.

Miles opened his eyes. The girl was mostly invisible but her bottom and legs lay on the pillow beside Miles' head. They looked good. Absentmindedly Miles leant out to touch her. Her bottom pushed back against his hand as he massaged her wetness. A muffled moan came from below as his hand slipped inside her. The head began to move with a new urgency and Miles felt the occasional sharpness as her teeth caught him. The hangover was forgotten now and he pushed himself against her. With the thumb of his right hand he rubbed the girl's anus before slipping it inside. Now he had her completely, and she had him. Again he wondered what she looked like as he felt the orgasm rise within him. He would soon find out. Sensing the situation, the girl slowed her movement. Miles gripped her more tightly, his hand deep within her as his climax exploded in wave after delicious wave. They lay exhausted for a few minutes, their positions unchanged, before Miles threw back the sheets.

'Good morning,' she said brightly. 'I bet you've got a hangover.'

'It's improved dramatically,' said Miles, impressed by her coolness and noting the pert mouth and twinkling eyes. 'I'm afraid my memory of last night's events is a little hazy,' he added weakly.

'I picked you up in Tokyo Joe's,' said the girl simply. 'You were pretty out of it – so I drove you back here.'

Miles was encouraged by this. The girl was clearly totally in charge of herself and, what's more, the intractable problem of how she could be got out of the flat was solved by the fact that she had her car outside. Paradoxically, he was not quite sure that he wanted her to leave immediately. It was the ones who stuck like glue and needed dynamite to dislodge that were the bane of his life. Perhaps he should take her to lunch at Mark's Club and pass her on to Rupert. The girl, however, had other ideas.

'Good God, it's nine o'clock and I've got a photographic session at ten,' she said. 'Look, I hope you won't think me rude if I rush off.'

Miles attempted to protest.

She was dressed in a flash – an ability honed to perfection at countless fashion shows. 'Call me at the Model Agency sometime,' she said cheerfully over her shoulder as she left the bedroom. 'I enjoyed it.'

For some minutes Miles lay still. Tokyo Joe's? No recollection at all. And if the girl had driven him home, then where on earth was the Porsche? He attempted to reconstruct the evening. Drinks with Willie Piggot Brown off Eaton Square. Always a dangerous start. Dinner at Langan's with 'Bear' Dene and a couple of fantastic-looking Brazilian girls who were supposed to expect 'presents'. That was where the rot had begun to set in, thought Miles. A great deal of champagne had been drunk. He remembered one of the Brazilians suggesting they go on to the Sombrero, an amusing gay bar and discothèque in Kensington High Street. Cheap red wine had replaced the Bollinger of Langan's Brasserie. There, to the delight of all, the Brazilian duo had revealed a little suspected interest in each other and had performed an erotic dance of considerable promise. The three men had agreed immediately that such an exhibition was more properly for private consumption and they had all returned to Willie's Belgravia house to enjoy the home entertainment while making serious inroads into a large bottle of thirty-year-old Armagnac.

From this point on Miles seemed to have lost the thread. The Brazilian girls had gone at each other like hammer and tongs and, through the mists, Miles picked up a few visual vignettes that even now had power to excite. Shy ventricles, illicit amulets of love, legs intertwined, endless tongues, musky scents, erotic noises. After that, total amnesia. How he had got to Tokyo Joe's and met that surprising model he would try to find out at lunch. Perhaps in exchange he could fill in a few gaps in Rupert Dene's evening.

Miles dragged himself out of bed at last, pulled on the rough white towelling dressing gown from the Georges Cinq in Paris, and went into the kitchen to face the rigours of Mrs Baker's mock disapproval.

There was only one place on a morning such as this and after picking up the matt black Targa Porsche from Belgravia, where he deduced it had been left, Miles headed for the RAC Club in Pall Mall.

'Good morning, m'lord,' said Anwar, the small Pakistani

Turkish bath attendant, in that impeccable English accent that only those of his race seemed able to master.

Throughout the morning Miles dragged himself back together. Hot room with the morning papers, steam, cold plunge – these last two repeated endlessly in sequence. Thirty lengths of the long marble pool, a distance of exactly half a mile. More heat and now, as the physical hangover lifted, time for a little contemplation. Miles stretched out on the cream deckchair and stared up at the ceiling. He let out a deep sigh that was not one of contentment. From experience he knew that this was when the metaphysical part of the hangover set in. Now he was filled with doubts and fears about his behaviour, his direction in life, his future. He couldn't go on like this. He was wasting it, throwing it all away and for nothing. Again he thought of the pointless evening, its immorality, its wanton hedonism, the physical damage that it and others like it had inflicted on his system. He did not admire his behaviour, did not like himself for having indulged in it. There had to be a better way, had once been one.

Not for the first time Miles surveyed his past, looking for clues, searching for the reasons for his spiritual decay. It had all started so well. His father, the sixth Lord Parmere, he remembered with great affection although he had died when Miles was only fourteen. Miles had wanted nothing more than to carry on the family military tradition, started when the founder of the title had served with such distinction as commander of a regiment in the Peninsular War. The family were always intensely proud of Arthur Wellesley's supposed remark about his subordinate: 'With Gerald Parmere at one's side, one could enter the very gates of hell unafraid.'

Miles had always lived up to his family's expectations after his father's death. At Harrow he had more than measured up to the 'giants of old' of the school song. Straight, brave and good-natured, he had impressed everybody he met. He was a superb athlete, too, and had played cricket for the school for three of his five years. He had decided against university much to the horror of his masters and despite the offer of places from Magdalene and Trinity, Cambridge, the latter his father's old college. He had been eager to get into the Army and had gone straight to Sandhurst and then into the second battalion of the Scots Guards, the finest battalion of the best regiment of the Queen's Foot Guards. Now Miles wondered vaguely if this had been his first mistake. He had preferred to be a man of action rather than of contemplation – perhaps that made him an anachronism in an age obsessed by qualifications and expertise.

He had been stationed in Kenya with the Scots Guards where he had learned to drink with some of the best friends he had ever made, but again his desire for action precipitated an unorthodox decision. Miles' family had not merely gone into the Army. When they got there they had fought and fought bravely for ideals, for God, for King and country. Miles had been brought up to believe in freedom, capitalism and the 'British way'. Such thinking was conditioned by his environment, but it was also deeply rooted in his genes. So he had volunteered for the crack Special Air Service Regiment founded in the North African deserts of the Second World War to operate secretly behind enemy lines. Since that time this secret and highly unorthodox organization had been involved in many clandestine operations when superb training, unorthodox approach and total ruthlessness had been required. At that time, in 1966, the war in Vietnam was hotting up. The 9th Marine Expeditionary Force, the first US combat unit to be sent to Indochina, had arrived the previous year and Lyndon Johnson was busy escalating the conflict and dispatching the Air Mobile Division to the fighting. For the Americans it was as important to win the war politically as it was to defeat the Viet Cong and the North Vietnamese Army on the ground, and they were keen that their allies should show support for the anti-Communist cause by sending their soldiers to participate in combat. The Australians had been involved since the early days when Kennedy had sent in the first American advisers, but the British, while happy to give verbal support to American aims, had stopped short of committing men to the fighting. The election in 1964 of the left-wing Wilson government had, on the surface, strengthened British resolve in that respect. However, too much strain could not be put on the Atlantic Alliance and so, secretly, the British had agreed to send a small token force of volunteers to show solidarity. This was exactly the type of mission for which the SAS existed and several of its officers were asked to volunteer. Miles had jumped at the chance to defend democracy and for two years had been attached as an adviser to a South Vietnamese Army Ranger Group.

In the steamy jungles of Vietnam Miles had confronted the realities of warfare and had not been found wanting. For days he would lead his patrol through the Communist-infested undergrowth, living off insects and roots, killing swiftly, often silently in the dead of night. Miles had loved this life, the cameraderie, the intense danger, the sense of purpose. He had become hard, determined, dangerous, at times more of an animal than a man, preferring the Italian diving knife with its rope-covered handle to the M16 rifle of standard issue. Miles thought now of the jungle fire-fights, the unseen enemy, the blood, the fear and the dying, the feeling of holding a knife at a man's throat, the throat of a man who had tried to kill you, had killed your friend.

During that period Miles had covered himself in glory. He could not be decorated for his heroism because of the secrecy surrounding his role. Instead he had been pro-moted. When he had returned from the jungle Miles Parmere was the youngest major in the British Army. He had learned his craft well, but in the peacetime army he had nowhere to practise it. After combat he found the boredom and pettiness of military life appalling and meaningless. After a few months he had resigned.

And yet here he was, a man who drank too much, his life dedicated to pleasure, sex, 'good times', mixing exclu-sively with men who shared these interests, sitting idly in the hot room at the RAC dreaming of a time when he had been made of sterner stuff.

Miles continued these reflections as he sat on the leather chesterfield of the upstairs room of Mark's Club where he was meeting Rupert Dene for lunch. The bellini and the morning's exertions were making him feel better. He ordered another of the delicious Venetian concoctions. Was there any better mixture than champagne and peach juice? He must discuss it with 'Bear', an *aficionado* of Buck's fizz, or what the Americans called a mimosa. Then the delicious guava juice at Harry's Bar ought really, he supposed, to be taken into consideration – while many of his City friends swore by black velvet, champagne and Guinness taken very cold from a half-pint silver tankard.

'Good morning, dear boy.' Rupert Dene would have been the first to admit that he was a relic from a bygone age, a laughing cavalier, a Restoration dandy, a Regency rake. His black, neatly cropped moustache also gave him a somewhat sinister air, that perhaps of a music hall villain or the d'Urberville that had seduced poor Tess.

Here was a man fighting single handed to maintain standards that had been dead long before he was born. Miles supposed there was a certain distinction in that. It was hard work, diligently pursued with considerable style and panache and at no small expense. It gave pleasure through the gossip columns to those who led a rather more humdrum existence and it undoubtedly offset to perfection the more pedestrian aspirations of an age that could easily have been said to have forgotten how to enjoy itself. Was anybody hurt by it? Probably not. The occasional trader found himself out of pocket from time to time, but this same shopkeeper would be the chief beneficiary of what was frequently conspicuous consumption in times of plenty. What about the girls whose affections were often 'trifled' with? On the whole, thought Miles, they gave as good as they got. Accustomed to life in the fast lane, they knew the score. Miles thought of one blonde aristocratic girl who had broken the heart of just about every *roué* in town. No, reflected Miles, the chief damage was to the pleasure-seeker himself and then only if, as in Miles' case, the life-style contravened conscience and decreased self-respect. Men such as Rupert and William Piggot Brown adopted an attitude of lofty scorn towards more 'worthy' members of society. They were above the rat race, far more concerned with spending money in an interesting way than in making it, living for the moment rather than for the future. Miles envied them their philosophy and their freedom from the guilt from which he suffered.

Perhaps detecting a hint of melancholy in his demeanour and seeing it as his bounden duty to abolish such treasonable feelings wherever they were to be found, Rupert summoned the waiter with a flourish. 'Now my child,' he intoned with affection. 'I shall create luncheon for us. This requires a little thought.'

He pored over the menu and the extensive wine list as if the secrets of life itself were contained therein. Perhaps for him they were, thought Miles. Certainly there could be few more important moments in Rupert's day than this. Miles thought about his own important moments. Most of them nowadays on the polo field, he supposed. For Miles Parmere was one of the most accomplished players in the land. With a handicap of nine he was as good if not better than most of the Argentinians and the last season had been spectacularly successful. He played for the Stowell Park team of his old army friend Sam Vestey and was largely responsible for their winning of the coveted Cowdray Cup, when they had beaten the Prince of Wales' team in the thrilling final. Polo took Miles all over the world, and that, together with his title, winning charm, bachelor status and classical English good looks, meant that he possessed a circle of friends that a social climber in any field would have envied.

Miles lived, ate, played and slept with the rich and famous. Villas at the Cap, chalets in Gstaad, Lear jets and Bahamanian islands were always at his disposal, but they were always provided by somebody else. The international rich regarded him as an expert in the art of enjoyment and his company was sought for the style that he could provide, the contacts that he could make. In this way Miles had set up many a business deal, but the payment had always been in kind; a holiday here, a private jet made available to him there. Miles lived like a rich man despite the fact that he was not one. This had always irritated him. He longed to have his own fortune, to be rich in his own right so that he could laugh in the faces of the peasants for whom he played so well the role of the court jester. For some time now he had been thinking about going into some business activity in which he could take advantage of his incredible connections. Banking perhaps. He smiled to himself at the effect it would have on poor Rupert if he were to reveal his ambitions over lunch.

'What price the Brazilian carnival last night?' said Rupert surrendering the wine list with some regret.

'I can't quite remember how it ended,' replied Miles.

'More with a bang than with a whimper,' sniggered Rupert. 'However you appeared not to appreciate it as you staggered out into the night muttering about "decadence"! How did your evening end up?'

'Rescued by a damsel from distress.'

'On the house was it?' queried Rupert. 'Just your luck. We had to bung those Brazilians a couple of "ponies" for their efforts.'

'Let's get stuck in – I could eat a horse,' said Miles.

'You'll have to get by on a dozen Whitstables and a cold lobster,' said Rupert as they made their way downstairs to the dining room. 'I thought we should probably struggle through a couple of bottles of the Puligny Montrachet, unless you feel strongly about it.'

Miles wondered if he would ever feel strongly about anything ever again. The hangover was making a comeback.

Food proved to go some way towards providing an answer and the white burgundy was terrific.

'We're relying on you for the South of France in June. What are your manoeuvres?' said Rupert. This was a serious question. Rupert was a great organization man. Every summer he would rent a grand house or a large boat, and occasionally both, fill them with rich, beautiful people and pay for them with a whip round. It was generally agreed that for the provision of this valuable service Rupert should be in for nothing.

'What's the scene?' asked Miles.

'I've got an option on the Aitken house at Cap Ferrat again – oh and I thought we might take that powerboat, *Tramontana*, for getting to St Tropez and places. Usual team. "Bugle", William, Bulmer, Flook probably. As usual the birds aren't exactly settled yet. Will you be with or without?'

Miles smiled. The turnover of women among the 'team' was high. Anything could, and most probably would, happen in the intervening few weeks with regard to existing relationships. To get around this Rupert usually arranged for a few unattached ladies of undoubted pulchritude and loose morals who would act as a sort of 'pool' from which unattached men could draw. The Brazilians, for example, might easily perform this function. Perhaps that pretty model too. Sometimes this was coals to Newcastle as the South of France in June frequently provided its own supply. However one had to be careful about these things.

'I think I'll take pot luck,' said Miles.

'More likely somebody else's bloody bird,' thought Rupert, not unkindly. He knew Miles' form.

'Well, anyway the house is huge so there's no problem if something turns up in the meantime,' said Rupert. 'What are your plans for May?'

May was a difficult month, neither one thing nor the other. Skiing was over and so was the Caribbean, more or less. Europe sun-wise hadn't really started.

'There might be a free-bee in Florida if you're interested,' said Miles. There's some banker down there whose opening a sort of a country club, near Palm Beach. They've got a polo ground and I've been asked to get together a European team to beat shit out of the natives. They want a few grand faces for the gossip columns, too. I suppose at a stretch we might pretend you're one of those.'

'Good old Miles,' thought Rupert. 'Could always be relied on to fill up a blank month.'

'Ages since I've visited the colonies,' said Rupert playing

down his interest. 'Still there should be some rather good deep-sea fishing. Let me know the details when you know more.'

'Are you going to Mark's dinner at Annabel's tonight?' said Miles.

'Yes. Should be fun. Best night club food in the world,' said Rupert.

They finished their lunch at a leisurely pace. Cockburns '60 and a fruity Stilton.

'I think a few hours' kip are in order,' said Miles. 'Shall we meet at Harry's Bar for a glass of champagne before dinner?'

Together they walked out into the afternoon sunshine.


## III


The Montgomerys' arrival at Claridges in London was not without ceremony. The blue and white Montgomery Chemicals Boeing 727 had been met on the tarmac by a silver grey Phantom 5 Rolls-Royce containing the managing director of the company's European operations. He had spent the half-hour journey to the hotel briefing Eleanor on recent developments on the UK industrial front. The hotel manager had been hovering in the lobby exuding pin-striped courtesy and bonhomie to usher them up to the huge suite, already bedecked with fruit, flowers, chocolates and champagne.

'May I say how pleased we are to see you again, madam. Please do not hesitate to let us know how we can be of help. There are two typists available on twenty-four-hour notice as your office requested and of course our telex is at your disposal.'

Eleanor signalled her gratitude. She was already on the telephone to New York although it was six o'clock in the morning there.

'The Swiss were very helpful. More than eager to lend

us the money. They agree that the loan will have to be in dollars in view of the size.'

'What do they think about the direction of interest rates?' asked the Montgomery financial director in New York.

'They're inclined to be bearish. Nicolas Baer even mentioned twenty-two per cent, though the Crédit Suisse people weren't quite so pessimistic.'

'Perhaps we should move at once,' said the voice from New York uncertainly.

'They have been wrong before,' Eleanor reminded him sharply. She did not rate this man's prognostic skills very highly, but he did what he was told and was a competent administrator. Eleanor preferred to hold the reins in her own capable hands as her husband had before her. She remembered Bill's dictum, 'Finance directors should have the mathematical ability of Einstein, the organizational skills of Napoleon and the morals of Christ, but the moment they have an original idea I fire them.' This financial director's job looked safe at least on the last count.

'I'll wait and see what the London lot have to say. I'm meeting Evelyn de Rothschild and Nick McAndrew tomorrow. See you next week,' said Eleanor as she put down the telephone.

'Have you decided what to do about borrowing that money?' asked Caroline.

She was lying sprawled on the oatmeal slubbed silk sofa. Faded levis clung to her legs and bottom, faithfully recording every voluptuous contour. One leg was pulled up beneath her, the trouser leg rucked up to reveal a rough, brown leather cowboy boot. A simple white tee-shirt did its best to restrain the braless nipples within. She looked, thought Eleanor, like a composite ad for milk, peaches and cream – hardly dressed in the height of fashion. That look was now hopelessly out of date, but Eleanor was resigned to the fact that she was unlikely to get Caroline to move with the times. Encouraged by her father, who believed that clothes should be functional, she had been dressing in jeans and Texan cowboy boots since the age of three. Three years ago Caroline's 'look' had been exactly 'right', although she herself had been the last to know or care.

'It's just a question of getting the timing right,' Eleanor explained. 'A wrong decision now could be expensive.' Montgomery Chemical was one of the most financially sound companies in the world, with a Triple A credit rating. The banks were queuing up to lend to them. Eleanor wanted a large five-year loan at a fixed interest rate to help finance the takeover of a small oil company. However, interest rates were high and opinion was evenly divided as to whether they would go up or down. If Montgomery was to borrow now and interest rates were to fall they would be locked into paying a high rate for five years. If the reverse happened and interest rates increased then Eleanor would look clever, having borrowed money relatively cheaply. This trip was primarily a fact-finding one, so that she could judge for herself, after consultations with the cagey Europeans, how much money was likely to cost in the near future.

'What would Daddy have done?' asked Caroline.

Eleanor smiled. This was a stock question which had a stock reply.

Together mother and daughter chorused, 'If we knew that we wouldn't have a problem.' Bill Montgomery had seldom been wrong even when Eleanor had disagreed with him violently.

Eleanor looked lovingly at Caroline. If all she could find wrong with her daughter was a deficiency in fashion consciousness then she indeed had reason to be grateful. Eleanor had but one worry. The other side of the coin to Caroline's enthusiasm and honesty was a certain naïvety, or at least a lack of worldly wisdom. It seemed that she was, for instance, largely unaware of, or perhaps disinterested in, the phenomenal effect that she could have on men. Eleanor did not herself care one jot if she left broken hearts and broken legs all over Europe, but what if one of these lounge lizards succeeded in awakening Caroline's interest? Once ignited that particular fire would burn with a frightening intensity.

'Have you got any plans for two o'clock, darling,' asked Eleanor, 'because I've got a man coming round from Cartier with some diamonds and I'd like your advice?' Eleanor said this rather sheepishly. She could imagine Caroline's reaction.

'*Diamonds?*' said Caroline, accentuating the word as if Eleanor had made an improper suggestion. She knew well Eleanor's weakness for beautiful jewellery and did not entirely approve. Mother and daughter played a game in which Eleanor would disapprove of her daughter's simplicity of approach to life while Caroline would retaliate by condemning her mother's sophistication. Each realized that the other had a point, but neither was going to admit it.

'Surely you're not going to buy more jewellery. You must have more than the Queen as it is,' she said with a smile.

'I was actually thinking of a little something for you.' This was cunning diplomacy. Now poor Caroline would have to turn down some bauble that might be worth $200,000. Caroline did not bat an eyelid.

'It's very sweet of you, Mummy, but I look terrible wearing diamonds. Don't you remember when I tried on yours last year? Even you had to admit it was a joke.'

Eleanor admitted defeat. 'Well, I suppose it is a bit of a weakness of mine – but do stay and meet Mr Brown. He's a wonderful man and the best salesman in Europe.'

At two o'clock sharp a knock at the door heralded the arrival of Mr Brown and the Cartier diamonds. Mr Brown, faultlessly dressed in the English style, carried a battered briefcase. Eleanor knew that it enclosed upwards of a million dollars worth of stones, but from its appearance and the casual manner in which it was held it could easily have contained Mr Brown's lunch. Perhaps, thought Eleanor, it encased both. This was the way with diamonds. Vast sums of money floating round the world with the minimum of pomp and ceremony. If the money had been in cash the whole floor would have been swarming with armed guards, a stark contrast to the diffident blue-suited assistant in his early twenties that was Mr Brown's only henchman. Diamond dealers thought nothing of sending the very largest parcels of 'goods' through the post and it was seldom that they went astray.

'Mr Brown, how lovely to see you as always,' said Eleanor. 'I don't think you have met Caroline.'

Eleanor was a very good customer indeed, a fact to which the courtesy and effusiveness of Mr Brown's welcome amply bore witness. She bought jewellery from two places only, from Mr Brown at Cartier in London and from Richard Winston, nephew of Harry Winston the legendary diamond dealer, in New York. These men were friends who liked her personally and valued her continuing custom. They would not lead her astray for short-term financial gain. For this alone it was worth paying the eighty to one hundred per cent mark-up over wholesale prices that these firms charged. Eleanor by now knew a very great deal about diamonds and their value, but she did not make the mistake of pretending that she was an expert or possessed a fraction of the skill that these men had by virtue of a lifetime's hard work dedicated to the recognition of beauty and quality. She knew, too, that if she wanted to dispose of or to change anything that she bought there would be no problem and many times in the past, when she tired of a particular piece of jewellery, Winston's or Cartier had offered her prices that had represented very considerable profits. There was another reason for dealing with these people. Throughout her life Eleanor had learned the wisdom of buying only the best, of dealing only with those of the very highest reputation. Winston's and Cartier bought only exceptional stones, employed the most brilliant cutters, such as Bill Meyer of Lazare Kaplan in New York, worked only with the world's finest designers. Cartier in particular produced settings of such consummate style and class that Eleanor was unfailingly able to recognize them wherever they appeared. The firm had done no wrong as far as she was concerned since the 1920s.

'You mentioned that on this occasion you were only interested in small-sized stones of the very highest quality and I have taken you at your word,' said Mr Brown, laying down the tattered case on the mahogany table.

Caroline peered inside expecting an Aladdin's cave of sparkling diamonds. Instead the briefcase seemed to contain little except many small packets all wrapped in identical blue-white paper held together with elastic bands. Each parcel bore incomprehensible hieroglyphics in black. There was also a folded copy of *The Times*.

Mr Brown rummaged through the tiny packages and selected six. He undid them carefully. Six shining diamonds nestled against the pale blue backgrounds. 'These are all finest white, or "D" as you'd say. Flawless except for this last one. They range from one to two carats.'

Caroline was intrigued. 'But they're so small,' she said.

'Small, and all but one absolutely perfect.' Mr Brown continued in the manner of a friendly schoolteacher addressing a more than usually clever pupil of whose progress he was extremely proud.

'When grading diamonds we consider the four "C's" – cut, colour, clarity and carat weight. Their value depends on how they measure up in these areas. Take these diamonds, for example. They are all cut in the 'brilliant' style, probably the most popular one. That is to say each stone has exactly fifty-eight facets. He picked up a stone with a pair of delicate tweezers. 'The light enters here through this flat top, which we call the 'table'. Each of these facets acts as a mirror which, by virtue of its exact geometrical relationship to its fellows, bounces the light backwards and forwards within the stone before throwing it out again through the table to give the characteristic sparkle of the perfectly cut diamond. If you get it slightly wrong the light can leak and be lost through the bottom or sides of the stone. The man who cut this one has made no mistake as I think you can probably see.' The salesman in Mr Brown had momentarily replaced the teacher.

It seemed true that the unknown cutter had indeed got

his facets right. Light seemed to blaze from the 'table' of the stone.

'Of course we prefer a north light for demonstrating these things. Or a south one if we happen to be below the equator.' Mr Brown was enjoying himself. This last remark was the mildest of rebukes to Eleanor who always insisted on diamonds coming to her rather than visiting the shops herself, where lighting conditions were more favourable.

'Now we look at the colour. We recognize seven different colour grades. All these stones are in the top grade. We English call this colour "finest white". The Americans call it simply "D". The Scandinavians prefer "rarest white".'

'Can people disagree about colour?' asked Caroline.

'Indeed they can,' replied Mr Brown. 'But disagreement among real experts is rare. It's a matter of opinion, but of highly qualified opinion. I would, for example, expect your mother to be right about a stone's colour nine times out of ten.'

Eleanor laughed at this courteous but totally unwarranted compliment. 'Flattery will get you everywhere, Mr Brown,' she joked.

'People do make "mistakes" from time to time,' admitted Mr Brown in tones that implied that such transgressions were committed exclusively by lesser mortals, none of whom were employed by *his* firm. Once again he turned to Caroline, who seemed to be thoroughly enjoying herself.

'Where were we? Oh yes, clarity. Now if you inspect the stone through one of these . . .' a small black eye-piece appeared as if by magic, 'you will see that the diamond is clean, literally "flawless".' He handed stone and magnifying glass to Caroline.

'What you are looking for are small scratches or pits near the edge, or dark blobs on the inside. Sometimes you see little groups of what look like bubbles, colourless crystals. There are five grades of clarity ranging from the top clear, flawless grade to those stones with inclusions that look like great lumps of coal – not surprising, I suppose, when you remember that diamonds and coal are made up of the same carbon atoms. Compare that perfect stone with this one, which has the very, very slightest imperfection. We call this clarity VVSI.'

'They look exactly the same to me,' said Caroline after studying both stones carefully.

'That's why your mother always comes to us,' said Mr Brown. 'It takes a lot of practice to find that tiny flaw and it's certainly not visible to the naked eye, otherwise it would come in one of the lesser clarity grades like "first piqué" or "heavily spotted". The one with the flaw is worth $30,000 less,' he added casually, 'so it's quite important not to miss it.'

Caroline whistled her surprise as Eleanor admired the English mastery of understatement.

'Actually,' said Mr Brown, 'only about one in ten gem stones are flawless. I should think that there are only about seven or eight hundred perfect stones of this approximate weight produced each year, so there's a certain rarity value.' He was getting round to price.

Eleanor took up the eye-piece and examined the stones quickly. 'They're very fine,' she said. 'I think that last one was damaged in the cutting. Unlike your cutters to have an off day. They look as if they are from Premier.' Eleanor referred to the famous mine thirty miles north of Pretoria which had the reputation for producing the finest gem stones in the world. The diamond pipe at Premier was 1700 million years old in contrast to the relatively 'new' pipes round Kimberley which could boast but 100 million years.

'Absolutely correct,' said a pleased Mr Brown. Premier was the original home of some of the most famous diamonds, among them the record-holding 3106-carat Cullinan; the superb Jonker, brilliantly cut by the virtuoso Lazare Kaplan and sold to King Farouk for a million dollars; the 354-carat Premier Rose and the 426-carat Niarchos.

'I know that you would not be interested yourself but I thought Caroline might like to see one or two "fancies".' Mr Brown always had his eye on the next generation.

'What on earth are *they?*' said Caroline, as Mr Brown sifted through the tissue-paper packets.

In answer to her question two stones lay exposed on the table top.

Caroline gasped at their beauty. They were several times larger than the diamonds they had examined so far, but that was not the only difference. One was gun-metal black like some exotic insect; the other was of the palest and most delicate pink – the colour, thought Eleanor, of Pol Roger's rosé champagne.

'Are they diamonds?' asked Caroline.

'Very much so – and extremely valuable if you like that sort of thing,' said Eleanor, demonstrating that in such matters she was a purist.

'But I thought you said that diamonds should be colourless,' said Caroline.

'In the normal way, yes. The lowest colour grades are "yellow" or "dark cape" but once in a while a stone comes along of a unique and completely desirable colour. Then the rules go out of the window. The highest price ever paid at public auction for a diamond was for a 22.5 carat pink stone. It went for over a million dollars in 1979.'

'Well, I have to admit that pink one is rather amazing,' said Caroline. Then, with the directness of youth, she asked, 'How much do all these diamonds cost?'

Mr Brown was not at all put out.

'The "D" flawless diamonds range from $100,000 to $200,000 depending on how heavy they are in carats. By the way there are 142 carats to the ounce. The pink stone is a little more at $350,000.'

Caroline looked appalled. 'How can they possibly be worth that?'

Mr Brown cleared his throat. He had been faced with this problem before and he had a stock speech ready to deal with it. Before he could embark on it he was pre-empted.

The hitherto silent assistant could contain himself no longer. He had been eyeing Caroline throughout the conversation and was clearly longing for an opportunity to make some favourable impression on her. This was his chance.

'In fact an investment in high-quality diamonds is totally without risk,' he intoned, in the pompous manner of a politician addressing a women's institute meeting.

'Daddy always used to say that there was no such thing,' said Caroline.

Oozing condescension, the assistant continued. 'I feel sure your father would have wanted to make a qualification in respect of stones such as these.' He had made a mistake. The women of the Montgomery family were not used to and were not prepared to tolerate disagreement with Bill's sayings, especially when they concerned business matters. This held true even when the speaker was an acknowledged and acclaimed expert in his own field, a description that hardly applied to Mr Brown's nark. Mr Brown himself noted the closing of the Montgomery ranks and settled back to enjoy the forthcoming spectacle. He did not like his assistant, feeling that he was too clever by half, or at least thought that he was.

Blissfully unaware of what was in store and determined to impress with his erudition the young man ploughed on.

'The diamond price is actually controlled by the De Beers company,' he explained, 'through their Central Selling Organization. It's a complete monopoly and has been in effective existence since 1949. The idea is that most of the diamond-producing nations such as Zaire, Russia, Angola, Sierra Leone, Tanzania and Botswana all club together with De Beers, whose major production is in South Africa and Namibia, and agree to sell their diamonds through the CSO. Because of this the CSO controls the sale of over eighty per cent of the world's rough diamonds. That, together with De Beers' phenomenal financial muscle, allows it to 'fix' the price of diamonds. When the Western and Japanese economies are booming demand for diamonds increases dramatically, tending to create a shortage and often large increases in price. The De Beers' policy is to create a stable market for the longer-term benefit of the industry and ultimately themselves and so in times such as these they release stones onto the market from their vast stockpile. This has the effect of keeping price rises within reasonable limits. They satisfy demand by increasing supply.'

The Cartier assistant paused for breath. This was going well, he thought as he warmed to his theme. He seemed to be holding his audience.

'Of course the other side of the coin is that in times of depression and economic slump the CSO reverses its policy. People have less money and the demand for diamonds falls. In a free market that would tend to put the skids under the diamond price, but the CSO begins to engineer an artificial shortage by withholding stones from market and increasing its stockpile. This stops the price from falling. The idea is that by ironing out wild price fluctuations the CSO can keep the diamond price moving steadily upwards, thus assuring the producer nations of a continued demand for their product in both good times and bad. Some of their economies are a bit shaky to put it mildly and it suits everybody to have De Beers controlling the market. Since 1949 the price of diamonds has only ever gone up. In fact there have been twenty-nine price increases since then. So you can see that any investment that your mother makes in diamonds is actually as safe as the Rock of Gibraltar.' For one second the assistant wondered if he had made an unhappy analogy – the Spanish were getting restless again about that particular piece of real estate.

He thought he might try a Parthian shot to show everybody who was in control. 'So I'm sure your father would have wanted to revise his maxim in the light of that information,' he said patronizingly.

Mr Brown braced himself.

Neat hydrochloric acid seemed to drip from Eleanor's tongue as she spoke. 'Well, Mr . . . I'm sorry I've forgotten your name but no matter,' she drawled, 'that's a nice little expression of the popular wisdom on the subject.' Her tone implied that she had seldom heard a more crass over-simplification, a more grotesquely misleading account of the true state of affairs in the diamond market. 'Of course I would not dream of buying diamonds as an "investment" nor would I advise anyone else to do so. The best reason for buying beautiful gems is because they can be made into beautiful jewellery.' Eleanor made it sound as if buying diamonds for investment purposes was a particularly degrading perversion, something akin perhaps to bestiality or necrophilia. The cause of her irritation was beginning to make him feel that he had made some sort of miscalculation.

'However, if you are trying to maintain that a diamond cartel is for ever and that the price of diamonds can never fall, then I suggest you are being a little naïve.'

'The monopoly has always kept the price up in the past,' protested the blue suit, a note of mild panic creeping into his voice. He looked round at Mr Brown for support. None was forthcoming. He was on his own, locked in debate about a business matter with one of the most acute business minds in the world.

'Nonsense,' said Eleanor. 'Cecil Rhodes had the first "monopoly" in 1887 when the Rothschilds lent him two and a half million dollars to buy out the French Company. The following year he bought Kimberley Central which gave De Beers ninety per cent of world diamond production – that's substantially more than they have now. He set up a sales consortium, the Diamond Syndicate, to manipulate the price. OK, it was a dealers' rather than a producers' cartel, but it worked well for about seventeen years. The thing you have to remember Mr . . . is that there are always two potential threats to commodity monopolies – increases in *supplies* from sources outside the monopoly and decreases in *demand* for their products. They can often ride out one of these, but when two come together disaster strikes. In 1907 that's exactly what happened. There was a stock market crash in America, by far the most important diamond market, and at the same time the Premier mine, the one that produced these stones, and which was outside the De Beers net, had increased production to over two million carats, more than all the De Beers' mines put together. The monopoly was broken.'

There was silence from the Cartier team.

This was Eleanor's style and many an opponent at a Montgomery board meeting had been defeated by it. She seemed to have almost total recall and could summon facts and figures to back up arguments that lent them a weight others could not match.

'What happened at the time of the Great Crash?' asked Caroline.

'Exactly the same thing,' said Eleanor. 'Immediately after World War I there were some very good years. Then they discovered diamonds in South-West Africa, what we call Namibia now. What's more they were very high-quality gem stones and they were sold independently of De Beers. At first the market was able to cope with the increased supply in the boom leading up to 1929, but when the crash came bringing the Great Depression the diamond price collapsed. There was nothing the monopoly could do about it. The price dropped from £3.15 per carat in 1930 to £1.74 in 1932. If you had bought diamonds in 1912 and sold in 1932 you would have been lucky to get your money back. De Beers had only one alternative. They closed their diamond mines and didn't effectively re-open them for five years. The industry was so desperate that the diamond sorters would grade the stones into different piles during the day and mix them up again at night just to give themselves something to do. They played marbles with the round ones.'

Mr Brown smiled nervously. It was time to come to the rescue of his beleaguered assistant, who had begun to open and close his mouth like a fish, searching to counter Eleanor's arguments.

'There is much in what you say,' he said, 'but I think you would agree that Oppenheimer has got things pretty well under control at the moment and for the foreseeable future. After all, the CSO does represent all the major diamond producers now and it's in nobody's interest to break ranks. The company, too, is so big that it can buy up any amount of diamonds that could conceivably come on to the market and prevent the price from falling.'

'I must disagree with you,' said Eleanor firmly but with a warm smile that left nobody in any doubt that she was prepared to regard the opinion of Mr Brown with infinitely more respect than she could extend to his assistant.

'If you look carefully there are all sorts of signs of trouble, even now. You say it's in nobody's interest to break ranks, but Zaire has done just that.' She shot a look of scorn at the chastened assistant who had included that country in his list of CSO members. 'All right, so they produce mainly industrial diamonds rather than gem stones, but in terms of carat volume they are the largest producer nation. And what about Russia? Technically they withdrew from the CSO in 1963, although they still sell most of their stones through the organization. At the moment it makes commercial sense for them to do so and they need the foreign exchange, but they produce more stones than South Africa and thirty per cent are gems. Nobody knows how many diamonds they have got stockpiled, but if for some political reason they decided to get awkward they could make things very tough for De Beers. After all they are not exactly in love with the South Africans. Then there's Botswana. They will be producing half of De Beers' total output by the mid-1980s. At the moment the Botswana government is only taking fifty per cent of the profits. They'll probably want more, perhaps much more. And what about Namibia, which contributes about fifteen per cent to De Beers' total profit? If they get independence and the SWAPO guerillas are in control it will probably mean nationalization.'

Caroline looked at her mother in astonishment. She knew of her formidable reputation but this *tour de force* of concentrated information displayed with absolutely no preparation was nothing short of remarkable. If she knew this much about the diamond industry how much did she know about chemicals? No wonder growth at Montgomery had been so explosive.

Eleanor had not finished.

'The diamond cartel make very strange bedfellows indeed,' she said. 'At the moment it makes economic sense for them to pull together. If circumstances changed the whole thing could fall like dominoes, and the diamond price with it. Even if they held together they could probably succumb to really unfavourable supply and demand factors. If Wayne succeeds in curing inflation in America and restoring faith in money then gold and diamonds will be out of favour. Already the economy is headed downwards, pushed by high interest rates, and diamond sales are going down with it. Some vast new diamond discovery outside De Beers' control could be the final straw.'

The blue suit thought of Custer's last stand as he summoned from somewhere the strength to say, 'That's very unlikely. The De Beers' geologists have combed the globe for nearly a hundred years. There won't be any more big finds.'

Eleanor shot him a look of withering scorn. 'Clearly you'll believe anything. There are probably hundreds of "pipes" in the Kalahari just waiting to be discovered. And where did all the Namibian diamonds come from? They're all in alluvial deposits, so somewhere along the Orange river lie the kimberlite origins.'

Eleanor piled it on. 'Perhaps you didn't see the estimated 1985 productive capacity of the new Australian Ashton venture. It is 22 million carats which compares with total 1980 world diamond production of 47 million carats. That's certainly a "new" discovery that eluded the geologists in whom you appear to place so much faith.'

'It sounds to me as if diamonds are for never,' said Caroline, parodying the catch-phrase that De Beers spent $60 million a year promoting.

'They remain extraordinarily beautiful,' said Mr Brown mildly. He, too, disapproved of diamond investors and was inclined to agree with Eleanor's prognosis regarding the diamond monopoly. However he also wanted to make a sale. He need not have worried.

'I quite agree,' said Eleanor. 'I'll take the five "D" flawless stones. Could you send them to New York in the usual way?'

There was no further mention of price, nor would there be. Eleanor knew from experience that the price would be a fair one. From Cartier's point of view it had to be if they wanted to keep her as a customer. She knew they would not overcharge her because at some future date she might want to trade in the stones. Then she would expect a reasonable profit if she had held them for several years. When Cartier failed to offer her that profit she would draw the conclusion that she had been over-charged initially. At that point she would go elsewhere. It was unlikely to happen and both Eleanor and Mr Brown knew it. A very rough calculation told Eleanor that she had spent about $700,000. For her that was petty cash. It would hardly make a dent in the Crédit Suisse account that collected the income from her Eurocurrency deposits. Her real money was in America tied up in the company. This was just the icing on the cake.

Mr Brown looked mildly relieved, his sweating assistant flattened. He stowed 'the goods' away in the tattered case and made ready to leave. Eleanor went with him to the door as goodbyes were said.

'Could I ask what plans you have for the stones?' asked Mr Brown. This was his real interest.

'I've got Mr Gardner drawing up some plans for a very original bracelet. He said we needed some excellent small stones. I promise to send you a photograph as soon as it's finished.'

Mr Brown smiled his satisfaction. Gardner was Cartier's top designer. The stones would be shown to their best advantage.

In the corridor outside the suite Eleanor took his arm. 'Now Mr Brown – not a word to Caroline – she probably wouldn't approve – but I think you'd better put that pink stone on one side for her. Add it to my account.'

With a conspiratorial nod Mr Brown signalled his consent and was gone.

# IV

The moment could be put off no longer. All afternoon the Emmanuel scarlet taffeta frock had hung sadly on its silk hanger in the depths of the cupboard – lonely and unloved, although not forgotten. Caroline had delayed until the last minute before rescuing it from its isolation. Now she stood in front of the long gilt looking-glass holding it with distaste in front of her tall, statuesque body.

'Oh God,' thought Caroline, 'this is a disaster.' Her shoulders were not wide but this off-the-shoulder dress seemed to accentuate their undoubted strength. She looked, she thought, like a cross between Liberace in drag and Scarlett O'Hara in time-warp.

'Mother,' she shouted to the next room, 'come and take a look at the sugar plum fairy.'

Eleanor smiled grimly to herself as she walked through to her daughter. She would need all her considerable diplomatic skills here.

'But darling it looks *wonderful*,' said Eleanor, her jaw set in determination to instil in her daughter some sense of fashion. 'So chic,' she added rather lamely. The truth of the matter was that although Caroline looked very beautiful there was a certain indefinable quality about her movements and posture that signalled to the world that this was not her normal mode of dress. It was not that Caroline was masculine or 'butch' – more that she lacked that coquettish languor, that aura of feminine caprice that the dress seemed to demand.

Caroline immediately caught her mother's uncertainty. 'Mother you *know* this sort of thing doesn't suit me. I look like lamb dressed as mutton,' she said appealingly and with some resignation as it was getting late and there was really no viable alternative to this awful dress. Disdainfully she began to climb into it.

'You're quite wrong, darling,' said Eleanor. 'It's fashionable. Everyone will love you in it. You must remember that this is London and Annabel's, not Aspen and André's.'

'But mother I can't *stand* the sort of women who wear dresses like this – simpering witches with dollar signs in their eyes, only interested in hooking men, all blushes and pouts – frills on the outside, steel on the inside; nothing to do all day but gossip and sleep, nothing to do all night except pose and screw.'

Eleanor laughed out loud at the violence of her daughter's characterization. 'Nonsense, darling. Anyway you can't possibly go in jeans and cowboy boots.'

The telephone rang in the next room and Eleanor went to answer it.

'We'll be down in two or three minutes. Darling the car's ready – hurry,' she called to Caroline.

Caroline gave one last despairing look at herself in the mirror. Suddenly an idea occurred to her. Rebellion. She aimed a scornful kick at the delicate black, satin pumps. Sitting down on the edge of the bed, slowly and deliberately she pulled on the comfortable, scuffed cowboy boots beneath the frilly dress.

# Chapter 2

## I

'Eleanor, how *lovely* to see you,' said the gaunt, patrician Englishman with the worried expression, as Eleanor and Caroline swept into the basement club.

'This must be Caroline,' he enthused, shaking her hand and staring deep into her eyes. 'I've been in love with your mother for years,' he joked. 'Now I can transfer my allegiance. You're both sitting at my table, so see you later.'

Mark Birley was something of a legend in English society. An old Etonian, well born and well connected, he had decided on a whim to open what he intended to be the best night club in the world. He had named it after his wife Annabel, the Marquess of Londonderry's sister, and it had lived up to his expectations. Recently the club had become in some ways the victim of its own success. Rich men with more money than class had cajoled their way onto the membership list and Mark's friends had persuaded him to open another club, 'Mark's' where Miles had lunched the day before. Tonight there would be no Arabs or parvenus to dilute the 'quality' of the party. It was private, the guest list carefully chosen. Eleanor knew, too, that there would be no gossip columnists. This breed had recently achieved celebrity status in England as the unfortunate populace sought light relief from the economic gloom that engulfed them. Mark Birley, however, had suffered personally at their hands and would have preferred to burn his club to the ground than to allow one of them through the front door. As a result members of his clubs felt free to relax, to let off steam, free to spend money without the uncomfortable feeling that their behaviour

54

might be the topic of conversation at a million suburban breakfast tables the following morning. Mark gave the rich aristocrats who frequented his establishments the two commodities they found most difficult to buy – exclusivity and privacy.

The fact that the food, service and ambience of his clubs were second to none was in a way incidental. The English upper classes had never cared much about those things.

The guests were gathering around the bar in the rabbit warren of small rooms that led off the main corridor to the dining room and dance floor. Each room was immaculately designed in the incomparable 'English country house' style, whose main characteristic was that one felt it had not been 'designed' at all, rather thrown together by somebody who had inherited good taste, not learned it. Deep leather sofas, fireplaces and fenders, hunting prints and the occasional sporting canvas depicting horses or grand country houses, mahogany tables. The rooms were comfortable, lived in, warm and inviting, as far removed from trendy aestheticism as it was possible to get. They were the sort of rooms into which wet dogs might easily burst at any moment, muddy and tired after the day's shoot.

Eleanor and Caroline took a glass of champagne from the waiter's tray and joined the throng.


Miles Parmere took the steps to the basement two at a time. He greeted Mark warmly.

'This has got to stop, Mark. Do you realize that this is the third "greasy spoon" of yours I've been in today? It'll be the death of me.' Harry's Bar was the latest addition to the Birley chain.

'Cirrhosis?'

'No, boredom,' Miles laughed.

'Well, if you die of boredom at dinner tonight you will confirm my worst suspicions that you are a secret poof. You're sitting next to the most beautiful girl in the room and, what's more, you've never met her before.'

'Nonsense,' said Miles, as if it was a contradiction in

55

terms to imply that there was a beautiful woman in Europe he had not met.

'What's her name?'

'Caroline Montgomery.'

'Never heard of her.'

'Ah, but you lead a sheltered life, Miles.'

We'll see, thought Miles as he plunged through the swing doors into the middle of the party.

Mark Birley's table was filling up. Guests were wandering about the subterranean dining room trying to find their places for dinner. 'A bit like a lottery,' thought Miles. The prize could be an introduction to a potential conquest or, alternatively, hours of boredom sandwiched between two ghastly women that in the ordinary way wild horses could not bring him to look at. For this reason it was more exciting than a lottery because there were potential penalties as well as possible rewards. Of course it was always possible to employ the ultimate sanction and leave during the soup if the 'draw' was too appalling, but that would entail the counter-move of being banished from Mark Birley's invitation list – not a wise move in present economic conditions. There were few enough party-givers as it was. On this occasion Miles had the advantage of knowing that he had been awarded some sort of prize in the shape of the mysterious but 'devastating' Caroline Montgomery. Past experience, however, told him that one could never count on the judgements of others, especially where feminine beauty was concerned. On the other hand Mark Birley had a good track record in this field. Far better, though, not to let expectations ride too high.

Caroline's attributes, or lack of them, took on a far greater significance for Miles when he read the name card of the lady who was to sit on his right side at dinner. It was not encouraging information. Lady Camilla Ponsonby, it was undoubtedly fair to say, bored for the Home Counties. It was not just that she was plain and mousey. That alone could not be held against anybody. Nor was it that she showed absolutely no awareness of this fact. That could be

regarded as a redeeming feature, showing a worthy determination not to be phased by the unfair distribution of
nature's assets. No, thought Miles, Lady Camilla's
undoubted failing was her dreadful, placid self-satisfaction
based for some weird reason on the fact that she was the
child of one of the more obscure Dukes. Certainly it was
not based on any talent for work, for life, for conversation,
for anything at all. Three husbands had left her. All had
married her because they were snobs and were attracted to
the substantial trust fund that it was rumoured she lived
off. None had been able to withstand the numbing tedium
of life with Camilla. Oddly enough, Miles remembered,
the considerable number of children of these unsatisfactory
unions already possessed a reputation for wit and brightness, an example perhaps of compensation for the awful-
ness of their parents. Bolstered by the fact that Caroline
Montgomery would, at the very worst, provide some
amusement, Miles, in charitable mood, tried to dredge up
from the depths of his memory some redeeming feature of
Lady Camilla. He failed completely. At that very moment
he heard the flat, calm, colourless voice over his shoulder.

'Hello, Miles,' said Lady Camilla. 'We seem to be sitting
together.' Camilla said this with all the self-satisfaction of
an Einstein discovering the theory of relativity – as if it
were her own personal achievement, triumph even, to have
learned this stunning fact.

'So it would appear,' said Miles coldly and without
enthusiasm, wondering whether the accurate location of
her place for dinner was indeed the most momentous
achievement of Lady Camilla's day. The burden on the
unknown Caroline Montgomery to save the situation was
mounting steadily. Miles turned in his chair to scan the
milling throng, searching for the 'most beautiful girl in the
room' of Mark's description. She would have to be quite
something if she was to better the home-grown competition.

And then he saw her and knew immediately that he had
done so. He was vaguely aware of some biochemical
adjustment deep within him as he contemplated Caroline

Montgomery's spectacular beauty. Miles savoured the moment. He was the 'voyeur', he could see her, and he knew who she was, while he remained unseen, unknown. He watched her carefully with the eye of the connoisseur, as Caroline moved from table to table searching for her place. He did not call out to her, or help her in her quest, not because of any uncertainty as to her identity but because he wanted this time to analyse her, wanted to savour the moment of mystery and anticipation that is all too often shattered by the first conversation as reality intrudes on fantasy, as the 'here and now' replaces the 'might have been'.

The face, Miles conceded immediately, was unbeatable, and even across the candle-lit night club Caroline's inner vitality shone from it. About her body Miles could only speculate because it was hidden from view beneath a ghastly red dress. Certainly the shoulders and bare arms were very fine, thought Miles, noting their strength. She probably took a lot of exercise. His eyes returned to the dress as he tried to pinpoint its problem. Then, as he did so he began to realize that the dress itself was not at fault, rather it was some unfortunate chemistry resulting from the interaction between frock and wearer that was responsible for a certain unease of effect. On Bianca Jagger it would have looked wonderful. On Caroline Montgomery it was not right. Miles wondered why this was so. Clearly the girl was not used to wearing clothes of that sort. But why? What sort of clothes did she usually wear? Perhaps she had no money, had been invited to the party for her beauty alone, the dress lent to her by a sophisticated and older friend. Or maybe she was one of those people with no fashion sense at all, who would slavishly wear the 'latest' thing whatever the expense, but who lacked the style to carry it off.

In view of the waves of enthusiasm and zest for life that seemed to emanate from her in such a disturbing way Miles was inclined to the former explanation. She was a naïve girl unused to the milieu and props of high society. At the same time she was clearly pleased to be there – out, no doubt, to do herself a bit of good. She would be quite impressed by him, thought Miles. Girls usually were. This was going to be fun. Good old Mark. Miles leaned across the empty chair where Caroline would sit. He should know the opposition. He was not entirely pleased to see the name of Kiko Hohenlohe, son of the Marbella Club owner Prince Alfonso Hohenlohe. Miles did not know him personally, but by reputation he was a force to be reckoned with. Still, Miles was not afraid of competition.

He began to work on his tactics. It might be no bad thing to play initially on her weakness, show her who was boss, and then, her defences down, demonstrate a gentle knowingness, a considerate concern for which she would be suitably grateful. Miles was used to such strategic planning sessions, a legacy of his Army days, and held that campaigns of seduction no less than military ones depended for their success on such careful appraisals.

Caroline advanced towards the empty seat, her athletic stride scarcely disguised by the frilly frock. She smiled her hello as she read her name card.

Miles was on his feet, pulling back his chair. 'Why it's little Bo Peep,' he said facetiously. 'You appear to have given your sheep the slip.'

Caroline's face grew stormy as she picked up the patronizing, mocking tone. 'Drop dead,' she said.

Miles stepped back and sat down heavily. He had not expected that. He felt that he had been ambushed, and now, his ranks broken and in disarray, he prepared to fall back on a defensive position. Something in his reading of the situation had gone very seriously wrong. 'I do apologize. I didn't mean to sound . . .' but he was left contemplating Caroline's superb back. Kiko Hohenlohe had arrived at the table at the same time as Caroline and had made a far better start.

A few minutes later he was shattered to hear Caroline say in response to Hohenlohe's polite inquiry as to who was on her other side, 'Oh, I don't know – some klutz.'

Miles could cross his heart and say with a clear conscience that he had never been called a 'Klutz' by anyone. He had certainly never been insulted so comprehensively by one so beautiful. In several respects this was a first night. With a feeling of mounting alarm Miles began to realize that he minded about all this. Why he did not know but a gut instinct told him that something important was going on. It could not be laughed off. The situation must be retrieved, but how? Miles munched morosely on the Beluga caviar, his appetite quite gone. Surprisingly, too, he seemed to have lost the taste for the excellent ice-cold Stolichnaya that accompanied it.

'Are you still out of work, Miles?' intoned Camilla Ponsonby in a loud, definite voice which, thought Miles, Caroline must have heard. Lady Camilla's tone implied not only that Miles was idle but that he was also incompetent, that his lack of employment was in some way the result of his inability to get a job. Visions of endless and unfruitful interviews with the personnel managers of large engineering firms, of Miles shuffling unhappily in interminable dole queues were conjured up. This women must be stopped before she destroys everything, thought Miles desperately.

'Are you still breeding like a rabbit from all those husbands that come and go like the milkman?'

Lady Camilla smiled quietly to herself. No insult could disturb her grotesque placidity, but she decided that Miles was in a dangerous mood and she turned to bore the man on her other side. Miles was alone, effectively 'sent to Coventry'. It began to look as if he would spend the rest of the dinner in silence. Normally he would have resolved this situation by leaving, by getting drunk or by a subtle combination of both, but he was strangely unwilling to tear himself away from Caroline. He contented himself by listening to her conversation. He was quite aware that this was all very odd indeed as he pushed the filets of Dover sole bonne femme from one side of his plate to the other and ignored the flinty Sancerre. Occasionally Miles caught the scent of Caroline, and at those moments he breathed in more deeply.

He found her incredibly attractive. Her immediate

analysis of his conversational opening, and instinctive and completely fair response to it now combined with her unusual beauty to captivate him. The 1966 Haut Brion tasted to Miles like Algerian 'burgundy' as he chewed unhappily on the steak Bearnaise. Caroline and Kiko were getting on well. From their overheard conversation Miles was able to piece together a fairly comprehensive profile of Caroline. She was American; clearly rich, probably very rich; a much-loved father had died; she was very good at skiing, probably very good, possibly expert; her mother's name was Eleanor and she was the startling-looking dark-haired beauty sitting on Mark Birley's right (obviously a person of considerable importance on this count alone); she was in London for a few days; she was quite unspoilt, exceptionally charming and highly intelligent. And yet Miles had, through his own stupidity, distanced himself irretrievably from this delectable object. It was like being in a room with the *Mona Lisa* and unable to find the light switch. This could not go on. He lent across the table towards Mark Birley and said, 'Mark, you're a man of the world who knows about these sort of things. What do you do if through your own incredible stupidity and lack of sensitivity you have alienated somebody you would very much like to know?' He spoke seriously. It was a public confession.

Conversation at the table stopped. In the uneasy silence that followed Mark joked, 'Surely you haven't upset Camilla.'

There was general laughter at this, but Miles did not join in. He seemed to want an answer. The laughter died away. Mark Birley wondered if Miles might be a little drunk. The full glass of Graves said 'no'. The pregnant silence continued, and then, suddenly it was broken. The soft American accent said, 'You say sorry – and are immediately forgiven.'

'Sorry,' said Miles.

'You are forgiven,' said Caroline.

'Oh, God,' thought Miles. 'It's happened. I'm in love.'

Eleanor saw it happen and immediately recognized it.

61

At their own speed it began to dawn on the other diners too. It was as if for a brief moment the tip of the iceberg that is the collective emotional unconscious had become briefly visible above the waves. The sun had caught it, illuminating it for all to see. Miles Parmere had met his match at last.

When Caroline had approached the table she had noticed at once the lean, good-looking Englishman who was to be her neighbour for the next two hours. She had been shocked by his opening remark. She was uncomfortable in her dress; he had seemed to sense it and had cruelly drawn attention to it. He had been unkind and she had instantly dismissed him because of it. She had not quite succeeded. Throughout dinner she had remained aware of him, had noted his air of melancholy. She had heard him dispose of Lady Camilla, had recognized that the remark had hurt him just as she, Caroline, had been hurt. She had felt, rightly, that his angry response was in some way connected with the fact that he knew that she had overheard it. As time passed she sensed him watching her, listening to her, and was aware of his mounting discomfort. There was about him the quality of a sulky child. He had done wrong and had been told off. Now he wanted to make amends. Caroline had recognized the courage that must have been required for his touching little speech. It had not been easy for him and her heart had warmed to him during it and in the silence that followed.

'Can we start again?' asked Miles, fully aware that the line sounded as if it came from a 1920s 'B' movie.

Caroline threw back her head and laughed aloud. 'No more cracks about my dress or I'll whack you with my shepherd's crook!'

The discotheque sprang to life as if specially to mark the reconciliation. Caroline did most things well and dancing was on the list, but after a few seconds Miles' coroneted velvet evening shoe ended up beneath one of the brown Texan boots. He yelped in mock pain.

'What on earth have you got on your feet?'

In answer Caroline pulled up the red dress to reveal the boots and, incidentally, a generous length of immaculately constructed thigh. 'I wore these to counteract the dress,' she said. 'I am afraid I'm not used to dressing up in all this gear.'

'How long are you in London?' asked Miles.

'Till Friday.'

'And then?'

'Back to Aspen.'

'God,' thought Miles. 'Its Wednesday. There's not much time.'

Miles' phenomenal success with women was on the whole a function of his ability to do without them. He had about him the aura of a man who could, if necessary, survive happily on his own. Debonair, apparently carefree, there was a hardness, too. His whole manner intimated that he needed no one, perhaps even wanted no one. Girls tended to regard this as a challenge and would impale themselves with careless abandon on the sharp spikes of his indifference. This desire for forbidden fruits, this perverse preference for men who are hard to get was, on the whole, characteristic of a particular type of woman. In general such women were primarily interested in 'the chase' and devoted much time and energy to it. Often there were few other calls on their time and energy. Usually these women did not have high opinions of themselves, frequently with good reason, and, like Groucho Marx who did not want to belong to any club that would be prepared to have him as a member, these ladies were not particularly interested in men who thought highly of their qualities, on the grounds that this showed considerable deficiencies in judgement. Such people treated the whole business of 'romance' as a sort of a game, certainly a competition, in which other women were competitors. This gave them a certain frivolity, a frothiness that men such as Miles, in their continual quest for diversion and amusement, found superficially attractive. This inaccessibility came easily to the social class from which Miles came. Certainly at the 'better' public schools, Eton for example, with their

63

insistence on the avoidance of all outward expression of emotion, on the 'stiff upper lip', men such as Miles were carefully trained to demonstrate a sort of global lack of enthusiasm, an all-embracing 'boredom' of which disinclination to form heavy emotional attachments to women was but one example.

Caroline did not fit into this pattern at all. She was immune to any display of uninterest that Miles might employ because she was not looking for a man, and would not have looked for *that* sort of man anyway. To play hard to get when nobody wanted you was clearly no way to succeed. Caroline was not uninterested in men, the closeness with which she danced contradicted that; it was rather that she had other priorities, more important things on her mind, more worthy ambitions. This was a far more 'serious' approach to life than Miles was used to and he had little experience of it. In short, he did not know how to handle the situation at all and his nervousness and alien lack of self-confidence were uncomfortably apparent to him. This approach would have done him no good at all with the 'Mayfair Mercenaries' with whom he usually mixed. They were trained to go for the jugular at the scent of blood, the first whiff of weakness. Paradoxically it had quite the opposite effect on the self-confident and kindly Caroline. Strong herself, she was drawn to sensitivity and uncertainty in others. So, while Miles felt that he was doing badly, Caroline found her attraction to him increasing. He reminded her of the small boy who had been hurt but was determined not to show pain. His hard exterior exuded a sort of brittle worldly wisdom, but inside she felt he was not like that at all. He seemed lost, searching for some as yet unknown destination while at the same time pretending with a sort of desperate intensity that he knew exactly what he was doing. And so, through no conscious effort of his own, in fact despite his own intentions, Miles was projecting just that combination of attributes that is so invariably prized by the most superior kind of woman. In essence Miles appeared to Caroline to be a man of very considerable talents who had, for some reason, allowed them to go to waste. If he was a sinner who had not yet found redemption the reasons for his 'fall from grace' provided an element of mystery which was another essential ingredient in the 'mix'. For these reasons, quite apart from the more obvious ones such as Miles' exuberant good looks, Caroline found herself increasingly drawn to him. But if Caroline was interested, Miles was captivated, the biter bit. Few, including Eleanor, could have seen that.

They danced for as long as was decently possible, before returning to the table – leaving the music in order to face it. Mark Birley had a few points to score.

'Good Lord, I thought you two had left,' he joked. 'You seem to have found the right words for your apology, Miles.'

Miles wondered idly whether or not he could get away with throwing the Baked Alaska pudding at his friend.

Out of the corner of his eye Miles noticed that Kiko Hohenlohe was preparing to strike.

'Caroline, you must dance with me,' he insisted. She was gone.

Caroline was enjoying herself enormously, in contrast to the 'pleasure mixed with pain' that Miles was experiencing. She liked these Europeans, was intrigued by their complexity. With them nothing was as it seemed – there were endless layers of gay superficiality that had to be peeled away before the inner personality was revealed. It was a welcome change from the earnest, straightforward skiers of Aspen. Miles was certainly interesting and she wished there was time to get to know him better.

When she got back to the table he appeared to be waiting for her. 'That was the longest ten minutes of my life so far.'

'You say that to all the girls.'

'I've never meant it before.'

Then Miles did something quite remarkable. As if it belonged to somebody completely different, he heard his voice saying with absolute and total finality, 'Caroline Montgomery – I'm going to marry you.'

Caroline looked down at her plate. She did not laugh.

When she looked up it was with a quizzical expression, her head slightly on one side. Still, she said nothing. Then with a hint of a smile on her lips she said, 'Stranger things have happened.'

'Tell me about Lord Parmere,' said Eleanor as the Rolls turned out of Berkeley Square on its way back to Claridges.

'Interesting,' said Caroline non-committally. 'He's asked me to lunch tomorrow at a place called Odette's. I said I'd go.'

'Mark said he had a reputation for being quite a playboy.' Eleanor spoke casually. Mark Birley, a man wise in the ways of the night people, was a person whose opinion on such matters should be considered.

'I can imagine that.'

'He seemed to like you a lot.'

Caroline laughed and squeezed her mother's hand by way of a reply. It was her way of saying 'don't worry'.

Miles was worried. He had already demolished two plates of the delicious cockles and mussels soaked in vinegar that together with jugs of wild flowers adorned the tables at Odette's. Now he sat in the corner by the door gazing periodically at his watch like a teenager on his first date. She had seemed to want to come to lunch. Perhaps her driver had been unable to find the restaurant. He should have picked her up at the hotel. He looked at his watch again. One o'clock precisely. She wasn't actually late yet, but he had rather hoped she would be early. Overhead the bottle-green ceiling fans were reminiscent of some Far Eastern location, the background perhaps for a Maugham short story.

'What are you up to, Miles? Loitering with "intent" in the corner.' The polished tones of Patrick Lichfield, the Queen's cousin and a famous photographer, cut into Miles' thoughts.

'Hello, Patrick. I see you've recovered from the wedding. I liked the snaps.' Patrick had been the official photographer at Prince Charles' wedding.

Patrick was the advance guard of a large, noisily cheerful group who now burst into the restaurant. A shortish figure in faded blue denims with an impish grin and two weeks stubble on his face planted a wet kiss on Miles' cheek while playfully pretending to strangle him.

'Piss off, Bail,' said Miles with affection, attempting to wriggle free from David Bailey's embrace. There was no more famous heterosexual in the Western hemisphere than the man who had married Catherine Deneuve and Marie Helvin and 'discovered' Jean Shrimpton, but such camp behaviour was very much the norm in this group.

'Stop necking you two and let one of the girls have a go,' said a beautiful, stylish blonde. Pat Booth's personality came across like vintage Krüg – fizzy, bubbling and with a kick like a mule. Miles had known her for years and loved her dearly, but as she advanced towards him and kissed him with all the natural enthusiasm that always characterized her, Miles wished fervently that the ground might open and swallow them up, for over her shoulder he saw Caroline enter the restaurant. It was not an auspicious moment. While Pat disengaged herself and before he had had a chance formally to recognize Caroline's arrival let alone introduce her, Marie Helvin, a tall, statuesque and staggeringly beautiful model, now Mrs David Bailey, took her place.

'Darling Miles,' said Marie. 'Are you going to join us for lunch?'

Only blind instinct, the result of careful training and endless exposure to such socially daunting situations, saved Miles from disaster. 'Caroline,' he shouted cheerfully. 'The US cavalry to the rescue in the nick of time to save me from these rapacious women and ginger beers.'

Caroline laughed as he introduced her to the group, but found herself looking closely at Pat and Marie.

'God, Miles, you've done it again. Where on earth do you find such incredible women?' said Pat.

Caroline blushed at the compliment. At the same time she was aware of the reference to others with similar attractions, perhaps many others.

Pat turned to Caroline, whom she had immediately recognized. 'I saw that interview you did in *US* magazine. It was really good. I especially liked the bit about it being easier to get to the top than to stay there. How long are you here for? If you've got some time I'd love to do some pix.'

'Listen darling, if anybody's doing pix on this one it's me,' said Bailey giving Caroline a friendly squeeze. 'By the way, luv, don't listen to a word Miles says. He's all mouth and trousers – more front than Brighton.'

'Bloody hell, Bail. With friends like you . . .'

The party moved on, leaving Miles and Caroline alone at last.

'Who are they all?' Caroline asked. 'I recognized David Bailey and Marie Helvin.'

Miles explained the group. It was a lunch party being given by Barry Taylor, the head of UK operations for Olympus cameras.

'The man with the good-looking model is John Swannell. He used to be Bailey's assistant. Now he's the chief rival for the top fashion photographer spot. He's just done a great exhibition, shot entirely on his wife. We'll have a cold, red Sancerre – very unusual and particularly good, especially on a day like this.'

Caroline looked around the pretty room. The walls were covered entirely with old Victorian mirrors in ornate gilt frames, each one different; dried flowers cascaded out of a green chamber pot; an art deco lady leaned protectively over a huge bowl of white peppermints; in a corner of the ceiling a tight bunch of large silver balloons recalled the beach balls of the early Beaton photographs. 'Sounds delicious. I really like this place.'

Today Caroline was in her own clothes and she looked unbeatable. A big, burgundy-red Claude Montana soft leather jacket covered the white tee-shirt and light blue jeans. The leather boots that had injured Miles' velvet evening shoes provided some continuity with the previous evening.

'Last night was fun,' said Miles hopefully.

'And full of startling predictions,' said Caroline. She wondered how he would react to that.

'More a declaration of intent than a prediction.' He had never felt more serious. Nothing about Caroline's appearance or demeanour now gave him any reason to change his mind. This girl had devastated him, destroyed the rhythm of his life. At the same time she filled him with wild hope, gave him a thrilling sense of how the future could be different, of how life could become meaningful once again, not merely 'fun', but worthwhile too. Catching the earnest look in his eyes Caroline changed the subject.

'What should I eat? I'm famished.'

'You must start with the fried camembert – it's wonderful. Then it should be the chicken brochette.'

'Sounds great. What are these?'

'Cockles and mussels,' said Miles. 'The staple diet of every cockney born within the sound of Bow bells – sort of a national dish.'

'They're wonderful,' said Caroline, prizing a cockle from its shell with the pin provided for that purpose. 'I've just had an incredible swim at somewhere called the RAC,' said Caroline. 'I'm afraid that's why my hair's still wet.'

'Good God, I'm there most days,' said Miles, cursing inwardly that he had spent the morning at Blades ordering some new suits. Caroline in swimming clothes would be a sight a man might crawl five miles over broken glass to see, but clearly there was no delicate way of expressing that particular thought. 'How many lengths did you do?'

'I didn't count. I swim for an hour exactly.'

'Skiing training?'

'Everything is.'

Caroline began to talk about skiing. This was her subject and Miles listened, infected by her enthusiasm, charmed by her soft American voice, thrilled by her phenomenal beauty, freed by her presence from the gloomy slavonic melancholy that was the curse of his class and his heritage. Caroline showed him in the most simple way possible that life had more to offer if one dared to desire or demand it. She had a goal, a direction, an ambition. She wanted to be the best woman skier in the world, and as she talked there seemed to be no force on earth that could prevent her from achieving her objective. Nothing and nobody would be allowed to stand in her way, certainly not Lord Parmere, thought Miles ruefully. But he was not disappointed by such single-mindedness, despite its gloomy prognosis for him. Instead he was revitalized by it, more encouraged than he had been in years. For now he too had an objective. He would have Caroline as she would have the World Championship. There was no reason at all why both ambitions should not be fulfilled.

'Look, you musn't let me talk about skiing all through lunch – I'll send you off to sleep. What are your plans?'

When Rupert Dene had asked him that question at lunch a few days ago the short and most accurate answer would have been that Miles had no plans apart from wandering down to Florida to play some polo before perhaps joining the 'team' for some highjinks and heavy drinking in Cap Ferrat in June. Things, however, had changed since yesterday. Decision making, lately a difficulty, had never seemed easier. What he had not mentioned to Rupert, both because he had no real intention of accepting the offer and because he did not want to provide free ammunition for the Bear's amusing but sharp tongue, was that Harry Fox, the enormously successful Sun-Belt banker who had arranged the polo matches as promotion for a country club real-estate venture, had offered him a job. Miles was under no illusions about what was expected of him. In exchange for the $250,000 salary and virtually unlimited expenses Miles would provide the high-powered contacts and introductions without which no banking operation could hope to join the international big league. Harry Fox had no entrée into this world. He went down in high society like a fart in a space suit. Miles, in contrast, swam effortlessly in these waters. His accessibility to the captains of industry and commerce was total, for in their spare time they were snobs. Miles stayed in their houses, slept with their daughters and occasionally, and sometimes at the same house party, with their wives. He took their money at cards, exhausted them on the polo field and deflated their pomposity, and they loved him for it. For despite all this they knew that Miles posed no threat to them. At the bottom line Miles was harmless for one reason and one alone – he was not rich. However much he might appear to humiliate them, at the end of the day they owned him. Nobody understood this more clearly than Miles himself. So, although in other ways he and Harry Fox had about as much in common as a goldfish and a barracuda, both shared a secret desire – they sincerely wanted to be rich. Some obscure subterranean chemistry told each of them that the other might be able to do him a bit of good. Harry knew all about Miles. It was his business to know such things. He had seen in him the class and connections that he, Harry, knew how to turn into money. Miles had seen in Harry a rich and successful plebeian that he might be able to manipulate. He had agreed to come to Florida in May to play polo and, incidentally, to discuss Harry's job offer. He had never seriously considered accepting it.

In answer to Caroline's question about his plans Miles said simply, 'I'm coming to live in your country. I'm about to become a banker.'

Caroline could have no idea of her own role in bringing about this unlikely transformation, had no inkling that thirty seconds previously Miles had about as much intention of becoming a banker as he had of taking up rat catching. She was pleased.

'Oh, that's great. Where will you be?'

'Costa geriatrica. The bank's based in Miami. Its called the Union Bank of Florida, run by a man called Harry Fox. Apparently they feel they can't do without my renowned financial skills.'

Miles laughed recklessly. He had just made a decision that would totally change his life. What was there about this disturbing girl that seemed to make him say things, and what's more mean things, of such importance on the spur of the moment? Obviously there was some element in Caroline, perhaps her own intensely clear-cut sense of direction, that brought this out. Already he had told her that he intended to marry her. Now he had bound himself to take a job in a profession that he despised, in a particular geographical location on the other side of the world which previously had figured only in his jokes, working for a man who in any other situation he would not have crossed the street to piss on if he'd been on fire. This girl had a lot to answer for.

Caroline was no stranger to the world of finance in general and she had vaguely heard of the fast-moving Sun-Belt bank and its publicity-seeking president. 'You must talk to mother about it,' she said. 'She's meeting with bankers all week and talks about nothing except interest rates at the moment.'

Miles was listening. If he was going to be a banker he'd better start getting together some information on the subject. At the moment he hadn't much. A few minutes before his stupendous decision bankers were to Miles irritating little people who would never lend you quite as much money as you needed and occasionally, unless exceptionally well trained, asked impertinent questions about what you needed it for – in itself a startling comment on their collective naïvety with regard to the real world that he, Miles, inhabited. Now, two minutes into his new career he was already picking up information from the horse's mouth, as it were, if such a grotesquely inadequate metaphor could be used to describe the delectable source of Caroline's speech. A few telephone calls that morning had given him a great deal of information about the ladies of the Montgomery family. Victor Lamson, a close friend from Army days and a partner in Cazenoves, had told him that the Montgomerys were 'rich beyond the dreams of avarice' and that there wasn't a banker or business man in the Western world, or for that matter the Eastern one, who wouldn't have given his right arm to have dealings with them.

'Mother needs a billion dollars for something or other,' said Caroline simply. 'It's a question of getting the timing right on interest rates as to when she goes to the market for the funds.'

There was no hint that Caroline was aware, nor was she, of the 'send-up' value in her statement. Miles thanked God that 'Bear' Dene was not there and that Bailey was safely tucked away in the corner of the restaurant. Miles' crowd were not used to such casual talk from pretty girls about such very large sums of money, nor to semi-technical banking jargon from the same source. Caroline had made her remark feeling that it would be of interest to Miles, as a prelude perhaps to a more general discussion about the likely cost of money in the short term. After all, he was intending to be a banker and so presumably had all sorts of views on such things. Miles loved her for her lack of patronization, for her intelligence, her seriousness, her transparent 'goodness'. To Miles 'interest rates' were chiefly represented by unwelcome amounts added to his bank statements when least expected that seemed in some way to be related to the size of his overdraft. He was vaguely aware that they went up and down. Why they should do so was unclear to him. This was not, however, the moment to reveal his ignorance. 'Perhaps my bank will be able to lend it to her,' he offered, demonstrating, unknowingly, vast tranches of ignorance on banking matters.

'It's a lot of money,' laughed Caroline.

The rule that US banks could not lend more than ten per cent of their capital and surplus to any one borrower had recently been repealed due to the efforts of the fiercely pro-business President Wayne who was determined to reduce the role of foreign banks in the US economy. In theory, therefore, it was now possible for the Union Bank to lend Montgomery a billion dollars. After all, in the recent takeover 'feeding frenzy' in the oil industry Citibank had raised over $15 billion for customers, much of it from its own resources. However, for a relatively small bank like Union to lend a billion to a chemical giant like Montgomery would be a bit like a tin-pot banana republic granting economic aid to the United States. Clearly there was a certain amount that Lord Parmere had yet to learn about the intricacies of the American financial system.

Caroline was not about to waste time at such a pleasant lunch by enlightening him. Miles at any rate had just about exhausted his knowledge of things financial.

'So we'll be next-door neighbours, sort of,' said Miles, displaying a somewhat hazy notion of American geography.

'Well, Colorado and Florida aren't exactly "next door", but they're certainly closer than England.' Caroline found this Englishman very charming. She would like to see him again, but of course as soon as she got back to Aspen there would be no time for this sort of thing.

'You must fly up for the week-end. There's always a house full of people. I'm afraid I tend to be a bit preoccupied with training,' she added as a gentle warning.

Miles realized he had a long way to go. She liked him, no more. He thought for some reason of the family motto – 'Unto them that hath it shall be given'. It had always seemed grossly unfair to him, especially so in view of the fact that the remainder of the biblical prophecy forecast economic disaster for the 'have nots'. Miles wondered whether he could classify himself among those lucky people who had much and could therefore under the terms of the motto expect more. If so he would cheerfully accept Caroline as his 'bonus', thought Miles as the last delicious morsel of fried camembert slipped down.

Caroline was also thinking of family at that moment. What would her father have made of this apparently effete aristocrat? Would he have dismissed him as a well-born milk-sop, a lily-livered playboy with no spine. Certainly those whose character judgements were based on superficial considerations could have come to such a conclusion. But that was not Caroline's view and she felt it would not have been Bill Montgomery's either. There was about Miles Parmere the feel, the vibration of wasted talent, of mis-spent youth. Caroline detected both the warmth, the vulnerability and at once the almost dangerous strength behind the 'devil may care' façade. She thought of the saying, 'When the going gets tough the tough get going'. Certainly he would be good on a desert island faced with nameless disasters. Come to think of it he might be rather

74

pleasant on a desert island in the absence of any disasters at all. The chilled red Sancerre was delicious. She was having a wonderful time. Bill would have liked Miles, she concluded. Much, perhaps, as he had in the end come to like his father-in-law 'Devil' Lawrence, her rumbustious grandfather. After that initial meeting when Jack Lawrence had attempted to insult her father and had been roundly abused in return, there had, at first, been an uneasy truce. Then 'Devil' had chanced his arm a second time just before Bill's marriage to Eleanor. He had invited Bill to go riding with him and, hoping for disaster, had selected the meanest and most dangerous horse in the county for his prospective son-in-law. That evening at dinner, in the middle of what was in effect a vicious drinking contest, Bill Montgomery had complained to Jack Lawrence that the New England horses 'lacked the spirit' of those found in his native Texas and gave as an example the 'insipid' mount that he had ridden that day. He had proceeded to drink his future father-in-law under the table to the extent that the latter was forced to spend the larger part of the next day in bed, an unheard-of event. From that moment on they had become firm friends. At the wedding reception Lawrence had infuriated his drinking cronies, scandalized the county and thrilled Eleanor by describing Bill Montgomery as the first 'man' that his daughter had ever met and stating how relieved he was that, on seeing the real thing at last, she had had the good sense to recognize it. Caroline felt certain that if Miles and Bill could have met the end result would have been the same, although there might well have been similar false starts along the way.

She bit into the delicious chicken brochette, admiring the delicate flavour of tarragon and other, unknown herbs. As she did so she thought again about Miles' personality, about his carefully concealed toughness, the unmistakable aura of scarcely suppressed violence. Those hidden depths would be plumbed successfully only by the determined and the brave. Caroline wondered if she fitted into that category – if she wanted to.

Despite the desire of both Miles and Caroline to prolong

it, the lunch was drawing irretrievably to a close. That fact could not decently be overlooked for very much longer.

'So, next time we meet it will be on your home territory,' said Miles. It was a statement and a question.

'To the mountains of Aspen,' said Caroline. It was an ambiguous reply.

'To the beaches of Florida,' said Miles Parmere with quiet determination.

# Chapter 3

## I

Miles leaned in heavily with his left shoulder. The pony responded instantly to his command, nostrils flared, its coat steaming in the sultry heat. Nero Castelli was so effectively ridden off the ball that it looked as if he had never intended to approach it in the first place.

Miles kept his shoulder in the American's face for just that split second longer than the situation demanded – a fact that was lost on neither of them. It was not a foul or an infringement of the rules, but it spoke a warning. Miles smiled to himself. The American had had that coming.

European polo was a gentleman's game, played among friends, and the Parmeres had been involved in it for six generations, since its 'invention' by British soldiers stationed in the Imperial India of the mid-nineteenth century. The first Lord Parmere had been in some way responsible for coining the name 'polo' from the Indian word for ball, *pulu*. Miles' ancestors had been instrumental in the drafting of the formal rules in 1897 and his father had sat on the governing body of world polo, the Hurlingham Polo Association, since its creation in 1947. But it was not only because of his family's association with the game that Miles knew the score. He was generally acknowledged to be the best player in England, with a rare handicap of nine. Despite his brilliance Miles had a reputation for erratic play, and this, together with his taste for a rather faster style of life than polo players were expected to lead by the somewhat stuffy hierarchy that controlled the game, meant that his appearances for the English team were infrequent.

However, from time to time, when a particularly tough match loomed, Miles would be invited to parade his virtuoso talents to confound the opposition. Miles himself preferred to play for the Stowell Park team. There he could be himself, indulge his taste for the high life, and perfect his skills by playing with the world's greatest exponents of the game, the incomparable Argentinians, who would play for the Vestey team when the vicious heat of their own country's summer made play impractical there.

It had been a long way from the park of Parmere Hall, where at the age of ten Miles had started to learn the game with stick and ball sessions seated on a wooden horse, to the clipped lawns of the Guards' Polo Club at Smith's Lawn, Windsor Great Park, where he had received the coveted Cowdray Cup from the Queen the year before. Stowell Park had defeated the Prince of Wales' team *Les Diables Bleus* in a closely fought contest.

Miles thought of Prince Charles' advice when he had mentioned that he was going to play polo in Florida. A few years before the Prince had suffered a severe bout of heat exhaustion when playing at the Palm Beach Club and had been driven, almost pulseless, to a local hospital. Miles had heeded his friend Wales' warning that at all costs he should avoid dehydration. The Americans, not averse to a little gamesmanship, and well acclimatized themselves to the sticky, humid heat of their native state, had scheduled the match for three o'clock, when the sun would be beating down and the air so damp that you could almost drink it. In these conditions the skin was unable to cool itself as the sweat could not evaporate on the skin surface. On Wales' advice Miles had avoided lunch, refused all dehydrating alcohol, had eaten a couple of salt tablets that morning and had made sure that there was plenty of cool water available between the five seven-minute chukkers. He had taken one further step in getting Locks of St James' to design for him a special lightweight, aerated helmet that allowed more efficient air circulation. He was therefore well prepared and made a mental note to write and thank the Prince, using the envelope code that would ensure that the letter was opened by him personally rather than by a private secretary.

The match was going well for the European team, despite the fact that they were unused to the ponies, which had been provided by Harry Fox. This could have been a problem, but for the fact that three-quarters of Miles' team were superb horsemen. Two of them, the Domecq brothers, had been friends of Miles since childhood. During the holidays he had often stayed in their beautiful family *estancia* in the country outside the sherry town of Jerez de la Frontera in Spain's Andalucia. There had hardly been a time during those wonderful summers when they had got off a horse. He had learned fluent Spanish and fallen in love with the southern Spain of the bullfight, the haunting flamenco, so much so that when he had heard that the Domecqs had a small farm for sale on one of their estates near Seville he had bought it. Now it was his retreat from the high society world in which he moved, the one place on earth where he could feel at peace. Miles and the Domecqs appeared to the crowd to be sewn into their saddles and were able to extract the maximum from their mounts. The other Englishman on the team was less happy, being used to the faster acceleration, greater speed and 'attack' and at the same time more placid temperament of the English ponies.

The Americans were already trailing by four goals at the end of the second chukker and one player, the huge, bull-necked Nero Castelli, a swarthy, blue-chinned American of Latin descent, was not taking it well. He had imagined that these Europeans would be a push-over, all class and no guts. He was being proved wrong and was reacting in a way more appropriate to a street corner than to a polo field. At a goalmouth mêlée a few minutes into the previous chukker he had indulged in some dangerous 'bumping and boring' and as a result Miles' team had been awarded a penalty goal by the two umpires. That was rare. As Miles drank water and changed his pony between chukkers one of the other Americans, a charming, patrician Southerner, John Charlton Pell, had apologized to Miles for his team-mate's behaviour. Miles had already evened things out to some extent by his enthusiastic riding off of Mr Castelli, which, although within the bounds of legality, had made its point.

During the next chukker Nero Castelli began to swear horribly when he mis-hit a ball or failed to make a clearance. He was playing in the 'back' position and so was subjected to the full onslaught of the European attack. Now, as Pedro Domecq bore down on his goal, Nero Castelli did something very dangerous indeed. Riding in from a sharp oblique angle he crossed the line of the Spaniard's pony and, at the same time, hit hard at the ball underneath the neck and across the front legs of his opponent's mount. Pedro Domecq was himself leaning low, his face next to his pony's neck, to aim a near-sided back-hander at the American goal. Castelli's fifty-five-centimetre bamboo stick arched up in a bow beneath the neck of the Spaniard's mount and caught him full in the face, instantly shattering his nose, for he wore no visor. The chukker was halted as a blood-bespattered Domecq was led off the field for medical attention. Later, bravely, he was to return to finish the match.

Miles could not remember when he had been more angry. Nobody could say for sure that Castelli had intended to injure his friend. What could not be denied was that he had used very dangerous play and that his whole demeanour and attitude bore no relation at all to the sort of thing that was acceptable on the polo field. To add insult to injury the peasant seemed infinitely cheered up by the event despite the awarding of a second penalty goal against his team. Miles was far too well trained to retaliate on the field itself. That would come later. Instead he concentrated on winning the match by the largest possible margin. When the bell went at the end of the final chukker the margin of victory was a substantial ten goals to two.

Miles headed for the pink-and-white, candy-striped tent that stood incongruously beside the clipped, luxuriant green of the polo lawn. He pushed through the appreciative crowd and made for the bar. As expected Rupert Dene was already there, cutting an outrageous figure. He sat at a large table with two pneumatic, peroxide blondes, puffing on a vast Churchill cigar. Despite his anger at Castelli's behaviour, Miles had to laugh. How on earth did Dene manage it? He wore one of the loudest Hawaiian shirts that Miles had ever seen, depicting various fishing scenes among which, for some inexplicable reason, scantily clad hula girls performed erotic dances. His white and brown 'co-respondent's' shoes sported tassels and he wore a pair of pale pink poplin trousers with a teddy-bear motif. Dene's booming voice cut across the bar, drowning for a second the strident tones of his awful shirt.

'Milovitch, dear boy, come and join us. I have discovered this wonderful barman who *understands* about Pimms Number One.' Miles sat down heavily at the table. The two girls preened themselves, intrigued by the new arrival. Bear Dene's priorities demanded, however, that the possibilities of the Pimms conversation be exhausted before the secondary matter of the introductions arose. 'He knew all about adding some Gordons and a dash of Cointreau but we nearly fell out about the fruit.' Dene spoke as if failure on the barman's part to surrender on the question of the fruit was a matter of such vital importance that it would have led to total severance of any relationship, even to blows. 'People will insist,' he complained, 'on putting everything into a Pimms, including the proverbial kitchen sink. We nearly ended up with maraschino cherries, melon, slices of banana, strawberries – more like a bloody fruit salad than a drink.' The tone implied that violent death would be preferable. 'I finally got it across that the sole constituents of a good borage are mint, sliced cucumber if you must, oranges and lemons.'

The huge jug of Pimms Number One cup dominated the table. Around it were stacked several chilled silver tankards. Miles poured himself a glass and drank it down gratefully. Rupert had done well. Not too sweet, not too dilute, a good strong taste of gin, plenty of fizz, Schweppes lemonade. At this point Rupert showed signs of wanting to expand the conversation into a more general one in which the merits of the different Pimms concoctions were discussed in detail. What, for instance, of the vodka-based

Number Six, saved from extinction by the vociferous demands of the *cognoscenti* a few years before? Miles cut in – 'I think you should introduce these charming ladies.'

'Ah,' said Dene, 'Meet Maybelline and Sue Ellen, natives of this excellent state and excellent advertisements for it, I might add.' He puffed contentedly on his outsize Havana. Miles took them in. Maybelline had a pronounced Southern drawl, a see-through blouse and green hot pants. The blouse revealed *Playboy*-style breasts and nipples, ready air brushed. Her legs were, for Miles, a little too short, her bottom tending more towards the pear than to the peach that he preferred. There was no doubt about one thing. Maybelline was clearly a raver. Sue Ellen was taller, thinner, more sophisticated, more intelligent. Her breasts were almost as big as Maybelline's, but were more angular than rounded. Longer legs, smaller bottom, quieter clothes. She wore a copper bracelet around her right ankle. Miles wondered about the significance of that. If you knew what you would get from Maybelline, Sue Ellen's promise was more mysterious. Horses for courses, thought Miles. Sue Ellen would be for the earlier part of the evening before one had got too drunk – Maybelline for that later period when one needed all the help one could get.

As if in answer to Miles' unspoken question as to the origins of these two thoroughly acceptable girls Dene said, 'The ladies were introduced by that rather unsatisfactory person who failed to distinguish himself on the polo field – Canneloni or Castiogli, or whatever he's called.' Both girls giggled guiltily at this inaccurate rendering of Nero Castelli's surname. The impression was given that that was not something a native would have allowed himself to do.

'If I wasn't a guest here that parvenu might easily find himself munching on a knuckle sandwich,' said Miles darkly.

'I suspect he would understand such things. He told me that if the girls didn't "pleasure" me he would have their arms broken. I *suppose* he was joking – he did sort of leer when he said it.'

Maybelline and Sue Ellen exchanged glances which said

that jokes like this from Nero Castelli were the sort that they could easily do without.

At this point John Charlton Pell joined the table. Miles introduced the cool American who had apologized in the paddock for Castelli's behaviour.

'I couldn't help overhearing that last bit,' said Pell. 'I am afraid that Mr Castelli is a bit of a caricature – one of those Americans you get to know through old Bogart and George Raft movies.'

'You mean he's a gangster,' said Dene with enthusiasm, greatly encouraged by this development. 'My word, does that mean you two are gangster's molls?' He turned towards the two girls. His tone implied that to discover that they were Nobel Prize winners or prima ballerinas could hardly have been more exciting. Neither girl appeared at all at home with such levity concerning a subject which was for them very serious indeed. However the Pimms was strong and these Englishmen appeared to be quite immune from any of the nameless horrors that might be dished out by the disturbing Castelli. Perhaps some of the immunity would rub off on them. There were more nervous titters.

'Personally,' said Pell, 'I couldn't care how rich he is from peddling drugs and pushing his weight around. I thought his behaviour on the field was quite inexcusable.'

Miles liked the American enormously – the very best sort of person. Totally straight, honest and forthright, afraid of no one. Suddenly he thought of Caroline and his heart sank. Would there be wall-to-wall John Charlton Pells in Aspen? It was not a comforting thought.

Pell's words were still hanging in the air when the party became aware that they were not alone. A sense of foreboding descended as if for a moment a dark cloud had blotted out the sun. Nero Castelli towered over the table exuding an aura of menace. The two girls became very quiet, very still. It was as if the birds had stopped singing in response to the presence of a much-feared cat. Castelli stood there, hands on hips, jet-black hair slicked straight back from his forehead, his stubbly, blue chin thrust forward, greasy, glistening. Thick black hair hid his huge forearms, pushed like a doormat through the V-neck of his polo vest. Highly polished black boots, now scuffed and spotted with mud, gave him the forbidding appearance of an eighteenth-century plantation overseer whose job it was to discipline the slaves. It seemed merely an oversight that he carried no whip.

Miles wondered if ever before he had seen such an unattractive man. Behind and on either side of Castelli stood two equally discouraging figures. It would be hard to imagine how any casting director searching for two men to play classical 'hoods' could have bettered their appearance. They were almost too good to be true. He would have been accused of 'overkill'. Black suits, bulging pockets, expressionless faces chewing gum, wide shoulders, narrow waists. If Castelli was not a gangster then he was a consummate actor, who had taken the trouble to get hold of the right 'props'.

Now he spoke and it was immediately apparent that he was in conciliatory mood – the sight of blood earlier having satisfied some deeper desire than the need to be on the winning side. Like some latter-day werewolf he had had his fill. Nero Castelli in friendly mood was, however, if anything even more macabre than his earlier display of temper had revealed. He was cleary a person of such monumental nastiness that his attempted charm merely added hypocrisy to his list of sins. He wished everyone at the table nothing but evil. No superficial friendliness could disguise that.

'Well now, there are some gentlemen here I don't know,' he said in a hard, thick voice, looking pointedly at Miles.

'Ah, Castrolli, there you are,' said Dene, making much of the name, which he knew to be wrong.

Castelli's lip curled. He disliked being a motor oil as much as earlier he had objected to being a pasta, but he would let it pass. What did these foreigners know?

'May I introduce Lord Parmere – he's the one with the unbroken nose. Mr Pell you probably know, as of course you do the ladies.'

This limey could get hurt, thought Castelli.

Pell cut him dead. Miles said nothing as he looked him up and down as if he was something the cat had brought in.

Castelli held on to his temper with difficulty. 'Well, Lord,' he managed finally, 'what have you got to drink there? Lemonade?'

Miles said coldly, 'Lord is my title, not my Christian name.'

This was too much for Castelli. 'Tight hole. Tight ass,' he quipped without any humour at all.

To his two companions he might have been Bob Hope or Jack Benny on a good day. They fell about.

John Charlton Pell's aristocratic Southern tones cut into the conversation. '*Mr* Castelli,' he said, his voice ice cold. 'You have failed to behave like a gentleman on the polo field and you are failing to do so again now. It may be that this is because you are not a gentleman. I suggest that you leave us alone and take those two extraordinary figures with you.'

The veins in Nero Castelli's neck began to fill with blood. Miles had the definite impression that he had begun to pulsate. He appeared to grow larger although his individual components were all contracting. His eyes narrowed, his fists clenched into tight, white balls, his mouth became a neat surgical scar across his face. The smiles on the faces of the henchmen melted as, mentally, they prepared to earn their keep. It was a very nasty moment indeed. Miles felt his adrenalin flow. Dene worried about the fate of the jug of Pimms. Pell, clearly a man of very considerable courage, continued to stare haughtily at Castelli as he completed his metamorphosis into a throbbing beetroot. Broken noses paled in comparison with what might be expected now. Miles braced himself, muscles tightening. Surprisingly he was rather heartened by all this. His mind suddenly was crystal clear – the SAS unarmed combat training flooding back at lightning speed. The trick would be to prevent the henchmen from drawing their guns. With Dene not much use at this sort of thing and Pell at best an enthusiastic amateur, it would be, like Waterloo, a close-run thing, thought Miles. Some sixth sense, some street cunning, gave Castelli the same message. He paused for a split second before giving the sign.

'I am so glad you are all getting acquainted,' said the authoritarian, severe voice. It was a command, not an observation.

Harry Fox stood before the potential combatants like a ringmaster in the wild animal cage. Nobody was going to spoil *his* party. He intended to be obeyed. The bomb was defused. The moment had passed. Castelli stared hard for a second at Harry Fox and then back again at the table. Great waves of cold malice shot from him before he turned abruptly and, trailing his two bodyguards behind him, was gone.

## II

Harry Fox had taken in the scene instantly and had as quickly acted to draw its sting. Nero Castelli was a gangster, but the richest one in Florida and, far from incidentally, a very large shareholder in Harry's Union Bank. Harry knew his character well. They had come much the same way from similar origins. But Miles was also of potential value to him, a possible source of the respectability that Fox craved. It would be no disaster for Castelli and Parmere to dislike each other. That was to be expected. To have them half kill each other at the opening of Harry's new club was another thing altogether.

Harry Fox was a ghetto boy made good. Born in the slums of New York City and neglected by his impoverished alcoholic parents, he had graduated *summa cum laude* from the academy of petty street crime to being at the age of twenty-three a man with 'Mob' connections. Good with his fists, he was better with figures, and these two attributes, coupled with a burning desire to succeed, led him through a succession of jobs in the vast business conglomerate that was organized urban crime. He had started by organizing dope pedlars and prostitutes, moved on to gambling dens and night clubs until, by the time of his twenty-eighth birthday, he was running a large insurance company that provided cover for 'legitimate' Organization businesses. In the late 1970s and early 1980s the growing business was cocaine. The drug was smuggled into Florida from South America and the sums involved and the profits to be made were huge. This enormous business had to be financed, its rewards hidden away from the prying eyes of the IRS. Money needed to be deposited, laundered, reinvested in the dangerous but lucrative cocaine trade. Mob money was therefore provided to start the Union Bank of Florida whose initial purpose was to finance this rapidly developing drug traffic. Harry was made chief executive and chairman, was allocated twenty per cent of the shares and given total freedom to run things his way. He had proved himself to his masters in harder schools. This delegation of responsibility had been an inspired one. Since Harry's appointment, growth at the bank had been phenomenal and expansion had taken place into all areas of local business. Cocaine remained at the heart of the operation but Harry was diversifying away from it fast. Men such as Castelli did not look good on the shareholders' register. When the time came Harry would buy him out. The old men of the Organization liked this approach. After all, they were only interested in money and the power that it brought them. If money could be made legitimately there was no point in criminal activities. So now Harry chased respectable growth like any other respectable capitalist and he did it well. Although his experience of traditional banking was limited, he was in the right business at the right time and, if rumours circulated about the quality of some of the depositors, nobody was inclined to argue with the profits. That was where Miles Parmere came in. He would provide some respectability, help with the thrust into the international arena, provide contacts with people who would not be seen dead in a ditch with Harry Fox. Harry wanted him and what Harry wanted he usually got, English aristocrats not excluded.

Harry had spirited Miles away from the polo match at the first opportunity. He could not risk one of Castelli's hangers-on attempting to do himself a bit of good with his boss by indulging in some free-enterprise violence. Now they sat by the pool of Harry's Palm Beach house, drinking Bloody Marys. A party was scheduled for later in the evening.

Harry Fox was a more socially acceptable figure now, but the raw, pungent aroma of the ghetto still clung to him and one could sense the violent ruthlessness and determination to succeed beneath the fashionable suits and shirts that now clothed him. Miles could sense it across the few yards that separated them and was intrigued by it.

'That Castelli and his friends looked like something out of *Guys and Dolls*,' he said. 'I am afraid there was nearly blood on the walls.' The way Miles said this carried with it the intimation that it would have been Castelli's blood rather than his that would have defaced the candy-coloured tent. Harry knew all about Miles' SAS career. The professional skill and bravery that organization had shown in the British storming of the Iranian Embassy in London hinted that its members knew a thing or two about self-protection.

'Castelli's a throw-back to the old days,' agreed Harry. 'But he shouldn't be under-estimated. Miami has a higher murder rate today than Tombstone did in the days of Wyatt Earp. Castelli does his share.'

Miles marvelled at the way this man could talk so casually of his invited guests as ruthless killers. He was not used to playing polo with such people, although come to think of it he had enjoyed a few chukkers with 'Lucky' Lucan.

'He has a big holding in the bank, too,' Harry added. He thought of the early days when Castelli's presence had been not only useful, but vitally important. On several occasions the policemen and judges that Castelli 'owned' had helped solve problems for Harry and the bank. On others Castelli's hired muscle had 'discouraged' debt defaultors, had 'persuaded' people that the Union Bank was the best place for their spare cash and had 'suggested' to talkative employees that they button their mouths, take a vacation. Those who had not taken notice of Castelli's warnings had not prospered, and, more important, the information that they had not done so was public knowledge. Some had suffered nasty little accidents that had cost their medical insurance companies large sums of money. Some had moved to other states, other countries, often leaving suddenly. Harry seldom required these services now. He had lawyers and accountants to do his dirty work. But he would never forget the days when a casual word in Castelli's ear could have dramatic effects. One never knew when such favours might be required again. So, for the moment Harry was content to leave Castelli on 'hold', a sheathed sabre, a caged animal. There were, after all, many different kinds of insurance policy.

Miles got Harry's message. If he was to work for him he had to keep his personal feelings about Castelli to himself. Miles could live with that. He didn't have to mix with the man. He wondered if Harry Fox had the power to control the mobster and if so why. Men like Castelli tended not to forget being insulted in front of an audience of their own retainers. There were, after all, many different kinds of honour.

Miles looked around him. Harry had done well. The Spanish-style *hacienda* surrounded the sixty-foot pool on three sides. Tall palm trees rustled in the late afternoon breeze, a welcome respite from the steamy heat of the polo field. Mixed fragrances, jasmine, frangipani, orange blossom, hung on the air, the soft whirr of the pool filter the only sound disturbing the tranquillity. Miles sipped at the blood-red drink. Harry had done well, indeed.

'I've decided to accept your offer,' said Miles. Caroline's spell had not lifted.

'You won't regret it,' said Harry. For a time they discussed the details of the job. Miles was to be a roving ambassador for the bank. Based in Florida with an office and secretary in the Miami headquarters, he would spend much of his time on the road, or rather in the air. His brief was simple – to spread the word that the Union was the best small bank in America and was about to become one of the biggest. Miles was to score deposits, produce deals, pass on information, make introductions. He would report directly to Fox and answer to nobody else. He would not need to involve himself in the day-to-day affairs of the bank and indeed would be encouraged not to do so. Harry did not want the English lord turning over too many stones. One never knew what he might find – how he might react.

Harry thought back over the past five years. He had not dared to dream of the success that had come his way. The Sun-Belt population explosion had been under way for several years as the sun-starved northerners headed south to escape the fuel bills and the unions, to experience the 'good life'. Ten of the twenty-five fastest-growing cities in the US in the 1970s had been in Florida. The explosion in property prices that had resulted had been largely financed by banks like the Union. Tourism and the retirement industry had also been growth areas. It had been a licence to print money. New deposits had flowed into the brash new bank with its opulent offices and pretty tellers. The cocaine money provided the base on which a fast-growing pyramid had soon been built. Now the bank's thirty-eight branches covered the whole of Florida, handling deposits of $8.5 billion with total assets of $11 billion. Already there was a London branch in Bishopsgate and representative offices in Tokyo, Singapore and Bahrain. But it was only a beginning. The McFadden Act, still unrepealed, meant that within the United States deposit-taking banks could operate in one state alone. President Wayne, a firm believer with Calvin Coolidge that the business of America was business, was bitterly opposed to the Act and soon it would be no more. Fox would be free to move into Texas, and into the glittering world of California banking, the most lucrative in the world.

Unlike many other small operations, the Union was not afraid of competition from the big money-centre banks.

Harry welcomed such competition because he believed in himself, knew that he could outwit them in the scramble for deposits. He could make a better turn on deposits than the big boys. For instance, the net interest rate margin at the large banks in New York and Chicago was roughly two and a half per cent. That represented the difference between what they had to pay out on money deposited with them and what they received as interest on their loans. Harry, however, had access to much cheaper deposits and reckoned on averaging a four per cent 'turn'. Nor would the battlefield be confined to the States. He would expand abroad until he could compete with the majors, with Chemical, Citibank and the Chase. It would be a long time before he could draw level with them, but this was the stuff that dreams were made of. For although the Union Bank was now the biggest in Florida, nationwide it was a minnow, its assets a tenth of Citibank's. It needed to number big industrial borrowers among its clients before it could walk with the mighty, needed to appear as lead manager on the underwriting advertisements in *The Times* under names like Exxon and IBM.

Harry had the cash to do it but not the caché. Union had been unable to shake off entirely the reputation for having disreputable customers. It was a question of image, and image in banking was everything. Harry remembered an old Rothschild mentioning to him once that in England there was no substitute for a 'lord on the board'. The point had been taken. Miles might not cut a great deal of ice in Florida, but in New York and Europe he would earn his keep. After all, the top ten banks in the United States relied on abroad for, on average, half their deposits, while Citibank's overseas business accounted for more than seventy per cent of its deposited funds.

Miles poured himself another Bloody Mary from the ice-cold silver shaker. The job didn't sound too taxing and $250,000 a year would solve a lot of problems. He began to think about where he would live.

'No particular reason for you to stay in Miami,' said Harry. 'I don't think it's really your kind of town, but I suppose you ought to have a base in Florida for when you're not travelling.'

'I once stayed in a superb place in Key Largo for a fishing week-end. I'd thought of pitching my tent there,' said Miles. 'Travelling wouldn't be a problem,' he continued. 'There's an air strip where you can rent helicopters and planes.'

Miles thought of Roy Felty, the tough, laconic ex-Navy captain, and of the week-end they had spent together reminiscing on wartime experiences, drinking Budweiser and catching sailfish in some of the most beautiful and best fishing waters in the world. It would be good to see Roy again.

'The place is called Ocean Reef. Heard of it?' asked Miles.

Harry knew of the ritzy development at Key Largo, where Burt Reynolds and ex-President Nixon stayed. That would be just the place for Miles. Harry vaguely remembered that one of the Saudi princes had a house there too, next to Bebe Rebozo's place. 'Yeah. Lots of money around there. Should be able to pick up a lot of business.' Harry made it sound as if Miles would be selling insurance, if not encyclopaedias.

There were some things that Harry simply did not understand. Miles made a dismissive gesture. 'I don't really think that I'm going to sniff out business for your bank by hanging about the bars and marinas of smart apartment complexes.'

Harry didn't like the tone of Miles' remark, but then he had never expected to *like* him. What he wanted to do was to *use* him. It was a question merely of how best to do so.

Miles was thinking much the same thing.

Harry lapsed into a moody silence, staring at Miles balefully.

'I had dinner with Eleanor Montgomery and her daughter the other day,' said Miles.

Harry sat up. Eleanor Montgomery, Walter Wriston, David Rockefeller, Donald Regan, these were names to conjure with. He cheered noticeably. This was the stuff he was paying a quarter of a million a year for, and so far he hadn't parted with a cent.

Miles noticed the change. He paused.

'Oh, what's she up to?' said Harry, trying to sound casual. Eleanor Montgomery's brand of toothpaste would have been of interest to him.

'She's thinking of going to the market for a billion dollars of five-year money. I think they want to buy a small oil company to secure their supply of animal feedstuff. Apparently petrochemical products can be used for that.' Miles felt proud of his retentive memory, but was not totally sure that he had got it right. Caroline's delicious face filled his mind.

'Oh?' said Harry. He wanted more.

'She's rather concerned about the level of interest rates and is delaying because she wants to do the best possible deal.' Miles could see that he was doing well. 'I suggested to her that we might lend her the money,' he continued. He didn't see why he shouldn't bend the truth a little bit.

Harry laughed and slapped his thigh. The thought of the Union Bank lending Montgomery Chemical a billion dollars would have made any banker laugh. And then, quite suddenly, he stopped laughing. Harry Fox was not a conventional man. He had always fought shy of the mainstream, avoided where possible the dedicated following of fashion. Why should he laugh at the idea of his bank making a vast loan to a big company like Montgomery? They should be so lucky. With mounting excitement he savoured the idea. If he could swing it, it made sense. For years he had craved the big time, yearned to be part of the New York scene with the big board quote that would signal the 'arrival' of the Union Bank, its acceptance into the inner sanctum. At the moment the shares were quoted on the infinitely less prestigious 'over-the-counter' market. By lending a billion to Montgomery he would achieve respectability at a stroke. There would be lunches at Salomon Brothers and First Boston, membership perhaps at one of the grand clubs like the Knickerbocker, telephone calls from the *Wall Street Journal* to ask his views on the credit markets, inside information, walks along the corridors of power. Doors would open for Eleanor Montgomery's banker. It was a glittering prize.

And he had the money. That was the glorious truth. He had it in Florida, in short-term loans that could be called in at maturity. In a few days he could lay his hands on a billion dollars. Few small banks were in this position, and there were special reasons why the Union Bank was so well placed. Firstly there were the enormous drug deposits. These were often deposited in non-interest-bearing accounts, their owners anxious not to stimulate the interest of the IRS and prepared to forgo interest in exchange for secrecy and the 'no questions asked' attitude of the Union Bank. Harry knew these depositors well. They could be relied upon to keep their money with the Union, which had always been good to them. Then there were the deposits of the unsophisticated and often extremely rich retired population who had for years flocked to Florida. Harry had always courted them with his special 'Senior Citizens' advertisements, his separate high-speed counters for the over-sixty-fives, his employment of janitors who would help the elderly with their shopping baskets, his insistence the bank staff refer by name to the smallest and least significant customer. The result of this careful wooing was that the bank was popular with this extremely important group. These people, although often very rich, had on the whole little interest in financial matters, health, or the lack of it, being of more pressing concern. They tended to leave their money on deposit, mistrusting the stock market, nervous of bonds. Many of the old people, through disinterest, left their money in checking accounts on which Harry paid them a return of a fraction over five per cent. It was a fantastically cheap source of funds as there was nothing to stop Union lending that money on at rates of twenty per cent or more in present market conditions. It always seemed incredible to Harry that these people would be happy to leave their money earning such an insignificant rate.

These two sources would provide the lion's share of the

billion dollars, but there were other sources of funds too, such as short-term loans to rich individuals, to various state agencies, to small businesses. It would take some scraping of the barrel, would irritate some of the locals, and would leave the bank in an exposed position, short of ready funds, but the potential rewards were enormous. Administration would be significantly simplified by concentrating the lending to one powerful company, while Montgomery's impeccable financial position would abolish any worries about bad debts. The share price would improve dramatically on the announcement of the deal, making Harry by virtue of his twenty per cent shareholding in the bank a significantly richer man. Above all the Union Bank would gain immeasurably in reputation, that intangible asset that meant more to banks than gold in their vaults.

If Harry could pull this off Miles Parmere had already earned his first five years' salary in his first five minutes of work. Harry looked across at Miles – a new respect in his eyes. There was another angle, too. Harry wondered if Miles knew about it.

'Of course you know that the Secretary of State has got the hots for Eleanor. He might marry her.'

Miles nodded. He knew that. He had made it his business to know a great deal about the Montgomerys. He also remembered Caroline mentioning at lunch that 'Uncle Charles' was a frequent visitor to the Aspen house – that Miles could expect him as a fellow house guest if he was to week-end there.

That was an added bonus, thought Harry. Mingling with the mighty, knee-deep in dropped names, gossip about the President, digests of 'top secret' CIA reports discreetly referred to. It would all be within the grasp of the banker who lent Eleanor Montgomery a billion dollars. But why would she borrow it from him when a thirty-second telephone call would secure it from half a dozen banks within spitting distance of her New York office? Harry knew the answer. Eleanor Montgomery was first and foremost a businesswoman, perhaps the best in the country. She thought about the bottom line. Harry would make her an offer that she had to accept. He would lend her the money cheap, would undercut the opposition. The potential rewards justified it. In general it was expensive to borrow money from banks. A first-class borrower like Montgomery could expect to pay a fraction above the prime rate, presently twenty per cent. If, as Eleanor was intending, she was to sell a five-year bond, then she could have the money for around seventeen per cent. However, that seventeen per cent would be fixed for five years whereas money borrowed from a bank would be tied to fluctuating interest rates represented by the New York prime or the London interbank rate. The future direction of interest rates, notoriously difficult to predict, would determine the wisdom of the decision. In the absence of hindsight Eleanor would take the view that *this* bird in the hand was some bird. If she could get bank finance for the cost of floating a loan she would go for it and be considered clever to have done so.

Harry would lend Eleanor the billion at three and a half per cent under prime. She would not refuse him. It was very cheap borrowing indeed. 'Can you set up a meeting?' said Harry scarcely able to disguise the shake in his voice.

'I can try,' said Miles.

As an afterthought Harry added, 'There's that skiing daughter too, isn't there? I wouldn't mind throwing my leg across that one.'

Miles decided, not for the first time, that he did not like Harry Fox.

The swimming pool lights lit up the surrounding royal palms and carefully concealed spots picked out the magnolia trees. Heavy scents impregnated the night air, country music played low. Harry's guests were gathering by the pool and already white-uniformed Cuban servants were plying them with drinks. Iced martinis, mimosas, delicious *piña coladas*. For the *aficionados* there was coke too, laid out on silver salvers with silver spoons. This coke was the real thing – pure pharmaceutical – unobtainable on the street. It was going well and the party was going with it. Harry often gave parties like this. They were very popular, and not just for the excellent food, drink and drugs. Most of the girls at Harry's parties were hookers, or inhabited that no-man's-land eternally disputed between prostitutes and enthusiastic amateurs. They had been paid in advance for services to be rendered later. Harry liked this way of selecting his 'guests'. It meant that there was a solid core of the party that he could control – when they arrived, when they left, what they did and to whom in between. It also meant that there were no 'dogs' at Harry's parties. Every girl looked good and was prepared to do you good. It was a happy arrangement, although not cheap.

Scattered throughout the crowd were the targets of Harry's hospitality – men to whom he owed a favour or from whom he wanted one. These men would find during the course of the evening that they had 'got lucky'. Miles, for example, would definitely get lucky. Harry Fox, a firm believer that charity began at home, would get very lucky indeed.

After his bath Miles had watched the early guests arrive from the balcony of the guest house that made up one of the corners of the Fox compound. Lots of pretty girls arriving by themselves or in twos and threes and driving open Mercedes roadsters could only mean one thing, he noted with satisfaction. He sipped at the Louis Roederer Cristal 1973, several bottles of which nestled in the bedroom refrigerator. Things were looking good. They would look better. Miles slipped out of the rough towelling dressing gown. It was time to join the party. He dressed quickly. Double-breasted navy blue blazer with the regimental buttons, Guards tie. Turnbull and Asser cream silk shirt, faded blue soft levis carefully ironed, black cotton socks from Harvie and Hudson, dark blue velvet slippers, the single initial 'P' surmounting the Parmere crest. 'Unto them that hath' – indeed. He splashed on some Cerrutti cologne, poured himself another glass of the superb wine and went out into the night, pausing to breathe in the heady fragrance that enveloped him. The well-watered grass was springy beneath his feet as he approached the party.

Harry Fox detached himself from the crowd to welcome Miles. Since their conversation that afternoon Harry had been in a turmoil of excitement and anticipation. Now his good humour homed in on Miles. 'Miles, Miles,' he bubbled. 'Come and join us. Meet some of these young ladies.'

Two of them he had met before. Sue Ellen and Maybelline had made the transition from the polo match to the Palm Beach house. Both had been at the coke and were now well and truly wired. There were two other girls in the group to which Harry introduced him – a tall, gangling black girl with an arse so high that it seemed to belong to the middle of her back and a sensational-looking blonde whose most remarkable feature, apart from a faultless face and body, was her very extreme youth. An optimist could just have put her at sixteen. The smart money said thirteen. She was not the sort of girl that had come with her mother to the party. In California they called girls like her jail bait. Miles wondered what Florida laws were like in this respect. It seemed in some way that she 'belonged' to Harry Fox because before he moved off he patted her bottom and said, 'Now you behave, Susie, until I get back.' It was his way of saying 'hands off'. Miles would not have dreamed of putting his hands on. Screwing kids was not his bag. It began to look as if it was Harry Fox's.

'Can I get you some coke?' said the black girl to Miles.

'Never use it, but thanks anyway.' As an afterthought he added, 'But I think I could handle one of those rather good-looking mimosas.' He admired the retreating arse as she went off to fetch the drink.

'I just love your funny accent,' said Susie, the thirteen-year-old, with a precocious pout. She stuck both thumbs in the waistband of her skin-tight jeans and pushed out her pert, pre-adolescent bottom. The white cotton tee-shirt was undone to the waist and she made no effort to hide the jutting breasts with their rose-pink nipples, breasts that if anything pointed upwards rather than straight ahead.

The black girl came back with the mimosa.

'Mind if I taste it?' she asked as Miles reached for the drink.

With her eyes boring deep into his, the coloured girl darted her pink tongue at the yellow, fizzing drink. She ran it along the edge of the tulip-shaped glass and then, suddenly, plunged it deep into the sparkling liquid. She threw her head back and swallowed. There was no mistaking the meaning of this charade. Miles felt himself harden in the tight blue jeans. The thirteen-year-old picked up on it immediately. In a second she was beside him. Her hand rested casually on his bottom. 'Say,' she said in a mock Mae West voice, amid general laughter, 'is that a pistol in your pocket or are you just pleased to see me?'

'Things are moving fast,' thought Miles. 'Time to slow down.'

Sue Ellen and Maybelline clearly worked as a team, and now that the cocaine had loosened them up a bit Miles could see why. Sue Ellen, the taller girl, had her hand between Maybelline's shoulder blades and was massaging them gently, the other girl squirming with pleasure. All tastes appeared to be catered for at Harry Fox's parties.

Susie of the tender years was old enough to know the importance of keeping up momentum. She put her hand around Miles' waist and moved in close, her front against his side. Her thin limbs straddled his right leg and he could feel the warmth of her cunt through the soft, tight levis.

'Save it for Uncle Harry,' said Miles cheerfully as he disengaged himself. 'Why don't we all go and find a table?'

Susie was not at all put out by this apparent rejection. She reached up on tiptoe to whisper something in Miles' ear. He bent down to hear what she had to say. He was rewarded with a probing tongue thrust deep into his ear. As it withdrew she whispered, 'How would you like me to stick my tongue right up your ass?'

Before Miles could answer Harry's voice cut in from the edge of the group. Miles could not help wondering if he specialized in dramatic entrances to avert potentially dangerous situations. After all it was the second time in one day. In a commanding voice he said, 'Susie, why don't you go and wait in my room? I have something for you. I won't be long.' With a sulky toss of her long blonde hair Susie disappeared.

'Unlikely to be a teddy bear,' thought Miles.


# III


Harry stormed into the bedroom. Susie had already put on the handcuffs. She knew the scene.

'What did you say to him?' he screamed.

Susie stood forlornly in the middle of the room her hands fastened together in front of her. She wore a pair of black silk briefs and nothing else. She swallowed guiltily.

'Answer me,' Harry barked. 'Or you know what will happen.'

Susie knew. 'I told him I wanted to suck his ass.'

Harry shuddered with pleasure. 'Did you? Did you?' Slowly, deliberately, Harry unzipped his fly.

'And that I wanted to swallow his load,' Susie lied in her little-girl voice.

'You're a tramp, a child whore. You're only a baby and you've got a mind like a sewer. Children like you should be treated like sewers.'

She knew what was coming – had learned to like it. She knelt on the carpet.

'Don't . . .' she pleaded.

Harry stood in front of her, his zip undone, his limp penis in his hand. She stared at it, mesmerized. The golden stream hit her between the breasts, cascading down her beautiful stomach, soaking the black underpants.

'This is all you're good for,' he yelled. Susie squirmed.

'I got carried away,' she mumbled. 'I guess I just wanted to feel his prick.'

Now she took it full in the face. This was the bit she liked, that always made her come. She turned her head from side to side to escape the warm, stinging liquid. At last it stopped, but Harry Fox had not finished.

He walked towards her. 'Open,' he barked.

Dutifully she opened her mouth. Between her legs she was wet with both his urine and the juices of her own desire. Harry pushed into the open mouth holding her roughly by the hair. Susie's eyes widened as his erection filled her throat.

'You filthy whore,' he shouted.

From past experience she knew it would not be long now. This was the tricky bit. She would have to swallow fast to avoid choking. And then Harry was coming. He pushed her backwards onto the carpet as he did so, pinning her head to the floor until the last delectable spasm was spent.

Miles was correct about the absence of teddy bears. Susie's 'present', apart from one phenomenal orgasm, would be $500.

The party was loosening up. The inevitable nude swimmers had already started disporting themselves in the pool. 'Very 1950s,' thought Miles. He was determined to eat a good meal at the very least before succumbing to the waves of kamikaze women that seemed to be aiming themselves at him from every side. Miles was under no illusions. Clearly the word was out that he was to get well and truly fucked. He had already made his selection. It would be the double act from the polo field, Maybelline and Sue Ellen, who continued to flash smouldering glances at one another, looks – Miles felt – that were not merely for his benefit. He sat with them now at one of the tables by the pool, in front of him a vast plate of Florida seafood – clams, giant 'king' prawns, cracked crab, half a lobster and a bottle of well-chilled Muscadet, shipped by Sichel. Afterwards he would attack the ripe, runny imported Brie he had nosed out among the rather tasteless, bland American cheeses with names like 'Dart' and 'Kraft', soon, perhaps, to be known as 'Daft' as the two companies had recently merged. With that he would try a glass of the Napa Valley Californian burgundy that Harry swore by. Miles' experience was that the more distinguished older French reds seldom recovered totally from their long journey, were anyway too heavy for the humid heat of Caribbean-type climates such as Florida's.

'Tell me about Nero Castelli,' he said, cracking a lobster claw in his teeth.

'He bears grudges,' said Sue Ellen simply.

'He makes a lot of people nervous,' added Maybelline. She spoke from first-hand experience.

'I thought all that gangster stuff went out with Prohibition,' said Miles.

'Not in Miami.'

'Well, it's all rather encouraging to know that grand old institutions continue to survive in the face of what's laughingly called progress . . . gangsters, the House of Lords, nude swimming at midnight . . .' He looked over his shoulder towards the pool. A statuesque Puerto Rican girl was sitting astride a rubber lilo. Firmly wedged between her legs was the head of the black girl whose tongue had showed such promise earlier. From the ecstatic moans of the girl on top it was hard at work. Miles watched as the Puerto Rican, showing considerable dexterity and balance, shifted her position to lower her anus over the black girl's eager mouth. Sue Ellen leaned forward in approval, her erect nipples pushing angrily against the cotton tee-shirt. She licked her lips. Beside her Maybelline shifted uncomfortably in her tight white shorts. Sue Ellen turned and shot her a look of pure, unadulterated desire. Under the table her hand sneaked out to Maybelline's crotch. Once there it was immediately gripped vice-like by the smaller girl's legs.

'Enjoying the show, you two,' observed Miles.

There was a loud splash. One of the more uninhibited guests had jumped in and was swimming towards the lilo. When he reached it he dropped his head down and buried it between the black girl's legs. There was spontaneous applause for this piece of enterprise. Now the aquatic live show drifted towards the side of the pool where a small, thin man with a large prick was ostentatiously masturbating. The Puerto Rican, her arse still covering the black girl's face, managed with some difficulty to manoeuvre the onlooker's penis into her mouth.

Miles was going to have to miss out on the Brie. Pushing his plate away from him he stood up. 'May I invite you both to a glass of champagne in my room,' he said.

Both girls looked relieved. 'Thought you'd never ask,' said Sue Ellen.

They never did get to the champagne. Within seconds of entering the bedroom Sue Ellen had unzipped Miles' fly and his erect penis was in her hand. Not a word was spoken. All three remained dressed, standing by the doorway. It seemed there was not a second to lose. Maybelline moved behind Sue Ellen, fiddling with her friend's belt. Then, very slowly, as if unveiling for the first time some exquisitely sculptured monument, she lowered Sue Ellen's jeans. The small round arse jutted out. With her right hand she rubbed gently between Sue Ellen's legs, until the silky brown pubic hair began to glisten with moisture. Sue Ellen turned to face Maybelline, presenting her bottom to Miles.

As she did so, hands behind her back, she guided him inside her, whilst her open mouth sought Maybelline's. Still standing, and fully clothed, Miles thrust into her, caught tight in the grip of her unusually strong pelvic muscles. As he did so he watched the two girls necking with all the enthusiasm of teenage lovers. He quickened his movements. Sue Ellen groaned. Maybelline sank to her knees at this signal and thrust her head into her friend's crotch, her chin resting on the jeans that hung around Sue Ellen's knees. Miles felt her warm tongue on his prick as he pounded into Sue Ellen, the occasional rasp of teeth adding exquisite pain to the silky softness of his pleasure. Sue Ellen had both hands against the wall now, pushing back at Miles with all her strength and at the same time bearing down hard on Maybelline's tongue. Her orgasms were coming rapidly, showering her moisture onto Maybelline's face and hair. Suddenly she stood upright and once more her hands reached backwards for Miles' prick.

'Try this.' The voice was thick and husky with desire.

With a deft movement she took Miles out of her, but not for long. Miles watched her bottom pushing out again and in seconds he was deep within her anus, thrusting into her bowels. The increased tightness was the final straw. He could hold back the orgasm no longer. It seemed to take for ever as he pumped into her and then it was over.

'The end of the beginning,' thought Miles.

'Let's get undressed,' said Sue Ellen.

Miles abandoned himself to ecstasy under the practised tuition of the two American girls. He had never experienced anything quite like it before – doubted that he would again. No area of his body was left unexplored, untouched by passion. Maybelline and Sue Ellen were deeply in love and the genuine nature of this mutual desire provided the background for an almost total experience in lovemaking. In between they had drunk Crystal, and had toasted their sensuality. At some stage of the night Maybelline had slipped away. One final time Miles made love to Sue Ellen and then, buried inside her, he fell into a deep sleep.

Some ghostly reveille sounded in Miles' brain. He was wide awake. He lay still, searching for the cause of his sudden consciousness. Then he heard the noise that had awakened him. Somebody was moving about downstairs on the ground floor of the guest house. The girl lay beside him, her back towards him. She had not stirred. Miles' mind raced. Burglars? Possibly. More unwelcome visitors? Probably. Keeping absolutely still otherwise, his hand moved slowly to the bedside table. Now it closed over the hilt of the Italian 'Grisbi' diving knife that since Army days he had kept close to him while he slept. It was a wicked weapon. The six-inch Inox steel blade was curved on one side, with a serrated edge near the point. The other side of the blade he kept razor sharp. On several occasions in the past when he had run out of Wilkinson Sword blades he had used the Grisbi to shave.

Miles shifted slightly in the bed. He should get out without waking the girl. There was an added difficulty in that he appeared to be still inside her. She moaned gently as he withdrew but did not wake. In an instant Miles was at the door, stark naked, knife in hand. He paused, turning his head from side to side, listening carefully. Two men were searching the empty ground-floor rooms. Soon they would try the stairs. Miles had come alive. This was his world. He was back in the jungles of Vietnam, living on his wits, his life in the balance. He was the hunted but he was also the hunter – it was an attitude of mind. He felt no fear, just intense excitement. His mind worked with the speed and precision of a computer, assessing the situation coolly, calmly, the complete professional. It was two to one. They probably had guns. He on the other hand had surprise on his side when they were under the misapprehension that it was their ally. They would be on their maximum guard going up the stairs and entering the room. If they found he was not there they would relax for a moment. Possibly they would question the girl. That would be the moment for him to strike.

Catlike, he crossed the room to the open windows and slipped out onto the little balcony. He stood poised for a second on the balustrade and then, feet wide apart, legs braced, he dropped down twelve feet onto the grass outside. For anybody else it was a dangerous jump, especially at night. Miles thanked God for the three-month parachute course the SAS had put him through at Oxford. He had spent three weeks doing jumps like this in all conditions before anybody had even mentioned the word parachute. He paused by the front door of the guest house and listened again. Silence. All around him the compound slept. Only the crickets kept up their tireless commotion. He went in through the door, stopping again at the foot of the stairs. As he did so he saw the light come on in his bedroom. He heard a voice say 'He's not here.'

'Where the fuck is he?'

Sue Ellen was awake.

'What the hell . . .' she exclaimed.

'Shut up or I'll blow you away.'

'So at least one of them has a gun,' thought Miles. Clearly these were no burglars. They were after him. He was after them. Very slowly he began to climb the stairs.

'Where's the limey?'

Silence.

Then Miles heard the sound of a terrible blow. Sue Ellen's scream pierced the night.

'Talk, fuck rat, or I'll beat your brains out.'

Like a panther Miles took the stairs two at a time, but despite his speed he made no noise.

For a split second he lurked on the landing outside the bedroom taking in the scene. The man with the .38 he recognized as one of Castelli's mobsters of the previous afternoon. He was standing in the same dark suit with his back to Miles, the gun dangling loosely from his wrist. The other man Miles had not seen before. Immediately he recognized the type. Body-building homosexual. The man wore pink sneakers and tight white levis. Short powerful legs, a small upturned bottom. He was shaped like an inverted triangle, huge shoulders tapering down to a narrow waist. He wore a grey tee-shirt, the sleeves cut away to reveal strong muscular arms. He, too, had his back to Miles. It was he who had hit Sue Ellen. She lay on the bed, her hand to her mouth, staring in disbelief at the two jagged white teeth that lay among the frothy blood she had just spat out.

Miles was cold inside. There would be time for anger later. Now was the time for action and it had to be right. Miles braced himself against the door and launched himself into the room. SAS anatomy lessons flashed through his mind as he went for the drop kick. His right foot took off on its long upward curve with the whole of Miles' weight behind it. With perfect timing it exploded with maximum momentum just beneath the gunman's right kidney. Such was the force of the blow the gangster seemed to stand for a split second, like some apprentice ballerina, on the tips of his toes. He had lift off. And then he was going forwards, his mouth crashing into the sharp corner of the heavy glass bedside table as he fell.

'You'll piss blood for six months after that kidney punch,' thought Miles with satisfaction. There wouldn't be much change out of $10,000 for the dentistry either.

The queer stood there, his mouth wide open, rooted to the spot. As he tried to gather his thoughts Miles stepped quickly towards him. The sharp point of the Grisbi rested on the man's throbbing right carotid artery. Miles saw the fear in his eyes.

'Don't move, darling,' he rasped, 'or Mr Fox's nice room will be redecorated red in about five seconds flat. Castelli?'

The man tried to nod.

'Well,' said Miles, 'grubby little boys like you should learn to be more polite to ladies. I'm going to perform a little service for you. The good news is your boyfriends will love you – that's if they don't mind fucking the Blackwall Tunnel. The bad news is you're going to need a cork.'

He moved like greased lightning. With his left hand he grasped the mobster's left arm and, spinning him round, forced it up between his shoulder blades in the classic half-nelson grip. He pushed upwards on the arm, bending the gangster forwards. The Grisbi knife flashed. With surgical precision Miles pushed the knife into the man's anus like a red-hot poker into a snowdrift. One twist and the superficial external sphincter ceased to exist, another and the vital and all but irreparable internal sphincter was no more. It would take a brilliant proctologist to prevent this man from being faecally incontinent for life. A series of terrible screams rent the night air.

Harry Fox sat up in bed. He had heard the girl scream – thought nothing of it. The English had a reputation for that sort of thing. But there was no mistaking the urgency of these male noises. If this was fun and games it had clearly gone too far. There was another explanation and, as Harry hurried past the pool on the way to the guest house, he feared the worst – that Castelli had prematurely 'retired' his most recent employee.

As he stood in the doorway of the wrecked bedroom he immediately recognized Castelli's two men. Huberto was lying on his stomach moaning and clutching at his bottom where a fast-growing red stain was soaking through the white jeans. Franco was deeply unconscious next to the bed, blood pouring from his mouth onto the beige carpet. Miles, still totally naked, was dabbing at Sue Ellen's mouth with a wet towel.

He looked over his shoulder at Harry. 'I hope these boys have got Blue Cross,' he said. 'My God, they're going to need it.'

Harry dialled Castelli's number. A sleepy voice answered.

'Nero? Harry Fox. Listen, you'd better get an ambulance over here. Huberto and Franco are bleeding all over my carpet.'

Castelli grunted.

'It seems they went private enterprise and tried to do over my Englishman,' Harry added by way of explanation.

Harry knew the way things worked. Castelli had not actually commissioned Huberto's and Franco's mission. He had merely intimated that it would please him greatly if something unpleasant happened to Miles Parmere – that way Huberto and Franco would score extra points and yet Castelli would not be directly implicated.

'Oh, and, Nero, let's call it quits on this one now. Parmere can be very useful to us. I'd like him protected. I'll be the first to let you know when anything changes in that respect.' Harry smiled to himself. It seemed that the English lord needed protection about as much as Attila the Hun.

# *CHAPTER 4*

## I

The warm, stuffy New York air hit Harry in the face as he
left the cool comfort of the Eastern Airlines first-class
cabin. His mind had been in turmoil on the flight from
Miami as the details of the audacious business deal he was
about to attempt crowded in on him.

Eleanor had agreed to see him immediately, despite his
refusal to discuss the purpose of their meeting. Miles
Parmere had done his bit and, reflected Harry, it did not
hurt to have a cover of *Fortune* and an article in *Forbes* in
the same week.

Absentmindedly, Harry wandered out of the terminal
building, his shirt already sticky from the humid air. The
uniformed chauffeur from the Charmont Limousine Company led him to the stretched Fleetwood Cadillac sedan
and Harry sank gratefully into its air-conditioned comfort.
He switched on the Hitachi television and caught the news
as he poured himself an iced Lowenbrau from the well-
stocked drinks' cabinet. The drive from Kennedy would
take about an hour.

The vast car powered along the Van Wyck Expressway
towards Manhattan. The view through the smoked-glass
windows was strictly one way and Harry enjoyed the
peering necks of the lesser mortals who, as they came
alongside, tried in vain to recognize the celebrity who
could afford such grand transport. Harry smiled inwardly.
He knew what it was like to be on the outside looking in
and he was determined never to be there again. Over to the
right, as they approached the East River crossing, lay the
Bronx, in which Harry had fought his childhood. That
battle, Harry reflected, had been won against very consider-

able odds and now this limousine acted as one of the victory medals. The campaign, however, would never be completed. Getting to the top was hard, staying there harder. One could never relax and, perhaps, Harry thought philosophically, it was as well that life was like this – that the journey was the thing and never the destination. No chance of boredom in this war.

He settled back into the cushions and drank deep on the delicious lager allowing the bubbles to sting the back of his throat. The steamy streets of the Bronx would always be there to drive him on. It was as if they exerted a constant unseen magnetism, a siren call that if he weakened would suck him back into the quagmire from which he had with such difficulty escaped. He remembered that El Cordobes, the brilliant bullfighter who had known hunger as a child, was never separated from a giant ham which accompanied him everywhere but into the ring itself. Harry's money was his insurance policy and he would kill to retain it.

He was now but a few miles from that derelict tenement building. He remembered the freezing cold in winter, the stifling heat of the summers, the roaches that crawled across his face at night, the smells of sweat and urine, the rubbish and rotting vegetables in the street. And he remembered too the aimless loitering on the street corners, and the bursts of sudden violence that afforded some brief respite from the numbing tedium of urban poverty.

Harry had allowed himself the luxury of these reminiscences because he knew of the contrast that awaited him. At the Plaza Michael Gafford, the assistant manager, would be there to greet him and take him personally to the corner suite that he regularly used. The bottle of Taittinger Rosé Champagne 1971 would be cooling now in the silver ice bucket, the room would be full of the red baccarat roses that he loved. Harry was returning to the city of his birth, not as a street-sharp urchin but as a man who was in a position to lend someone a billion dollars. He had come a long way.

# II

Harry Fox woke suddenly at seven. He had got to bed late and the Plaza suite still smelled of cigars and whisky, relics of an energetic evening with a soft-skinned hooker, whose delicate appearance had concealed a prodigious appetite for hard liquor and exotic sexual activity. Today Harry needed to look good and feel good if he was to persuade Eleanor Montgomery to take his money. Already he had made the final decisions as to which loans would be called in to make the cash available. The board of directors, stooges to a man, had readily rubber-stamped the proposed deal. They had pointed out that it would leave the bank dangerously short of liquid funds, but Harry had convinced them that the risk/reward ratio was acceptable. There was no doubting the fact, however, as he put one foot on the rust-coloured carpet of suite 323/5, that he had a slight hangover, the legacy of that last rather too generous measure of Hine brandy.

Harry Fox was not a man to let a little thing like a hangover interfere with his single-minded pursuit of riches and he made for the bathroom in a determined way. Ten minutes and several gallons of iced water later he emerged from the shower to contemplate his wardrobe. Harry Fox was a vain man and also a shrewd one. As a banker he knew the importance of appearances and he spent a great deal of money on clothes. Miles was fond of applying Oscar Wilde's dictum to Harry – that he knew the price of everything and the value of nothing, and indeed a connoisseur of men's fashion would have viewed the contents of the closet with not a little alarm. The two-piece, single-breasted lightweight suit was of an unfortunate colour that tended more towards yellow than the subtle shade of tan that Harry, and possibly its maker, had intended. The brown tie with its loud white stripe did little to redeem the suit and it was left to the stylish cream cotton shirt made by Turnbull and Asser to prevent total sartorial disaster above the waist. Things did not improve on the journey south. The trousers were marginally too long and broke precipitously on the brown lizard-skin shoes which were themselves separated from Harry's feet by a pair of brown silk socks. A heavy gold bracelet, a chunky gold watch and a sickly after-shave added to the unhappy effect. On the whole it was as well that one could not see the heavy medallion that nestled among the plentiful hairs of Harry's chest, and for the performance of this function alone it was possible to be kindly disposed towards the otherwise disastrous tie. Later, however, Eleanor was able to deduce its presence from a general consideration of the persona of Harry Fox.

In blissful ignorance of the effect that it would have on the sophisticated Eleanor, Harry studied his appearance in the looking-glass and liked what he saw. He peered at himself, noting the rugged, craggy features that he thought distinguished but others described as cruel. The stomach was flat and hard and it was obvious that he was fit. A moment's doubt as to the success of the jacket's fit across his broad shoulders was instantly suppressed, for Harry recognized that self-confidence was the most valuable asset that he had and that nothing must be allowed to devalue it. He was uncomfortably aware that Eleanor, whose wit, beauty and fortune were a legend in the Western world, would perhaps, through no intention of her own, test his most prized commodity to the limit.

Harry ordered a large breakfast and read through the *Wall Street Journal*, noting with satisfaction that the Union Bank stock was holding steady in an otherwise dull market. Growth at the Union Bank had been phenomenal, but it was only the beginning. A pleasure of almost sexual intensity coursed through him as he allowed himself to imagine the results that must surely follow from the billion dollar loan to Montgomery Chemical.

He allowed himself to imagine the press conference at which he would announce the details of the advance, visualized the news appearing over the tapes, anticipated the feverish trading in the share price as the bank analysts in the brokerage houses made upward revisions of Union's status. Harry's adrenal cortex pumped again, sending a bolus dose of neat epinephrine into his bloodstream. He would make a lot of money on his shares.

A glorious vision unfolded as Harry dreamed of seeing the stock on both the *Journal*'s 'most active' and 'biggest percentage movers' list. And then he thought of the downside risk. The bank would be unable to make any substantial loans for many months to come. His freedom to manoeuvre would be strictly limited in the short term until new deposits provided fresh funds. Harry dismissed the thought as easily as he had ignored the unsatisfactory cut of his coat. Such thoughts were for losers and he, Harry Fox, was about to become one of the biggest winners of all time.

Lost in his reverie he ignored the cooked breakfast that had arrived unnoticed and now sat congealing on its tray. He wandered to the small window overlooking Central Park and stared out at the trees, pitying the tourists and early morning joggers, their Sony Walkman stereo cassette players glued to their ears. What could they know of the importance of the deal that he must do today? How could they suspect that they were privileged enough to be part of the visual field of a man who was about to make banking history? Then Harry thought of Eleanor, for it was she who held the key to treasure beyond the dreams of avarice.

Unknown to both of them, Eleanor was sharing Harry's view as the two were separated by only a few hundred yards. She had been woken by her Filipino maid at eight o'clock and had breakfasted in bed – her usual half grapefruit and pot of Earl Grey tea. Now she stood before the vast picture window of her bedroom on the fiftieth floor of the Solo building and gazed out at Central Park from her vantage point far above the roof of the Plaza Hotel that encased Harry. Eleanor had not slept well. She was preoccupied with the vitally important decision that would have to be taken at the board meeting the following day. Could Montgomery delay any longer in its borrowing operations?

She walked back to the bed and picked up the manila

folder that contained the day's press cuttings. Since five o'clock that morning an aide had been hard at work scouring the papers and magazines for any story that might conceivably be of interest to Eleanor. She flipped through the pages of photostats. Nothing new on interest rates that could help her in her decision. A few articles on Dow and DuPont that her practised eye told her she could ignore. There seemed to be a whole separate section on Caroline and Eleanor devoured the articles. As she did so she looked at them from two quite separate angles. In her role as a businesswoman, who understood the vital importance of good PR, she assessed their likely effect on Caroline's career. In her capacity as a mother she searched for remarks that might hurt her beloved daughter and, more important, those that would please and comfort her. When they spoke later that day, as they always did, it would be the positive side of the interviews that she would emphasize.

Not for the first time Eleanor reflected on the differences between the American and the European press in their attitude towards celebrities and said a silent prayer of thanks that it was not digests of the London morning papers that she was reading. The articles were full of optimism and excitement for Caroline's prospects and the writers were not ashamed to admit that they both liked her as a person and admired her achievements. The *People* article in particular was generous and fair. It told the truth and did not attempt to make cheap jibes. In England the journalists would miss no opportunity to make snide and niggling comments, their jealousy and envy at another's success warping that sense of fair play that no longer could be considered an English characteristic as far as the gentlemen of Fleet Street were concerned.

The last photostat caught Eleanor's eye because it concerned her lunch appointment and she made a mental note to commend the unseen aide who clearly did not allow the early hours that he kept to hamper his efficiency. The article was from *Forbes* magazine and it detailed the meteoric rise of Harry Fox and his Union Bank. The magazine ended by tipping the bank's stock and Eleanor wondered if she might buy a block if she found herself impressed by Harry over lunch. Otherwise she had no very clear idea why she had been asked for such an urgent meeting at which, Mr Fox had hinted conspiratorially, he would make a very important and extremely valuable proposal. Eleanor had learned to take such remarks with a pinch of salt, but she felt on the whole it would be worthwhile to see the thrusting banker with the growing reputation if only to pick his brains about the likely course of interest rates.

Eleanor's bathroom was of a size that few but an ancient Roman could have expected. The walls and the floor of the vast room were of Carrara marble. At the far end stood a single slab of stone on which each evening her personal masseuse would spend twenty minutes rubbing away the stresses and strains of the day. Another room leading off the main body of the bathroom contained the hot room providing dry heat, while a heavy brass door separated off the steam cubicle. Eleanor loved these rooms but she was no hedonist. Before she allowed herself the luxury of heat treatment and massage she would punish herself with half an hour of strenuous exercise in the gymnasium along the corridor. Now as she stepped into the shower the effect of her self-discipline was clear. Eleanor was forty years old but any twenty-five-year-old athlete would have been happy to have her figure. Her long legs were superbly sculptured, firm but not over-muscled. She was thin, but unlike most thin people, her breasts were full and pointed. Her skin glistened with good health. Her personal maid handed her the dressing gown and together they entered the huge closet with its racks of frocks and dresses. Eleanor slipped on the silk Dior briefs and stockings. She wore no bra. Then she picked out the red-and-white, polka-dotted Yves St Laurent silk dress with the white scalloped collar and cuffs. With it she wore a pair of red Maud Frizon court shoes with peep toes and a fine white line around them. A black silk double-breasted St Laurent blazer completed the outfit. Eleanor splashed some Opium perfume on her wrists and slipped on the five oblong gold bangles to balance the antique watch – both by Cartier. Then she turned, and, vaguely aware of her maid's admiring glance, walked briskly along the corridor to the anteroom where two aides waited to brief her for the first of the day's meetings.

Harry spent the morning on the telephone to Florida but his mind was on his lunchtime meeting with Eleanor. At twelve-fifteen he left the side entrance of the Plaza and walked the few yards to the Solo building. He checked with the driver of the stretched limo that he had arranged to take them for lunch before striding into the lobby. Harry was expected and a Brooks Brothers-suited Montgomery executive materialized at his elbow.

'Good morning, Mr Fox. Mrs Montgomery is expecting you,' said the clipped Boston Brahmin voice. Harry grunted. In the express lift to the fiftieth floor the businessman tried to engage him in conversation, mentioning the *Forbes* article. But Harry Fox did not cast his pearls before swine – he was keeping his powder dry for Eleanor and he studiously avoided the struggling executive's half-hearted conversational sallies. Harry avoided mediocrity as if it was a highly contagious disease. Both were relieved that the elevators in the Solo building were among the fastest in New York.

The double doors to Eleanor's apartment were already open as Harry left the elevator, and an English butler hovered in the entrance. The trio strode along the corridor in perfect silence after the butler had made his country's traditional observation on the inclemency of the weather. Harry wondered how a corridor could be so long in a town in which space was so expensive. He took in the photographs that lined the magnolia walls, noticing that all were by the same artist, André Kertész. Beneath his feet lay Persian silk runner carpets covering the highly polished oak boards. An Ansel Adams screen depicting snow-covered trees in winter separated half the corridor from the huge salon in which they now found themselves. Another faceless minion introduced himself and Harry began to wonder if the whole of Montgomery Chemical had taken the day off to welcome him.

'Welcome to New York, Mr Fox,' said Eleanor as she swept into the room. It was instant impression time.

'Too yellow,' thought Eleanor, focusing in on the suit, the gold bracelet, and the exuberant tan. 'I bet there's a medallion beneath that ghastly tie.'

'Stuck up bitch – hard as nails but what a looker,' thought Harry, as influenced by the quality and type of the hired help and the apartment's visuals as by Eleanor's appearance and demeanour.

Two seconds had passed but Eleanor and Harry both felt they had known each other for a long time.

'How kind of you to agree to see me,' Harry mouthed insincerely. Perhaps to bolster his self-confidence he allowed an erotic thought to surface. As they stood there making small talk he imagined what it would be like to make love to her, perhaps after lunch, on the brown carpet of the Plaza suite, Eleanor's red dress round her waist, her briefs at her knees as he drove into her. Her imagined screams of ecstasy contrasted cruelly with her cool measured tone as she inquired as to whether or not he was comfortable in his hotel.

'Not as comfortable as I'd be with you going down on me,' thought Harry crudely.

Eleanor picked up the vibration immediately. This awful man was leering at her. She became aware that she wasn't wearing a bra. Usually she thought nothing of it – she seldom wore one because her superb figure did not require it. Damn. Fox had played one of the oldest tricks in the book and she had fallen for it. For a second he had made her feel like a sex object rather than the brilliant head of a multi-billion dollar corporation. This lunch had all the makings of a duel after only two minutes. She repaired her defences and mentally sharpened her offensive weapons.

She looked him up and down very slowly and allowed her lip to curl faintly. She breathed in and caught the pungent after-shave, wondering as she did so whether she had ever disliked anybody so much on a first impression.

'I thought we might have lunch at La Goulue. Do you know it?' said Harry allowing, with some reluctance, the steamy vision of a sweating, howling Eleanor to fade.

'I used to go there a lot.'

Harry did not miss the condescending tone and inwardly cursed the trendy young Florida banker whose opinions on New York restaurants he had previously valued.

'Perhaps I'd better mend fences,' thought Harry, suddenly aware of Eleanor's growing hostility. There was no angle in trading sophisticated insults with this mother, especially when he wanted to lend her a billion dollars. He decided that he would be charming. Charm, however, was not an attribute with which Harry Fox had been generously endowed and Eleanor, who knew that this man had in some mysterious way undressed her and violated her body, felt that she was behind on points.

'That's a very beautiful drawing,' said Harry picking out a superb Egon Schiele nude.

'Oh, do you like the Bauhaus?' said Eleanor wickedly.

For a desperate moment Harry wondered if she was suggesting an alternative restaurant for lunch, a thought that was immediately replaced by the notion that Eleanor was asking for his opinion on the penthouse apartment.

The hitherto mute aide who had watched with growing alarm the deterioration of relations now feared the imminent outbreak of open hostilities and leapt in to separate the combatants. 'May I respectfully remind you that Mr Schapiro will be here at three, Mrs Montgomery,' he offered.

Harry grasped the opportunity and spirited Eleanor into the bowels of the vast black limousine.

Eleanor cursed herself for allowing this brash vulgarian to prize her out of her domain. She would have far preferred a light lunch in the private dining room at the corporation, the food lovingly prepared by the French chef poached from Allard in Paris. Or they could have crossed the road to the wonderful Oyster Bar at the Plaza for a dozen mixed Cherrystone and Littleneck clams and a bottle of Muscadet. The frenetic hurly-burly of fashionable New

York restaurants was not her scene at the best of times. Now she had to brave it in the unacceptable company of Harry Fox.

Then she thought of Caroline and could not suppress a smile at the reaction she would have when Eleanor told her all about it that evening. Caroline often joked with her mother about the degree to which Eleanor was protected by her wealth and position from life in the raw. For a moment she even hoped that her awful escort might commit some dreadful *faux pas* like grabbing her under the table – it would make a good story better.

They swept into the restaurant and were seated at one of the best tables that $100 pushed into the eager hands of the head waiter was able to secure. Eleanor noted that nothing seemed to have changed. The polished dark panelling, the white tablecloths, superior glasses, and brown leather banquettes were all as she remembered them. So, too, were the brass handrails, the mock Lalique glass, and the art nouveau lamps. She looked around and waved to young Spiros Niarchos, a great friend of Caroline, who was having lunch with his beautiful dark-haired Brazilian girl friend, Yelitze.

Harry hated her and fancied her at the same time. How he would love to humiliate her, to abuse her, to destroy her composure. He stared at the outlines of her breasts through the silk dress and longed to handle them. His eyes wandered down to her lap where the long brown legs flowed from the demure dress. He wanted to part those legs, to see the vulnerable, exposed look on her face, to hear the choke in her voice, to smell the scent of her desire. But Eleanor was up to his tricks now. She threw back her head and laughed at him rather than with him, using her sexuality to tantalize and discomfort him. She knew now that he at once loathed and wanted her and she knew, too, that he could not touch her – that she was as inaccessible to Harry Fox as was the State of Grace.

She ordered moules marinières and noted that the sauce needed a little more white wine. The escalope de veau au citron arrived with potatoes, carrots and beans and Eleanor sent them back because she had not ordered them. She had one glass only of the Bâtard Montrachet white burgundy for which Harry was paying $48 and she ordered some Perrier to dilute it.

Harry was out of his depth and he knew it, but he also knew that at the end of the day he had something to offer Eleanor that she could hardly afford to turn down. So he let the charade continue, allowed Eleanor to parade her superior class and *savoir faire*, let her think that she had avenged herself on him for his lascivious chauvinism and then, as she haughtily refused a glass of champagne, he sucked noisily at his brandy and said, 'The word is that Montgomery are about to take the plunge for a billion dollars of five-year money.'

Harry could see from her expression that he had for the second time that day succeeded in thoroughly destroying her equilibrium.

'God,' she thought, 'I mustn't relax with this man for a second.' Her mind raced. No point in denying it. It was probably common knowledge on the street. But why had he said it? What next?

'I might be able to help,' said Harry simply, enjoying her discomfort. Then he laid it on the line and as he did so he knew that she would accept his proposal.

Eleanor could hardly believe what was happening. This parvenu was sitting next to her in a trendy New York restaurant trying and occasionally succeeding in making her feel as if she was totally naked and at the same time offering to lend her a billion dollars. Where on earth could the Union Bank find that sort of money? She searched her mind for all the information that she had on Harry and his bank. A file had been prepared on him as a matter of course when the lunch appointment had originally been made. Now Eleanor attempted to re-create the pictures of the Dun and Bradstreet credit report, the Value Line card, the numerous press clippings. The *Forbes* article had spoken of explosive growth and innovative banking techniques, but a billion dollars just had to be bullshit. She peered into Harry's face with an entirely new interest, trying in vain to tune in to his thoughts. Was he merely trying to impress her? Could he be so crass as to be trying to pull her? Was it a joke?

Harry had already endured her scorn. He could live with her disbelief, knowing as he did that there were three pieces of paper in his pocket that would dispel it. He produced them slowly. Transfixed, Eleanor thought of conjurors, hats and white rabbits. In a detached way she noticed that her hand shook slightly as she accepted the three letters. Morgan Stanley said simply that they had $300 million of call money on account for Harry's Union Bank and would be more than happy to provide the financial advice on any projected loan by Union to Montgomery. The letters from Chase Manhattan Bank and Citicorp confirmed that Harry's billion was sitting in New York as they spoke.

'We ought to be able to save you a bit on the underwriting,' said Harry casually, savouring his moment of triumph.

The point was not lost on Eleanor. She calculated quickly that she would save $15 million or more on underwriting commissions by borrowing the entire amount directly from Harry's bank. She leaned forward in her chair and her mouth opened. Which question should she ask first? But Harry was at the controls and she was the passenger.

Rather in the manner of an affable airline pilot pointing out some landmark of greater or lesser interest to his captive audience, he said, 'I suppose you'd have to pay about seventeen per cent for five-year money right now. I think I could let you have the billion at three and a half per cent under New York prime for the period of the loan.'

'Game, set and match,' thought Harry, and Eleanor was thinking much the same. No Texas Instruments calculator could have processed the figures faster than Eleanor Montgomery in the La Goulue restaurant that day. She knew Harry was right about the rate she would have to pay on the street. The deal that he was offering was extremely generous. Over the full five years of the loan the saving on interest costs alone would be $25 million. She added on the $15 million saving on the underwriting fees. $40 million.

'Can I change my mind about that glass of champagne?' she asked meekly.

Eleanor knew at once that the deal made sense from Montgomery's point of view. The dealings would be simplified enormously and the savings would be vast. She saw no advantage to Harry in the deal at all. That was no concern of hers. It was not after all the job of a borrower to worry about the financial stability of a lender and the loan would be structured so that Montgomery was totally protected should Fox and his bank go down the tubes. Then there were the letters from three of the most powerful financial institutions in the world, the clean bill of health from Montgomery's own financial department. Eleanor did not have many problems in the board room at the corporation. Quite apart from the Montgomery family holdings, which accounted for a solid twenty per cent of the equity and provided a secure power base, old Bill Montgomery, who had founded the company single handed, was a man who had always preferred subordinates to equals. The composition of the board reflected this preference. Eleanor's remarkable business acumen, widely regarded as being the main factor behind the recent explosive growth at Montgomery, was another factor discouraging criticism from a board which was already constitutionally disinclined to provide it. She knew she could and would deliver on the loan.

'Do we have a deal?' asked Harry.

'Subject to contract, yes,' Eleanor replied.

Harry leaned back on the leather banquette and drew deeply on one of the torpedo-shaped Montecristo Number Two Havana cigars that he had had smuggled in specially from Cuba. Once again he had got what he wanted. Tonight there would be Taittinger Rosé 1971 and three of the most expensive hookers that New York could provide in the Plaza suite. 'And, my God, they'll have to work for their money,' thought Harry. Eleanor was dismissed from the equation. She would deliver because it was in her interest to do so. He need concern himself with her no longer.

Eleanor was not entirely sure what she felt. Clearly she had made a great financial coup and she had solved a problem that had been worrying her for weeks in a way that could only benefit her company. Yet she did not feel like a woman who had just been lent a billion dollars. In some mysterious way she felt that she had lost rather than won, had been worsted in the duel with the surprising Mr Fox. The points that she had scored off him earlier seemed trivial and irrelevant now and she sensed the indifference to her that seemed to have descended on him like a Scots mist since she had given him what he wanted. Strangely, that indifference was even less acceptable than the barely concealed desire for her body that had exuded from him a little earlier. There was another feeling, too, deep within her, and with not a little alarm Eleanor found herself wondering what it might be like to be screwed by Harry Fox, perhaps on the floor of his apartment, her Yves St Laurent dress hitched up, her silk Dior briefs at her knees, as he pounded into her.

# Chapter 5

## I

Caroline was running for her life. Sweat poured from her face, ran down her chest, dripped from her heaving and naked breasts. Still her speed increased – flat out now, her body working to maximum capacity. The messages flooded into her brain from the hard-working muscles as she fought for breath. She forced herself to ignore the pain as the muscle accumulated lactic acid building the oxygen debt, tried instead to concentrate on the music – hard, pounding rock from Tom Petty and the Heartbreakers that blared from the huge speakers in quadraphonic sound.

'OK, so now we ease, Caroline.' The guttural Swedish accent cut through into Caroline's consciousness promising sweet relief from her torture. Ingemar Jorgensen, who had been running on the spot next to Caroline, his short, powerful legs rising and falling like pistons, now slowed to a jog. He reached out and moved the treadmill running machine lever to a slower speed. Caroline's torment eased as she filled her lungs, returning oxygen to the beleaguered tissues. Ingemar watched her closely. He glanced up at the second display of the digital wall clock and then at the green QRS complexes on the screen of the electrocardiograph machine to which Caroline was connected by suction chest leads. His eyes moved back to Caroline as he checked the muscle groups one by one, noting their development, their interaction, showing a purely professional interest in the exquisite body. Caroline was stripped to the waist. Her tiny cotton briefs, now soaked through with perspiration, long white socks and Adidas running shoes were her only clothing. She was fifteen minutes into her morning training programme and the concentration of both pupil and coach was total.

That morning Caroline had risen, as usual, at seven o'clock. She had eaten a grapefruit and some bran, drunk fresh orange juice and two cups of sweet, strong tea. For an hour she had relaxed with the papers and skiing magazines and then, at 8.30, she had walked over from the main house across the helicopter pad to the vast barn that had been converted into possibly the best-equipped personal training area in the world. Ingemar, her coach, friend and mentor, had been waiting for her. The programme would start at 8.45 sharp, the time never varying. The barn was as big as an aeroplane hangar, one hundred feet long, fifty feet wide, and was perched on the edge of a steep, grassy slope that in winter served as Caroline's quickest route to the town of Aspen, nestling in the valley far below. The carefully designed gymnasium had already featured in a six-page spread in *Architectural Digest* and anybody who saw it could understand why.

Along the side overlooking Aspen ran a narrow sixty-foot mosaic pool that had clearly been built for swimming lengths rather than for cooling off. A long picture window ran parallel to the pool, giving a breathtaking view across the valley to the mountains on the other side. At one end of the pool was the relaxation area where Caroline would recuperate after the training session. A circular jacuzzi was lined with the same mosaic as the pool. Next to it stood a white marble massage slab on a stone pedestal. Across from the jacuzzi on the other side of the barn was the changing area equipped with Finnish sauna, showers and a cold plunge pool. A door led off from this cluster of rooms to the dark, cavern-like equipment room with its racks of skis and sticks, shelves of boots, helmets and goggles, cupboards of parkas, racing suits and a bewildering array of equipment for fine tuning and hot waxing skis and for adjusting bindings. Beneath the central skylight was the square exercise area. Around it were arranged the jogging machine, a static bicycle, a Cybex muscle-strength tester, and a complete exercise centre made up of counterbalanced weights, pulleys and platforms for body building. Against the far wall stood a gigantic $75,000 Ski-Dek conveyor belt skiing machine that allowed Caroline to experience the actual sensation of skiing in the period from April to Thanksgiving when there was no snow in Aspen.

In the remaining far right-hand corner a comfortable sitting area was arranged around a projector, video-console and hi-fi system. Here Caroline and Ingemar would discuss and analyse films of Caroline in action, carefully dissecting her mistakes, weaknesses, triumphs and strengths. The styles and techniques of her World Cup competitors and of great former champions such as Killy, Sailer, Thoeni and Klammer would also be subjected to careful analysis. Occasionally the star of the tape would be Ingemar himself, a man who in the early 1960s had elevated slalom skiing to the level of a fine art form.

Ingemar had stood up from the sofa of the video area as Caroline had walked into the building. He was a short man, but his height was the only small thing about him. Eyes were immediately drawn to thighs that appeared at first sight to be deformed in their enormity. It seemed that they had been designed for some unusual, esoteric purpose, as a giant nutcracker perhaps. The warm, craggy face with its exuberantly broken nose offset the rather humourless sky-blue eyes that hinted at Slavonic melancholy, possibly even Nordic cruelty. Certainly no one would have wanted to be on the receiving end of that, as the massive shoulders and spade-like hands signalled nameless dangers no less than the outrageous thighs. Whoever might have cause to fear Ingemar Jorgensen, Caroline was not among them. He worshipped her. She was his life. She had, after all, given him back his own.

Jorgensen's face glowed with pleasure at the sight of her as she stood in the doorway, the white sweat-shirt making its usual half-hearted attempt to restrain her magnificent breasts.

'Good morning, Caroline,' he intoned formally.

'Hi, Ing. Sleep well?'

'Always.' 'Since I met you,' he might have added.

Ingemar pointed at the video screen. 'Come and look at this – I've been playing the Moser tape again.'

Annemarie Moser, the great Austrian skier, had been the woman to beat in the downhill for ten years, but despite her achievements in the World Cup she had never won an Olympic Gold until 1980. Moser was that increasingly rare animal in these days of specialization, a genuine all-round skier. She was as capable in the slalom and giant slalom as in the completely different downhill discipline, although running downhill was her first love. Previously Moser had used downhill techniques in her slalom and GS racing. For the downhill Olympic Gold she reversed that process.

'The Lake Placid Downhill Gold on Whiteface?' asked Caroline.

'Yes,' said Ingemar. 'It's very interesting. Remember the conditions, cold, hard, fast man-made snow; clear, gusty and very cold weather.'

Caroline remembered.

They watched the tape. The white-helmeted Austrian, wearing number 6, streaked down the 3200-foot Whiteface run on Atomic skis.

'Now, Caroline. Look how she brings her slalom technique in here. It's incredible. She's turning at seventy miles an hour and she's carving the turns to get the shortest downhill line. Watch how she angles the knees to get the edge set.'

Caroline leaned forwards. 'Yes, she's counter-rotating pretty strongly – look how she uses *avalement* to start the turn. It certainly worked on Whiteface, but I'd be in real trouble with that technique.'

Ingemar slapped his mammoth thigh to emphasize his point. 'But Caroline you must be in a position to use any technique when the conditions dictate it – that's the secret. You must be perfection in all three events. You will not just be a champion, you will be the great champion. It will happen. It *must* happen.'

Caroline walked over to the tape rack whose six shelves stretched across ten feet of wall. She pulled out a tape.

'Let's look at my race,' she said, pushing the cassette into the Betamax. She stood tensed at the starting gate on the lifesize Mitsubishi projection screen. The Lake Placid wind plucked at the insulated racing suit and Caroline remembered its cold fingers on her spine, the butterflies in her stomach.

It was a great run, a classic downhill descent. One did not miss the Bronze by a tenth of a second with anything else. The secret of successful downhill technique is to keep the skis flat on the snow for as long as is humanly possible. The downhiller should glide, maintaining the best possible aerodynamic stance to cut wind resistance. Caroline hurtled down the initial steep descent known as Hurricane Alley. Things were going well as she rode out the compressions, pre-jumped the bumps, screaming down the precipitous Snow Field decline. In the perilous Wilmington fast turns that came immediately after the first sharp drop, her line was outside Moser's as she used hip rather than knee angulation to edge the ski and carve the turn. As a result the turns were wider and time was lost. Eagle eyes on the course ahead, searing concentration, her powerful thighs straining against the centrifugal and gravitational forces, Caroline flashed downwards. And then, in the Niagara stretch, the mistake that cost her the Bronze or Silver. At high speed ramming even the smallest bump in the snow with ski tips can slow you down. You must pre-jump them by springing up just enough to clear the bump. Three quarters of the way down the course Caroline failed to pre-jump. The front of her skis flicked up and at the same time a gust of wind accentuated the process. Her knees pushed her chest up and, as she fought for balance, she put her arms to her side. Her aerodynamic position was in ruins and, although she did not fall, the increased wind resistance cut her speed those tenths of a second that made all the difference to the result.

'So near but yet so far,' said Caroline.

Ingemar looked at her. 'You're the best in the world now, today,' he said. 'By Christmas the world will realize it.'

Caroline smiled. There was not an atom in her body that did not throb with desire for the overall World Cup. Sometimes they both wondered, the rough, peasant former champion and the beautiful, young aristocratic heiress, just who wanted it the most.

And then the training session had begun. First the pulse check. Caroline had the low resting pulse of the athlete, her heart pumping fifty times a minute. At maximum exertion it would not go above 120. Next were the vital warm-up exercises that would prevent muscle strain and pulled ligaments – walking and then jogging on the spot, side bends, trunk rotations, arm swings and windmills. Now Caroline pulled off the sweat-shirt as she walked towards the jogging machine. A thin film of perspiration already covered her torso like the morning dew in summer. She was totally unselfconscious in front of Ingemar whose eyes roamed over her semi-naked body with approval and appreciation but without a flicker of desire. He attached the suction electrode of the EKG machine to record the apex heartbeat immediately below her left breast, smoothing on a scoop of electrode jelly first. He switched on the stereo and Caroline started to run. Longer periods of slow jogging to build muscle endurance and to strengthen the cardiovascular and respiratory systems were interspersed with fast sprints to build explosive strength. Both would be needed on the slopes.

Ten minutes later she was off the treadmill. A short rest and then the swimming. This was the bit that Caroline enjoyed. A perfectionist in all things athletic, Caroline swam with total dedication, caring that the style was right, that bad habits did not creep in. At the mid-point of the long pool the mosaic side wall had been replaced by glass, next to which a fifteen-foot observation well had been sunk allowing a spectator to watch the swimmer's movements under water as she passed. Ingemar now stood in this area as Caroline got ready to enter the pool. She slipped off the track shoes and socks and pulled down the cotton briefs. For a moment she stood at the end of the pool totally naked, her body glistening with sweat. She brushed wet hair from her eyes and knifed into the water. The crawl was textbook – legs straight, elbows high, hands cutting into the water either side of the mid-line, the forward reach and the straight downwards push towards the thighs. Ingemar watched her as she swam by, noted the lithe thrashing limbs, the flash of golden pubic hair, the boyish bottom. He yelled instruction and encouragement as Caroline alternated between rhythmic swimming and flat-out sprints.

Later, after another rest, it was time for hexagon obstacle jumping, a skiing exercise to strengthen thighs, calves and ankles and to develop balance and agility. A perfect hexagon was marked out on the oakwood floor in red. At each point on the hexagon stood plywood blocks of different heights joined at the top by bits of string. Feet together, Caroline stood in the centre and jumped alternately in and out of the hexagon over the string. As if on the slopes she varied her pace, sometimes jumping clock-wise, sometimes counter-clockwise. During periods of rest Ingemar would vary the height of the blocks. Muscle function studies had shown that this was the exercise in which muscular activity most closely simulated the actual patterns found during snow skiing.

'OK,' said Ingemar at last. 'That should be it for this morning. Now let's stretch and relax.'

Together they performed the litany of cooling-down exercises, stretching in sequence the different muscle groups – hamstrings, quadriceps, groin, arms, shoulders, neck.

The next bit was pure pleasure. Caroline eased herself into the 100-degree jacuzzi and immediately felt the tensions ease. Ingemar knelt beside her, gently kneading her bare shoulders. Neither spoke as he massaged her neck, his strong fingers digging deep, probing for knotted muscle, squeezing it away when he found it. The powerful water jets played over Caroline's body, plucking and pummelling her skin. It was a deeply sensual experience and Caroline could feel the desire coursing through her. But desire for what, for whom? Not for the first time

Caroline found herself thinking of the strange Englishman with his hard body and wistful eyes, imagined him making love to her – at first gently and then . . . not so gently. She shifted her position, splaying her legs apart to allow the warm jets to touch her, caress her. The warm glow began to spread as she pushed against the probing finger of water. Ingemar gripped hard on her shoulders. He knew what was happening – wanted it for her. An orgasm was the perfect finale to training, the ultimate and most natural relaxation. And this way there were no complications, no feelings, no humans to intrude, to get in the way of the final goal. Neither Caroline nor Ingemar had discussed it. They had not needed to. Caroline was eighteen and a virgin. She had no boyfriend. She needed release from sexual tension. It was as simple as that. Slowly Caroline began to arch her long powerful back, pushing her shoulders against Ingemar's hands. She drew up her knees and thrust herself out at the warm, hard stream. She began to moan quietly, the sound of her own pleasure increasing her satisfaction. She opened herself up to the water jet, allowed it to ravage her, enter her, take hold of her mind. She felt the orgasm grow, sensed its distant rumblings, braced herself for the storm of pleasure that would soon break over her. And then she was coming, her whole body shuddering with the force of its thrill. As it exploded she groaned her satisfaction, squirming as she did so in Ingemar's strong grip.

Later, on the massage slab, as Ingemar rubbed the scented oil into her back, over her buttocks, her reverie continued. Imperceptibly her desire merged into dreams of mountains and valleys, of virgin powder, and within minutes she had fallen into a deep sleep.

Ingemar felt her body soften as she lost consciousness, but he continued to massage her, now in the Swedish rather than the Japanese style. He stroked her skin, smoothed her muscles, patted her softly with cupped hands. He had never seen such a perfect body, such a consummate piece of art. Ingemar regarded himself as the curator of some mythical museum in which Caroline's body was the only exhibit. It was his sole purpose to protect it, to develop it into the ultimate skiing machine. Caroline would have it all because, grafted onto her exquisite physique was an awe-inspiring determination, a naked desire to win, without which no ski racer could become champion. He loved her for her skiing potential, but he loved her for much more than that. No desire for her body sullied Jorgensen's adulation of Caroline, for he had one flaw, a fault that had once destroyed him as a person and left his skiing career in ruins.

Ingemar was a homosexual and he hated himself for it. He had never freed himself from the guilt and self-loathing that always accompanied his furtive forays into the homosexual *demi-monde* where he could satisfy his unwanted appetites. Every few months the awful, black desire would be on him, growing in him, mocking him, resisting all attempts at sublimation and repression, demanding discharge in the deed that disgusted him. He cursed the accident of biochemistry, the unknown combination of environmental factors that had made him like this, but he could not resist them. He wished with all his heart that the juices would flow at the contemplation of Caroline's sleeping form, but at the same time he knew his wish would never be granted. He was condemned to his sexual fate, and he had learned to live with it.

Caroline knew this, too, and it allowed her a physical intimacy with Jorgensen that she had with no other man. He knew her body better than his own, and cared for it more. They had never spoken of his disability or admitted to each other that it existed. It was better that way and Ingemar was grateful for Caroline's sensitivity. Some things were better left unsaid, unexamined.

The stereo softly played the country music that Caroline loved, but she slept on and as Ingemar rubbed her with the gentleness that only extreme strength can achieve, he thought back on his life and of how Caroline had saved him from disaster.

Born the son of a construction worker in the Swedish skiing town of Arë, two hundred miles south of the Arctic circle, he had started to ski at about the time he had learned to walk. Unlike Caroline's, his family were poor and uneducated, typical peasant stock, but they had the good sense to recognize and indulge Ingemar's talent. Skiing was the only competitive sport for schoolboys in Arë, and the young boy loved to compete. After school he would practise on the slopes until late at night, skiing always in artificial light as it was dark by two in the afternoon. Determination and natural talent, that unbeatable combination, meant that by the age of twelve he was training with the Junior National Team and by eighteen he was the best slalom skier in Sweden. His famous string of World Cup victories in the slalom and giant slalom had put him in all the record books and given him the overall championship three years running. And then it had happened.

One year, while on the grinding four-month World Cup circuit, he experienced one too many lonely hotel rooms. An excess of schnapps after a slalom victory in the German town of Oberstaufen and a chance meeting at the bar with a wildly good-looking blond German skier had culminated in them both ending up in Ingemar's bed. It had been a watershed, a revelation, nothing could be the same again.

Ingemar had always ignored his sexuality, banished it to the back of his mind in his single-minded obsession with becoming a great champion. Sex didn't win races, but frequently he had seen it lose them. Now, having reached the pinnacle, with its dampening effect on his ambitions, he would pay for his neglect. The shame that accompanied the wicked hangover of the next morning was swamped by a more primeval and infinitely more powerful emotion. Ingemar Jorgensen, the skiing champion of the world, was an emotional child, immature and naïve, hopelessly out of his depth and unable to swim in the waters into which he had fallen. The intensity of the sexual passion, the release of latent, pent-up desires was too strong a drug for him. He spent the whole day in bed with the German and by the evening he was in love – in love for the first time in his life.

Many clichés exist to describe the adolescent experience

of first love. Ingemar was thirty years old but he proved them all to be true. Unhappily he had made an unfortunate choice in the object of his adoration. Kurt Muller was a sociopath, charming and attractive, but with no conscience and the morals of an alley cat. He lived by his wits, which were sharp, and had an insatiable appetite for the good life. In Jorgensen, the rich and respected champion, he had found his meal ticket. He played the Swede like a fish on a line, taught him sexual tricks that made Ingemar almost faint with excitement. In return Muller was showered with presents, a new Porsche, a Rolex watch, cameras, skiing equipment, Ralph Lauren clothes. Ingemar insisted that Muller go with him on the remainder of the Cup circuit and Muller gladly agreed. He enjoyed basking in the reflected glory of the champion. All night long they would make love, even before important races, and in the evenings when Ingemar returned exhausted from the mountain Muller would drag him out to parties, to the gay bars, anywhere Muller could see and be seen. The effect on Ingemar's skiing and reputation was dramatic. Never again did he win a World Cup race. By March he was bringing up the rear in races that earlier in the season he would have been ashamed not to win. Despite his earlier triumphs and his commanding lead in points the championship began to slip away from him and by March he had lost it.

No hypocrite, Ingemar had committed the ultimate sin, indiscretion. Encouraged by Muller, who wanted to demonstrate publicly his hold over the champion, he would indulge in public displays of affection in bars and restaurants. The world, scandalized, exacted its retribution. The ski manufacturers who had been so keen to sponsor him the previous season withdrew their support and there were no other takers. The Swedish team asked him to resign and the pro circuit turned him down flat. As his career toppled so his sources of income dried up. Nobody wanted a faggot endorsing their products and a faggot was what Ingemar had become. The conclusion was inevitable. With no reputation and no money he had nothing to offer the ambitious Muller. One day he packed the Cartier jewellery and other trophies into his Louis Vuitton luggage, threw the bags into the back of the Carrera Porsche and drove out of Ingemar's life.

As his parting shot he subjected a weeping and disbelieving Ingemar to a vicious and devastating little speech spelling out how he had never loved him, had only wanted to use him, that he had despised him as a man, been revolted by him as a lover. Ingemar had gone to his room and drunk a whole bottle of Scotch. For five long years he had done little else. He had gravitated towards Aspen where he lived in a filthy room, the floor covered with vomit and excrement as he tried to drink himself to death. He paid for the drink and the apartment by hiring himself out as a freelance guide. There was always some young dentist ski bum who would pay for the privilege of boasting that he had been up the mountain with the once-great Jorgensen. He could still get down the mountain, but he fell a lot and the week-end skiers who hired him were better than he was. Every day on the slopes was a constant humiliation. Then one morning as he lay in his bed at eleven there had been a knock on the door. He had lain there, comatose, vomit on his pillow, vaguely aware that he had been faecally incontinent during the night but too weak to say 'come in'.

The door had opened and a tall, gangling fifteen-year-old girl had stood there. Ingemar had known her instantly from the slopes of Aspen where already Caroline Montgomery had a reputation as a potential world-beater, but he had never spoken to her. Caroline's personality had filled the room, rendering its squalor and rankness somehow irrelevant, of no consequence. She had looked him in the eye and said simply, 'Mr Jorgensen, you have been the greatest slalom skier in the world. I want you to work with me to make me the champion.'

Ingemar had known at once that he would accept. It had been his rebirth. Ten minutes later he had walked from that room with Caroline, never to return. He took nothing with him. He had entered a new life. He moved into quarters in the Montgomery's Aspen house and never drank again. For six months he had trained harder than anyone had ever done before, conquering the pain and psychological *Angst* of alcoholic withdrawal. At the end of that period he was as fit and capable as he had ever been. From that moment on he had merged his ambitions with Caroline. What she wanted he wanted, nothing more, nothing less. As he traced a gentle slalom track with his fingers down her spine, he thanked God that she had wanted him.

## II

'. . . And although I have often used Rossignol skis and found them excellent in every way I am afraid I must, as a matter of policy, decline your kind offer of sponsorship in the coming World Cup competition. I would like to add that this has nothing to do with your support for the Russian team.' Caroline paced up and down in her office. Nigel, her and Eleanor's secretary, leaned over his shorthand pad, pencil flashing. He looked up as Caroline paused in her dictation. Like everyone else he was a bit in love with her. It was just like the Montgomery women to employ a male secretary, he thought – completely uninfluenced by tradition, by the 'done' thing. Of course it made sense, especially to him after he had been selected from 120 applicants, all of them female.

Nigel was no freak. He was highly intelligent, with a degree in English literature from the University of California where, among other things, he had learned the power of lateral thinking. The job market had been a disaster after his graduation and he had immediately recognized that cunning would be required if he was to avoid the ranks of the great unemployed. After all, English literature was hardly computer science. Thumbing through the job ads he had been struck by the considerable wages being paid to secretaries and personal assistants. How long would it take to learn to type and write shorthand? A fraction of the time it had taken him to earn a worthless degree. He had borrowed from his parents, gone on a course and in one short year of hard work he was the equal in proficiency of any secretary in America. He never suffered from periods, was unlikely to get pregnant, was never jealous of Caroline's and Eleanor's good looks and style and he could carry skis and hump electric typewriters and luggage without a murmur of complaint. Like most Californians who had been born by the beach he took good care of his body, was a great tennis player, a good intermediate skier, and a useful man to have around in a tight corner. He could be porter, bodyguard, skiing companion, tennis partner, and authority on spelling, punctuation and syntax – it was not a bad combination. And, at the end of the day and perhaps most important of all, he looked good. 'Life is fleeting,' Eleanor would say. 'I don't see why we should be surrounded by "dogs". After all we don't buy ugly paintings or furniture.'

The clatter of the helicopter, flying low over the sprawling house, interrupted them.

'That'll be Uncle Charles,' shouted Caroline, walking over to the window. Two secret servicemen were already on the landing pad waving in the chopper. The Montgomery helicopter, with Skip at the controls, had picked up the Secretary of State at Aspen airport to where he had been flown by the Air Force. Caroline ran down the stairs to meet him. She loved it when Charles was staying. The great house came alive and began to hum with activity as the paraphernalia of government descended on it. The scrambler telephones had been installed the day before and for three days the advance guard of secret servicemen had probed every inch of the house and its grounds. Now they would swarm all over the place – hard, lean men with suspicious eyes. Caroline enjoyed them being there. They would teach her to shoot and she would show them how to grass ski. Often in the afternoons there would be hilarious competitions with the Aspen household team of Caroline,

Ingemar, Nigel and Skip, the ski technician and helicopter pilot, pitted against four of the secret servicemen. Despite the laughter, everyone played to win and played hard. It would be a pentathlon – pistol shooting, where the opposition had the advantage; grass skiing, a shoe-in for the home team; and the bitterly contested no-man's land of swimming, sprinting and tennis. Visits to Aspen were popular with his bodyguards and Charles Cabot Lodge used to joke that after Caroline had finished with them they were so tired out that if any trouble came up he would end up having to protect them.

There were other reasons why Charles' visits were welcome. Eleanor became her old self when he was there. The mealtime conversation would sparkle and shine as affairs of state and politics were seasoned with Charles' dry wit, subjected to Eleanor's sharp, analytic mind. Not since the days when Bill Montgomery had been there to fill the house with his energy and laughter and support them all with his wisdom and strength had the atmosphere been so good. Caroline wanted her mother to marry Charles almost as much as he wanted to. They were both working on it.

Caroline rushed into his arms as he came through the big oak door. He swung her off the floor. Charles Cabot Lodge was Boston Brahmin and looked and acted the part. Short, brown hair; round tortoise-shell glasses; two-piece grey pin-stripe from Brooks Brothers; white broadcloth shirt; sober striped tie; Church's shoes. He was wiry and rather stooped, but rangy – a tough old bird. He would have won no beauty contests but then, with $20 million, a pedigree that only just missed the Mayflower, a Navy Cross in World War II, and the State Department thrown in, he did not need to. More important, he was kind, considerate, bright, witty and open and he was deeply in love with Eleanor. A prospective stepdaughter could not ask for much more and did not. 'There's only one better-looking girl in the house than you,' he laughed. 'Take me to the leader.'

Eleanor was walking down the stairs to the hall – cool and crisp in a classic navy-blue coat and skirt, her hair swept back from her face to reveal the fine bone structure. 'So the intrepid traveller returns, spewn out from the bowels of darkest Africa.' Her radiant face spoke her warm greeting.

'Be careful,' said Charles. 'Those long, lonely nights in the throbbing bush give one a fiendish appetite for white women.' He hugged her.

'I think you just lost Washington,' she joked.

Charles Cabot Lodge had just returned from the Pan-American tour that Eleanor had originally suggested. The State Department position paper that Charles had commissioned had been strongly in favour of his going and President Wayne had given the go-ahead for the multi-nation tour, whose purpose it was to reassure both friendly and not so friendly states that the election of a right-wing president did not herald a new pro-South African foreign policy. By all accounts it had been a brilliant propaganda success. The Africans were flattered that the trip had been thought necessary so soon after the presidential elections. As Eleanor had predicted, it had been a considerable blow to Russian and Chinese influence throughout the continent and it had opened up new areas for American financial investment. Cabot Lodge's stock had risen and already there was talk of his becoming the favourite son for the next Republican presidential nomination as the seventy-year-old President Wayne was not expected to run again. The only people who had been upset were the South Africans, but they were used to it – captive allies with nowhere else to go but Israel and the West.

It was a tradition in the Aspen house that all house guests were free to do their own thing, with one proviso. Mealtimes were sacred. At 12.30 drinks were served in the oak-beamed drawing room before lunch and there the party was gathering.

Eleanor made the introductions. 'Charles, have you met Marvin Davis? I think Mr Davis owns very nearly everything in Aspen so we will all have to be very nice to him.' She smiled. Marvin Davis, the Denver oil man, had just bought Twentieth-Century Fox, one of whose subsidiaries was the Aspen Skiing Corporation, the largest landowner in Aspen. 'And this is his daughter, Patty.'

A pert blonde dressed from head to foot in a silver jump suit that looked as if it had been made from parachute material shook Charles' hand.

'Do you know Arch and Di Cummin? Arch and Di are neighbours in the Hamptons and are building a stunning house in Sun Valley.'

'I envy you,' said Charles. 'I used to ski there in the Hemingway days. It's a wonderful place.'

'David Frost – I seem to remember you met some time ago.'

'Hello David. I'm *so* pleased you're staying. I haven't seen you since that dreadful fund-raiser in Florida. Still we carried the state and it was an important one.'

The other guest was Dr Axelrod, a brilliant young anatomist from Harvard Medical School employed by the Montgomerys to do research into the biomechanics of ski racing using Caroline as a model.

The white-coated, pin-stripe trousered butler handed round the drinks and canapés – smoked salmon rolled in brown bread, pistachio nuts, black olives, and 1971 Dom Perignon. At one o'clock sharp the booming of the brass gong from the hall announced that it was time for luncheon.

They filed through into the long dining room that appeared to be, and was indeed, hovering on the brink of a steep abyss. The room had been built out from the side of the mountain on stilts and from the window that ran the entire length of the outer wall could be seen the same staggering panorama across the valley of Aspen that Caroline enjoyed from her training barn. Eleanor sat at one end of the highly polished mahogany table and her professional eye checked it out – Georgian silver, Crown Derby porcelain, Waterford glass, white linen napkins. Charles was sitting on her right and Marvin Davis on her left. Caroline sat next to Charles on his other side, with Dr Axelrod on her right. She never wanted to get too far away from skiing.

'So Charles,' said Eleanor, 'what's the bottom line on Africa?'

'Oh, mother,' said Caroline, 'you can't possibly expect him to encapsulate a whole continent in a sentence or two.'

'Nonsense,' laughed Eleanor. 'Charles has the happy politician's knack of reducing all great complex truths to a few simple, home-spun sentences, don't you, Charles?'

'I can call platitudes from the vasty deep.' Charles borrowed from *The Tempest*.

'What I want to know,' said Eleanor, 'apart from whether or not I get credited for having suggested this trip, is when Africa is going to be safe for long-term investment.' She never wanted to get too far away from business.

Most of the table had a glass of chilled Amontillado with the turtle soup. Caroline drank Perrier.

'Well, of course it depends where you are,' said Charles in serious answer to Eleanor's question. 'For instance, I would rather have a chemical factory in Kenya than in France right now. That's the most amazing country, highly civilized, and Moi, the Prime Minister, told me they're bending over backwards trying to get corporate America to invest. Cheap labour, hard workers, a stable social infrastructure and with leaders that believe in capitalism – what more could you want? Everybody thought there would be disaster when Kenyatta died and, not for the first time, everybody was wrong.'

'Unfortunately rather unlucky in its neighbours. Not much market for product in places like Uganda and Tanzania,' commented Eleanor.

Charles nodded. 'Wait a minute, Eleanor,' he said, remembering suddenly. 'I've got exactly the right investment for you – I know you're a sucker for diamonds. How would you like to finance a diamond mine?'

Eleanor and Caroline were listening. Caroline remembered the beautiful pink stone that Mr Brown had shown in the Claridges suite, which, unknown to her, now nestled in a Cartier vault with her name on it.

'How fascinating. Where?' asked Eleanor. Her mind

raced through the list of countries that Charles had visited. It had to be a country outside the De Beers' cartel, otherwise there would be no problem with the financing. A rich, credit-worthy country would either have the development money or would be able to raise it, which meant she was looking for a poor country with a bad or non-existent credit-rating. To be looking for Western funds it would have to be at least superficially neutral. That narrowed the field.

'No, wait,' she said. 'Let me guess. Umpala.'

Cabot Lodge had long since ceased to be surprised by Eleanor. Thank God she had never gone into politics. She would never have settled for the State Department. 'Yes, of course you're right,' he said, shrugging his shoulders in mock resignation. It seemed superfluous to ask how she knew.

Eleanor was intrigued. This was hot, new, insider business information – always a delectable morsel.

'Of course I'm not much of an expert on either business or diamonds.' He paused. Before he had graduated to the State Department from the Senate Charles Cabot Lodge's Boston law practice had sold superb business advice to the cream of corporate America, while before she died Muffy Cabot Lodge's diamonds had been the envy of every White House reception. There were few people in the country who knew more about the two subjects of which he professed ignorance. Eleanor was one of them.

'But it seemed like one hell of a good deal to me,' Charles continued. 'The man who really runs Umpala is a very sharp cookie called Seretse Mwamba, a sort of *éminence grise*, power behind the throne. He's thoroughly Westernized – you know, French university, course at the London School of Ecomomics – and he has the President in his pocket. The country is on its knees, no foreign exchange, no tourism, no minerals and above all no oil. Since the 1974 oil price hike things have gone from bad to worse. The people scratch about trying to farm, relying on Western grants to prevent starvation. The Communists aren't particularly interested in them because there are only two million people and strategically they're not well placed. Apart from anything else Seretse actually believes in free enterprise. He must be just about the only graduate from the LSE who's ever done so, and I can assure you its pretty rare in Africa. The rest of them seem to believe in straight embezzlement. I felt that I could trust him and he's undoubtedly the man in control and that in my book is the absolute *sine qua non* of any deal. It's no good either trusting somebody who hasn't got the power to deliver the goods or dealing with a top man who's crooked.'

Eleanor nodded her agreement.

The crown of lamb came on enormous silver serving dishes, ready cut, each cutlet pink at the centre. There were roast potatoes, spinach *en branche*, and baby courgettes. The 1961 first-growth Haut Brion, the superb red from the Graves district and therefore not technically a claret although a Bordeaux, was much admired by the connoisseurs present, David Frost and Arch Cummin noticeable in this respect.

Charles' story continued to unfold. 'Well, apparently, seven years ago some dirt farmer came across a 127-carat diamond lying beside a river bed – you know, the classical alluvial find. They managed to keep it quiet and set off to look for the kimberlite origin.'

'I don't want to miss any of this. What's kimberlite?' Caroline interrupted.

This was Eleanor's territory. 'Diamonds get crystallized from carbon in molten rock called liquid kimberlite about a hundred miles down into the earth,' she explained. 'If volcanic activity weakens the crust above, igneous rock and the diamonds it contains explode upwards in a narrow column or 'pipe', blowing a neat hole in the earth's surface. Immediately it collapses back in on itself, cools off, and solidifies into hard blue-black kimberlite rock. The diamonds are scattered through the kimberlite like raisins in a plum pudding. If you find diamonds you might be right on top of a kimberlite pipe, although rivers can wash the stones hundreds of miles from their original source.'

'Anyway,' Charles continued, 'three months later they

found one kimberlite pipe, five hundred yards across at the surface. Apparently many pipes aren't worth mining, but this one was stuffed with diamonds. It had an incredibly high yield of the very finest gem stones, and big ones too.'

Eleanor could hardly contain her excitement. 'De Beers must have offered to buy it. They'd have to protect their monopoly,' she said.

'They simply never found out about it,' said Charles. 'Umpala had never had any diamonds before and the De Beers' geological teams had been over it years before with a fine-tooth comb and found nothing. They weren't in the CSO because they had nothing to sell, until now. Seretse bothered to find out all about diamonds and came to the conclusion that in view of the exceptionally high quality of the stones and because De Beers were doing such a good job in keeping the price of gems on an upward course that Umpala ought to mine the stones herself and stockpile the diamonds. His plan was to go to De Beers eventually and to put a gun to their head by threatening to unload vast quantities of fine gems onto the market, the theory being that they would have to pay through the nose to support the price, safeguard the paper value of their vast stocks and protect their monopoly.'

'But there was a problem,' Eleanor carried on, predicting the outcome of the story. 'They hadn't got the $200 million or so that it would take to develop a diamond mine.'

'Precisely,' said Charles. 'But they knew they were on to a good thing. So they scratched and scraped, and, incidentally, diverted a lot of our agricultural aid to raise enough money to get the mine going from their own resources, and they held on to all the stones that they mined. They kept the whole thing a complete secret. Nobody knew what was going on. It wasn't as difficult as it sounds. The pipe was in the middle of the country, which few foreigners visit anyway, and they had tight security. Of course De Beers, who make it their business to know such things, had an inkling that something was up from things like machinery orders and the five-year disappearance of people like geologists and engineers, who were put on special contracts not to leave the country. What De Beers have never found out is the quality and size of the mine.'

'So Umpala is about to become an ex-poor country,' said Eleanor. 'If Seretse Mwamba ever gets retired there will be a place for him on the Montgomery board. But you said they still needed finance. How come?'

'It's the old, old problem. Cash flow. Umpala have a treasury full of diamonds, but at last they are totally out of money and the mine is at a standstill. They can't afford to repair the machinery, put gas in the trucks and excavators or pay the engineers' wages. They've simply got to get hold of some cash.'

'Why don't they raise it on the international capital market?' Eleanor already knew the answer to that one and she answered her own question. 'Because loans to small central African republics collateralized exclusively by uncut gem stones don't look too kosher to bank stock analysts, or anybody else for that matter.'

'Right again,' said Charles. 'They sniffed around the conventional lending outlets and came up with a big zero. They haven't even got the money to pay the interest on a loan. It begins to look as if the only thing they can do is get hold of De Beers, eat humble pie and ask them to bale them out. Dealing from weakness like that they'd be lucky to get the development costs back, and they could kiss their dreams of a diamond coup goodbye.'

'And they can't flog the diamonds they have stockpiled so far because they haven't got enough at this stage to threaten the monopoly and get De Beers to pay a fancy price. That would just depress the market and at the same time alert De Beers to the fact they were sitting on a vast, high-quality diamond mine. De Beers would immediately start organizing to head off the threat to their position.' Eleanor was enjoying this little financial problem. There was an elegant conclusion to it and she voiced it. 'What Seretse needs is a friendly, innovative banker with a lot of balls who's prepared to take a large risk and his interest payments in diamonds.'

'Seretse's thinking entirely. He knows it's decidedly

unconventional but the logic is good. He's prepared to hand over annually the diamond equivalent of thirty per cent interest on the loan principal, and he'll put up twenty-five per cent of the mine as collateral. Obviously the diamonds paid over in interest will be subject to independent valuation.'

'How much and for how long?' asked Eleanor. She had been dying to ask the most important question.

'They need $300 million for five years.'

'So the lender takes $90 million worth of diamonds a year for five years, $450 million, and then he gets his $300 million back. That sounds like a fantastic proposition,' said Caroline.

Charles was inclined to agree. 'If, for some odd reason, the interest isn't paid, he gets to own a quarter of one of the richest diamond mines in the world, a snip at $300 million. That's pretty unlikely though, as they have enough diamonds stockpiled to pay the interest on the first two or three years of the loan.'

Caroline remembered the Claridges conversation in which Eleanor had destroyed the upstart Cartier man. 'What if the diamond price were to collapse?' she asked.

'The lender would have to have very deep pockets, because he'd own a whole lot of nothing. He'd have to say goodbye to any interest payments and hang on in, hoping the price would recover. It's not a deal for widows and orphans,' said Eleanor.

She turned to Marvin Davis, who had been following the conversation closely. 'What do you think, Marvin?'

The shrewd Denver multi-millionaire thought carefully.

'Buying Twentieth-Century left me a little short of loose change,' he said at last, 'but it's a good deal for a gambler. Of course you have to have faith in the diamond price which just about everyone does as a result of De Beers' careful advertising and good track record in keeping the price up. Otherwise the gamble is that Seretse's honest and that he can deliver.'

'What about you, Charles? I get the vibe you're pretty enthusiastic.' Sometimes Eleanor lapsed into her company presidential style, searching for the consensus at the board meeting.

'Well, I have faith in all three of the factors that Marvin mentioned. What's more I've got a vested interest in getting the deal financed by Americans so I suppose I'd better declare it. Firstly, on a philosophical level it's exactly what America is all about – the frontier spirit. Here are a bunch of shrewd, poverty-stricken, hard-working guys attempting to turn an honest buck and at the same time put the boot in on one of the richest and most successful monopolistic cartels the world has ever known, a cartel incidentally composed very largely of South Africans – not mine or Seretse's favourite people. They're in trouble and they've come up with an adventurous capitalistic scheme that promises the lender a more than adequate return on his investment with reasonable safeguards for his principal. I think it would be entirely in keeping with the great entrepreneurial spirit of this country if somebody chipped in with the cash. If we don't, who will? The Russians? The Chinese? If they do it'll be another foothold in Africa lost to the free world, and lost needlessly. So frankly, I'm going to push hard to get this deal off the ground, although God knows where. David Rockefeller very nearly laughed in my face when I mentioned it to him. I think the idea of being paid interest in diamonds made him think of the coloured beads that the British used to buy their Empire on the cheap, a sort of natives' revenge. I don't know where he got the idea that dollars were better value than tangibles like gold and diamonds.'

'Juuuuu . . . st a moment,' said Eleanor, drawing out the first word in a long drawl. 'I have the man for you. Do you remember a pushy Sun-Belt banker called Harry Fox, who was on the cover of *Fortune* a few months back?'

'Vaguely,' said Charles. 'But surely he isn't in the $300 million league.'

'One certainly wouldn't have thought so,' said Eleanor, 'but he's just lent Montgomery a cool billion at three and a half under prime.'

'Good God,' said Charles. 'Has he?'

147

'Isn't he the man that Miles Parmere works for?' Caroline did not miss much.

'Certainly he is. In fact Miles telephoned to make the introduction.'

Caroline felt a strange twang somewhere inside her. Head? Stomach? Lower? She wasn't quite sure, but something had happened, molecules had definitely re-arranged themselves on this news.

'Have you heard from him at all?' Eleanor asked. Was there the faintest flush on Caroline's cheeks? 'We should invite him for the week-end now that he is here permanently.'

'That might be nice,' said Caroline uncertainly.

Charles was not going to let go of the diamond conversation. Harry Fox to the rescue of US foreign policy, another domino propped up in the nick of time, the bugles of the cavalry.

'Can you get this Fox character to come and see me in New York next week, I've got to talk to the UN. Seretse's going to be in town, too. If you think he's got the cash and the *chutzpah* I'd like to put them together.'

'I am afraid you won't like him, Charles, but he might easily be the man for the job. I'm sure there won't be a problem getting him to New York, especially if you can lay on some motorcycle outriders, promise him a visit to the White House, signed photographs – you know the sort of thing.'

Eleanor remembered Fox's lascivious eyes burning into her, shifting uncomfortably in her chair as she did so. Somewhere in the deepest depths of her subconscious there was a vague awareness that she had done the wrong thing in recommending Harry Fox to Charles. She could scarcely have dreamed of how dreadful the consequences of her action would be.

The rest of the table had been busy with their own topics, leaving the politics and high finance to the Montgomerys, Charles and Marvin Davis. David Frost was attempting the Herculean task of explaining the intricacies of Nixon's personality to Di Cummin. Dr Axelrod, a

Broadway buff and something of a star-gazer, was intrigued by Di Cummin's inside accounts of life on the international *haute café* society circuit, names like Andy Warhol, Jack Nicholson, Calvin Klein and Brooke Shields peppering the conversation. It was just as well, thought Charles, as the information that he had provided was pretty sensitive, not at all the sort of thing that you wanted to read about in the newspapers the following morning. He turned to Caroline. 'I suppose, as usual, you are going to leave me unguarded this afternoon at the mercy of every terrorist and lunatic in the Western hemisphere while you exhaust my escorts with your fiendish games.'

'Right on,' said Caroline. 'This is the fifth meeting of the Aspen Challenge Cup and we're two all. It's a needle match. They always win the shooting but' – she held up her hand – 'Ingemar got hold of a gun licence and we've been practising. Also we're negotiating to have the sprinting uphill, making it more a test of endurance than speed.'

'Sneaky,' said Charles.

Eleanor smiled. How like Caroline – always playing to win. She hadn't touched a drop of alcohol throughout lunch and had eaten sparingly, her mind on the afternoon competition.

The lunch was over. A delicious chocolate mousse, a moist half Stilton, a gum-tickling Cheddar, a runny Camembert, and an eye-watering Port Salut. Coffee and liqueurs were in the drawing room.

'Please excuse me,' said Caroline. 'I have to go and organize my team. If you hear shots, don't worry, it's only us.'

In the gymnasium Ingemar had already marshalled the others. Nigel and Skip were limbering up. Skip Warner, tall and wiry, was, like the others, an enthusiastic member of the Caroline fan club. During the season he was with her at every race, fine tuning the skis lovingly until the last minute. For years he had worked as an engineer in the racing ski research and development division at the Atomic Ski Company. There he had been largely responsible for the development of the sophisticated dual wood core, bionic skis in which use was made of a metal/fibreglass hybrid reinforced by carbon and Kevlar fibre. He had been lured away to work for Caroline but his links with the company remained close. He had access to all the latest technical information and was a walking encyclopaedia of ski science. Skip was vital to Caroline, for she had no sponsors and had refused all requests to endorse particular equipment. She could therefore pick and choose from the very best. But the range of available products was enormous and she needed Skip's wisdom and expertise to help her identify the equipment that best suited her technique. For the moment she used K2 skis, Salomon bindings, Nordica boots and Carrera goggles, but that could change. While her skis were being made, Skip would be there in the factory supervising every step. Later, on the slopes, he would arrange elaborate trials to identify the skis that best complemented her individual style, for no pair of skis, however standardized their construction, is ever totally alike, and in races where fractions of a second separate winners from losers such perfectionism paid dividends.

An artist with skis, Skip was no less talented at the controls of a helicopter. He had learned this skill in the ultimate training ground, the bullet-torn skies of Vietnam. He had served there with the 17th Air Cavalry as command pilot in an Assault Helicopter Company based at Pleiku. He had gained a reputation among the Marine grunts for coolness and bravery that he valued more than the Air Medal which was the official recognition of his courage. Unlike many of the helicopter pilots, he was prepared to fly his Cobra attack helicopter through fog and heavy rain to the hottest landing zones to give support to combat platoons pinned down in firefights. Time and again he would risk his life and his machine to evacuate wounded men from perimeters saturated with incoming mortar fire, and yet miraculously he had survived.

On his return from Vietnam he had decided to use his master's in engineering to go into ski development and design and had gone to Austria to work for Atomic. In his spare time he had continued to fly helicopters for a charter company and by the time he joined the Montgomery team he had seven years experience of Alpine flying. It had given him the ability to land on a sixpence in a snowstorm.

He navigated using some highly developed sixth sense that he himself did not understand. It was as if he had an inbuilt homer beamed in on Caroline and on more than one of those early-morning trips to the mountain tops to seek out the virgin powder he had discovered her at the foot of some deserted descent when a blizzard had reduced visibility to a few feet. There had been the time, too, when Caroline had slipped into a deep crevice, becoming wedged at the bottom. Skip had manoeuvred the helicopter into the narrow mouth of the ravine with snow and ice one foot either side of the churning rotor blades and held it rock-steady while he dropped a rope-ladder to her. On another occasion, sensing avalanche, he had swept down on her as she rode the powder, and, hovering two feet above the ground, had made her sit on the landing gear, skis dangling, as he whisked her away to safety. A few seconds later they had watched the mountain disintegrate. In Ingemar and Skip, Caroline had the best back-up team in the world. She was lucky but, in the words of Goethe, 'Fools do not know how clearly linked are luck and merit.' As Bill Montgomery was fond of saying, 'It's the damnedest thing, the harder I work the luckier I get.'

The secret servicemen ambled into the barn dressed in a variety of track suits. They looked casual but they were ready for action and they wanted to win badly. Their leader, a rangy former special forces major, opened the negotiations with Caroline. This was traditional. Ground rules could be changed if all agreed. The secret servicemen had discovered the spent shells of the clandestine target practice on their careful search of the grounds before the Secretary of State's arrival and had worked out that their usual lead in this might be jeopardized. They had a proposal. The shooting category would include a section using the Israeli Uzi submachine guns that all agents carried. Caroline would trade. OK to the Uzis in exchange for their agreement to the sprinting course taking place up the steep slope that was used for the grass skiing. The major would deal on that if the grass skiing became a straight downhill rather than a slalom. That way naked bravery might go some way towards countering the natural superiority of the home team in this event. They would shake on it, said Caroline, if the Aspen team were allowed fifteen minutes' practice with the Uzis first. After much playful bantering the ground rules were agreed.

Grass skiing was first. This was relatively new in America. The skis are made up of two-foot-long narrow platforms beneath which are attached a single row of ten rubber wheels of the roller-skate type. The ski boot is bound onto the platform some eight inches above the ground. The technique is remarkably similar to snow skiing and in previous matches this had meant a walkover for Caroline's team. This time there would be no need to master the art of the turn. The secret servicemen launched themselves like suicide jumpers onto the steep incline, prepared to do or die. Psychologically they were well prepared for this as at any moment they might be required to throw themselves unthinkingly in the path of a bullet to protect their charge. Expert skiers, however, know that there are three speeds in downhill. Firstly there is the speed when you are consciously holding back, using your edges to slow your descent. Secondly there is so-called 'gravitational speed'. Here you just let yourself go and gravity pulls you down the slope as fast as it can. Finally there is the speed you can achieve through hard training and mastery of the downhill technique – the ability to go faster than the hill naturally dictates. Caroline and Ingemar travelled at speed three, the others at speed two. One up to the home team.

Charles Cabot Lodge was feeling expansive. It had been a good lunch. He sniffed appreciatively at the Courvoisier and rolled the Havana between his thumb and forefinger. Should he remove the band or not? It was always an agonizing decision. At this point his tranquillity was rudely shattered by the frantic burst of machine-gun fire from the woods a few hundred yards to the left of the house. Eleanor paled. Conversation stopped dead. Charles' mind raced. Was this it? The revolution? Government leaders attacked separately, picked off by synchronized hit squads. He stood up quickly. Time for decisions. As he did so, a blushing secretary entered the room and whispered in his ear.

'You forgot to warn me that Caroline and Co would be firing machine-guns between 3.00 and 3.30,' he repeated aloud in disbelief.

There was general laughter with which a strong element of relief was mixed. Charles spread his hands open. The gesture said it all. Only in the Montgomery household could one's post-prandial digestive repose be shattered by a little casual machine-gun fire from the woods. He wasn't angry. In fact he was proud that Eleanor's daughter was like that. He loved them both so much he would do anything for them. Kill? Betray his country? He wondered. But Eleanor had never asked anything of him, to his eternal disappointment. That was the problem. She liked him, respected him and occasionally desired him, but she had never needed him.

'I suppose that next month it will be hand grenades, or bazookas.'

'For God's sake, don't suggest that,' said Eleanor half seriously.

'I must speak to that major,' Charles muttered. It was tradition not to mention secret servicemen by name.

Eleanor reflected that she didn't really have one moment's concern about her eighteen-year-old daughter playing with machine-guns. It was a very remarkable fact, a testimony to Caroline's monumental competence and self-control. Eleanor stood in awe of very few people. Her daughter was one of them.

# Chapter 6

## I

SNAP! The sudden noise was music to the ears of Miles Parmere and Roy Felty as they trolled the waters at the edge of the Gulf Stream seven miles off Sugarloaf Key. The big fish had struck in a crashing blind rush, taking the plastic yellowfin tuna lure without any foreplay. The long Dacron line had sprung from the wooden clothes peg that had held it suspended from the starboard outrigger twenty-five feet above the boat. The additional thirty yards of slack given to the line by the outrigger loop provided Miles with time to organize himself in the fighting chair of the fifty-foot Hatteras Sport Fisherman. In these vital seconds his mind was underwater, visualizing the sinewy slither as the huge fish raced away with its prize. Must avoid the head-on collision of forces as the powerful fish came up against line resistance. He could lose it that way. Miles free-spooled the line, adding manual dropback to that provided by the outrigger. And then the fish broke the surface. The leap was spectacular, the bright sun catching the shining surface of the vast billfish, reflecting in a cascade of brilliant colours from the webbed dorsal fin. This was what they had wanted – *Makaira nigricans* – the toughest, most determined and aggressive fighting fish of them all.

'Blue!' Miles and Roy shouted in unison.

'Boy, watch that fish go!' Roy was excited. They had been looking for blue marlin and now they had found one, and it was big.

In the brief moment of aerobatics Roy's professional eye had assessed the fish at more than three hundred pounds. He thanked God they had used the eighty-pound test line

and the heavy class rod. Even so the odds were on the fish.
It would be a long battle.

'He's running hard, Roy. For God's sake get the boat
around.'

Roy had anticipated this and already the *Happy Hooker*,
which had been cruising with the Gulf Stream at seven
knots, was turning about to follow the fish. In two minutes
Miles had watched several hundred yards of line streak
after the marlin. On a 6/o reel he would be down to the
arbor knot by now. He blessed the foresight that had led
him to use the additional capacity widespool-type reel.

Roy gave the wheel to his boatman and moved to Miles'
side. He knew that the Englishman was no novice, but
then this blue marlin was no ordinary gamefish. He would
need all the advice he could get.

Miles reeled in fast. Already he was worrying that the
boat might overrun the fish. As if reading his mind the
boatman throttled back.

For twenty minutes the big blue sashayed wildly all over
the ocean, and Miles gave him his head. There was no
alternative. But after half an hour he was beginning to
assert some control. The muscles on his forearms stood
out like ropes as he fought the fish and sweat coursed down
his face with the effort of the struggle.

'That's it, Miles. Bend his neck and keep him coming.'
This was the fashion in fish fighting today. To hell with the
dainty touch. It was no longer considered enough to keep
a tight line and let the fish wear itself out. You had to go
out and get him. 'Keep the line as short as possible,' Roy
added.

'He's beginning to fade a bit,' Miles gasped.

'Keep him close. That way you sap his confidence. Out
in the ocean with a long lead he feels he can do anything he
wants. Don't worry about the boat. We'll follow him
wherever he goes.'

The battle raged on for over an hour with Miles keeping
the line at about a hundred feet. With this length of line he
could use a lifting action to cramp the fish's freedom of
movement. As it tired Miles wondered about tightening

the drag on the reel, increasing the resistance on the line to apply more pressure. 'Should I go a little tighter?' he asked.

'No way. Don't fool with the drag. Thumb the spool if you must.'

Miles looked down at his heaving abdominal muscles through the mist of sweat that covered his eyes. The rod handle was grinding away at his skin and already there was a large blister from the friction, but he felt no pain.

One and a half hours into the fight and Miles was on top. He found that he could turn the fish from side to side and took advantage of this to tire him, stopping him shorter and shorter in his runs. Relentlessly he began to establish his mastery.

'Don't relax when you stop him, Miles. Make him go where you want him.' Roy was pleased. The contest was going well. He had his money on Miles now.

Wearily the tired fish approached the boat. This was a dangerous time. A bungled gaff now could give the fish a second wind, stimulating him to summon up those final reserves of extra strength in a break for freedom. For another half hour Miles fought him, trying to break up the pattern of laborious runs that the exhausted fish embarked on no more than fifty feet from the rod tip. At last the blue marlin was in the boat, the battle won.

'My God, I need a drink,' said Miles.

'You've earned it,' said Roy, disappearing into the cabin to get the ice-box.

Roy and Miles sat side by side in the two fighting chairs, the insulated plastic box between them. Inside, packed tight in the ice, were the beaded tins of lite beer. Miles took the first Budweiser fast. He had lost about four pounds fighting the fish and he needed to make up blood volume. He let the fizzy liquid hit the back of his throat, leaned back in the chair, one leg hooked up over its arm, and contemplated his situation. It looked good. A fickle breeze went some way towards relieving the oppressive heat of the steamy Florida summer, while overhead the blue sky was dotted with powder-puff clouds whose purpose was clearly decoration rather than rain. There was a gentle, lazy swell and the big boat rode it easily, the twin Mercedes diesel engines throbbing reassuringly. A hundred yards off the port bow a pelican took slowly to the air. Further away towards the land, in the shallow waters that bordered the Gulf Stream, cormorants dived for fish. Miles was at peace. The big blue marlin lay defeated in the bottom of the boat. He had a friend next to him, cold beer at hand. What else could there be?

As he asked the question he knew that there was an answer. Caroline. Miles had tried to forget her. It would have made sense. The girl was obsessed with skiing and he could contribute nothing to her ambitions. Since he had arrived in America he had begun to understand the extent of her fame and accomplishments. Her face stared out at him from the magazine stands, at supermarket check-out counters, from the covers of *People* and *US*. She was the great skiing hope, the all-American girl who would finally show the effete Europeans and the unscrupulous Communists just who was boss. Rich, famous and beautiful was a magic combination that Americans loved and admired more than life itself and Caroline had all the attributes. Miles had bought some of the magazines and had read the interviews, but he had found no encouragement in them. It was true that she appeared to have no steady boyfriend and the gossip columnists had been driven to distraction by their failure to rake up anything even remotely scandalous in her private life. That Miles supposed could be regarded as a bonus point. On the other hand there was nothing to bolster the hopes of potential suitors either. From the tone of the interviews it sounded as if Caroline would have been totally at home in a nunnery, her sexual desires apparently so successfully sublimated that they had to all intents and purposes ceased to exist.

And yet Miles remembered the Annabel's evening. He thought gratefully of the hard body pressed against him, recalled the exquisite pain of the cowboy boot on his foot, the smell of her hair, the touch of her skin, the smooth, powerful shoulders framed by the incongruous, sophisticated dress, the contours of her leg when she had raised the dress on the dance floor. He remembered the soft lilt of her voice with its hint of the Texan drawl that she had never entirely lost, saw again the anger flash into the blue eyes when he had unwisely tried to patronize her. He thought of the almost physical discomfort he had experienced until she had forgiven him, of the warm, intimate smile, the reassuring squeeze of her hand. In his mind he re-created the lunch at Odette's, the delectable mouth, her enthusiasm as she had talked of skiing, the sensitivity that had seemed to understand the predicament of Miles himself, the strong mutual desire that the lunch should not end, the unwilling acceptance that they could have no more time together.

Not for the first time Miles contemplated the effect that she had had on his life. Here he was, bobbing in the Gulf Stream, a bank executive earning a quarter of a million dollars a year, a man of prospects, far from the social round, the jaded life of decaying European capitals. On his first day in the job he had set in motion a phenomenal financial coup, and that too had been courtesy of the Montgomerys. Harry Fox and the Union Bank had, at a stroke, joined the big league with the billion-dollar loan to Montgomery, and Miles' prestige had risen with the bank's share price. Eleanor Montgomery had been cool when he had telephoned her to set up the meeting with Harry Fox and he had sensed that she disapproved of him. However, she had done well from the deal and she was a businesswoman as well as a mother. She had written him a charming letter of thanks for his part in it and had suggested that he must visit them one week-end at the Aspen chalet or their Southampton home. There had been no mention of Caroline in the letter and Miles heard again the Odette's conversation when Caroline had gently warned him that if he came to stay he should not expect to see too much of her. Miles was not the sort of man to stand that sort of treatment, being wheeled out to provide light relief at mealtimes or in the gaps between training. A thousand times he had wondered if she ever had any time off, time that he could use to mount a frontal attack to capture her emotions, to saturate her with his personality, creep stealthily around her defences to kidnap her feelings. If he could have enough time alone with her he felt certain that he could win her.

He knew exactly where he would take her. It would be far from America, far from the ski slopes, from the eyes of the media, of sophisticated people, of anybody who would recognize her or interfere with his campaign. He would take her to the farm outside Seville where they would ride, walk and swim, go to the bullfights, spend evenings in the flamenco bars where Miles had more good friends than in London or Paris. She would get to know him and learn to love him. Miles made an instant decision. He would call her up and invite her to Spain. He had nothing to lose.

Roy Felty's voice cut into his day-dream. 'Sure as hell you're not thinking about that fish any more.'

'More like how to catch a bird,' said Miles, smiling gently.

Roy Felty reached for another beer. With his other hand he pushed the worn blue forage cap further back on his head. He wore a blue tee-shirt, cut off at the shoulders and the midriff, bearing the name of his boat, the *Happy Hooker*, in orange letters across front and back. Sawn-off levis and dirty tennis shoes completed the outfit. Embroidered in gold across the band of the blue cap was the legend 'US NAVY SEAL'. Dark mahogany was the background against which Roy Felty would have been best camouflaged. Salt, sun and hard work had left their marks on his body, but there were other marks too – shrapnel scars and a jagged bullet wound just beneath the right collarbone that must have taken lung. The eyes hinted at other wounds, invisible but nonetheless real. There could be no doubt, and there was none, that Felty was a very hard man indeed. Hard in the sense of enduring, indestructible rather than cruel or insensitive. It would have been difficult to conceive of any physical discomfort that would phase him or of any set of circumstances that would rattle him. He had the look of a man who had seen the pit, the ultimate horror, who had survived the worst hand that a human could be dealt and yet had gone on to finish the game, who had been tested in the hottest fire and had emerged strengthened, not weakened.

Roy looked quizzically at the Englishman. Miles and he had fought in the same war, although they had not known each other then. They had a lot in common. Both of them had refused to write off their Vietnam experiences as a ghastly interlude of horror, death and destruction, and instead had chosen to gain and learn from them. Roy liked Miles for other reasons too.

'And this "bird" that needs to be caught has something to do with you taking this banking job in Florida?'

'You wouldn't believe me if I told you.'

'Try me.'

So Miles told him about Caroline. He had never discussed it with anyone else before and what seemed curious in thought was even more strange when expressed in words.

Roy tended to cut through to the heart of things. 'So you're in love,' he said.

Miles had never really thought about it like that before, but on the whole he supposed that Roy was probably right.

Roy Felty remembered the time when he too had been in love. The war had put an end to that. Towards the end of his second tour in 'Nam he had been badly wounded. When he finally got out of hospital and returned to the States it was to find that his wife had fallen in love with his elder brother. He had lost both of them, but the pain had never gone away. He had been there, still in a way was, so he knew what Miles was talking about. 'When you're in love with a beautiful woman, it's hard,' he said. He wasn't particularly thinking about the song.

'Especially when you're risking your life in stinking jungles thousands of *kliks* from anywhere.' He knew about Roy's marriage, wanted to show solidarity.

They both started on their third Budweiser.

'It's a funny thing,' said Miles. 'There are similarities

between love and combat. There's a sort of manic ecstatic quality to both. I always remember that when the danger was greatest you got a kind of adrenalin high, an incredibly clear consciousness when reality seemed to be intensified. It was terrifying and awful, but at the same time fascinating, almost addictive. Ordinary life seems colourless by comparison. Now this Caroline thing has sort of charged me up again, given me the type of receptive alertness that you get in a jungle firefight, the feeling that life is worth a lot and you really want to hang on to it.'

Roy drank deeply. There weren't many people who understood this kind of thing – not at all what you learned on mother's knee, at high school, or in basic training for that matter. It was good to talk about it to someone who had experienced it first hand. 'You're never far from 'Nam. I know what you mean. It's difficult to get a buzz from life after the experiences one had there. Everything mattered so much when your life depended on it and other people's lives mattered too. Guys would get killed going out into fire to bring back the dead bodies of their friends. You don't get that close to people in the "real" world. Somehow whether or not your M16 was going to jam in combat was a more fundamental worry than whether or not you can afford the mortgage payments or whether you locked the back door.'

Miles laughed. He felt that too. What was the point in struggling through this watered-down rat-race when you had competed with infinitely superior rodents in a far more serious competition, where the stakes were your own blood and guts, not the country cottage and the second car? The psychiatrists talked about delayed stress reactions and reactive depressions, about personality disorders and 'problems of readjustment'. Miles did not object to their jargon. After all, they had to carve out a living like everyone else. But the problem was really a simple one. Men who had lived for very long periods of time with the realization that at any minute their brains might be splashed all over the jungle, that their balls might be blown off, their guts turned inside out, were irrevocably changed by the experience. It would have been odd if they had not been. It takes more than an aeroplane ride to change a professional killer into a model citizen.

'You can even plan love like a military campaign,' said Miles. 'Situation. Mission. Execution. Administration. Command. Logistics. It's all there.'

Roy laughed. 'Right on. Situation – you are in love with Caroline. Mission – to get her to fall in love with you. Execution – invite her to Spain. Administration – telegraph the servants to get the house ready. Command and Logistics – I guess that would be to do with aeroplane tickets and things.'

The Budweiser was hard at work. Miles and Roy were enjoying themselves. They were both keen fishermen but drinking ice-cold beer in the Gulf Stream was as fine a way to pass a couple of hours as any other.

'I had a lot of plans for my life before Vietnam,' Miles confessed, 'but afterwards most of them didn't seem worth the effort. The regular Army was impossible. A peacetime Army has about as much relevance to a real war as a country church to Heaven or hellfire. So I've really drifted until now. Caroline has sort of given me a sense of direction again.'

Roy nodded. 'It's like after you've had your most intense experiences in your very early twenties, there's not much to do with the rest except to grow old disgracefully. There's not much call around the place for the things I'm best at. Nothing for M60 machine gunners in the classifieds. Nobody wants to know that I can hit a mortar position with a forty-mike mike grenade at sixty yards or take out a hooch with an M79 launched Willie Peter from a sampan in thick fog.'

Miles laughed. 'You're right. Slitting throats with a K-Bar and busting caps in a firefight go down like lead balloons as topics for conversation at job interviews.'

'Mind you,' said Roy, raising a finger. 'I keep myself prepared. As you know we're in the Bermuda Triangle right now and something like four hundred ships have disappeared without trace. All the wisest boat captains carry weapons. It's just that I've gone a little over the top.' He stood up. 'Let me show you something.'

Miles followed Roy into the dark, teak-panelled saloon. The air conditioning whirred gently and the cold, dry air went to work on their sweat-covered bodies. Roy moved over to the cushioned seating, threw off the detachable upholstery and opened the wooden lids of the storage spaces. Miles drew in his breath sharply. Roy Felty was carrying enough military hardware to equip a Marine combat squad.

Miles picked up one of the M16 rifles and eyed it professionally. 'I see you've got an M203 40mm grenade launcher attachment on this one. I hear they're phasing out the old M79 launcher and replacing them with these. God, Roy, this stuff is in good condition.'

'They're mint,' said Roy. 'I clean them regularly and blast them off too. Never let a wasted talent go to waste is my motto. Of course, it's illegal to have them, but no pirate or drug-runner is going to mess with my boat when it's got an M60 mounted on the flying bridge.'

'That would be the definition of bad luck,' thought Miles, 'picking Roy Felty's boat to hijack.'

They went back outside and as they did so the crack of the line leaving the outrigger told them that they were back in business.

The white marlin lay beside its blue cousin on the floor of the Hatteras. This was turning into an exciting day's fishing. If they could catch a sailfish now they would achieve the prestigious billfish grand slam. A swordfish as well and it would be a super grand slam, only the second time that a single angler would have caught the four billfish in the course of a single day.

It was time for lunch. Roy Felty's Hatteras was the best-equipped charter boat operating out of the Florida Keys and as a captain his reputation was formidable. A week before he had poached Paul Newman from Skip Bradeen at Whale Harbour. When you could do that you really knew you had arrived. Roy and Miles were close friends but Miles had chartered the boat and was paying the going rate of $400 for the day, so he was the customer as well.

'What have you got for lunch, Roy?'

'You name it. There's shrimp, conch chowder, fried grouper, chicken salad, salad Niçoise, and Key lime pie of course.' This last local delicacy was a delicious cheesecake flavoured with limes grown in the Keys.

'Sounds good,' said Miles. 'What are you having?'

'I'm afraid I've got to admit to a perversion,' Roy answered. 'Since 'Nam I've had this thing about "C" rations. I just can't get enough of them. I've got a guy up at Homestead who gets me the odd case, but not nearly as much as I'd like.'

Miles roared with laughter. The processed, dehydrated, preserved, tinned food, known in the Army as 'C' rations, were for many soldiers ranked, with mosquitoes, leeches, rain, booby traps and Viet Cong, among the very worst experiences of the war. Miles had eaten them without much enthusiasm, but with no real distaste. Anybody who had survived an English public school would never again be faced with a meal that he could not eat. No prison would have dared to serve the food that hit the tables at Harrow. In the Guards, while on exercises, he had quite enjoyed British Army compo rations, especially the rice pudding and condensed milk. 'C' rations were only marginally worse. There was one particular meal that was dreaded by all combat soldiers, generally recognized to be of peculiar and consummate nastiness, setting new standards of gastronomic ghastliness. This was the all but inedible ham and lima beans. Miles had never met anybody who had actually liked them, although there was a rumour that there was a fire team leader in the 1st Battalion of the 26th Marines at Khe Sanh who would actually trade 'C' ration peaches for them.

'Knowing you, Roy, you'd go the whole hog. I bet I know what you like best.'

Roy nodded, smiling broadly, and they both chorused – 'Ham and motherfuckers.' That was what the lima beans were called.

Miles settled for conch chowder, fried grouper, a mixed salad and a slice of Key lime pie. Roy prised open a tin of 'C' with a Navy K-Bar knife. They stuck to the lite beer. Minutes later the seductive smell of simmering seafood began to waft through from the galley as the chef went to work, a smell that kept the two men talking about food.

'What did you do for food in the jungle?' Roy asked.

'Mostly we got rice from the villages, heavily laced with Agent Orange – that defoliant the Air Force used to scatter about. We used to be out for a week at a time, so no way could we carry "Cs". We'd toss old Mark 80 grenades into the rivers to score some fish when we weren't in close contact.'

'That was the way to go. You had to be as much like the VC as possible if you were going to get to waste them.'

'Yes,' said Miles. 'Of course my job was easier in a way because the whole platoon was Vietnamese. They knew the language and the natives. I was the only round-eye. We never once got mortared because we never stayed still and we moved fast. The name of the game in the main war was to announce your presence with a noisy helicopter landing and in effect use the troops as live bait. We just crept around like the VC. With us it was the enemy and especially the North Vietnamese Army who represented the mono-lithic, large formation regular troops and *we* were the guerillas. Our Vietnamese were as good if not better than theirs because we got a great team spirit going. We were small enough for that, independent and totally flexible, and there were no corrupt ARVN officers to set a bad example. We kept the same platoon together and operated over the same large area so that at the end of two years we knew it like the backs of our hands. We were the ones that laid the booby traps and they were the guys who got blown up. Of course we didn't have to bother about the Cambo-dian border like the regulars. We could go right in and zap their supply trails when they thought they were safe and then just melt away into the jungle. Some of the platoon would actually go and live in VC-controlled villages from time to time. That was really role reversal.'

Miles paused, lost in thought. The damp, dripping forest closed in on him, buzzing, biting insects at his face and neck. Like taking a warm shower in dirty water fully clothed. Hack at foliage with machete. Walking point, leading from in front in platoon formation – two flankers out. Head turning from side to side – total concentration, hearing senses on maximum alert. Sniffing the foetid air. Cooking smells? Not far from the trail now. VC base camp up ahead. Whisper back to gun team. Bring up the M60. Complete silence. Very slow movement. Creep, crawl, hardly breathing, listening to heart. Unexpected, unannounced, one hundred per cent alive, fear, loathing, excitement, exhilaration, stomach fluttering, muscles tensed, mouth dry, pupils dilated, mind racing. Fan out platoon. Where were their outposts? Who would die? A million dollars to be out of this? A million dollars' worth of experience. Visual contact. Ten men, eating rice, sitting about. No sentries. Incredible. Bad soldiers, thank God, about to pay the price. Safety off AK47. Slow-motion ballet. Blood, rice, brains, cooking pots, tissues, ex-people – theirs. Momentary spurt in world death rate. How long to replace? Ten new babies. Ten minutes? Zero to ten kill ratio, high body count. Screw that crap. Get away fast. Walk for hours. Lie low. Disappear.

'Lunch is ready when you are.' The chef's head peeped out from the saloon.

Miles was back in the real world. Or was he?

The conch chowder went some way towards answering the question: hot and spicy, thick chunks of meat.

'So, how's business this summer?' asked Miles.

'Good at the top end. Luckily I'm well established now and I've got real loyal clients. The guys who are just starting out are really hurting. Most of them have gone into drug or people smuggling. There's no recession in that.'

'I've heard that drugs is the state's biggest industry right now,' said Miles, who was unaware that the bank for which he worked had a not insignificant role in the drug traffic.

'Sure is. Since last year they've seized $600 million worth

of cocaine. The drug enforcement people reckon they only get about one per cent of the market so on that basis it's a $60 billion-a-year business.'

'So coke is the real thing.'

'Yep, marijuana is old hat. But quaaludes are pretty big, too. Heroin's getting real cheap.'

Neither Roy nor Miles used drugs of any kind except alcohol. They made up for it there.

'How does the whole cocaine thing work?' Miles asked.

'Well, the coca leaves grow mainly in Bolivia and the north-western jungle area of Peru. The next step is to turn it into coca paste – quite a crude process. You stick the leaves into oil drums, add potash, kerosene and water, drain off the liquid and you're left with a gummy, brown paste. That sells for $2500 a kilo in Peru and Bolivia. The paste is smuggled into Colombia, to laboratories in places like Medallin and Bogotá, where it gets converted into cocaine base. The paste has doubled in value by this time. It takes about two pounds of paste to make a pound of base and it's rather a sophisticated and expensive conversion. You add all sorts of acid to the paste and then boil the mixture in a cauldron until there's a brown, syrupy liquid, the cocaine base. That gets mixed with hydrochloric acid, acetone and household bleach and when it dries you're left with large crystallized chunks of pure, white cocaine. Reckon about $10,000 per kilo of pure cocaine by the time the producers, border guards, smugglers and refining costs have been paid. The couriers by the way are known as "*traficantes*" or "mules" and the whole chain is known as "the train".'

'And the next step is to get it to America?'

'Yes. The "mules" either use regular public transport and just smuggle it through, stopping off first in the Bahamas, Guatemala or Panama to avoid suspicion, or they bribe a boat captain, or fly it in by light aeroplane. Sometimes they hijack a boat on the open ocean, throw the crew overboard, use it for a couple of drug runs and then scuttle it. Beach value in the US is $50,000 to $60,000 a kilo against a total production cost to the Colombians of $10,000, so they can afford to pay the boat captains well.

Guys I know have picked up $100,000 a trip with no trouble. Once it's landed in the US, often in northern Florida and Georgia where the beaches are less crowded, it gets sold to one of the wholesalers in Miami. They're mostly organized into "companies", although there are independent operators known as "mustangers". They pay $60,000 for the smuggled kilo and pass it on to the users at $139,000, or $139 a gram.'

'And when they all fall out it's open warfare on the streets of Miami,' said Miles.

'Precisely. That's why it's murder capital USA right now. All the killing gets done by Colombian hit men. They fly them in to torpedo the target and then hustle them out again. That Castelli guy you were telling me about uses them all the time. In fact there's a rumour that he keeps a bunch of them in a sort of murderer's doss house on a small island that he owns just north of Key Largo – a place called Soldier Key. So the days of private armies are not entirely dead. If I had my way I'd napalm it.'

Miles smiled. Castelli was a formidable enemy. It was remarkable that in the 1980s a gangster could keep an island full of foreign killers just off the coast of the USA and that nobody could, or would, do anything about it.

'Of course the money is so big that they own several of the judges, quite a few policemen, many of the politicians. They're pretty well organized. And I suppose you could argue that cocaine's no big deal. After all, it was part of the recipe for Coca Cola until they outlawed it in 1906. I just object to a whole load of greasy South Americans turning our cities into free fire zones and us not being allowed to do a damn thing about it.'

Miles could see that Roy had a point. It would be considered generally unacceptable in London, certainly frowned upon in the Home Counties.

'Well,' said Miles, 'maybe after a few more beers we'll tool on up to Soldier Key and blast the shit out of them. We've certainly got the fire power.'

They both laughed.

*

It was evening as they put in to Bud and Mary's marina where the *Happy Hooker* was based and both Roy and Miles were flying high. Prodigious quantities of beer had been consumed, the Vietnam war refought and won, the enemies of good and the forces of evil isolated and destroyed. They had not made the billfish grand slam but they had caught some blackfin tuna and bonito to add to the two marlin. There did not seem to be much wrong with the world that chopped cherrystone clams and soft-shell crabs at the Marker 88 would not put right. After dinner they had driven up to the Pilot House and listened to the girl playing the guitar as they hit the *piña coladas* in the moonlight. There was only the one thing missing, thought Miles, and that would be taken care of. Already he could hear the wail of *saetas*, feel their harrowing melancholy. He saw the arched backs and the brightly coloured dresses as the flashing fingers of the guitarists conjured up the bubbling gaiety of the Sevillanas, felt the thrill of anticipation unfailingly evoked by the *pasadobles*. Would Caroline love Andalucia as he did? Would she learn to feel as much for him as he did for her?

II

Susie sat in the aisle seat one row back from the front in the almost empty first-class cabin on the flight to New York. In front of her Harry Fox had the two seats to himself. She liked it when he took her on trips and this one promised to be something special whichever way you looked at it. It was not the easiest thing, or even perhaps the wisest, to travel across state lines with 'juveniles', expecially when they were to be used for 'immoral purposes'. Susie smiled at the phrase. If there was any corruption to be done it was usually she that did it.

Harry Fox had solved the problem of her youthful appearance with characteristic efficiency. She was his 'daughter' on trips like this and Harry had paid the $3000 going market rate for the false passport that proved it. This way there were no problems with hotels, immigration officials or anybody else. For the last year she had effectively 'belonged' to Harry Fox, who had come to rely on her for satisfying his somewhat eccentric sexual proclivities. This suited Susie fine. She earned a very considerable income and she enjoyed every minute of it, but it was no nine-to-five job and she had to work hard to earn her keep. She twirled rings in her long blonde hair and stretched out her legs across the empty seats next to her. So Harry Fox was going to New York to have lunch with the Secretary of State and some important spade politician to discuss a business deal. That was all she knew but it sounded impressive. How much higher could you go? It seemed to Susie that she had caught the right bus.

'Hello, I'm Paula. I'll be looking after you on this flight. May I get you a soft drink, Miss Fox?'

Susie looked up and took in the stewardess. Paula was tall, brown-haired, sun-tanned and with an open smile. About twenty-four, thought Susie. A touch flat-chested, but a small, firm boy's bottom and great legs. The beige skirt was pulled tight over her narrow hips. Bending over would be a problem. Flesh-coloured stockings, bolero jacket matching the skirt, white silk blouse. Paula looked outstandingly healthy, uncomplicated, good looking, without actually qualifying for the adjective beautiful. The same could not have possibly been said about Susie. She was a card-carrying, fully paid-up member of the beautiful people club and there was no questioning her credentials – long blonde hair, blue eyes, pert nose, pouting rosebud lips. Today she was dressed like a schoolgirl but she was as much a woman as a child. White shirt, blue blazer, long white socks and flat, 'sensible' shoes. The skirt was rather too short for the rest of the ensemble and she wore no underpants. Harry liked that. It meant he could touch her in elevators, on cab rides, in restaurants. Her pubescent breasts were probably a size larger than the stewardess's and Paula could see most of them through the half-open shirt as she stood over Susie.

'I'd love an orange juice. Oh, I'm so excited. This is my very first flight and I've just been longing for it,' she lied, injecting a winning note of unsophisticated enthusiasm into her voice. 'I've always dreamed of being a stewardess like you. I can't think of anything I'd rather be.' She stared deep into Paula's eyes, lost in admiration.

The older girl laughed, pleased by the indirect compliment. 'Well, it's not all glamour and excitement.' She managed to imply that actually it was.

Susie reached out and touched Paula's arm lightly. 'Listen, Paula, would you tell me all about it? You know, what it's like and things. You're so incredible looking, I'm sure you're absolutely the best person to give me the low-down.'

The stewardess laughed again. 'Of course. I'd be glad to. Luckily the cabin's more or less empty so I've got lots of time. I'll get you that orange juice and sit down with you for a bit if you like.'

Susie liked. She knew exactly what she was going to do and so did Harry, who was shifting about in the seat in front, strenuously pretending not to have overheard the conversation.

Paula went back to get the drink. It was far from unusual to be told that she was incredible looking by the male customers. That was part of the job, the best part in Paula's view. She had lost count of the one-night stands, expensive dinners and, on occasion, lingering affairs that had resulted from such opening gambits as she served the drinks.

The truth of the matter was that Paula liked to make it most nights and if she missed out for a day or two she tended to get a headache. Sometimes she had even worried that she was too promiscuous and had discussed it with the other girls but they had reassured her that she was not particularly unusual in this respect and that the real problems would start when the invitations dried up. Still, it was the first time she had ever been called 'incredibly beautiful' by a woman or, more accurately, by a young girl who appeared to be only about sixteen. Somehow the compliment made her feel better than it usually did.

Paula sat down next to Susie and was immediately aware of the intense, saucer-like blue eyes boring into her. There was an aura, a force-field of throbbing sexuality that seemed to charge the atmosphere around the young girl and Paula picked up on it at once. Susie had often been told about it and she knew how to control it, project it, switch it on. From the very earliest days she had been obsessed with the giving and receiving of sexual pleasure, had never really been interested in anything else. All day long, in every situation, she looked at people and events as potential sources of physical gratification. Her id had taken over her ego and her conscience, if it had ever existed, was now nowhere to be found.

Susie broke the pregnant silence. 'Paula.' She breathed the name. 'You don't mind my asking, do you, but how do you get your hair into such fantastic condition?'

The stewardess's hair did look good. It glistened and shone and the short, urchin cut offset the angular bone structure of the sun-burned face. Paula touched it self-consciously and said, 'I think it helps to keep it sort of short.'

'It's just beautiful. May I feel it?'

Paula felt helpless, disarmed, a bit out of her depth. Very slowly Susie reached out and ran her fingers through the stewardess's hair. It was unmistakably a caress. There was a slight pressure on the head and before she withdrew her hand the fingers had lingered suggestively on the lobe of Paula's ear. Paula felt the tingling burst of electricity pass through her, noted it almost as a dispassionate observer.

What was *happening* here? But nothing had happened. A young, affectionate, enthusiastic and probably lonely girl had paid her a couple of compliments. That was all. Yet the messages from Paula's body told a different story. She was intrigued and was adventurous enough to wait and see how this one would turn out. Susie watched it all in the stewardess's eyes. Not too fast.

'I guess it's really difficult to get a job as a stewardess.' That was pretty neutral.

Paula produced the stock answers. She was always being asked this sort of question. As she did so she became sure that she had got it wrong. The girl was quite straight. Then Paula noticed, with interest, that she felt a little disappointed, but by what? That a sixteen-year-old wasn't trying to pick her up after all? Dear God, this was a very curious situation indeed.

'There's something else I'd like to ask, but I'm rather shy,' said Susie, blushing deeply. Time to move things along again. She reckoned she could have got the Oscar for this one. Little-girl time. Eat your heart out, Brooke Shields.

Paula laughed. 'Go on,' she said. 'No secrets. Ask away.'

Susie leaned over and put her mouth on the older girl's ear. Her lips touched it and she made sure that lots of warm breath went right inside with the sound of her whispering voice. As she did so her hard, erect nipple pressed into Paula's shoulder and she squeezed her arm. 'Do you get to go with lots of gorgeous men?' she asked in a voice laden with scarcely camouflaged sensuality.

This time the wave of electric current flashed up and down the stewardess's body, setting off a cacophony of jingling alarm bells that could not be ignored. When it was gone it was replaced by something much more easily recognizable. Paula felt the warm glow of sexual arousal spread through her, in her nipples, between her legs, at the nape of her neck. This time there was no mistake. Miss Fox was trying to pull her. That was certainly a very extraordinary state of affairs, but there was an added component that was far more unusual, absolutely unique in fact. In a flash of blinding and totally unexpected intuition Paula realized to her horror and incredulity that she was not at all averse to being pulled. She seemed to have no control at all. Susie was in the driver's seat and she was merely a passenger with no vote as to the journey's destination. It was a very exciting feeling.

She heard her disembodied voice attempt an answer to

Susie's question as the delicious feelings continued to vibrate within her. It seemed totally appropriate that they should be discussing sex at last, the sun breaking through the clouds of meaningless small talk that constituted their conversation up to this point. She knew that she was blushing deeply, and that it was not going unnoticed, as she replied, 'I guess I do get lucky quite often.' She licked her lips. They were quite dry. Her voice was decidedly strange.

Susie pressed home her advantage. Paula was on the run. This time as she headed towards the stewardess's ear there was total contact, her body pressing urgently against Paula's side. The throaty whisper said, 'Have you ever done it in the john?'

She was no longer the little girl. She pushed her tongue into Paula's ear as far as it would go and rolled it around. The stewardess squirmed. Oh God. What next? She'd got to get herself together. She tried to get up, to protest – but she couldn't. She was held to her seat by a magnet of pleasure too powerful to resist. It was the point of no return. Until that tongue had gone into her ear she could just about pretend that she had no idea about what was going on. In a few more seconds she would be a willing accomplice. She opened her mouth to speak, wondering what would come out. Pleasure versus principle, sex versus safety, physical senses versus common sense. Susie knew that this was the vital moment. She pulled her tongue out of Paula's ear and whispered again, 'I'd really like to make you come.'

Game, set and match. The only sound that came from Paula was a very soft, very acquiescent moan.

Susie continued to nibble at the stewardess's ear and her right hand reached out for the elder girl's crotch. Beneath the flat of her hand she could feel the warm, throbbing mound. Slowly and deliberately she moved her hand from side to side. There was no turning back now. She would keep Paula wanting it, pile on the pressure, fine-tune her to a pitch of uncontrollable excitement that would leave her weak and trembling, desperate for more. Paula moaned again as Susie rubbed her.

'I want you in the john – I've got to see your body.' Susie's voice was husky.

Paula knew she would do it. She had gone too far. Never in her life before had she been so sexually excited. She just wanted it to go on and on, but it was really dangerous here in the cabin, behind the girl's father. Paula fought to get her thoughts straight as Susie continued to whisper obscenities in her ear. She was already soaked between the legs. Any minute now and it would be seeping through the tight skirt to Susie's probing hand.

'I'll go back to the one on the right. Give me two minutes and when you knock I'll unlock the door.' Paula's voice was hardly working at all, but she managed to get it out.

With an effort she stood up. She looked at Susie uncertainly and Susie smiled back, encouragement mixed with simmering sensuality. Susie watched her head towards the back of the aeroplane, admiring the tight ass and the long brown legs. 'Oh, Paula,' she said quietly to herself. 'You're sure going to remember this.'

Paula stood in the tiny lavatory like a condemned prisoner waiting for execution. She couldn't believe it. Some schoolgirl was going to make her in the john at twenty thousand feet. Had she gone mad? She should get out now while she could. But the spell was too strong and her hand was between her legs as she looked at her watch.

Susie was an expert in such things and it was exactly five minutes before she knocked on the door. Paula had all that time to wonder what was going to happen to her. Susie squeezed into the small space. As she went in she looked briefly over her shoulder. Nobody had noticed what was happening. Thank God for the empty compartment. It would really hit the fan if she was caught in the loo with a flight attendant!

The two girls stood facing each other, breasts touching. Paula was already breathing fast, the long wait having taken its toll as it was intended to do. Her hands were by her side, her mind in turmoil as she waited for Susie to call the tune. What was this girl going to *do* to her?

Without taking her eyes off the older girl's face Susie used both hands to slide Paula's tight skirt up to waist level. Only then did she look down, taking in the red briefs already soaked through with the stewardess's desire, the sheer nylon stockings, the red suspender belt.

'Oh, Paula,' she moaned in delicious anticipation, 'we're going to leave those beautiful stockings right where they are.' She spoke in the voice of an expert who had discovered a particularly rare fine painting in an old curiosity shop, and indeed to Susie suspender belts on stewardesses in airline lavatories were choice morsels.

With her right hand she eased the briefs away from Paula's crotch, exposing the glistening brown pubic hairs. The sensual, musky scent of her excitement filled the air of the enclosed space.

'Boy, are you hot for it,' Susie whispered. The sight of the older girl's passive abandonment, the smell of her desire, the fear and excitement in her eyes was turning her on, winding her up. Until now the chase had been a parade of her seductive skills, but now she wanted the pleasure, wanted it for Paula. It was a test of her ability to please, of her skill in bringing another human being to undreamed-of heights of sexual ecstasy. That was what Susie liked to do. She just loved to make people come. On the whole that was a pretty selfless ambition. The nice, easy-going, pretty American stewardess was going to have the time of her life. She guaranteed it.

Her fingers slipped deep into Paula's wetness, no strangers to the anatomy of the region. The older girl opened up to her gratefully, her bottom braced against the washstand, bearing down as hard as she could on the inquisitive fingers. A low-pitched moan announced that Susie had found the magic button, the pivotal centre of the erogenous zone. Susie bent down a little and suddenly her whole hand was inside Paula as her vaginal muscles relaxed under the expert touch. She looked up at the stewardess's face bathed in sweat, eyes half closed, tongue protruding slightly from

176

the half-opened mouth. With her free hand Susie reached inside the tight blouse in search of the small breast, taking the erect nipple between her thumb and forefinger, squeezing gently. Inexorably she led Paula towards the mammoth orgasm and she watched her whole body tense, poised for the ultimate experience. Steadily Susie brought her on and like a puppet on a string Paula danced to her tactile commands. Her right hand moved rhythmically now – long, slow, deliberate strokes – and Paula pushed against it, gripped it in the vice of her pelvic musculature, striving to increase the pressure and the friction. Her liquid poured down her legs, soaking the stocking tops. She had never been so wet – a slave to the teenage hand that had invaded her most private area and made itself master of her will.

'What does it feel like, Paula. Do you love it?' Susie liked to hear girls talk in this condition.

'Oh yes, I do. Don't stop. For God's sake, don't stop. I'm nearly coming.'

She had her now. Paula would do anything for the orgasm.

'You know I'm only thirteen,' said Susie cruelly. 'What's it like being fist-fucked by a thirteen-year-old girl?'

'Christ!' thought Paula, through the artillery barrage of pleasure that was saturating her brain from every area of her body. 'What sort of a crime am I committing here?' But it was far too late and both girls knew it. The threat of prison, degradation, dishonour were nothing compared to the over-riding concern of the here and now. Paula wanted to come with a desperation that involved every fibre of her being.

'Should I stop? Does it worry you?' said Susie as she increased the piston action of her right hand.

Panic.

'No, you mustn't stop. Please go on. Go on doing it to me. Please. Please.'

Coloured lights burst in front of Paula's eyes and the moan started from the pit of her stomach. She rode the orgasm like a surfer crouched on the crest of a breaking wave, crushing the sublime hand that was its cause with her powerful legs. It seemed as if a tap had been turned on deep within her vagina as the juices cascaded from her. Susie whispered encouragingly as the orgasm rolled on and on.

'That's it, honey. You're coming beautifully. Isn't it good? Isn't it great? That's right. That's right.'

Paula could hardly stand, her legs shaking with the effort of her orgasm. She sank back against the washbasin and surveyed the wreckage of her clothes. Her stockings looked as if she had taken a shower in them and great beads of wetness rolled down the inside of her thighs. Her make-up was a disaster area and her hair in total disarray.

'You're only thirteen?' she said in disbelief, looking guiltily at Susie. 'You know I've never done this before with a girl,' she added, looking away.

'Don't worry, I have and anyway I prefer virgins.' She smiled and, leaning forward, took Paula's face in her hands, kissing her softly on the lips, running her tongue suggestively against the older girl's teeth. Then, reaching up, she began to lick gently at the beads of perspiration that had formed above the upper lip, savouring the salty intimacy, stoking the glowing embers of Paula's desire. The stewardess returned the kiss, probing the inside of Susie's mouth, tasting her saliva. It was going to happen all over again.

Susie sank to her knees until her face was level with Paula's upper legs and, with infinite tenderness, as she knelt before the stewardess she began to lap at the moisture that continued to slip down the inside of the quivering thighs. Slowly she moved upwards and then, hooking her chin over the soaked red briefs, she buried her face in Paula's crotch, licking lasciviously at the abundant wetness, drinking in her desire.

Susie kissed the lips of Paula's vagina as before she had kissed her mouth, nuzzling, nibbling, tasting, coaxing them apart. Now with her tongue she explored the musky interior, revelling in its warm softness, its silky mystery. At first it was a gentle voyage of discovery and then, as the terrain became more familiar, it merged imperceptibly into an expedition of conquest. Susie's tongue seemed to Paula to grow in size as it began to impose its will on her vagina, licking now with long hard strokes that seemed to start and end on the most sensitive centimetre of her body. She put both hands behind the young girl's head and pulled it against her, rubbing Susie's nose and mouth against her crotch, forcing her to continue. Susie revelled in this attempt at coercion. She loved to be made to do things. That was how she saw herself. The ultimate pleasure machine. Dedicated to the sexual service of humanity. Old, young, rich, poor, male or female, Susie would do anything to satisfy their desires – anything at all. It was her job to spread happiness in the ultimate form, in the mystery of the orgasm. And so she continued to tongue Paula mercilessly, building her up, turning up the rheostat of the dimmer until once again the stewardess shone like a beacon with sexual intensity. Her right hand reached around and found the puckered opening to Paula's anus. Two of her fingers invaded the relaxed sphincter and were soon luxuriating in the slippery warmth of her bowels. Paula moaned as the knowing tongue played with her and Susie's fingers explored the inside of her bottom. She had never been had like this. Nothing had been asked of her except that she give herself up completely to the pleasure. That seemed to be the way the young girl liked it. OK, she could have it.

Paula took Susie roughly by the hair and crushed her face between her legs. 'That's right. Lick me. That's good. Put your tongue in deeper. Go on. Go on.'

But the moment of self-assertion put Paula right over the top.

Susie knew she was going to come. It was her business to know such things. She positioned her mouth so that it covered the entire opening of Paula's vagina. She wanted all of this.

Paula's knees shook and her mind stopped as she gave herself over to the orgasm. Once again she felt the waterfall deep inside her as she climaxed, exploding torrents of liquid desire into Susie's waiting mouth.

Slowly Susie brought her down, comforted Paula as she wept with the intensity of the experience, licking away the salty tears, helping her get her clothes back to some semblance of normality. Then on tiptoe she planted a light kiss on the corner of Paula's mouth and, one finger on her lips to signify the secrecy of the passionate encounter, she unlocked the door and slipped outside.

It was time for the second half of the game plan. She sat down next to Harry Fox who glowered angrily at her. 'Where have you been? What have you been doing?' he rasped.

'Oh, Harry, please promise you won't be cross,' pleaded Susie.

'What have you been doing?' Harry's voice was thick with menace.

'Well, I've just had that stewardess in the john.'

'You did what?' Harry spat out the last word. The game was unfolding.

'She was so pretty and she wanted it so much I really thought I should make her come. I thought as she was a girl you wouldn't mind.'

Harry went red. Susie watched the erection grow inside his trousers. He spoke through clenched teeth. 'Are you really trying to tell me you've just balled the stewardess? I don't believe you.'

He wanted more. Susie was ready for this one.

'Yes I did, really. You see I've sort of got all of her stuff over my face. You're not angry, are you? I kinda felt I was doing her a favour, relieving tension – you know.' That ought to do it.

'I'll deal with you just as soon as we get off this aeroplane,' he said ominously.

Susie sat little-girl style at Harry's feet on the floor of the black limo. 'Oh, Harry, please don't hurt me. I didn't mean any harm. That girl really needed what I gave her and I didn't let her touch me.'

'Susie, you're a wicked, promiscuous little girl and evil little girls like you need to be taught a lesson.'

Susie felt good inside. She really liked this. Harry fumbled in his briefcase. He lifted out a false bottom. Susie licked dry lips. What would it be? She gasped in shock at the size of the black rubber dildo. God, it would split her apart. The moisture gathered between her legs as she waited patiently, preparing her body for the intrusion, the trauma that she knew to expect.

'This will teach you not to go with girls. Now you can experience what real whores feel.' He signalled to Susie imperiously. Dutifully she lifted her skirt, and pushed herself forwards. In a vicious sudden movement he thrust the huge phallus deep into Susie's vagina. She let out a mock scream of surprise as the fearsome weapon penetrated her and concentrated on controlling the orgasm that threatened to engulf her despite the exquisite pain. With deft fingers Harry secured the base of the dildo to her skin with surgical tape. 'You'll have that inside you until tomorrow. You'll learn.' Then he began to masturbate and Susie watched him carefully as her insides began to acclimatize to the alien intruder. When he was ready he said one word. 'Now!'

Dutifully Susie lowered her mouth over the tip of his erect penis and as Harry emptied himself into her she pushed down hard, forcing the artificial cock deep inside her. Violated from both ends in the way that she loved, Susie achieved a racking, thunderous orgasm.

## III

The doorman at the '21' was expecting Harry Fox and he was escorted with considerable ceremony through the hallowed portals of the world's most exclusive restaurant and presented to the courteous commissars of the reception desk.

'Welcome to '21', Mr Fox. The Secretary of State is waiting for you inside. Please follow me.'

From a discreet distance the professional eyes of the two secret servicemen scanned Harry for concealed weapons as he passed through the lobby with its comfortable chesterfields and old wood.

'The Secretary prefers to eat in the bar rather than the restaurant,' said the dark-suited '21' employee over his shoulder by way of explanation to an 'out of towner'. Harry Fox might be a country cousin but he knew that the bar at the '21' was where the action was.

Harry had arrived in more senses of the word than one. This was the inner sanctum, Nirvana, Mecca, the right hand of God the Father Almighty as far as he was concerned, and as he glided across the thick carpet towards table fourteen where the Secretary of State of the United States of America was already on his feet preparing to greet him, Harry knew with absolute certainty that he had made it. He had got there. He would never leave. They would have to carry him out of the big time feet first. There would be no other way. And he would take any bastard who wanted to try along with him. As waiters bobbed and ducked, making little noises and gestures of welcome, Harry Fox vibrated with pleasure. He was surrounded by familiar faces although he knew no one in the room – Owen Atkins of Ashland Oil; Bill Levitt the builder; Nelson Doubleday the publisher. Soon he would be familiar to them. He was in the process of making his mark. Who was this man that Cabot Lodge was making such a fuss of? The sharper spectators made the connection to the *Fortune* cover. Wasn't this the up-and-coming banker who had just lent Eleanor Montgomery a billion dollars? What was he about to do for the State Department? Something African from the appearance of the third man at the table. Already there were people in that famous room who knew his name.

'How very kind of you to lunch with us, Mr Fox. I have heard so much about you from Eleanor Montgomery.'

The dividends from that billion-dollar loan were pouring

in, thought Harry. The telephone had not stopped ringing since the press conference when he had announced its details and now the financial community were bending over backwards to court him. They did not know, nor would they, the extent to which the loan had stretched the Union Bank, had left it vulnerable to short-term deposit withdrawals. Nobody had any idea that Harry had committed the cardinal sin of banking, that of borrowing short and lending long. For Harry had failed to match up his deposits and loans in terms of time and had tied up what were essentially short-term deposits in the mammoth five-year loan to Montgomery. Harry, however, did not care. He was riding the tiger, going for bust and his streak was a winning one. He would capitalize on the Union Bank's surge in reputation to pull in new deposits and rebuild the lending base. He would expand out of danger. What's more, he would enjoy the process, savour the success, drink the heavy wine to the full. He was not like other men. He was an original, a one-off, as hard as a harlot's golden heart. Compared to him the other bankers were as tough as noodles soaked overnight in condensed milk. Christ, that Susie had better watch out tonight. Sex and success were inextricably intertwined for Harry Fox.

Harry thought a lot about both. What was it Oscar Wilde had said? 'Nothing succeeds like excess.' Well, he was not averse to over-indulgence. Harry Fox, however, preferred to say that nothing succeeded like success. It fed on itself – one of the few examples in nature of positive feedback, perpetual motion, self-generating energy.

Harry sat down surrounded by the aura of his own self-importance. What on earth did this cunt Cabot Lodge want? Not that it mattered much. Being there was the thing. And who the hell was the expensive-looking spade?

'May I present His Excellency Sir Seretse Mwamba of the Republic of Umpala. Mr Harry Fox.'

The tall black was on his feet, his long, thin fingers extended towards Harry.

'Now, Eleanor says that you are a great connoisseur of

fine wine,' said Charles, 'so I have persuaded Mr Kriendler to look out a bottle of his Pétrus 1961.'

'Sounds expensive,' thought Harry. He smirked at the thought of that haughty bitch Eleanor Montgomery discussing him with Cabot Lodge. He imagined them in bed together, the Secretary of State making love like a bird, all darts and swoops, a wise old owl perhaps. Then he remembered Eleanor's gravity-defying tits and how he had mentally stripped her to counteract her attempted patronization, speculated how she would perform *in flagrante delicto* on the floor of the Plaza suite. In his mind he could hear her saying to Cabot Lodge, 'I seem to remember he's rather fond of expensive wine – but you'd better tell him it's good. He won't know otherwise.' Something like that. Harry didn't care a twopenny fuck. She'd borrowed his billion and put him on the map. People knew where he was now.

'How is Eleanor?' asked Harry. A solicitous inquiry from an old friend. What he wanted to ask was 'Does she scream when she comes?' or 'Do you go down on her, you pompous old ass? What does she have to do to get you straight?' Such thoughts were never far from Harry's mind and he used them to even up the score in situations where the cards were stacked against him.

Cabot Lodge thought that he picked up on the supercilious curl of the lip as Fox made his ostensibly polite inquiry, but he must ignore it if he was to get what he wanted. Nevertheless he made an entry in the vast notebook that was his mind. No favours for this man. Careers had been destroyed for less.

'Wonderful.' He gave his politician's smile. The hand snaked out and caught Harry's elbow. Sincerity time. 'I just want you to know that she is extremely pleased, as I am, that your bank was able to get together with Montgomery on that loan.'

When would he get to the point? But Harry could wait. He was scoring points just sitting there, being handled by the Secretary of State. The meter was already running.

Cabot Lodge was a man who believed in observing

certain conventions where business was concerned, and the conversation remained general over the pea soup. With the New York prime cut he got down to the principles of the deal. Harry had to admire the man's skill – the suave, sophisticated delivery, the well-turned politician's phrases, the constant references to the wider picture, the world view. Then there were the accomplished psychological components – the subtle flattery, the hints, implications, innuendoes, that substantial but non-specific rewards and favours would be made available to Harry if he fell in with Cabot Lodge's plans. The droning Boston accent also managed to convey in the most oblique way possible that it was not the wisest thing for a man who wanted to get ahead to refuse a Cabot Lodge request. With the pudding came the hard-nosed business man, the bottom-liner, the honest Christian with the Puritan ethic who was not averse to turning a buck or two if it was to the greater glory of God and America. He spoke 'man to man' now, rather than Secretary of State to parvenu banker, American aristocrat to ghetto rubbish, patrician statesman to brash guttersnipe. Harry liked his style but all the way through he had felt like doing him an injury.

Bit by bit the diamond deal had emerged until, with the coffee and liqueurs, it was all there, on the table, cards face up. Seretse Mwamba had said little. From time to time Harry had interrupted with pertinent questions. Now at last he was in a position to consider it in its entirety. In essence it was quite simple. That was the way Harry liked it. He was being asked to lend Umpala $300 million that would be returned to him after a five-year period. In exchange for this they would give him $90 million worth of diamonds every year for five years. If for any reason they did not do this then he would own twenty-five per cent of their diamond mine. The Union Bank would make a profit of $450 million on the deal. More if they held onto the diamonds and the price went up as it always had in the past. Harry knew all about the De Beers company and its price-fixing methods that so far had guaranteed a rising diamond price. The transaction looked to be a good one.

But there were other considerations that appealed to Harry. There would be considerable scope for fiddling the taxes. The deal could perhaps be a secret one and the IRS would not know the exact value of the stones that the Union would be receiving as interest. A much lower figure than $90 million could be declared, and the tax bill significantly reduced. And then there would be the kick-backs, commissions, consultancy and 'introduction' fees. Some of those stones would find their way into the Zurich strong box whose purpose it was to receive such offerings. Fox was a big shareholder in the Union Bank, but the bulk of the stock was publicly owned. Harry was not averse to shaking down the other shareholders to the advantage of his personal account. After all, without his entrepreneurial skills the share price would be languishing at a much lower level and big block holders like Castelli would not be sitting on such sizeable capital gains. Still, it would not do to let such people discover that he was indulging in a little personal private enterprise. Such things were advised against for those interested in their continued good health. He looked hard at Mwamba, noting the knowing smile that played on his lips. His instant impression was that the black would not throw up his hands in horror at the suggestion of the 'sweeteners'. It would be as well to have something on him to make sure his mouth remained buttoned. A videotape of his doing unmentionable things to the thirteen-year-old Susie perhaps. That was an old KGB trick, but maybe worth a try. Cabot Lodge of course would have to be kept well out of any such transactions.

Harry threw back his head and took the thirty-year-old brandy at a single gulp. He produced a theatrical burp, noting that his two table companions winced as he did so. This was a very good moment. Now they could wait for him.

'I think I could handle another glass of that rather good brandy,' he said in a scarcely veiled imitation of Cabot Lodge's Boston accent and patrician style. Fox's fan club had gained no additional members during this luncheon.

The speed with which the waiter arrived would have

shamed the genie of Aladdin's lamp. Inside Harry the excitement grew. There were of course two problems. What if Umpala reneged on its foreign debts? Bigger and better countries than Umpala had done so. Then there was always the possibility of a coup. Not unheard of in Africa. After all, Seretse Mwamba might well be dish of honour at some future state banquet for a jumped-up sergeant-major if Harry knew anything about the uncertainties of Third World politics.

The collateral of twenty-five per cent of a diamond mine was pretty meaningless when that mine was situated in the middle of somebody else's country far from the jurisdiction of American courts. But Harry had already thought of a way round these obstacles.

'So I'm right in thinking that you have about $300 million worth of diamonds right now, from mining operations to date?'

Seretse nodded his assent.

'And that you can't or won't sell them because firstly it would depress the price and secondly it would prejudice your chance of cornering De Beers later on.'

'That is correct. So there would be no problem about paying the interest on the loan as the first three years' payments are already in our vaults.'

'You would presumably have no objection to those stones being placed in a mutually agreeable escrow vault in a neutral country, say Switzerland, to be held for your account but to be released to me if there was any default for any reason on the interest payments.'

'That was brilliant,' thought Harry. If there was close to $300 million in diamonds backing up the value of the loan outside the control of the Umpalans, he would be on a winner to nothing. He would be making a totally secured loan at an interest rate of thirty per cent. It would be a considerable coup.

What about the downside? For a second Harry allowed himself to contemplate the awful effect of an actual fall in the price of diamonds. It would be nothing less than a disaster. The interest payments could not be kept up and the value of the collateral would sink as well. A small drop in the price might be supportable, a significant one would be a tragedy. Immediately Harry dismissed the thought. Everybody knew that the diamond price went in one direction only. Upwards. De Beers saw to that.

For long seconds Cabot Lodge and Mwamba looked at each other. This man Fox was obviously a sharp cookie. However they were both acting in good faith. It was a shrewd insurance policy that Fox had suggested. Only the politically naïve or the congenitally stupid would overlook the realities of political life in Africa. Seretse Mwamba broke the silence.

'That should be no problem. I'm sure we could find an acceptable institution to hold the kitty, as it were.'

Harry Fox was no waster of time. He liked the deal. Liked it very much. Things that he liked he wanted and things that he wanted he got. He was about to say 'yes' when the awful thought struck him. His mouth was open to reply, and it stayed open as the wheels turned inside his brain. He hadn't got the money. The Union Bank had no way of getting hold of $30 million, let alone $300 million. The loan to Montgomery had cleaned him out. He was the poorest banker in the big time, a minnow in a pool of giant fish. Damn. Damn. Damn. He'd have to stall for time. There was always a way. Certainly he could not let on to Cabot Lodge and the black man that he had already shot his bolt in terms of lending. That could only be counter-productive.

'Well,' he said at last. 'I'm very interested in principle. Of course I'd like time to discuss it with my advisers and with the board. Perhaps we could be in touch again in the next few days.'

That was the prudent approach. The two men would not have expected an immediate decision although Harry would have liked to have been able to give them one.

'I'm at the Pierre for two weeks and of course I'd be more than happy to discuss this further with your advisers. I'm very encouraged that your attitude is positive and feel certain that we can all do well from this deal,' said Seretse.

'Was there a hint there? Probably,' thought Harry.

Charles Cabot Lodge, uneasy in his role of honest broker, was relieved that the lunch was over and that some sort of successful conclusion had been reached. He wanted no further part in the deal and would have none. Already weightier considerations were on his mind. Tomorrow he would address the UN before returning to Washington in the afternoon. He signalled the waiter. Lunch would be on the State Department.

Harry walked back to the Plaza despite the sickening heat and the drinkable air. His mind was in overdrive; he felt that he might well be emitting a high-pitched whine audible perhaps to passers-by as his mind processed the information. He started from the basic premise that the deal was too good to be refused. Harry was not about to let a measly $300 million stand in the way of his single-minded pursuit of profit. If he hadn't got it he would borrow it. It was the American way. The alternative was to steal it but that, Harry had come to realize, was as inefficient as it was unnecessary. Especially when you could borrow it from people who had already stolen it.

By the time he had walked into the lobby of the Plaza he knew what he would do. As he crossed his suite to the telephone his thinking was purely positive. Perhaps this was the best way for everybody. Pass round the honey pot. Make some friends. Influence some people. He dialled the number. As he did so his eyes fell on Susie as she catnapped on the sofa. The dildo had not encouraged sleep the night before. After this call he would wake her up. Who knew? She just might have something to confess. After all, the place was rotten with waiters and chambermaids, bell boys and desk clerks. He felt the stirrings of desire.

The number was ringing now. The harsh voice answered.

'Castelli? Harry Fox. Listen, Nero old friend, I think I may be in a position to do us all a bit of good.'

Harry Fox would return to the hand from which he had originally fed, for which recently he had had no need. He would once again take from the hand that, if bitten, exacted a terrible retribution. He would borrow the $300 million from the Mob.

## IV

Miles sat on the lawn of the Ocean Reef house watching the spectacular sunset over Florida Bay. He sipped appreciatively at the planter's punch. A light breeze had freshened up the air and driven away the mosquitoes that all too often kept him inside the screened pool area in the early evening. The cold rum punch was making him feel good. Really the only drink in this part of the world. He eyed the cordless telephone that sat accusingly by the side of his chair. For two days now he had put off making the call. What if she said no? And then he found himself reaching for it. Decisions were often like that, he reflected, not necessarily preceded by ghostly dialogues. Suddenly you just found yourself doing it.

'Montgomery residence.' The English accent indicated 'butler'.

'This is Lord Parmere calling for Caroline Montgomery.'

'I'll see if she's in, m'lord.'

The two fellow-countrymen knew each other intimately, although they had only talked together once before. There are few more clearly defined relationships in the world than that between English butler and peer of the realm.

There was a delay and Miles pictured the pin-striped trousers and immaculately polished, black lace-up walking shoes padding deliberately across the priceless Persian rugs that he imagined would adorn the natural wood floors of the Aspen house.

'Miles Parmere. How great to hear from you again. How's Florida?' Caroline's voice sounded genuinely excited. It was a promising start.

'Hot and sticky, but the fishing's good.'

'And the banking, too, by the sound of it. Listen, Lord Parmere, the next time you have a billion to lend think of me, will ya? My bankers are always complaining about how much I spend.'

Miles realized that by referring to his role in the billion-dollar loan she was paying him a compliment.

'Well, we aim to please,' said Miles. That was what it said on the Union Bank's TV ads. 'Always happy to attempt to smooth the financial path of our impoverished transatlantic cousins.'

Caroline laughed.

'I've missed you,' said Miles simply. That said a lot.

There was a pause. 'England was fun, wasn't it? Annabel's, Odette's. I really enjoyed those places.'

The response was neutral. Neither one thing nor the other.

'Listen,' Caroline continued. 'It would be really great if you could come up to Aspen for a few days. I've got some holiday coming up and I could show you the Rocky Mountains.'

'That's really why I'm ringing,' said Miles. It was time to take the plunge. He couldn't have asked for a better opening.

'I have to go to Spain for the first two weeks of July. I don't remember if I told you but I have a small *finca* there near Seville, and I was very much hoping that you would come with me. It would be very quiet, just lots of riding, swimming, bullfights and things – sort of traditional Andalucian living. Would you be able to take the time off from training?'

Caroline did not hesitate. 'God, Miles. That sounds like absolute paradise. I'd love to come. It would be really good. It just happens that I've got the time free and I've vowed to get as far away from skiing as possible. I can't think of anything I'd like to do more.'

'That's wonderful, wonderful.' That was it, thought Miles. Caroline Montgomery. Lady Parmere. Unto them that hath.

# Chapter 7

## I

*Aunque pongan en tu puerta*
*Canones de artilleria*
*Tengo que pasar por ella*
*Aunque me cueste la via.*

With severe and serpentine elegance and a monumental dignity, the dark-haired gypsy singer communed with Caroline's very soul as the rythmical stanzas of the *allegrias* curled through the air. Soft and delicate, like the long fair plumes of sugar cane tossing in the wind by the banks of a river, the strains of the flamenco song filled the air of the small cellar. Hundreds of years of history were etched into the man's face and all the joy and sorrow in the world seemed to Caroline to be contained in his harrowing song. The old, black corduroy jacket worn smooth by the passage of time, the soft Cordoban grey hat and the brown and battered boots spoke at once of his poverty and his style. He leaned forward, his body flowing out towards the object of his song, as broken tobacco-stained teeth, framed by swarthy, stubbled lip and cheek, twisted and turned the subtle syllables of the chant. Both hands were clasped at his chest as if in prayer, and indeed the intensity of his song was such that he seemed frozen in an attitude of eternal supplication, begging Caroline to grant him some fundamental favour, some forlornly unexpected dispensation. By his side the nimble fingers of the guitarist picked out a dashing accompaniment, while behind the third member of the trio, tall and saturnine, contributed a restrained and intricate *zapateado*. Caroline sat enthralled by the spectacle while around her old men sipped petulantly at their manzanillas, muttering occasional criticism of the gypsy's delivery, smoking studiously at small caramel-coloured cigars.

> *Mas desgracio que yo*
> *Creo que no nacio de madre.*

Infinite sadness poured from the singer's very essence, saturating the room with melancholy. Miles' eyes were far away but his hand was in Caroline's, fingers intertwined. A man and a woman pushed forwards from the back of the smoky café and, addressing each other solemnly, they began to dance. No smiles softened their coarse features, but there was a delicacy, a piquant grace and lightness, about their movements. If the content of the song was serious the form of their dance belied it.

Caroline turned to Miles. 'What is he singing?' she asked as she squeezed his hand.

Miles smiled at her. 'He says that even if they put cannons by your door to guard it he will pass through even though it may cost him his life.'

Tears appeared in Caroline's eyes as she said, 'God, that's a beautiful song.'

'He also says that no mother ever gave birth to a man as miserable as he since he has been separated from you.'

They were silent for a time, lost in the haunting melody of the *allegrias*, keenly aware of the bond that hour by hour, minute by minute, strengthened between them. They had been in Spain for two days only, but already the spirit of Andalucia was working its magic.

In a final flourish the song was at an end, the dancers still, and the guttural, growling chorus of *olés* rose like the crackling of burning grass from the weatherbeaten crowd.

Caroline and Miles were the only people in the room who had not been born in southern Spain and Caroline alone looked a foreigner. Miles wore a dark, lightweight suit, white shirt open at the neck, and soft black leather ankle-length boots. His dark colouring offered no contrast with the sons of Africa, offspring of the Moor, who formed the main contingent in the Sevillan flamenco bar. Miles was no stranger to this and similar cafés, and many of the locals remembered him from the days when, as a rumbustious teenager, he would frequent the bars with his aristocratic Spanish friends, a couple of bored ranch foremen as escorts to ensure that they did not get into too much trouble. This was feudal Spain where rank was recognized and respected for the continuity and security that it guaranteed. No bitter class envy polluted this agrarian community – that was for the souless businessmen of Catalonia, the middle-class 'rubbish' from the northern industrial towns. So Miles was honoured and esteemed as an *hombré*, a predictable man on whose behaviour one could rely. He was moreover *un hombré simpático*, a man who understood the important things in life – honour, courage and plain dealing, the love of beautiful women and of the *canté jondo;* an *aficionado* who appreciated the importance of a full belly, a tight wineskin and a clean kill; an aristocrat who was so at home in his position that he was at ease with any man, who was not afraid to call a man a fool because he came from a lower rank or an imbecile because he came from a higher one.

Caroline's blonde hair and blue eyes proclaimed a totally different racial mix, but she was nonetheless welcome for that. Her transcendent beauty spoke an international language that the dark Spaniards understood and appreciated. She was the *senorita linda* who came to visit them with the English *condé* Miles, friend of the Domecq. She was thus a welcome and an honoured guest who would know how to behave, who would appreciate that they were proud, simple men who believed in a code of conduct and a social system long since abandoned by the 'sophisticates' of Europe and the Americas. Caroline had not disappointed them. She had not got drunk or tried to take their photograph. She had dressed with quiet decorum in a white ruffled cotton shirt, bolero jacket and black calf-length skirt and their hearts had gone out to the earnest beauty who vibrated with an inquisitive eagerness to experience their lives and their relaxation. Miles could have no clearer corroboration of the wisdom of his heart than to see the respect for his choice in the knowing eyes of these cunning gypsies.

Miles' good wine had lubricated the tongues, hands and feet of singers and dancers, and they enjoyed themselves as the best way of giving enjoyment, some of them already a little in love with the tall, fair beauty from just north of Mexico.

Miles had been right, thought Caroline. The nearest thing to this was southern Texas. The language and the smells were different and the people could hardly be compared, but the all-important attitude towards life was the same. Country music and flamenco and those who played and listened to it were more or less indistinguishable.

'What kind of song was that?' asked Caroline. She wanted to remember everything.

'It's called an *allegrias*, a nineteenth-century song from Cadiz. Now they're going to do a *Sevillana*. There's no better place to hear it.'

> *A dibujar tu cara*
> *me puse un dia*
> *cuando llegue a tus labios*
> *ya no podia.*
> *Porque tus labios*
> *necesitan pinceles*
> *pa dibujarlos.*

'I think this man has fallen under the Montgomery spell,' said Miles. 'He says that he wanted to draw your face and was doing fine until he came to your lips at which point he realized that a real artist would be required to do them justice.'

The dancers came to life again. Liquid fingers threshed the guitar strings and the sublime melody filled the soul with the frivolous gaiety of the time-honoured dance.

'Oh, I want to stay here all night,' said Caroline.

'I think we just have,' said Miles. He looked at his watch: four o'clock.

On the pavement outside they said goodbye to the gypsies, with many promises of future encounters. One friend of the evening, a fiend for the brandy, addressed an incompetent *saeta* at a wall of old bullfight posters. Another coughed the contents of tuberculous lungs into a large red handkerchief. A third held onto his friend as he tried first to remember, and then to explain, where he lived. The quick-eyed gypsies alone seemed still on maximum alert. Creatures of the night, they appeared uneasy before the approaching dawn, anxious to scurry away, vampire-like, to dark, overheated rooms where they would hide from the sun's tyranny until once again nightfall released them, unleashed again their torrents of song.

Miles and Caroline made their way to the dark blue Land Rover, its unlocked doors proclaiming the nature of the society in which they found themselves. It was half an hour's drive to the *finca* through the orange groves beside the meandering mystery of the Guadalquivir river. Caroline breathed in the scent of the orange blossom, the *azahar*, which, mixed with the fragrance of rosemary, impregnated the heavy night air. Later, as the dawn stole away the night, she could make out the clumps of carnations growing wild by the side of the dusty, red road, nestling beneath hedges of aloe and prickly pear. And in her ears rang the wild rhythms of the *Sevillanas*, the virile anguish of the *fandangos*, the trembling peaks and abysses of the *tientos* in which the singer had confessed that life itself had no meaning in the absence of his love.

> *Ay que to quiero*
> *lo que yo te quiero*
> *Sin ti mi vida*
> *pa que lo quiero?*

Miles turned to look at her and she looked steadily back at him. There was no need for words.

Caroline lay still in the big four-poster bed, fighting off

sleep, thinking of the myriad of experiences and emotions that had flooded her consciousness since her arrival in southern Spain. The angry, unforgiving heat of the day had relented now, but the night air was solid, unmoved by breezes, a warm dry blanket that clung to her naked body. The tireless *cicadas* provided a soothing background to her thoughts. The sweet scent of jasmine filled the old room and through the semi-darkness Caroline watched the moon, nearly complete, through the open windows that led to the small balcony. She left the bed, the cold, stone floor comforting beneath her feet, and soon she was standing, naked, among the overflowing flower pots, her hands on the ancient wrought-iron balustrade as she looked out over the *finca*. The outline of the dark river bordered and imprisoned the olive groves where serried ranks of sturdy trees stretched in straight unyielding lines to the outskirts of the small village. Caroline breathed in deeply, taking inside her the spirit of Spain, and she thought of Miles, asleep now in the room across the wide-beamed corridor.

It was all so confusing. She had always been attracted to him, right from the start, but she had been in control of it, had had other things on her mind. It was incredible to her that this was the same Miles Parmere – the toast of the smart nocturnal watering holes of London and Paris, the callous womanizer, the heartless dilettante, the roistering *roué*. In the evenings they would dine quietly together at the long refectory table with Arturo, the butler, pouring the thick red rioja wine, eating gazpacho and suckling pig while Miles explained to her the intricacies of running the small farm, talked of the Spanish character, of the civil war and the region's Moorish history.

After the meal they would sit together and read in the dark library, or talk until the early hours, close, the atmosphere charged with subterranean electric currents, their gestures pregnant with the unspoken language of desire. Miles had been the perfect English gentleman.

Now, naked in the moonlight, she wondered if she really welcomed such restraint. She was a superbly confident young woman, a believer in herself and her abilities, but in this situation she was no expert. Could it be that Miles Parmere had already tired of her attractions? After all, he had a fearsome reputation in that respect. Perhaps he found an eighteen-year-old American girl rather lame after the exotic delights of the worldly-wise women of Europe, a group who knew a thing or two when it came to stimulating a jaded palate. Certainly he was unfailingly courteous and he seemed to be enjoying himself, but there were times when she caught a distant, sombre expression in his eyes, as if he were contemplating some onerous burden that weighed him down and crushed the gaiety in his soul. At times she had sensed his physical longing for her, in the flamenco bar and on the night of their arrival. Then, in the early hours, he had put on the swimming pool lights and they had bathed together, casting off the dust of the long journey. She had felt his eyes on her firm yet voluptuous body and had seen the hard evidence of his desire. She had wanted him, too, and there had been every opportunity for him to cross the gulf into intimacy. He had held back then and at every minute since.

Caroline was not sure why, and now, separated from him by the thick walls of the *finca*, the insecurities of the night played tricks with her natural self-confidence. There was no escaping the fact that she wanted the door to open and Miles' voice to whisper her name. She wanted to walk with him to the big bed and to lay down beside him as he told her that he loved her.

There was another feeling – one that could not be denied. For Caroline lovemaking was indeed virgin territory – for him, presumably, it was well-trodden ground. Would she be able to please him in the way that he was undoubtedly used to being pleased? Would he have desires that she could not satisfy? Would it destroy rather than cement the relationship that they now enjoyed? One thing was certain. Things would not be the same afterwards. They might be better, but they would be different.

Caroline felt the desire rise within her and she pushed against the cool, iron grille as an artificial substitute for Miles' warm, hard body. For a second she allowed herself to wonder how Miles would react if she went to him now in the middle of the night. The short answer was that she could not be sure.

And what if he did want her, loved her even? She was not entirely sure how to handle it, having no experience of such things.

Back in bed the thoughts crowded in on her until, finally, a deep sleep released her.

Caroline had already worked out a routine for her days. Although even the thought of skiing was taboo she had to keep fit or she would undo the hard work of the previous months. The fifty-foot pool was perfect for that and she would swim for an hour in the early morning and again in the evening just before sunset. Miles and Caroline rose with the dawn and would go riding in the hills to get up an appetite for breakfast. She marvelled at Miles' ability on horseback and, as a native Texan, born on a cattle ranch, she did not give her admiration lightly, nor was it ill informed. It was just another side of the remarkable Miles Parmere whose multi-faceted personality and latent talents revealed themselves in surprising stages at unexpected moments in the most unlikely situations. They would return to the *finca* for breakfast together on the verandah – eggs, grapefruit, toast and the delicious powder-covered pastries so dear to the Spanish heart.

Miles would sometimes sit and watch as Caroline powered up and down the pool after breakfast, lost in concentration. It was, he thought, an extraordinary aesthetically pleasing spectacle. On every level Caroline Montgomery had fulfilled and exceeded his most exotic dreams and fantasies. In vain he tried to list her faults and, finding none, began to wonder about his objectivity. He was in love with her. There was no doubt about that. But now he was in love with flesh and blood, with reality rather than with a memory. At the time when Roy Felty first diagnosed his condition he could have been accused of projecting his inexperienced emotions of affection onto an idealized, conceptualized person who only existed in his imagination.

Now there was evidence to back up his heart's case and no honest jury could have failed to find in its favour. All the facts pointed to Caroline's superiority as a human being, were unaminous in supporting her claim to a truly remarkable beauty. The evidence was not circumstantial, hearsay, incomplete. It was hard and fast, watertight, corroborated at every second by the fact of her presence.

Miles had decided to play the waiting game and it was taking its toll. He was nervous, jumpy and, occasionally, lost in reverie as he ruminated on what might be. He longed to hold her in his arms, to cover her with his kisses, tell her how he felt. But he wanted it to be her decision. Sometimes he felt she was on the verge of making it. At others he could not be sure.

And so the fire of thwarted desire was steadily built, the kindling stacked higher and higher, the breeze already up that would fan the potential flames, the wood soaked through with gasoline waiting only for the spark that would ignite the conflagration and consume them both in the burning fiery furnace of their passion.

Caroline emerged, dripping, from the pool. Miles walked towards her with the big, rough towel. As he did so she came at him, both hands at the side of her head, forefingers and thumbs extended to portray a bull's horns. Miles sidestepped gracefully and the white towel billowed like a cloud in the classic veronica pass, his legs stiff and still, back straight as Caroline followed the 'cape' past him.

'*Olé*,' she laughed, 'Toreador.'

'Only in the opera,' Miles corrected. 'It's matadors we'll be seeing this afternoon.'

'*A las cinquo en el tarde*,' said Caroline, who, typically, was learning Spanish fast.

They had decided to go into Seville so that Caroline could see her first bullfight. It promised to be a good one. Jaime d'Aragon, the star of the decade, was top of the bill and the bulls to be fought were from the ranch of Don Eduardo Muira. A Muira bull had killed the legendary

Manolete and they had an awesome reputation for their courage and strength.

No bullfight could be properly appreciated if not preceded by an excellent lunch and Miles had decided to take Caroline to a restaurant in the narrow Calle de las Sierpes which boasted the finest *paella* outside Valencia, and whose pavement tables were a mere twenty feet from the beautiful baroque façade of the Capilla de San José. This church was the most richly ornamented sanctuary in Seville. They would spend some time there before eating.

Caroline sank down on one of the sun beds. 'Miles, you know this is one of the most beautiful places on earth. How do you ever tear yourself away?'

Miles gazed out over the productive fields to the distant hills where they had ridden that morning. He turned back to look at her. The early morning sun, gathering its strength for the tasks of the day, was already decimating the beads of moisture on Caroline's skin. 'If you were here with me all the time I never would,' he said.

He did not smile. Caroline turned her head to one side, a quizzical look on her face. Was this the moment? Electricity crackled between them, the chemical cauldron bubbled, but neither of them moved. And then, suddenly, Caroline was on her feet. One moment she was lying, apparently relaxed, on the sun bed – the next she was bending down close to Miles. He did nothing. His whole being was suspended in time, his muscles frozen, not daring to breathe. This was it. The super-charged reality of the jungle. Caroline's face came towards him and he breathed in deeply as it did so, capturing the natural scents of her body in a forlorn attempt to imprison a portion of her essence within him. Then, at last, her mouth was on his. Slowly, calmly and with agonizing tenderness she kissed him – warm, dry lips of infinite sensitivity nuzzling, teasing, reassuring, loving his own. For the first time in his life Miles experienced intellectual ecstacy. His body had not yet had time to acclimatize to the state of unbridled physical desire that would surely follow, but with Caroline's chaste kiss he had known the sublimity of paradise.

Whatever happened they both knew now that they would be lovers. The uncertainties were banished for ever by that simple kiss.

Miles took Caroline's head between both his hands and stared deep into her eyes. 'I love you,' he said.

'Oh Miles.'

They stood together before the high altar of the Chapel of San José, holding hands in the cool gloom of the church. In front of them the cherubs and the seraphims danced attendance on the central figure of Christ their Maker. Saints and angels looked on with quiet, reverential dignity – ever faithful, ever sure, like the mercy of God Himself. Among this pious contingent hundreds of candle flames shed their light, testifying to the loyalty of the true believers. The skill of the carpenters who had worked these figures was without equal in the Western world. They had achieved astonishing splendour in their decorative art, the richness of their material and their inventive genius giving an escape into the world of dreams for the humble who sought to distance themselves from the misery of their earthly predicament. Miles and Caroline needed no such transport to delight. For them it seemed that paradise existed here, there, everywhere, whenever they were together. But in their own private state of grace the altar could not help but have inescapable connotations and, as each increased the pressure on the other's hand, their thoughts were in unison.

They walked out across the sunbathed street, saying little but thinking much, to the corner restaurant with its round tables, chequered table-cloths and bent-wood chairs. Miles ordered chilled *fino* and some black olives, shrimp and vinegar-soaked mussels. They smiled at each other as the taciturn waiter brought the *tapas*. Caroline sipped at the cold, dry wine. Already she had taken on the mantle of Spain. Apart from the high-necked, long-collared canary yellow shirt, she was dressed from head to foot in black. The tight-waisted jacket hugged her figure while the trousers traced the line of her thighs before flaring at the knee to end in broad bottoms just above the level of the ankle. Long black leather boots complemented the shiny black wide-brimmed Cordoban hat that she had borrowed from Miles. It was the riding outfit of the Sevillan aristocracy. God she would look good on the back of a stallion at the *feria*, showing off her beauty and her horsemanship, curling the lips of his Spanish friends with envy and jealousy.

'It's a beautiful chapel,' he said at last.

'Everything's beautiful,' said Caroline.

They ate *calamares* before the *paella* with which they drank a dry Monopole. Caroline gasped as the huge *paella* appeared in its traditional flat, black dish. The large-grained saffron rice stained rusty red with paprika glistened with moisture. Nestling among the rice like rubies and emeralds were chunks of red and green peppers. There were big pink shrimps, mussels, succulent pieces of chicken, small cubes of pork. Thick, coarse, crusty bread and a bottle of Marqués de Riscal completed the gastronomic assault course. Later there would be tiny wild strawberries eaten with lemon juice, black coffee and *fundador*.

Miles and Caroline talked little as they ate, but no one could have mistaken their quietness for the silence of the long-married couple. It was plain for all to see that theirs was the silence of lovers. They sat close to each other, and their hands were not long apart. When they spoke they leaned towards each other, voices lowered to protect their intimacy. Their laughter was soft, controlled, measured, hinting that humour was not all that was between them. All their gestures hinted at the smouldering sensuality that encompassed them while the incomparable food and the good wine fanned the sparks of the underlying passion. Across the restaurant an old and distinguished looking man sipped pensively at his sherry as he watched them. Wistfully he remembered when he had felt such things, the days of the spring of his life now replaced irrevocably by the bittersweet twilight.

Miles and Caroline walked through the narrow, irregularly

cobbled streets towards the Plaza de Toros. On either side the blinding white façades of the houses rose to meet the powder blue of the sky, revealing occasional tantalizing glimpses of their mysterious interiors as elaborate wrought-iron gates displayed vistas of flower-encrusted patios, rich with fresh-water pools and fountains panelled with intricate tiled mosaics. This was the Seville of the Arabian Nights and it provided a fitting background to Miles' and Caroline's happiness as they approached the bullring. Immediately they sensed the mounting excitement as the crowd thickened, as they became part of the *ambientado*, the self-forgetful collective joy of the *corrida*, that intersection where art, courage, life and death meet in the awful finality of the bull's majestic sacrifice.

Ticket hawkers, street vendors and all the other human effluent spawned by the fight clustered around them, importuning, soliciting, posturing, pleading. Miles hired two small green cushions and bought one of the tight wineskin gourds known as *botas*. Bullfights were thirsty work. Disdainfully he scorned the proferred posters while both their stomachs rebelled at the otherwise delicious sugared nuts and sweets that surrounded them in colourful profusion. As intended, they were early, for Miles knew that in Spain only mass and the bullfight would start on time, and he wanted to show Caroline the bull corrals and the *patio de caballos* where the horses were kept.

Three picadors stood in the gateway, smoking nervously. They were plump old men, members perhaps of the matador's family or the fathers of people to whom he owed favours, dressed traditionally in heavily brocaded jackets, bowl-topped hats and cream-coloured buckskin-buttoned trousers opened at the ankle to reveal the steel-leaf armour that covered their right legs.

'Those boys ride the horses,' said Miles. 'It's their job to spear the bull's neck muscles with a modified lance known as a pic. That way the bull has difficulty in keeping his head held high and the matador can get in over the horns to kill cleanly when the time comes.'

Miles called out to them, knowing that it would be the

size of the bulls and nothing else that was on their minds.
'*Que tal los toros?*'

   '*Son grandes.*'

   '*Grandes?*'

   '*Muy grandes. Muy malo.*'

The fat old picador who had answered Miles smiled wanly at his predicament and drew deeply on his cigarette. If he was to be unhorsed, his own weight, lack of agility and the burden of his armour would immobilize him like an upturned tortoise until others distracted the bull's attention away from him. It would be a discouraging moment.

They found their seats on the *barrera* in the shade. These *sombra* seats were the most expensive in the Plaza – cool, yet right on top of the action. The brass band played exuberant *pasodobles*. It was nearly time for the opening parade.

'Party trick time,' said Miles. 'Watch this.' The leather wine skin was held at arm's length above his head, stopper removed. With a flourish Miles squeezed with his right hand, injecting a pencil-thin stream of ruby wine with uncanny accuracy into his open mouth. 'This stuff is bad enough in your stomach. In your eye it's a tragedy,' he laughed. Once again the tense wineskin ejaculated its sticky contents at his epiglottis.

   '*Hombré,*' said Caroline, fighting back a desire to tickle his ribs.

   'Your turn.'

   'Listen,' said Caroline. 'I don't practise with a loaded gun. I'll get this one right poolside in an old bikini.' She took the *bota* and, wrapping her lips around the nozzle, filled her mouth with the warm sweet wine.

The president of the *corrida* had taken up his position in his flag-bedecked box and the white handkerchief in his hand caused the trumpet blast that signalled the start of the fight. The three columns of men walked out onto the sandy floor of the arena preceded by two men on horseback dressed in the court costume of the reign of Phillip II. These were the president's agents, the *alguacils*. Leading each column were the three matadors, serious and solemn, bearing their richly adorned decorative capes over one arm, the other swinging loose and free across their bodies. On the sunny side of the ring in the cheaper seats of the *sol*, the noisier *aficionados* were alive with excitement. The crowd hummed with activity, a sea of colour and movement as fans waved and tiny parasols on stems of reed were manoeuvred to provide shelter from the searing heat.

'God, look at those clothes,' said Caroline.

'*The traje de luces* – suit of lights,' said Miles. 'Its a good name.' The sun's reflection flashed from the gold and silver of the matadors' costumes.

Jaime d'Aragon, who, as senior matador, had led the right-hand column, would fight first. Standing alone in the middle of the arena he swept off his hat and, pirouetting in a complete circle, right arm extended to embrace the crowd, he dedicated the bull that he was about to kill to his appreciative audience. Another fanfare of trumpets and suddenly the big Muira bull was in the ring. For a second it stood still, adjusting to the brightness and strangeness of its new environment before rushing with awesome speed and power towards the floating capes offered it by the men of Jaime d'Aragon's *cuadrilla*. These men did not stop to play the bull. Having initiated its charge they jumped in apparently cowardly fashion behind the guarded openings that were placed strategically around the wooden barrier fence. In trying to reach them the irritated bull crashed his right horn into the hard wood and splinters flew.

'They're getting the measure of the bull for the matador,' said Miles. 'Each bull is different. This one for example likes to hook upwards with his right horn. Its important to recognize things like that early on. Also the bull tends to set up a *querencia*, an area of the ring which for some reason he makes his home and where he is particularily dangerous. This one seems to have taken a fancy to the patch where he hit the *barrera* with his horn. Another reason that the *cuadrilla* don't indulge in any fancy capework is that they'd probably get the sack for attempting to upstage the boss. Job security in bullfighting is not all that it should be.'

Jaime d'Aragon was in the arena now signalling for his

henchmen to hold back. He made a few preliminary testing passes with the big yellow and magenta cape. As he began to know the animal he started to work closer to the bull, sculpting the passes, raising the spectacle to the level of ballet. A series of carefully executed veronicas and the crowd began to respond, the chorus of *olés* growing progressively louder as the razor-sharp horns moved nearer to the frail flesh. D'Aragon's body struck poses of effortless elegance despite the pointed instruments of potential death that passed within inches of his femoral arteries. He finished the moving series with a *rebolera*, gathering the cape towards him and turning the bull so short that it was momentarily brought to its knees. Then, the bull fixed in place, he turned his back on it and walked away arrogantly to the cheers of the crowd.

Caroline felt immediately the emotion of the moment. As yet there had been no blood spent to confuse the beauty of the spectacle. That came next. Jaime d'Aragon signalled to the president for the arrival of the picadors. With great precision the bull was manipulated by the capes into making a frontal charge against the padded horses, which looked to all the world like the fiendish floats of some outlandish carnival, or ungainly pantomime animals containing human beings in tandem. The leathery old picadors dug their lances into the bull's trapezoid muscles and soon the red blood coursed freely down its black coat. Caroline was not enamoured of this part. Its artistic value was zero and pain had been injected into the equation. She looked at Miles questioningly.

'Not pretty, but necessary,' he responded to her look. 'D'Aragon has told the picadors to concentrate on the muscles around the right shoulder to neutralize that tendency to hook. He must judge carefully how much to give the bull. Too much and he half kills it which wouldn't be popular with the crowd. Too little and he risks getting wounded by horns that are held too high.' As Miles finished speaking the trumpet sounded again for the removal of the picadors.

'This next bit is interesting. They're going to place the

*banderillas*, short, barbed spears that go into the same place as the pic, and for more or less the same purpose, to wear down the neck muscles. If the bull has his head held high when the matador goes in with the sword the window to the heart will be closed by a door of muscle and bone and the bull has to be "assassinated" by a sword in the lung, or worse. You've never seen an angry crowd until that happens. It's every matador's nightmare.'

Jaime d'Aragon liked to do this part himself and made a bit of a speciality out of it, running between the bull's horns and the *barrera* in a fast closing space in which, if he had been caught, he would have ended up pinned to the wooden fence like a butterfly in a display cabinet. In a typically *macho* gesture he chose to place all six *banderillas* with the bull standing menacingly in the centre of his *querencia*, bravery that was not lost on the knowledgable *aficionados* of the sol, but meant nothing to the tourists in the expensive seats. Miles pointed out d'Aragon's courageous action and commented on his style, the arms held high, the body straight, the closeness to the horns, the accuracy of the cluster.

'Hey, pass that wine, Miles. This is really good.'

Miles was thrilled that Caroline was enjoying it, but then he had always imagined that she would. She wanted to know about everything and Miles was in a position to tell her, pointing out things that it would have taken one hundred bullfights for her to discover for herself.

The dark-red *muleta*, a blood-coloured square of material attached to a stick along one side, the other edge supported by the matador's sword, was altogether smaller and more businesslike than the graceful, billowing cape of the earlier passes. D'Aragon stood in the centre of the ring now and stimulated the charge, lifting the red cloth above the passing horns with his left hand, the bull's head thundering beneath his left armpit, his midriff rubbing against the animal's bleeding back.

'That's the *pase de pecho*,' said Miles. 'You can tell that this guy's got balls because he's just risked getting them skewered like a couple of maraschino cherries on a stick.'

There were other ways of telling that Jaime d'Aragon had balls, thought Caroline. Apart from anything else you could actually see them clearly outlined through the tight blue trousers of the *traje de luces*. Bullfights were aphrodisiacal she concluded, shooting a hungry glance at Miles. Not that she needed much help.

'He's doing well,' said Miles. 'The early capework was distinctly distinguished; he didn't pic the bull too hard, placed the *banderillas* with style. If he keeps this up with the *muleta* and kills cleanly he should get a couple of ears.'

A series of brave, severe left-handed natural passes had the crowd in uproar and led d'Aragon to try a few tricks such as passing the bull from the kneeling position, to the delight of the newcomers and the infuriation of the purists.

'This is El Cordobes stuff,' said Miles, indicating that he was in the latter category.

It was a momentary aberration and the matador returned to his classic style, building the excitement of the crowd to fever pitch.

At last the bull was ready for the kill, and d'Aragon changed swords, arranging the curved killing weapon carefully in the folds of the *muleta*. Now for the all-important positioning of the bull – front legs square on to open up the heart – d'Aragon's left hand held low across his body, flicking occasionally to keep the bull's attention on the moving *muleta*. He turned sideways on to the horns, profiling himself for the kill. With his right hand extended towards the target, he took aim along the sword shaft, head, arm and sword in perfect alignment. He cocked his left leg out, knee bent pointing towards the bull's lowered nose, and shifted his balance so that he could follow the sword thrust, his whole body poised to pass over the horns in the forward momentum that would carry the sharp Toledo steel blade to his heart. With a prayer he launched himself towards the target.

'A superb kill,' said Miles. The bull was still on his feet but the sword was sunk to the hilt in his back and Miles could tell from the angle that it was in the right place. A few seconds later, as the matador stood glowering at the conquered animal, it toppled over feet in the air to howls of appreciation from the grateful crowd. To a storm of applause the brave bull was dragged from the ring and the tumult began as the spectators shouted to the president to reward the hero of the moment and a sea of white handkerchiefs danced beneath the clear blue sky. First one ear, and then, as Miles had predicted, a second were awarded to the matador, as he started on his lap of honour. Flowers, wineskins, hats, even loaves of bread rained down into the arena. Most of the offerings d'Aragon threw back, but a few he accepted, handing them like royalty to a member of his *cuadrilla* for safe keeping. The ring was eventually cleared, sand brushed over the red blood stains to prevent slipping. The trumpet sounded once again. It was time for the next bull.

Hand in hand Miles and Caroline walked towards the house. Peaceful and silent they mounted the tiled steps. Miles pushed open the heavy oak doors and stood back to let Caroline pass, but she had stopped and stood now, looking back over the orange groves, lost in her private dreams. For a second he stood and watched her, all the love and devotion in the world shining from his eyes. This girl had bewitched him, captured him completely. He walked quickly towards her and encircled her waist from behind. As if expecting him, Caroline leaned back, her head on his shoulder. Gently, but firmly he turned her towards him.

At first the kiss was warm, tender, hesitant as if he feared that his touch might harm her. Their lips brushed together in delicate exploration, like the timid touch of the hummingbird at the face of a flower. Miles wanted to know the taste of Caroline, to smell her, to hear the soft, reassuring noises that she made as she gave herself over to the emotion of love. His lips traced the contours of her face, the upturned nose, across the half-opened eyes, back once more to her mouth. And then the fire began to burn. Miles' lips became more courageous, his tongue invading Caroline's mouth as his hands, which had until now lain softly on her firm breasts, began to explore them, sending messages of exquisite sensuality to Caroline's besieged mind. She made no effort to stop him. She knew that never again in her entire life would she feel this way about a man. Deeply in love, she wanted Miles with an almost feverish desperation as her body shuddered beneath his touch.

Miles' hands ran tenderly through her hair before resting at the back of her head. He pulled her towards him, strongly now, as if he wanted nothing more than to merge her face, her mind, her whole being, into his – so that he could own her, be her, have her for ever. His tongue deep within Caroline's mouth, Miles fought for control of his destiny, trying to slow the pace, to prolong the wild happiness of the moment, to know fully the extent of his bliss.

As if in slow motion he bent Caroline backwards and then, suddenly, he lifted her up into his arms without removing his lips from hers – his kiss full of love and devotion as he cradled her like a baby. Then he smiled down at her, as he watched the flush of passion spread across the bronzed cheeks, the red glow of the setting sun reflect in the golden hair. He wanted desperately to reassure her, to comfort her at this, the moment of her abandon. Caroline had lost control of herself, had wanted to lose it as Miles himself had wanted her to. He needed to tell her that it would be all right, that any nameless fears that she might have were groundless, without a base. His look said, 'Trust me. Believe me. Love me.'

Miles kicked open the ancient doors and slowly, deliberately, he carried Caroline up the circular stone stairs.

Her arms around his neck, she watched his face, lips parted, breathing fast, her expression full of expectancy, the beginnings of a mischievous smile playing around the corners of her mouth. For the first time in her life she was going to make love to a man, to the man she loved. She knew, too, that it would be beautiful.

Her whole being was permeated with a lascivious sensuality as love strengthened desire, as desire strengthened love. Even at the threshold of her ecstasy Caroline was aware of the faintest element of competition. She loved Miles with all her heart, had suffered horribly at the hands of her own insecurity about her ability to please him in the face of his widely publicized 'experience'. But she doubted herself no more. From the look on his face and the enormity of her own need, from the phenomenal power of her own feelings, Caroline knew that she would not disappoint him. Never before would he have made love to a woman like her. In a sense it would be the first time for both of them.

Miles laid her down on the cool, linen sheets. She lay still. It was the moment she had been waiting for ever since her arrival in Spain, but once again she felt a momentary shyness, the child-like fear of the unknown that Miles' touch seemed to have the power to banish.

Miles saw the apprehension creep into her face, but he knew how to still her anxiety, was not alarmed by her hesitancy. He knelt down and brushed the hair from her eyes. With slow deliberate fingers, he unbuttoned her skirt. Not for one instant did his eyes leave hers. His hands traced a pattern over Caroline's proud breasts and he watched her pink nipples become erect, alive beneath his fingers. For a second he was still, in simple awe at her remarkable beauty and then, once again, his need for her was driving him on. He undid the buttons on the gaberdine trousers and, as he pulled them down, Caroline lifted her bottom slightly to help him. Through the white lace pants he could see the blonde pubic hairs already moist, glistening with the wetness of her desire.

To Caroline this lovemaking was so new, so different, that she could not know of the dangers of haste – but Miles knew. He would not rush her. Instead he would build her to a pitch of passion that she would remember forever. Deftly, softly, he slipped off the pants and the long black boots and then his hand was on her, rubbing gently with a slow, circular motion.

With quiet reverence he laid his lips on the firm, flat stomach and kissed her lightly, his mouth poised above the damp, blonde triangle. Quickly he stood up and in seconds was standing naked above her. Caroline watched him in admiration, gazing in fascination at the stiff, erect penis – like the rest of his body the colour of sun-kissed honey.

Miles lay down beside her and she felt his hardness against her leg. His tongue explored every inch of her mouth. Next he kissed her neck and then his tongue was on her naked breasts, journeying untiringly from one to the other, leaving only enough time for one nipple to flatten imperceptibly before returning to it once more, manipulating it again to its erect position.

Caroline could not believe the extent of the raging sensuality that enveloped her. She was in some wonderful alien world, on the very borders of consciousness, a world of heightened and yet in some way also of diminished reality. The room, the bed, the external universe did not exist – only Miles' tongue, his hard body and her own thoughts and sensations.

Remotely aware of her desire to give pleasure as well as to receive it, Caroline reached for Miles' penis, but his hand stopped her. This first night of their lovemaking would be hers alone. His tongue followed the mid-line downwards towards the perfectly sculpted tummy button. For a few seconds it lingered there, buried deep in the skin of her stomach and then, as Caroline braced herself for what she knew she would soon experience, his mouth was between her legs, his tongue plunged deep within her. He kissed the lips of her vagina at first lightly, mimicking their first kiss. Then he saw the muscles of her stomach tense and felt the surge of wetness.

'Oh God, Miles . . .'

Caroline's voice tailed off in a despairing shout as the force of the orgasm took her. Miles held her tightly as she disintregrated in his arms.

For a few minutes they lay together side by side, luxuriating in their closeness, in the warmth of their love. Caroline broke the long silence. 'Make love to me, Miles.'

As he positioned himself over her she took his penis and

guided it into her, drawing up her legs as she did so and staring deep into his eyes. For a second he hovered there, uncertain, unsure, on the brink of her virginity. Caroline nodded gently. He needed reassurance, too. Suddenly Miles plunged into her and the searing pain shot through Caroline's brain only to collide with a wall of pleasure at the feeling of Miles deep within her. Slowly at first and then with increasing confidence she began to move, feeling the delight of the warm hardness that had penetrated her so completely. Miles took her with slow, long strokes, but, as he felt her respond, he quickened his pace. Together they climbed towards orgasm. And then it was upon them. Swearing his love Miles exploded into her and Caroline shuddered with her own climax as she felt the delicious hot liquid saturate her.

'Miles, Miles . . . God, I love you.'

# Chapter 8

## I

It would have required a fertile imagination to liken the two sweating figures to a couple of Roman senators relaxing after a hard day's politicking on the Capitol in ancient Rome, but there were elements in the scene that lent weight to the analogy. Certainly their immediate environment was on the side of the comparison – wall-to-wall marble, the design of the tiles undoubtedly inspired by early Italian motifs, the steamy air, at least to the naked eye, little changed from Roman times. Even the appearance of the two men did not at once give the lie to the comparison with ancient Rome. There was about Castelli – swarthy, stocky, dark chinned – the unmistakable whiff of Italy, although the serious student of history might have worried about the heavily greased hair, not widely recognized as a characteristic of the ancient Roman. With regard to his companion there was more room for doubt. Goebbels would not have been caught dead describing him as of Aryan stock, but at the same time the man would have, and indeed often did, stand out like a sore thumb at Mafia weddings. Not exactly semitic and yet hardly a WASP, Harry Fox inhabited some no-man's land of physiognomic appearance, the competing blood lines having seemingly cancelled each other out like the opposing armies of the First World War bogged down irretrievably in the mud of the Flanders trenches. It was left to the conversation to indicate without a shadow of possible doubt that this was the Florida of the 1980s rather than Augustan Rome.

'If this deal turns sour the fish'll be lunching on our balls. You realize that,' said Castelli, as his long finger foraged around in the moist recesses of his hairy nostril.

Harry realized that. He drew mild encouragement from Castelli's use of the word 'our'. If it ever came to the defence of life and limb he would be a not insignificant ally.

'Don't worry, Nero. How can you go wrong with diamonds?'

'Listen, if I hadn't liked the deal I wouldn't have set it up with the Mob. I just want it clear that there's as much room for error as there is space in a virgin's cunt. We'd be so full of lead they wouldn't need weights when we hit the Gulf Stream.'

'Come on, Nero. I've been around.' Harry had gone in with his eyes wide open. Borrowing from a Godfather was not the same as taking a loan from a grandmother. There were risks attached and he knew what they were – didn't need Castelli to spell them out.

Grudgingly Castelli changed the subject. He liked to fantasize about violence. 'How much did you have to kick back to the nigger?' he said, the finger that had recently invaded his nose now in hot pursuit of an elusive piece of salami that had taken temporary refuge among the discoloured molars at the back of his mouth.

Harry tensed a bit at this despite the soothing steam heat of the Turkish bath. He had known that Castelli would ask but the answer had to be just right. 'Funny guy,' said Harry evenly, 'he didn't want anything and I wasn't about to offer. I think the cunt's got religion or patriotism or something.' He said the last words as if describing some contagious and physically disgusting social disease.

Castelli peered at him nastily through the steam and grunted. OK, so he hadn't invested money buying the spade. Maybe. 'And do you get to score a few stones on the side – sort of under the counter, if you get my meaning?'

A genius IQ was not required to get Castelli's meaning. His transparent nastiness was on the surface for all to see. It was both his strength and his weakness. If there existed some imbecilic cretin who could fail to grasp the thrust of Castelli's question he was not present that morning in the steam room at Harry Fox's Palm Beach house. Castelli and

Harry thought alike, had learned to do so in travelling similar paths from common origins. It was only over the past few years that those paths had diverged – Harry taking the high road, Castelli preferring the more lowly one where the flora and fauna more nearly approximated the habitat of his earlier days. It was a moot point who would be 'in Scotland' first, but the race was indubitably on.

'Really, Nero, you can't think I'd go behind your back to do that. It would be taking your money.'

If sarcasm was the lowest form of wit nobody had told Castelli. If they had he now showed a considerable disregard for the hierarchy of humour. 'My dear Harry, I know you would be the last person to take money from anybody, me or the Organization in New York.'

Nobody had turned the thermostat up, but had there been a third person in the room he would have felt the temperature rise. Fox held on to himself. This was no time or place for emotions. The stakes were far too high. He had sold the deal to Castelli and in turn Castelli had gone to the New York Mob with whom he had always retained close ties. Fox, on the other hand, with the tacit consent of the top men who had been his initial backers, had allowed his relationship with organized crime to loosen as he struggled for the respectability that would bring the mega bucks to the Union Bank and incidentally to its low profile 'Family' investors. By using Castelli as an intermediary, Fox had, to some extent, cushioned himself from the unfavourable publicity that 'consorting with known criminals' could bring, coverage that he could ill afford in his new position, which could hit him in that most sensitive of all areas, the pocket.

There was another advantage to Castelli. Certainly he was a reptile, but a reptile that Harry knew. To a limited degree he was predictable. The faceless gangsters in New York represented quite a different proposition. Harry was too far away to navigate the quicksands, submerged rocks and treacherous shallows that constituted Organization politics. Castelli, however, was always nosing about in such waters, had secured his position in the life-chain of that dangerous and hostile environment.

Harry knew that Castelli knew that he would have tried for a 'sweetener'. The smart money said he had asked for it and got it and the smart money was right. At a late night whisky-drinking session in the Pierre, Sir Seretse Mwamba had agreed to pay Harry $5 million in diamonds as his commission if the deal went through – just over one and a half per cent. Mwamba had promised total secrecy and Harry intended to make sure that he kept his word. Nestling beside the carefully wrapped stones in Harry's personal Crédit Suisse strong box lay an eight-millimetre movie film that showed, in glorious technicolour, thirteen-year-old Susie biting off much more than she could chew. Harry smiled as he thought of the metaphor. Seretse Mwamba had been left in no doubt that both the New York vice squad and his political opponents in Umpala would have copies of that film if news of his 'commission' leaked out. Harry could have sworn that the black man had gone white at the news that his sexual antics with a juvenile had been immortalized for posterity on celluloid.

From the beginning Harry had realized that Castelli would have to be cut in on this secret part of the deal, but it was a tricky business. If Castelli's loyalty to the Mob was greater than his interest in enriching himself, then he, Harry, would be in bad trouble. He must admit nothing, but instead cast a seductive fly upon the water.

'Of course, I feel that in a perfect world I would be due some sort of introductory commission, and, in consideration of your role in finding the principle, half of that ought technically to be yours.' 'God,' thought Harry, 'I'm beginning to sound like some smart-assed eastern banker with a long pedigree and a short prick,' but through the steam he could see that Castelli was watching him carefully.

'Certain people in New York might say that anybody who took a commission without cutting them in would be stealing.' Stealing from the Mob. The long goodbye. Harry held his breath. Castelli continued. 'Unless, that is, you *were* intending to let them in on it.'

This was a game of poker. Harry would bluff it out. He laughed nervously, but said nothing.

'What sort of figure might you put on this hypothetical commission?' Castelli was nibbling.

'I'd imagine $5 million in untraceable stones – half each – would be fair,' said Harry.

Castelli reached down and scratched his balls. Harry wondered about the finger's next destination. There weren't many orifices left unexplored. 'Like they would kinda turn up in my box in Switzerland,' Castelli said at last. 'And it would be just between the two of us. Not even the spade would know that you'd shared your commission.'

Castelli was hooked. Harry Fox began to breathe again. It had been a nasty moment. Now the two men would be partners in crime. If the fairy castles should ever start to fall he would have all of Castelli's resources at his disposal, the army of Colombian dagoes he kept on that island Soldier Key, his fearsome reputation, the luxurious ocean-going, high-speed yacht that could put them, Vesco-like, beyond the reaches of all interested law enforcement agencies and, above all, out of the vengeful hands of the Mafia. At a cost of $2.5 million in diamonds it was cheap insurance.

'I might be interested in that sort of deal,' said Castelli cautiously.

'I could probably arrange it,' said Harry.

Castelli laughed. It was a very remarkable phenomenon in that he managed to do this without smiling. The noise was there but the expression was absent. 'Rather like Edward Heath,' thought Harry. 'You piece of shit,' he said at last. It was the nearest that he could come to an endearment. 'You know damn well that those diamonds are sitting like turds in your bleeding box right now.'

Harry slapped playfully at the wet, hairy back and laughed too. 'Oh Nero, it's good to do business with you again. Just like the old days. Takes me back.' Harry felt a tiny spark of emotion in his cold heart. Could one be fond of a crocodile?

Castelli peered suspiciously around the steam room. 'If one word leaks – we're hamburger.'

They both knew that.

Harry lay back on the marble slab and took stock of the situation. He had pulled the fat from the fire. Everybody had liked the deal and now it was done. The Mob had put up $250 million, Castelli $25 million and Harry himself had borrowed against his Union Bank stock and mortgaged himself up to the hilt to come up with the $25 million balance. Financially he had stretched himself to the limit, but it would be worth it. However, there was no room for error, none at all. He was paying through the nose to borrow the money to lend the Umpalans, even though the yearly payment of diamonds would more than cover the outgoings.

It was costing Harry twenty per cent for the money, but he would be getting thirty per cent from the Umpalans in diamonds. That represented an annual profit of ten per cent on his $25 million, $2.5 million a year for five years – a total of $10 million not counting the $2.5 million worth of stones that would be left in his Swiss deposit box after paying off Castelli. And if interest rates dropped his profit margin would be far greater. Not bad for a week's work. But if anything happened to the diamond price he would be finished. He would lose it all. He wouldn't be able to convert the diamonds into cash to meet the interest payments. The banks would call in the loan and he would have to unload large quantities of Union Bank stock onto a weak market. It would be the end of everything that he had dreamed of. Nor would the tragedy be purely financial. The New Yorkers would make an example of him *pour encourager les autres*. There would be a contract out on him within the hour. He would be a dead man, unless he moved very fast indeed.

Harry forced the unpleasant thought from his mind. The die was cast. The Union Bank had acted as a front for the deal and a suitably woolly statement had already been issued to the effect that it was 'entering into a co-operative venture with the government of Umpala to help in the development of mineral resources'. It had sounded impressive and been well received, the more so because the Secretary of State had put out his own press release. In it he had welcomed the actions of the Union Bank, stating that the country needed financiers of the calibre of Harry Fox, men who were not hidebound by tradition, not afraid to look farther afield, in whom the American pioneering spirit was not dead. It had done Harry Fox's image no harm at all and already the deposits were flowing into the Union, rebuilding the lending base. The Crédit Suisse in Zurich had received the Umpalan's $300 million worth of stones and their value had been confirmed by independent experts. Now they sat in a large escrow vault within sight of Harry's own box with its $5 million worth of 'commission'. The Umpalan diamonds were to be controlled by the board of Crédit Suisse who had agreed to act as arbiters and referees in the event of any dispute between the two parties with regard to the terms and workings of the loan agreement. If the Umpalans defaulted on the interest or principal then the Union Bank would be able to draw out the collateral. It was a comforting thought. On the day that the value of the Umpalan diamonds was certified the $300 million loan had been paid into the account of the government of Umpala and immediately transferred to Africa.

Even now, as Harry luxuriated in the steam, the tankers and freighters would be heading for Umpala with new drilling equipment, mining machinery spares and supplies of fuel that would put the huge mine back on stream. He, Harry Fox, with a little bit of help from his friends, had made it possible. He was bringing aid and succour to the world's poor, and far from incidentally, to the world's rich as well. Everybody was pleased, everybody was grateful, everybody would make money. That was as it should be, thought Harry, as he contemplated his star high in the firmament. All was well with the world.

Castelli would be an invaluable buffer between himself and the Mob and a useful ally in time of trouble. His price had not been exorbitant. But there had been another price too and as Harry thought of it a cloud disfigured his otherwise clear horizon and he frowned as he remembered. Castelli had made one condition when he had agreed to act as go-between for Harry and the Mob.

'What's the name of that little piece of cunt you have hanging around – you know, the child nympho? 'Cos if I'm going to get this deal together for you I want her for six months. You can have her back after that,' the crude voice had said over the telephone.

Harry had not liked it. Susie had learned how to turn him on like an electric light. It would be difficult to find and train an adequate substitute. After six months with Castelli all she would be good for would be the knacker's yard despite her tender age. Castelli's ex-women tended to be ex-people as well. By turning her over to Castelli Harry would be depriving himself of the ultimate pleasure machine and signing her psychological death warrant all at the same time. But Harry was a man of principle, of unshakeable ideals, a man who lived his life according to a rigorous code of conduct.

'Of course, Nero,' he had said. 'Come by anytime and pick her up.'

There was to Harry Fox no greater God, no higher authority, no truer religion than the almighty dollar.

Today was the day. Before lunch he would tell Susie that, like some vassal in a medieval feudal system, she was to be transferred to another liege lord. No hard cash had changed hands but she had been sold as surely and as certainly as any southern plantation slave of the previous century and she would become the posession of a man who had cultivated a reputation for boundless cruelty and evil, especially towards women, who revelled in physical violence and macho-chauvinism of the worst kind. Harry Fox realized that he was not doing a very nice thing. Susie would not take it well. She knew all about Nero Castelli.

Castelli and Fox, retreating from the heat, stood side by side beneath the ice-cold showers.

'Well, Harry,' said Castelli, 'I feel a richer man today.' He was not talking about spiritual values.

'We both are, Nero.'

'And that little girl of yours. I've got some plans for her.' He looked at Harry slyly. He sensed that he was not pleased to be losing her. Castelli was a man who couldn't resist the opportunity to cause discomfort whenever it arose.

Harry owed him one for that. 'How are those two powder puffs that tried to top my house guest the other night?'

Nero Castelli frowned. Touché. 'They're costing me a bomb in the university hospital,' he admitted grudgingly. 'It's caused me a few problems on the street – you know – image is everything. Where's the English cunt now?' The last question was meant to sound innocent. Innocence, however, was not Castelli's strong suit.

'He's fucking the ass off Eleanor Montgomery's daughter in some Spanish love nest.' Harry made it his business to know such things. 'Word is it's a love trip,' he added.

'He'd better use his balls while he's still got 'em,' said Castelli bleakly.

'I wouldn't like to be the one to try and take them away from him,' said Harry. 'Hospitals don't get any cheaper you know.'

Castelli glowered. The reference to Miles had thoroughly upset his equanimity as Harry had known that it would. He salted the wound. If this fuck rat was going to wind him up by talking about Susie he would get as good as he gave.

'Yeah,' said Harry. 'You know I've never seen people bleed like those two boys of yours. Had to have the wooden floor sanded in that bedroom. Right through the carpet. I expect you'll have to retire them permanently.' He chuckled.

'That Susie had better watch out,' thought Castelli. His natural foul temper had now reasserted itself with a vengeance, blowing away the uncharacteristic good humour with the effortless ease of a hurricane disposing of an artificial sand beach.

Susie wept gently in the back of the big black limo on the way towards Miami. She couldn't believe what was happening to her. She had learned not to expect too much from life. In the circles in which she moved there were few white knights. But she had allowed herself to believe that Harry Fox and she had a good thing going, thoroughly acceptable to both parties. She did not deal in affection, but in pragmatism, and it suited her just fine to be with Harry. She had imagined that it had suited him too. Now, like some second-hand dress, she was being passed on. In itself that was not necessarily a disaster, but Castelli . . . The blood ran cold within her at the contemplation of her fate. Castelli liked to beat up on women. It was not just a rumour. Susie had seen the results of his handiwork. What's more he demanded and got total and absolute sexual fidelity from his girls. He did not share Harry Fox's vice, although there were few enough vices that he did not lay claim to. Castelli liked his women incapacitated, immobilized, tied to him, unable to leave. They were guarded day and night, often actually locked up for long periods. There was no escape. There was another and even surer method of binding his mistresses to him, and Susie's tears intensified as she remembered it. Nero Castelli liked to get his girls hooked on heroin, a drug of which he had a limitless supply. In this way he chained their minds and owned them completely. In her time Susie had snorted a lot of coke and she had smoked grass regularly, but she had always avoided the hard stuff. Would she be forced to become a junkie?

Beside her sat Castelli, saying nothing, enjoying her tears, still thinking about Harry Fox's remarks in the shower. He had promised to return her after six months. Would Harry want her then? His face contorted into the leering counterfeit of a smile that accompanied his more pleasing thoughts. He tapped on the glass partition separating him from the driver and the bodyguard who was riding shotgun. The thin Colombian in the passenger seat pressed a button and the bullet-proof glass whirred back.

'Enrico – pass me a packet of that good snorting smack. My friend here is anxious to try some.'

It was pure powdered heroin that the unfortunate Susie was forced to take up her nose and into her blood stream as Castelli's powerful fingers bruised into her upper arm. It would be main-lining next. In the brief moment before the artificial high got to her Susie experienced the abject depths of total despair in which were planted seeds that would sprout and grow in the next few months of her torture and degradation. Their names were 'hatred' and 'revenge'. She would, she vowed, find a way to destroy Harry Fox and Nero Castelli in a way that would make them regret the accident of their births.

# III

Charles Cabot Lodge sat back in the comfortable arm chair of the President's small study. Across the room the distinguished, greying man sipped thoughtfully on his whisky and water – relaxed and at ease, exuding good humour and homespun wisdom. President Wayne had not been in power long but already there were those who were prepared to say that he would go down in history as one of the great American leaders – a man who could inspire others to greatness, the catalyst in the chemical transformation of the United States from a country of uncertain direction and self-doubt into a land of dignity, purpose, pride and self-respect. No bigot, he had revitalized respect for the old values, the traditional way, and his conservatism was as far removed from neo-fascism as from the woolly-headed permissive liberalism which he had been elected to dismantle.

'I am so glad that you and Eleanor could come to dinner,' he said. 'It's just the four of us and we've got a good pot roast.' President Wayne made it sound as if the country doctor was giving dinner to the local pastor rather than the most powerful man in the Western world entertaining his Secretary of State.

'Always a pleasure, Mr President,' said Cabot Lodge easily. He was no stranger to the White House and was not overawed by the majesty of the presidential office, whose power it was to make fawning backsliders out of many otherwise self-assured men. He knew that he had been asked over for this pre-prandial talk for a specific reason. Soon he would know what it was. It would be unlike the President to beat about the bush.

'I asked you here specially to put you in the picture about something that's really too sensitive for either cabinet or the National Security Council.' That sounded big, thought Cabot Lodge.

'Unbeknown to many I've been talking quite regularily with the Russians over the past few weeks. The talks have been direct and at the highest possible level.' There was only one thing that 'the highest possible level' could mean and 'direct' implied the hot line. This was dynamite.

The President continued. 'It's been what they call "a fruitful dialogue" – extraordinarily so. We've been talking turkey and we seem to be getting somewhere. I want it to continue and if it's going to then it must be kept totally secret. That's top priority.'

Cabot Lodge would publicize this conversation at the cost of his job, probably any future job as well. He nodded seriously to show that he had caught the underlying drift of the President's remarks. Friends should not need to spell things out too clearly.

'I thought you should know about what's been going down,' the President added.

'Are they going to take the pressure off Iran?' asked Cabot Lodge. Soviet troop movement on the Iranian border after the recent death of the Ayatollah Khomeini was the burning foreign policy issue of the moment, with its threat to the Arabian oilfields, producers of the life-blood of the American economy.

'That's the point,' said Wayne. 'I've got a verbal undertaking that they won't invade and that they will reduce military activity on the Iranian border. Satellite reports this morning indicate that they are keeping their word.'

'That's terrific. What's the trade-off?'

The President smiled. He had chosen his Secretary of State well. 'On the surface we haven't had to concede too much. They want us to stand back while they destabilize South Africa,' he replied.

Cabot Lodge thought fast. He could see the logic in that. The racist government in Pretoria were already in deep trouble, SWAPO guerillas were well established in Namibia and were growing stronger daily, mounting occasional raids over the South African borders. Recently Cubans had moved into Zimbabwe to prop up the Mugabe régime and there had been reports of a Russian airlift of supplies that had included tanks and anti-aircraft missiles. The pressure was on and already there was evidence of mounting and well-organized resistance within the borders of South Africa itself. There were daily bomb blasts in the major cities and the beginnings of guerilla activity in the countryside. At a recent meeting of the Organization of African Unity, speaker after speaker had implored the Soviet Union to increase its support for the struggle against the South Africans. The dividends for doing so could be huge.

'We can't have Soviet combat troops in Southern Africa,' said Cabot Lodge. 'The Cape route is vital.'

'So is Saudi oil,' said the President. 'But it won't go as far as that. I have their word and I believe them. They don't want to take on the South African Army. They've got enough trouble in Afghanistan and that's on their doorstep. No, what they want to do is to hit the South African economy, and hit it hard.'

'How on earth would they do that?'

'Well, I must admit that I didn't understand it at first but the boys over at Treasury say that their scheme is perfectly feasible. As you may know they have this huge stockpile of diamonds, far larger apparently than anybody had realized and a closely guarded secret. They intend to dump the whole damn lot onto the world market all at once. They are going to destroy the diamond price. By the time they've finished marbles will be more valuable.'

'But they'd be cutting off their nose to spite their face,' said Cabot Lodge. 'They desperately need the foreign exchange that they got for selling diamonds through De Beers to pay for their wheat imports.'

'That's certainly been the popular wisdom on the subject and the view that De Beers have been anxious to project, but the fact is they're playing for higher stakes, and they're prepared to pay the price. The political dividends and increased influence in Africa will, they feel, more than compensate them for the short-term financial loss. They aim to destroy the De Beers monopoly for ever and cut off South African income from diamond mining into the bargain. Later on when the dust settles they have plans to set up a new monopoly of their own – sort of beat the capitalists at their own game. De Beers and the Oppenheimers will of course be totally *kaput*.'

'Can't De Beers just buy up all the stones that the Russians sell and hold the price?'

'The contingency planners in the Treasury say "no way". The amounts in the Russian stockpile are vast, and all good-quality gem stones. De Beers just hasn't got the financial muscle to buy them all up. Their sales are well down at the moment and the cost of financing their increasingly large stockpile at today's interest rates is hurting them like hell. The Russians calculate that the mere announcement of their intentions will be enough to cause panic among diamond holders. Everyone will try to unload at the same time and supply will swamp demand.'

'Perhaps the banks would bail them out. After all, there must be a lot of loans backed up by diamonds that would go bad if the banks did nothing.' Cabot Lodge's orderly capitalist mind revolted from the thought of any form of chaos on the capital markets of the world.

'In my humble opinion you can never rely on banks when the going gets tough. They couldn't prevent phenomenal losses in the silver market at the time of the Hunt fiasco and no central bank has ever managed to hold up a currency in the face of overwhelming selling pressure. In 1929, by your argument, they ought to have supported the stock market. After all, stocks provided security for an awful lot of their loans. But they didn't, couldn't or wouldn't. It will happen so fast that they won't have time to get together and plan a response even if they wanted to. They'll just run for cover and call in or write off the loans as quickly as they can. They won't stand about and throw good money after bad to protect a South African monopoly. When prices are artificially maintained by a cartel and the cartel disintegrates, it's a free fall and a bumpy landing.' President Wayne, who held the Air Medal, liked his Air Force analogies.

'What about all those engagement rings on the fingers of American women? Don't we have an obligation to protect their interests?' Cabot Lodge was clearly fighting a rear-guard action, but felt there was something faintly obscene about the Russians' cynical use of capitalistic mechanisms to achieve their own ends.

'I don't think so,' said Wayne. 'In general people don't want to sell their engagement rings and they'll be just as pretty on the finger as before. Anyway it's a trade off. At least they'll be able to run their car and heat their homes. My information is that the effect on the US economy will be minimal. Of course Tel Aviv, Antwerp and places like that will feel the pinch.

'The main casualty will be De Beers of course. It'll be the end for them. But they don't have any US connections because of anti-trust problems. In fact their monopoly is pretty un-American when you think about it.' Cabot Lodge was beginning to see the logic of the deal, as the President continued. 'And anything that tends to undermine faith in the value of such barbaric relics as shiny stones and yellow metal tends to reinforce belief in paper money, which is anti-inflationary.' Abolishing inflation was Wayne's most cherished ambition.

Cabot Lodge took up the running, no slouch in the

analysis of the political ramifications of proposed actions. 'The black voters certainly wouldn't object if we stood back and watched South Africa sink.'

'Not many of the white ones either. South Africa is no big deal to anybody outside the John Birch society and half of them don't know where it is.' The President had considered most of the angles.

'The Jewish voters who might object to the financial blow to Israel are the same liberal democrats who hate South Africa.'

Wayne nodded in vigorous agreement. He could see that he was carrying his Secretary of State along with him on this one.

President Wayne paused. 'One of the reasons that I mention this deal now is that I am afraid it will not benefit the unfortunate Umpalans for whom, I gather, you have just arranged a loan from a Florida bank. I'm afraid they're going to take some losses, but will be in better shape to withstand them with the loan than without it.'

Charles Cabot Lodge sat up. Of course. He'd forgotten. In his general political and strategic analysis of the information, he had totally overlooked the effects on Seretse Mwamba and Harry Fox. The Umpalans would struggle through somehow. They were used to poverty. But the effect on Harry Fox might easily be disastrous.

The President hurried on before Cabot Lodge could speak. 'Now it would appear that the people at Justice have had their eyes on this man Fox and his Union Bank for some time. They tell me they're pretty certain that he has organized crime connections and so I'm not going to cry too hard if he takes a knock – might even manage to keep a dry handkerchief altogether – while we protect the wider interests of the nation. However, I must emphasize that we are all committed to total secrecy on this. If anybody gets word of Soviet intentions I will be blamed for the leak and my dialogue with the Russians will be at an end. So there must be no warnings to Fox, the Umpalans or anybody else for that matter, that the diamond price is about to take a tumble. Nothing less than national security is at stake.'

That was very strong stuff indeed, thought Cabot Lodge. He wondered what else the President had discussed with the Russians that made the continuing of the talks so vitally important.

The President softened his warning with a joke. 'I'm rather nervous, because I haven't even told the First Lady, and you know how she does love her jewellery!'

President Wayne took Cabot Lodge's elbow on the walk to the First Family's living quarters in the classic older-man's steering grip. In doing so he managed to suggest an intimacy and affection that was both flattering and intentional. It served as some small recompense for the undeniable fact that Wayne had been conducting the foreign policy of the country without consulting his Secretary of State, taking him into his confidence only after the decisions had been made. Cabot Lodge was a Washington pro, an aristocrat and no green politician. He was a man of principle but also a pragmatist, always prepared to see the wider view. He was not basically offended, but he reckoned the President owed him one.

'Well, Mr President, you seem to have got things pretty well worked out.'

'Sometimes these things can only be done man to man,' Wayne replied, picking up immediately on the mild rebuke. 'I'm pleased with the results.'

'Do we know the Russians are firm on this diamond thing?'

'Baked in the cake,' said the President.

'And the time scale?'

'Christmas sometime.'

Cabot Lodge would have to keep the secret for six months. It was a strange experience to know that a widely accepted store of value was about to become worthless overnight. He thought of the De Beers ads in the glossy magazines – 'A Diamond is For Ever' – that should read 'A Diamond is Until Christmas', after that it would be

'For Never'. Damn. He couldn't even tell Eleanor. That would be the hardest part. Ruefully, he thought of her magnificent jewellery, her buying sprees at Cartier and Winston's. Still, the collapse of the diamond price would hardly cause a ripple in the vast Montgomery fortune. A quarter per cent move in the Montgomery Chemical share price would be far more significant. Actually, he thought, Eleanor would be quite pleased. She was always saying that there was no such thing as inevitable upward movement in prices of any sort, that what went up tended eventually to go down, and her jewellery would be nonetheless beautiful because it was valueless. She had scorned those who bought precious stones for investment purposes. Nor would she blame him for his silence. Saving her a few million dollars would count for nothing if the price was to prejudice the foreign policy of the United States. After all, it was national security that was vital. Without that everything would be worthless, including Montgomery Chemical stock.

As if reading his thoughts the President said, 'Now, Charles, when are you going to marry Eleanor Montgomery? My administration could do with a White House wedding – good for morale all round.' He chuckled. It was an open secret that if Charles could have arranged it he would.

'I'm counting on you to use your formidable powers of persuasion this evening. I need some heavy guns in support.'

They were both laughing as they entered the private drawing room of the President's apartment. Eleanor Montgomery and Mrs Wayne rose to greet them. 'Now, you two, no more business,' said Mrs Wayne pleasantly, but firmly. She was a short, homely woman with a warm smile, her folksy appearance belying the sharp political brain that had on more than one occasion saved Wayne from making decisions that would have ruined his career. 'It's gossip I want to hear,' she added. In politics, of course, gossip *was* business and the First Lady's retentive memory would be used to store facts and information that would later be used to pressurize and flatter, to identify potential sources of danger, to recognize situations and people from whom help might be expected. Both the President and his wife did a lot of hard business when their whole external appearance said 'off duty'.

'I think I could handle another whisky. How about you, Charles?'

'Yes please, Mr President.'

'What I want to hear about, Eleanor,' said the President, 'is that beautiful daughter of yours. Word is she's going to cover herself in glory this winter in the World Cup competitions. What's the low down?'

Wayne was a sports buff and, with the rest of America, was thrilled that at last they had a female skiing star who had the potential to win. Skiing was a big international sport. Defeating the Communists and the Europeans meant a lot to everyone and the President was no exception. Victory would be especially sweet in that the standard-bearer of capitalism would be the daughter of his old friend Bill Montgomery, a man who embodied everything that was good and decent in the American character.

'We all feel that she can do it,' said Eleanor. 'If determination and hard work were enough she's champion already. I think she's got the skill, too, but it's always tough. Anything and everything can go wrong. At the moment she's taken two weeks off and is holidaying in Spain with a rather disreputable English aristocrat.' She laughed.

Mrs Wayne looked at her carefully. Did she detect a note of anxiety at the mention of the Englishman? 'And what's the name of this Restoration character?' said the First Lady innocently. Within two or three days she would know all about him. At the nerve centre of political Washington she could gather information at breathtaking speed. She would ask the British ambassador's wife to tea, had been meaning to for some time.

'Lord Parmere,' said Eleanor.

Wayne laughed. 'By the end of the week Missie will be able to tell you the colour of his face flannel,' he said.

'Nonsense,' said the First Lady, not at all put out by this unsolicited testimonial to her intelligence network.

'He works for the Union Bank of Florida, for a man called Harry Fox. Incidentally, he helped to arrange a big loan for Montgomery a little while ago.' Eleanor felt she had perhaps gone too far in painting Miles as a playboy. Not really fair to Caroline.

'Aha,' said Wayne, exchanging a glance with Cabot Lodge.

In his mind he debated whether or not to tell Eleanor about the information from the Justice Department. Yes, why not? Business was the business of America. It was his duty to protect large corporations, especially when they were run by old friends and generous campaign contributors. 'I was just telling Charles that Justice have a file on that man Fox. It would appear that some of the investors and depositors in that bank are not entirely *kosher*.'

Eleanor looked startled. 'My finance department didn't pick that up,' she said.

'One step forward all Montgomery personnel with secure jobs – not so fast finance department,' thought Charles.

'I don't think it's very well documented yet, but I'm told by the boys that ought to know that there are some organized crime connections there – you know drugs and all that.'

'You don't imagine the Englishman is in on it,' said Mrs Wayne, never far from the heart of the matter.

'Good Lord, no,' said Eleanor. 'He's employed in a PR capacity and I know he's only just taken on the job. He'd never met Fox before this year.'

Inwardly she was cursing the fact that she had accepted Fox's money. It was crystal clear to her now why he had lent it to her on such favourable terms. He was buying respectability at her expense. The Montgomery name was as pure as the driven snow and would remain so despite the Union Bank loan, but Eleanor did not like to deal with criminals and she disliked being suckered even more. Her first impression of Harry Fox had been spot on target. In future she would not give him the time of day.

'It looks to me as if we all had Mr Fox wrong,' said Cabot Lodge. 'Possibly Lady Luck will not smile on his business ventures.'

'Time to eat,' said the President quickly.

'I hope you're hungry,' said Mrs Wayne, leading them through to the dining room. 'We have some delicious smoked salmon from Scotland, caught by Walter Wriston on the Dee, and the President's favourite pot roast.'

'Sounds wonderful,' said Eleanor, still planning her revenge on Harry Fox.

The dinner was a happy one and afterwards Charles delighted them all with some wickedly accurate impersonations of the more flamboyant members of Congress and the more self-important of the network interviewers. All the time Eleanor felt herself drawing closer to him, nearer to making her decision. In the limousine on the way back to his Washington house, where she was staying for the week-end, she slipped her hand into his. 'They're a wonderful couple. We're very lucky to have them,' she said. The advantages of married life had certainly been well demonstrated that evening.

'I think we'd be a wonderful couple too,' said Charles.

'So do I. Are you going to buy me a ring?'

Charles could hardly believe his ears. She was going to marry him at last. He had, however, been brought up in Boston and could remain cool at moments of the most intense excitement. There was another legacy of his Boston upbringing, a quality that men of his class shared with the Scots.

'I thought rubies and emeralds,' he said quickly. 'You're rather long on diamonds.'

# *Chapter 9*

## I

'Look at them – the poor little rich girl's fucking Mafia.'
The small, mean mouth was contorted with envy and
malice as it spat out the words like hot peppers. Anne
Carpenter's looks would not have won the Helen of Troy
award for the launching of ships. The truth was that she
was a very plain girl indeed and her character had been to
a large extent shaped by her failure to come to terms with
this fact. Now, at twenty-eight, the senior member of the
US ski team, she was on her last legs and the decline of her
skiing skills had done nothing to sweeten a temper that, at
the best of times, bordered on the cantankerous. She could
have coped better with the falling off of her skiing abilities
if she had more success with men, because Anne Carpenter
just loved to fuck. The good Lord, however, had not been
generous in the lottery of life and had failed to provide
recompense for the florid ordinariness of her face by the
provision of an above-average body. No competitive skier
would qualify for the adjective 'fat', but Anne Carpenter
did her best to deserve it. Certainly one could have
described her as being 'well covered' or, perhaps more
accurately, 'inefficiently covered', because her body's pre-
dominant characteristic was its shapelessness – it being
difficult to delineate where buttocks started and finished,
where stomach merged with torso, breasts with shoulders
and arms. If she had good points at all, and there were
those who strenuously maintained that she did not, then
her mammary glands would probably have qualified for
the dubious honour. These at least attempted to compensate for their lack of aesthetic quality by their considerable,
even remarkable, size. Certain members of the opposite

sex, almost invariably late at night when blood alcohol levels tended to be high and the spirit willing although all too often the flesh weak, had been known to succumb to the American obsession with the quantity of these anatomical appendages and had taken her to bed. Few had not regretted it the next morning. The more discerning had discovered within a shorter time that the demon drink had not sharpened their critical faculties. Her sexual frustration and her voracious appetite were inflamed by the succession of drunken one-night stands it had been her lot to experience, and her general peevishness was enhanced by the unwillingness of any male who did not closely resemble the Hunchback of Notre Dame to return, like Oliver Twist, for a second helping.

Anne Carpenter had no insight into the reasons for her lack of success, although others had strong thoughts on the subject. Those unlucky enough to inhabit neighbouring rooms had to suffer the nocturnal screams as she gave herself up to her lusty passion. If temporary deafness was an occupational hazard of taking her to bed, there were others too. Someone had once told her that men liked a little pain with their lovemaking. As a result many of her bedmates, mercifully drunk at the time, had the next morning discovered wounds on backs and faces, and not infrequently on other even less acceptable portions of their anatomy, caused by the Carpenter fingernails at moments of total abandon. So well known had this phenomenon become in the environs of US ski camps that any small but noticeable abrasion or cut, whatever its cause, had come to be known as a 'Carpenter'. Much laughter would ensue when somebody held up their hand to demonstrate such a wound with the words, 'I fell over and got a Carpenter'. Mirth would be particularly generous when the speaker was female, because, it was rumoured, the gentle sex were not entirely immune in Anne Carpenter's ceaseless search for sexual gratification.

At the end of the day it was hard to avoid the conclusion that Anne Carpenter was a 'dog', and what's more of that least attractive variety of the canine species, the type that liked to bite. Caroline Montgomery was the natural target for the Carpenter bile. There were several reasons for this. Caroline was not only beautiful she was also incredibly attractive to men. Furthermore she was totally unwilling to capitalize on these attributes. Men tended to fall for Caroline in a big way and then, finding themselves gently but firmly refused but seeing that this rejection was scrupulously fair in its lack of discrimination, would become fiercely protective of her. Nowhere was this ability of Caroline's to first captivate and then to enslave members of the opposite sex without employing any cheap feminine tricks more visibly demonstrated than on the terrace of the open-air restaurant where she sat with the devoted members of her retinue: Nigel, her secretary; Skip Warner, tall and laconic; and Ingemar Jorgensen, once slalom champion of the world. The animated discussion that this small group was enjoying was doubly irritating to Anne Carpenter in that during the three weeks of the training camp she had conceived a strong physical attraction towards Skip whose long, lean body had got the Carpenter juices moving in a big way.

One night when she felt he had taken the required amount of Heineken she had tried a move on him, but although glass-eyed and thick-voiced, undeniably drunk in fact, he had turned her down flat in front of Caroline Montgomery and several others. Her beauty, together with her proximity to and influence over, the desirable Skip would alone have been sufficient to score for Caroline a high position on the Carpenter 'hit' list. To add insult to injury Caroline was also the indubitable star of the US team, the only triple seed in the competition. For four long months Anne would see nothing but Caroline's back flashing down mountains with a speed and grace that she could never hope to emulate.

So she was jealous and her jealousy twisted and turned within her, filling her soul with vicious venom. She had ammunition too. Caroline Montgomery was the centre of attention. She was the one who could win and the media, drawn like moths to the flame of success, had concentrated all their attention on her. To the world's press the rest of the American team had about as much relevance to the birth of the champion as the faceless donors at a sperm bank. The better adjusted of her team-mates realized that this was not a situation that Caroline sought but one that her natural talent had thrust upon her, and they did not hold it against her. Similarly, her faultless pedigree, influential friends, prodigious wealth and earth-shattering good looks might be hard to stomach, but were hardly her fault. Caroline's winning personality, her charm and total lack of any inflated sense of self-importance had helped to deflate any jealousy experienced by her team-mates, and she was popular with them. Apart from anything else, Caroline alone had the power to make the US team number one in the world and they all wanted to be winners. Anne Carpenter alone did not share this view. Having raised no particular support with her earlier remark, she tried again.

'I think it's really disgusting that she has the nerve to bring that army of supporters to a US ski team camp. Why can't she be like the rest of us?'

This was a cunning psychological ploy. It had already caused problems and several of the team coaches felt badly about it. Obviously Caroline's entourage was employed by the Montgomerys and there was no dilution of ski team funds, but it got up their noses that their own advice and training methods were to some extent indirectly questioned. Ingemar Jorgensen's stature as one of the great heroic figures of skiing had done little to quieten their discomfort.

Similarly it was felt that a personal private secretary was not a pressing necessity on a ski team camp, although Nigel had defused the objections by making himself indispensable to everyone, running errands, typing letters, and generally organizing people's lives. Then there was Skip Warner with his room full of tools and skiing equipment, his briefcase stuffed with the latest technical information, his mind full of magical methods for making two flat, narrow platforms travel down a hill just that few milliseconds faster than the competition, fractions of time that could transform a world class skier into a champion.

It was indeed an unusual situation, but there was little point in trying to ignore the fact that Caroline *was* different, completely different. If the ski team wanted the glory that she could bring them and the nation they represented, then they would all have to put up with it. It was not the sweetest medicine to take but on the whole it had been swallowed with a relatively good grace. Caroline had drawn the sting of the criticism. Nigel was needed to fend off the ubiquitous sporting press. Ing and Skip were old and trusted friends who were vital if she was going to bring home the bacon. There was another reason that Caroline was travelling with her retinue. At the end of the ski team camp in Portillo, Caroline would be staying on in Chile to set up her own training programme during the months of September and October before returning to rejoin the team for final preparations at Mount Hood in Oregon in November. Ingemar, Skip and Nigel had merely flown out a week or two earlier. Still, it was a sensitive issue and Anne Carpenter, with the sure-footed ease of the gifted trouble-maker, had seized on it.

A Caroline supporter at the Carpenter table answered back. 'Are you suggesting that she send them all home, Skip Warner as well?'

Anne Carpenter blushed. She hadn't realized it was public knowledge that she had the hots for him.

'I thought your knickers were going to burst into flames the other night when he stood next to you at the bar,' said somebody else.

That was too much. Anne Carpenter stood up and clumped away.

Her path of exit from the crowded deck took her past Caroline's table. If she couldn't get ahead she would have a crack at getting even. Spread a little unhappiness. She paused at the table, hovering over it like some ungainly, but nonetheless malevolent, bird of prey. The three men looked up but said nothing.

'Hello, Anne. Would you like to sit down?' said Caroline

pleasantly. 'We were just discussing whether or not it's a good thing to use a stone on edges after filing them. What do you think?'

'I think,' said Anne Carpenter maliciously, 'that you're full of bullshit and that it's disgusting that you use your money and stuff to try to be different from everybody else.' She gazed around the table smiling proudly at this achievement of new heights of nastiness, feeling perhaps that Skip Warner could not help but admire her *macho* plain speaking, her gritty determination. Actually Skip Warner thought she was a piece of shit and opened his mouth to tell her so. Ingemar's face darkened as he contemplated the quickest and most uncomfortable method of extinguishing the life of this loathsome creature. Even Nigel, normally easy-going, California laid-back, tightened his fists beneath the table. This lady was unbelievably uncool.

'Oh, piss off, Anne,' said Caroline quickly before any of her friends could do or say anything worse.

Ingemar, whose business it was to notice such things, thought that he detected a watery film in Caroline's eyes. This had to be stopped. Anne Carpenter's sniping had now turned into verbal assaults, and it was getting to Caroline. She was missing Miles but that was OK. Caroline had learned how to turn that into advantage. To have to put up with constant bad vibrations from this ugly skiing 'has-been' was another thing altogether and could not be tolerated. They were in the business of winning. Obstacles to victory would have to be eliminated at all costs.

Unwittingly, Caroline herself suggested the solution. 'It's all your fault, Skip. She's been twitching to get into your pants since we arrived and you turned her down, you sod. Now she's taking it out on me.' She laughed and lunged playfully at Skip's ribs.

Hell hath no fury like a woman scorned. The idea occurred to Skip and Ingemar at precisely the same time.

# II

'That's one beautiful sight,' said Caroline. She stood next to Ingemar three-quarters of the way up the highest mountain in the western hemisphere looking down on the treeless bowl that was the valley beneath, in which the large hotel nestled like a small pile of sugar cubes. The hotel itself was at ten thousand feet and Caroline's vantage point was seven thousand feet above it. Overhead the wap-wap-wap of the rented helicopter's rotors told them that Skip's watchful eye would be hovering over them during the descent, a guardian angel now, who had once been an avenging one. The three-week camp had been tough, but Caroline's personal training programme would be harder still. That was the problem with team training. The speed of the convoy as always was that of the slowest member, in this case the revolting Anne Carpenter. Today Caroline had the afternoon off from team workouts and could do what she liked best, ride the powder with Ing at her side, try out new skis with Skip, plan and work towards the achievement of her mighty ambition.

'I'm sorry about that dumb cunt yesterday,' said Ing. He wanted to assess the damage.

'It's no problem. I can handle it,' said Caroline, but the smile disappeared from her face as she spoke.

That settled it, thought Ingemar. He had a contingency plan to take care of that situation. 'OK, let's ski,' he said. 'Don't be kind to an old man.'

Caroline laughed at the compliment. Women still could not compete with men, especially with skiers of Ingemar's calibre.

Together they sped down the mountain, first Caroline and then Ingemar in the lead. When he wanted to demonstrate something that was going wrong he would move out in front and signal to Caroline that he was duplicating the mistake. Later she would pass him and show that she had corrected the fault. At the halfway point between mountaintop and valley their own descent would cross the regular *piste* and there was a hut there where they had agreed to stop for coffee, and an analysis of the morning's skiing.

'My God, those gates yesterday really got to my gastrocnoemius muscles,' said Caroline as she pulled off the racing goggles and arched her back. Ingemar bent down in the snow beside her while she stood, boots still in her skis, resting on her sticks. With both hands he rubbed soothingly at the tense calf muscles, first one leg and then the other.

'Oh, that's better, Ing. Thanks,' said Caroline as the stiffness began to ease beneath Jorgensen's expert fingers.

The coffee was strong, the caffeine adding to the natural mountain high. Caroline felt good – all thoughts of unpleasantness banished by the intense physical activity and single-minded concentration.

'Hey, this coffee reminds me of Spain. Their coffee is so good. You either have it *solo*, black as hell, or *cortado*, which means "cut off" – they sort of pass the milk over it, like the tiny dash of vermouth in a really good dry martini.'

She was quiet for a second. The coffee reminded her of Spain and Ingemar knew who Spain reminded her of. When he had met the New York flight to Denver on her return from Andalucia he had known at once that Caroline had fallen in love – that what he had feared most had come to pass. Caroline had seen the look on his face as, like the flamenco singer, he had peered into her soul.

'Don't worry, Ing,' she had said immediately. 'Winning still comes first. It isn't everything – it's the only thing.'

But if winning was still number one there was no shadow of a doubt about who was now number two and, thought Ingemar, everybody knows that number two tries harder. Over the intervening weeks Miles Parmere had emerged as a flesh-and-blood character, no longer existing as the caricature of the dissolute English aristocrat, and, although all his attributes were doubtless seen through the haze of love-tinted spectacles, there was enough hard fact to conclude that he was a very substantial figure indeed. Not that Ingemar had suspected that Caroline could have been captured by any other sort of person.

Many times Miles and Caroline had discussed how they would behave over the months that separated her from the triumph she so desperately wanted. They had decided they would not see each other or communicate in any way until she became the champion. On the day that happened Miles would fly immediately to wherever she was. They had not needed to discuss what would happen then. And so Caroline had made a strength out of what could have been a potential weakness. Every second that she spent training and practising would bring closer the time when she could have the two things that she wanted most in life. If she could win frequently enough and swamp the opposition she would accumulate sufficient points to win the championship by the end of January, or early February at the latest. So her absorption in the task at hand and dedication to it had been increased rather than diminished by her love – its energy harnessed firmly to the cause. That did not stop her thinking about him, but it prevented the thoughts from being negative ones.

Ingemar had never doubted that Caroline would beat the world, largely because she had the right attitude. There was nothing more important. Her reaction to being in love was just another example of it.

Miles Parmere had been as good as his word and had not tried to contact her. That in itself showed the sort of person he was, thought Ingemar. It never occurred to him that there was the remotest chance that Caroline's love was not reciprocated and, to see her now, her sunburned face vibrating with inner strength and power, blue eyes and short blonde hair glistening and shining, there would have been few who would have bothered to consider that eventuality.

They talked of how they would run the training programme when the ski team eventually returned home, leaving them behind in Chile.

'We should concentrate on the slalom and GS and leave the downhill for a bit,' said Ing. 'We'll attack it in four-day crash courses, running 850 gates a day. And we train like we race, no stopping, no giving up because of weather conditions, ruts, bent gates – nothing. We finish every course. The trouble with the team coaches is they let the skiers take a break if there's a good excuse because "it's only practice". You stop when you break your leg or your neck or hit the finish line. Nowhere else.'

'Thanks a *lot*,' said Caroline. 'I'm really looking forward to it. I always did enjoy a little torture.'

They both laughed. In the real world Ingemar would allow Caroline to give up if she had a cold. It would be Caroline who would never give up, who would continue long past the time when ordinary mortals would have considered discretion to have been the better part of valour.

'It'll be good to get rid of the others,' said Caroline. Actually Caroline enjoyed the company of everybody on the team with the one significant exception, but both she and Ingemar wanted to be free to concentrate exclusively on her, to give her limitless talent a chance to expand into skiing greatness.

'I wonder how the trailers are coming along,' said Ing.

At Ingemar's suggestion two big motor homes were being modified for Caroline's use on the hectic European circuit. It would be the answer to the noisy, depressing, overcrowded hotels in the God-forsaken corners of forgotten lands that had so undermined the young Caroline on her first World Cup tour. Like some latter-day singing star she would be able to sleep like a baby in air-conditioned comfort as the huge vehicles powered through the night, eating up the miles to the next competition site. Everything and everybody could be kept together. There would be the video machine for the action replays of the day's races, a conference room for the post mortems, a comfortable sitting area with tape decks, television and a sixteen-millimetre projector with the latest movies for after-the-race unwinding. There were rooms for equipment and for Skip's exotic ski machinery. Nigel had his own communications centre complete with Sony word processor and Apple home computer so that he could handle the press and keep in touch with Eleanor at home. There were hot tubs and showers and of course the vital massage table.

The galley with twenty-four-hour-a-day food service would make them completely self-sufficient. Caroline would not be bothered by the male skiing groupies that plague women on the World Cup circuit. Everything had been thought of to protect her from hassles, to allow her to concentrate totally on the job in hand. They had all enjoyed working on the specifications and Eleanor Montgomery had insisted that nobody even mention the price. The two mobile homes promised to be among the most expensive ever built, but every penny would be well spent, for now they were all looking forward to that part of the tour that everybody usually dreaded. Nigel, who cared about such things, had christened the two vehicles the NORTH and SOUTH CARO-LINERS, and despite half-hearted objections from the others had organized this legend to be painted on the outside. They were going to win, but they were also going to have fun doing it.

Two converted Ford Broncos would accompany the motor caravans, carrying security men, mechanics, and a British-trained doctor whose qualifications would be recognized throughout the European Economic Community. In each different country there would be close liaison with Montgomery Chemical officials who would put the organization and influence of the mighty international company at the disposal of Caroline's team.

'One thing's for sure,' said Caroline, 'the Russians won't have anything like them, or any of my other "disadvantages" for that matter.'

In some ways her remark was not far from the truth. Certainly the goldfish bowl of publicity in which Caroline was continually forced to swim was no problem for them. They were lean and hungry, fighting for comfortable flats and other privileges for their families, for prestige and fame in a country that valued athletic skills above all others, for the increased opportunities that success would bring to themselves and to their loved ones. They had incentives. Caroline had created her own incentives. She had nearly everything, but chose to believe that all she wanted was the one thing that she didn't have. It was in a way a superhuman *tour de force* of positive thinking, a triumph over the 'adversity' of her secure upbringing and environment. After all, it was not often that little rich girls became world-beaters. The poor were always doing it.

'I guess the Communists will be training as hard as we are,' said Caroline.

'They will be next month, but their coach, Tyagachou, likes them to have August off. Then they start with six and a half hours per day on the mountain with gymnastics in the evenings. They like to concentrate on technique and they do their practice runs quite slowly. That's a big difference. They're certainly going to be tough. They've got their eyes on the Sarajevo Olympics in 1984 and they badly want to do well this year.'

'It's Jana Soltysova I'm worried about in the downhill.'

'No problem. You're braver than her,' said Ingemar confidently.

'And Nadezhda Petrakeyva in the giant slalom?'

'She's the one to watch in my view. Still, by December the third you'll be better on the slalom than I ever was.'

'Let's watch those two tonight. I think we've got Petrakeyva at Waterville Valley,' said Caroline.

A few minutes later, the break over, they were rushing down the hill once again. It was the best feeling in the world, thought Caroline, as the wind resistance increased. Or so she had thought. Now she had something else to compare it with, and, as she tore down the mountain, the delicious warm glow spread upwards from her groin as she remembered the feeling of Miles murmuring his love into her ear as he penetrated to the very depths of her being. She squeezed her legs together, intensifying the sensation, at the same time willing her speed to increase. And then it all began to merge – the excitement, sexual desire, her love for Miles, the determination to win – building to a crescendo of 'synergy' in which the one became inseparable from the other. Every emotion, each thought, all her physical sensations were channelled in one direction, enlisted under one standard. By winning soon she would get to Miles more quickly, by giving herself totally to the

247

skiing she made possible the ultimate sexual fulfilment that she had experienced in Andalucia.

Surprised, Ingemar noticed her speed increase as he struggled to keep up. He tried in vain to analyse the shift in her style and technique that might explain it. Dear God, if she could reproduce this in the races it would be 'no contest'. But even as he sought for visible clues he knew that it was all in the mind. Caroline had achieved some potent synthesis of the will that would make her travel on skis faster than any woman had ever done before and his heart went out to his protégé – the girl who had given him back his life, made the future possible. God and he would protect her.

# III

Sunday mornings being the only ones on which a certain amount of fragility could be tolerated, Skip, Ingemar and Nigel tended to meet in Ingemar's room on Saturday night to talk things over, let off steam, and drink beer after Caroline had gone to bed. Now the three of them sat round a large case of San Miguel. They were talking about Vietnam.

'What I can't understand,' said Nigel, 'is why so many Vietnam veterans seem to be so screwed up. You can't turn on the TV or go into a bookstore without being assailed by some bleeding heart wimping on about the psychological damage it caused him – how he's been a lush or a junkie or both ever since. I can't believe you got all that after World War Two or Korea. What's so different about 'Nam? After all, Skip, you're the most normal freak I know.'

They all laughed. Nigel, coming from California, was automatically assumed by a Mid-Westerner like Skip to be totally off the wall.

'I think there are several reasons,' said Skip. 'First, nobody got any thanks for putting themselves through that hell. In fact you usually got abuse. You just didn't admit you were a soldier round that time. It could really screw up your sex life apart from anything else. You know, all the girls into peace, grass and flower power. You couldn't talk about it – all the bad experiences, the killings, the cruelty, the cowardice, the pointlessness of it all – because nobody wanted to know. A bit like the holocaust in Germany. When you can't talk about things they get out of perspective, and because you can't sort of work through them you begin to worry in an irrational sort of way. Like in World War Two everybody wanted to know what you did in the war, how many Germans you'd wasted. It was a real hero trip – saving America for democracy, preserving freedom and all that stuff.

'When you talk about napalming Vietnamese it sounds as if you've been beating up on the little guy, taking unfair advantage of somebody who was never a threat to Little Rock, Arkansas, in the first place. Nobody had any problems about atom-bombing the Japanese after Pearl Harbor. So if you can't get any respect for risking your life for your country, for putting everything you have on the line, you've got to get it some other way – maybe by becoming a patient. You know – "Look what you did to me. You made me a mental cripple by making me do all those terrible things. I was an ordinary gentle guy and it just destroyed me to do all that killing." That way you push the guilt back onto others. I know guys who are media stars for their Vietnam soul-searching and others who are model patients, really giving their shrinks something to chew on. "And then I took this woman that I'd just screwed and put my gun in her mouth – God, doc, I don't know whether I can tell you this . . . they called me a double veteran, but I don't know how I can live with all this *pain*." '

'That's right,' said Nigel. 'It seems to me that man has a pretty good capacity for being quite unmoved by dreadful deeds.'

Ingemar cut in. 'But, Skip, how do you feel about the war now?'

'With the benefit of hindsight, we shouldn't have been

there, but at the time it looked right to me. The South Vietnamese didn't want the Communists, but they weren't prepared to risk their lives to keep them out. I guess they hadn't got any spin dryers and washing machines to lose. Now they've had a chance to experience them first hand they're prepared not only to risk their lives to get out, but the proverbial fate worse than death as well. The Thai fisherman have done things to the boat people that would make your hair stand on end, encouraged incidentally by their own government. I didn't mind killing VC because they were as cold and callous as the Japs or the Nazis ever were. If you saw the things they did to the South Vietnamese villagers during the policy of intimidation in the countryside, you'd say that nothing was too bad for them. They were very nasty little people indeed. There were bits of the war I really enjoyed. I loved flying the helicopters – that was the most exciting thing on earth, and it was great to be really good at something. You were saving lives, too, getting the wounded off hot landing zones. If I believed in the cause enough it wouldn't be hard to persuade me to give it another go.'

'Wasn't Caroline's Englishman, Parmere, in the war too?'

'He was a Special Forces adviser, I think – you know, crawling around on his hands and knees slitting throats, and risking his balls. He must be a very tough cookie indeed. Should be able to look after her.'

Silence descended on the trio. Caroline was never far from their minds.

Ing broke it. 'This Carpenter girl has got to be stopped,' he said. He looked hard at Skip. 'Can you do it?'

Skip swallowed nervously. 'I don't know.'

'Nothing must get in the way, in November or on the circuit. If she keeps up that sniping at Caroline it could be a major distraction.' Ing was piling on the pressure.

'It'll be far tougher than Vietnam,' he added, the beginnings of a smile playing around his lips.

Greater love hath no man . . . thought Skip in quiet desperation.

# IV

Skip walked slowly into Anne Carpenter's bedroom with all the enthusiasm of a condemned man entering the San Quentin gas chamber. Unwillingly, he breathed in the unwelcoming scent of damp leather, old socks and other nameless but even more disturbing odours. The shapeless ass waddled in front of him, undulating unevenly. This was a bad business indeed.

Anne Carpenter sat down heavily and patted the bed beside her. 'Now come on, Skip, you just relax yourself while I get you a beer,' she said with what passed for a coquettish smile.

'Do you mind if I have some bourbon?' asked Skip. A last request? The bar in Anne Carpenter's room consisted of one warm bottle of beer, kept in a bottom drawer. Visitors to her boudoir had usually taken the precaution of getting well tanked up in advance. Skip had anticipated the poverty of liquid refreshment. To describe the whisky receptacle that he now produced from the pocket of his anorak as a hip flask would be grossly misleading. It looked like a cross between a jerrycan and a petrol drum. He removed the massive stopper and took in a few mouthfuls of Jack Daniels. It was not gin, but the courage was Dutch.

'Don't drink too much,' said Anne, her tone whining, wheedling, the 'don't spoil my fun' of the pampered child.

She returned with the opened beer bottle from which she now proceeded to drink. She wiped her mouth with the back of a podgy hand and Skip caught a glimpse of black fingernails. Beside him on the bed once again, her face contorted into a disgusting expression which, Skip imagined, must have sexual connotations, she began to fumble greedily, but inexpertly, at his zip. Skip muttered something about the lights.

'I like them on,' said Anne Carpenter firmly. 'It's better that way.'

Oh God. Fighting back a wave of nausea, which coincided with the overwhelming desire to poke both his fingers, rigid, into the pig-like eyes, Skip did nothing.

There was nothing delicate about Anne Carpenter and her fingers were no exception to this general rule. After a minute or two Skip's penis still lay accusingly on his trouser leg, as animated as a boiled shrimp. He took another swig from his flask. Had he got the dreaded brewer's droop?

'God, Skip, what's the matter?' His prick actually began to shrink.

'Hey, don't you like to ball?' Inexorably it shortened further.

Skip wondered for a second if it might disappear altogether, his penis, balls and scrotum all climbing back inside his body in a last-ditch attempt to avoid the rapacious attentions of this horrendous female.

He managed a sickly smile. 'It's just you make me nervous.' That was no lie.

This was the correct answer, immediately accepted as a valid excuse.

And then she went to work on him. With a few brisk, business-like movements she stripped to the waist. She was quite proud of her tits. Like a rabbit caught in the headlamps of a car, Skip watched, mesmerized, fighting back the desire to scream 'Don't let them out!' his mouth opening and closing fish-like as he contemplated his fate.

Like an avalanche, great mounds of flesh cascaded down, white and forbidding as the bra that had acted so valiantly as a dam was removed.

'Play with my titties while I give you head,' she commanded. Her teeth, vice-like, closed over the miserable appendage that now passed for his penis.

He'd simply got to get it up. Bo Derek, Brooke Shields, Jackie Bisset were all pressed into service. At last he felt the stirrings.

'That's better,' came a strangled mumble from between his legs.

Skip winced with pain as the tip of his awakening penis

sustained a 'Carpenter', and then, slowly but surely, he began to lose his temper.

If Anne Carpenter wanted to get fucked then he would make sure that she wouldn't be able to walk for a week. He'd put her out of commission that way. He reached down and took matters in hand, getting things straight. Anne Carpenter moaned her satisfaction.

Rock hard now, he toppled her back onto the floor where she lay on her back, panting, a beached whale, an upturned turtle, gross and grotesque. Leering up at him she parted her monstrous thighs, exposing the steaming jungle of her pubic hairs. 'Put it in me, Skip,' she pleaded.

Skip put it in. He rammed it in, stuffed it in, tore into her. His penis was like an avenging dagger, bent on overkill, inserted with all the considerable force of his powerful gluteal muscles. As Skip's piston hammered into her, Anne Carpenter began her obscene chant. Moaning, groaning, howling, yowling she urged him on to greater exertions, screaming for him to increase her pleasure. He took both dough-like buttocks in his hands and squeezed with all his might, pulling her towards him, impaling her even more deeply on his spear. She would have his finger marks on her ass for weeks. Still she yelled for more. He turned her over and stuck it into her bottom, but still the sweating hulk yelled her appreciation. Into her vagina again from behind, he crawled around the room violating her with all the strength at his disposal.

'Fill me up, Skip. Fill me up,' she shouted.

'I'm not some bloody gas station attendant,' thought Skip, his orgasm still as far away as ever.

Anne Carpenter came like a ton of bricks. Clearly she intended to experience many more orgasms as she continued to scream encouragement.

For what seemed like hours Skip gave it to her, until at last one particularly happy fantasy involving Bo Derek and a tub full of warm jelly helped him towards a massive, shuddering conclusion.

There was a long silence.

'Skip, you know, I've never been screwed like that

before – it was – really wonderful.' The love light was in her eyes.

'You won't be again, unless you lay off my boss,' said Skip. He had her by the short and curlies.

Caroline would have no more problems from Anne Carpenter or Skip would simply cut off her supply.

# V

Miles Parmere, looking bronzed and fit in a Huntsman lightweight suit, stood up to greet the fresh-faced fellow-countryman who bore down on him.

'Hello, Nicky. How very good to see you again. What would you like to drink?'

They both decided on gin and tonic – that old standby of Englishmen in the tropics – and Miles gave the order to the black waiter.

They settled back in the chintz-covered chairs of the Mount Nelson Hotel bar, the heart of Cape Town action, and talked of old times and mutual friends.

Miles was on a two-week tour of South Africa sharpening up contacts, dropping the name of the Union Bank, trying to do a little business and to avoid thinking too much about Caroline who, in a few days time, would be starting the World Cup competition at Val d'Isère in France. The months without her had passed at a snail's pace, but he had followed her progress in Chile and Oregon in the pages of the sporting press. In several interviews she had spoken enigmatically of somebody who was 'extremely important' to her and such insignificant morsels were sufficient to sustain him and to maintain his morale. He longed to talk to her, to write, to tell her how he felt, but he had kept his promise. After all, they would have a lifetime together.

He had known Nicky Oppenheimer for some years. Although the son of Harry Oppenheimer, mighty head of the De Beers empire, was a few years his junior, they had played a lot of golf together. On hearing that Miles was passing through, Nicky Oppenheimer had made a big effort to see him, and a company jet had flown him down from Kimberley that afternoon. There was something on Nicky's mind and Miles had picked up on it immediately. That suited Miles fine. He liked Nicky but he was a businessman now, whatever that meant. If there was something that he could do for Nicky Oppenheimer then maybe there was something Nicky could do for Miles. He was getting the hang of this commerce thing by slow degrees. Not very different from real life at the end of the day. Somebody asked you to shoot and you asked him back, or let him have a day's fishing. The difference was that in trade you had to keep reminding people that they owed you one.

Coming straight to the point was not, despite their protestations of bluntness and their desire to be thought 'down to earth', an Englishman's characteristic and it was not until halfway through dinner that Nicky Oppenheimer lent across towards Miles and became rather conspiratorial. Earlier they had talked of Miles' summer holiday in Spain and Miles had mentioned that he had met a 'marvellous American girl', nothing more. Now Oppenheimer put his cards on the table, face up.

'Listen, Miles. I've heard on the grapevine that you've been seeing quite a bit of Eleanor Montgomery's daughter, Caroline. Was she the American girl in Spain?'

The De Beers' grapevine was an extraordinarily sophisticated plant, shaming most of the exhibits in the botanical gardens at Kew.

'Good Lord, Nicky, how on earth did you know that?' Miles was astonished rather than shocked. There was no particular reason why his relationship with Caroline should be secret. In fact when you are in love the mere mention of the loved one's name by a third person has a certain charm. Love and possession, pride of ownership were never far removed.

Nicky's expression said that there were few things that De Beers could not know about if they set their minds to

255

it. The interesting question was why they should be interested. That would presumably emerge. Miles sipped at the delicious red Stellenbosch, noting that Nicky was hardly drinking at all. His curiosity was well and truly aroused. Oppenheimer ploughed on.

'Of course you know that Eleanor Montgomery and Charles Cabot Lodge are engaged.'

'I had heard that. In fact I sent them a congratulatory telegram the other day,' said Miles.

'Do you see a lot of them?' asked Nicky.

'Not as much as I intend to. To be quite honest I'm planning to marry Caroline. But why all these questions?'

'I'll be totally straight with you, Miles. We've been friends for a long time. Frankly, we're in a lot of trouble, or at least we could be.'

'Who?' thought Miles. 'You? De Beers? South Africa? The world in general? Us?' It was not entirely clear. Anyway Nicky had said he would be straight. Miles had indeed known him and liked him for a long time – long enough to know that he *would* be straight, by no means always the case when people prefaced their remarks by that particular promise.

'It may be that you are in a position to know something that could make the difference to the survival of our company.'

Heavy stuff. The survival of De Beers.

'Of course, if you were to give us the information that we are after, the Union Bank could become one of the most important financial institutions in the republic.'

Suddenly Miles's $250,000-a-year-salary began to look rather mean.

'And I am authorized to say that there would be a seat on the board of De Beers for you.'

'Good God,' thought Miles. 'I've been wasting my life. Hardly six months in my new job and I'm a star. But wait for it. No free lunches.'

'Come on, Nicky, spit it out.'

'OK, OK, Miles. Look, do you know anything about the diamond business?'

256

'I think I've digested most of your company's propaganda on the subject. Like everybody else I know that a Diamond is For Ever.' He smiled gently.

Nicky wondered how technical he needed to get. 'In the last few days we've had some very disturbing information from one of the Russians on our payroll. He's been very reliable in the past, and he's well placed to pick up the sort of information that he has just given us. He says that the Russians have every intention of dumping their very considerable reserves of fine gem stones onto the world markets in an all-out effort to destroy the diamond price. We don't know when and we don't know if it's a firm intention or just a contingency plan. We desperately need to know the answers to those two questions.'

'Can they do it?' asked Miles.

'Probably.'

'I'm not sure why you think that I can help. I don't sit in on Politburo meetings, you know.' At this rate it would not be long before he was invited to do just that, thought Miles.

'The word is that it's part of some US-Russian deal involving the Middle East and the destabilization of South Africa's economy. Cabot Lodge almost certainly knows, and possibly Eleanor Montgomery now that she's his fiancée.'

At last the fog was beginning to lift. Miles was closer to the horse's mouth than he had supposed. If he married Caroline, then, he supposed, Cabot Lodge would become some sort of surrogate father-in-law.

'If we know in advance we might be able to cobble together some sort of defence. Its a long shot, but otherwise we're dead.' He looked very serious.

'Listen, Nicky,' said Miles. 'I don't want to con you or mislead you into thinking I can deliver the goods when I can't. The fact is that I'm desperately in love with Caroline, but as you know she's immersed in this skiing thing and I've agreed not to see her until she wins. At the earliest that won't be until January. As far as Eleanor's concerned I'm afraid I'm guilty until proved innocent. I don't think that *her* grapevine has included much favourable information on me so far. I aim to change that, but at the moment I'm stuck with rather an unsavoury reputation, and you know what mothers are. Even if I was seeing them all the time I'm afraid it would stick in the throat to pass on anything that was told to me in confidence . . . and the information that you are after would presumably be very confidential indeed. I can't imagine Cabot Lodge blabbing it out over a rubber of bridge on a "guess what I heard at the White House today" basis.'

Nicky saw the logic in that. He looked desperately disappointed. 'I quite understand, Miles. It was a long shot. You know – I thought perhaps you might know whether or not Eleanor had been selling her diamonds or anything like that.'

'Not close enough,' said Miles firmly. 'Wait a minute,' he added. 'I've got a great idea. Get one of the branches of your grapevine to check the stones on her engagement ring. That ought to be public information. It would go against the grain for Cabot Lodge to lash out a quarter of a million on diamonds if he knows they're about to become worthless.'

'My word, you're right,' said Nicky. 'That's a very good idea. It's clutching at straws but fortunes have been won and lost on less.' He brightened up for a while but became a bit *pianissimo* after dinner, and it was not late when he left the Mount Nelson.

Miles walked thoughtfully to his room. He possessed no diamonds at all. No problem on that front. Most of his acquaintances did. He could not suppress a certain amount of *schadenfreude* on that score. He thought for instance of Camilla Ponsonby's family heirlooms, her pride and her joy, and, incidentally, the magnet to all those dreary fortune-hunting husbands. Diamonds would not be the only things to discover that demand had fallen off dramatically.

He telephoned room service. A whisky and soda would round off the evening well. No ice. He wondered if the Union Bank had any interest in diamonds. He had seen the earlier announcement about a mining venture with the Umpalans but had not bothered to discuss it with Harry. As far as he knew the bank had no exposure at all to the gemstone market, but it was hot financial information. Certainly they should know. Nicky had asked him to be discreet but had not sworn him to silence, the *quid pro quo* for his engagement ring suggestion. What would the time be in Florida? Saturday and a seven-hour time difference. It would be four pm in Florida. Harry would probably be knocking off the girl he had got to replace little Susie. Miles wondered what had happened to her as he dialled the number. She had disappeared during his time in Spain and nobody seemed to know where she was. He had rather liked her.

'Harry? Miles Parmere.'

'Yeah, what gives? How's South Africa? Picked up any deposits?' Harry sounded cheerful.

'I've seen a lot of people. Maybe something will turn up. The reason that I'm ringing is that I've just had dinner with an old friend of mine, Nicky Oppenheimer. He's on the board of the De Beers company and the son of the chairman. He's just come out with some amazing story about diamonds. I wondered if the Union Bank had any interest in that area.'

There was a long silence.

'Are you still there?' asked Miles.

'What story?' Miles could have sworn that Harry's voice had changed.

'Well, if I didn't trust him completely I'd have hardly believed it, but he maintains the Russians are about to flog all their diamonds and put the skids under the diamond price. Something about a secret deal with the American government involving Arab oil and undermining the South African economy – all sorts of things like that. De Beers are really worried. They seem to think the Russians have the power to do it.'

A strange noise winged its way across the wire. The strangulation of a cat? No, it sounded as if Harry had choked on a piece of steak. If that was the case Miles hoped, albeit half-heartedly, that somebody would be around to perform the Hemlich manoeuvre.

'Are you OK? Is this a bad time? Perhaps I should call back.'

'Stay on the line,' the voice barked. 'Say all that last bit again, very slowly.'

Harry was clearly on something, thought Miles. Carefully he repeated the potted version of Nicky Oppenheimer's story.

'Oh, my good God,' said Harry Fox.

There was another long silence.

'Listen,' said Fox at last. 'Do exactly what I tell you and you'll get a raise bigger than you ever dreamed of. Call this Oppenheimer first thing in the morning and pump him for all he's got on this. Get as much information as you can and write it all down. Everything. I want every word he told you – when he blew his nose, when he scratched his balls. The moment you've talked to him again get on the next plane back to Miami – charter a plane if there isn't one. I'll meet you at the airport. And Miles, don't mention this to another living soul. Not anyone. Understand?'

'Sounds as if you've just bought a diamond or something,' said Miles cheerfully.

'Or something,' said Harry as he rang off.


# VI


Miles was tired after the long flight from South Africa, but Harry Fox, meeting him at Miami airport, went for him like a pickpocket. Gripping him firmly by the arm, he half pulled him towards the waiting car, while porters and drivers fussed and hovered organizing the luggage. The big car pulled out and headed downtown on highway 836.

There was not a lot that Miles could add to the information that he had given Harry on the telephone, but he had to repeat it all again anyway.

'So this Oppenheimer guy is pretty sure that Cabot Lodge would know exactly what is going down,' said Harry at last, his face an unusual shade of grey beneath the sun tan.

'That's right. Apparently the US government is well and truly in on it – that's if the whole thing's not the figment of somebody's fertile imagination. Tell me, Harry, why is it so important to you? I had to cancel a very promising week-end with the Schlesingers to hurry back.'

'That's for me to know,' said Harry rudely.

Miles said nothing. Harry's manners were appalling. He had about as much charm as a London airport taxi driver.

'And Cabot Lodge and Eleanor Montgomery are going to get knotted,' said Harry almost to himself, thinking aloud.

'So it would appear,' said Miles coldly.

'Do you think Cabot Lodge spills the beans to her when he's on the job?'

Harry was in a foul mood. The Englishman's calm exterior was getting to him. Here he was fighting for his life, for everything that he possessed, and this supercilious cunt was looking at him with all the enthusiasm reserved for dog shit on the bottom of a shoe. Miles fucking Parmere, English bloody lord. He would like to feed him to the barracudas. So for that matter would Nero Castelli. Perhaps he would let him. But not yet. For the moment he was still useful.

Miles was furious. As far as he was concerned Harry was hovering on the brink. He had just insulted Caroline's mother and although he could not be expected to know the significance of that he would not get away with it again.

'Well, you'll have to go and see Eleanor,' said Harry abruptly. 'Find out exactly what she knows about this whole thing and if she knows nothing then get her to find out from her boyfriend.' He said all this as if he was sending out an office boy for the *Miami Herald*.

It was unlike Harry to be so undiplomatic but the strain of the last twenty-four hours had been unbearable. It was all beginning to unravel, to run away from him.

'No way,' said Miles firmly. 'Even if I could I wouldn't. I'm intending to marry her daughter. I wouldn't dream of asking her to prise such information out of her fiancé.'

'What?' said Harry, eyes narrowing.

'You heard what I said.' Miles spoke calmly, evenly.

'You're telling me,' said Harry, his voice loud and rasping, 'that you won't do as I say and ask some stuck-up whore what gossip she picks up from her prick of a boyfriend?' Harry was angry, deliberately trying to be offensive. 'God,' he went on. 'Fucking Cabot Lodge must be like making it with an ice-pick.'

Suddenly the fingers of Harry Fox's left hand did not feel like they belonged to him any more. They were being held tightly in Miles' right hand and it was not a fairy's caress. Already the intense pain was shooting up the nerve fibres in his arm and he watched with a detached fascination as the fingers went first red and then a bloodless white. He tried to move his arm and then his whole body to relieve the pressure and ease the pain, but both continued inexorably to increase. A flashback in his mind showed him the bloody guest room, Castelli's hired help lying in various stages of decomposition and disarrangement on the discoloured carpet. Oh God, he'd forgotten about Miles Parmere.

Miles pushed his face close to Harry as he spoke. 'You disgusting little man. Now say you're sorry like the gentleman you're not or I'll break your fingers one by one.'

Not for a millisecond did Harry doubt him. 'I'm sorry,' he said.

Like lovers they continued to hold hands. That was where the similarity ended.

'I'd tell you where to put your job,' said Miles, his voice as hard and cold as a glacier, 'if for one moment I thought there'd be room for it among all the other garbage. Just make sure,' he continued, 'that we never meet again. I might remember how much I dislike you.'

Despite himself, Harry, who had gone quite white, now began to shake. He was beginning to lose control. He'd got to get it back or he'd lose everything. Literally everything.

Caroline stood all alone at the starting gate of the giant slalom course. This was it. December 4th at Val d'Isère, France, and the second race of the World Cup tour. This was where the women would be sorted out from the girls. She knew she would win, but she intended to humiliate the opposition. Take them apart. Destroy their self-confidence. Flatten them. Psychologically it was important.

On the previous day she had demolished the other competitors in the downhill, but she had been expected to win there. Downhill was her discipline. She was the one to beat as holder of the Downhill Cup. What nobody had bargained for was her incredible time. Nobody had even come close, including Soltysova, and few if any of the spectators had ever before seen a woman go so fast on skis. It had been little short of devastating and the joy in the US camp had only been equalled by the alarm and despondency among the teams of the other nations. Still, the optimists among her opponents were clinging to the hope that her slalom technique would not have improved markedly from the previous competition, maintaining that she must have concentrated totally on the downhill in her training. Caroline intended to show them how wrong they were.

To produce crushing downhill and giant slalom victories in the first two days of the four-month marathon would give her psychological flying speed that would make her very difficult to catch. So they had concentrated on running gates in August, September and October in Chile and again in November at Mount Hood. It was a far harder and more comprehensive programme than anybody else would dare to attempt. Most coaches would have emphasized the danger of going stale, of losing the zest for skiing, that fatal malaise that had laid low many a potential champion and led many to cut back drastically on training. No such problems plagued Caroline. As she stood poised for the descent she was as eager and excited as she had ever been before. First she would win and then she would allow herself the luxury of telephoning Miles. After all, rules were made to be broken and she would have earned it. Even the thought of it would be good for a second off her time. She had a substantial lead already after the first run. If she wanted to she could play safe, take it slowly, diminishing the danger of a fall that would put her out of the running, but that was not Caroline's style at all. On this, her second and final run, she would make the first descent look as if it had been performed by a one-legged cripple with a glass eye.

A thousand cameras zoomed in on her and the crowd hushed in anticipation. Was the legend of a skiing superstar about to be born? Caroline tensed all the muscles in her body and stared hard at the third gate. Don't let the gates come to you. Go after them. Improve on gravity. Think speed. She drew herself up to her full height and then pushed down as hard as she could on the sticks. When her shinbone hit the timing wand she already had considerable forward momentum.

Caroline Montgomery came out of the starting gate like the cork out of a bottle of shaken champagne, skating and poling with her skis for added speed. She did not even bother to turn for the first three gates – instead she skated and stepped around them in what was essentially a continuation of her start. Hands forward to reduce wind resistance and crouched low, she kept body movement to a minimum as she ate up the gates. This was the steep part of the course and the spectators with stop watches were already chattering to each other that she was going very fast indeed. Heading for a fall, some pessimists thought. Caroline was actually enjoying herself. She was attached to the mountain, her skis an extension of her legs, no less a part of her body than eyes or fingers. In turn the skis were a part of the hill, joined to the snow like the sky to the sea. All the time her mind searched for ways to go faster as the computer in her visual cortex read the ground ahead processing the information, the motor neurones feeding it to the heaving muscles at what seemed the speed of light. She saw the flat coming up and took her skis off the hard edge so as not to lose downward thrust. At last she could see the finish. Hello, Miles. She didn't turn out of the last gate, keeping her skis pointing straight down the mountain. As she flipped a hand forward to break the timing beam the crowd went wild. Nobody had seen a giant slalom completed like that and already, before the official time was announced, the reporters were scurrying for telephones, talking frantically into short-wave radios. 'America's skiing Christmas present', 'Caroline Montgomery brings home the bacon', 'American skier conquers the world' – the phrases poured onto tape as the motor drives whirred and the networks hustled each other at the finish line to get the interviews. Caroline stood breathing heavily at the foot of the course as skiing groupies and journalists clustered round, and then, pushing through the crowd, came Ing, tears pouring down his cheeks.

'Oh God. Oh God, Caroline,' he wept as he held her in his arms. 'You killed them. You killed them.'

Skip and Nigel helped to clear the way through the ecstatic crowd as the official time was announced to delirious shouts of disbelief. Caroline had not only killed the opposition she had buried them as well. All across America in the bars of the skiing villages, in the ski lifts and on the slopes the word would be flashing from mouth to mouth. America had produced the greatest woman skier the world had ever known. Caroline Montgomery, home grown in San Antonio, Texas, and Aspen, Colorado, the genuine article, the real thing.

The CBS reporter thrust a microphone in her face as she was half-carried away. 'What are you going to do now, Caroline?'

'Call my boyfriend,' she said.

'Miles, Miles, I just had to call. I won again today. I'm so excited.'

'You bet you did,' said Miles. 'That wasn't winning, that was cold-blooded murder. I knew the second you'd finished. I had an open line through to Val d'Isère for both races.'

And then they talked of their love, stronger now than ever.

'The moment this is over, you know we're going to get married.'

Neither of them had actually mentioned it before.

Caroline did not pause. 'Of course we are,' she said. 'Didn't I tell you?' They both laughed with happiness.

That night as Caroline lay in the big bed, heading south towards Cortina in Italy for the next races, she tried hard to imagine how anybody could be more happy. There would be a break from the competition from December 20th to January 6th. She and Miles had agreed on the telephone to see each other then before the races started up again. He had fallen out with Harry Fox and resigned from the Union Bank, so the job wouldn't stop him coming to her the moment she had won. The future looked very good indeed.

# VIII

'Frankly, Mr Fox, the Secretary of State will not be available to talk to you. He has asked that you state your business to me.'

So much for Harry's breakthrough into the heartland of the establishment. He might as well have been trying to sell life insurance. Cabot Lodge had been all over him like a hot rash at '21'. Now all of a sudden he was a leper.

Harry, terrified of disseminating the diamond rumour too widely, protested bitterly, but to no avail. Eventually he passed a question to Cabot Lodge. Did he know anything about Russian sales of diamonds? The answer had been unequivocal. The Secretary of State had no knowledge at all of such a scheme, very much doubted that it existed. That had not reassured Harry at all. Cabot Lodge was bound to deny knowledge of the plan. If the government had done a deal with the Russians it would have been a secret one. What Harry wanted and expected was a nod and a wink, a gentle intimation, some oblique remark accompanied perhaps by a 'significant' expression that would tell Harry that from now on diamonds were strictly for the birds. Instead he was being avoided, and rudely so. Why? It was a bad sign. It seemed that the doors that had so recently opened were already slamming shut in his face. The 'Harry Fox as friend of the rich and powerful' show had not stayed on the road long.

Harry had spent the next twenty-four hours on the telephone to Umpala, a country whose telephone communications system posed no threat at all to Ma Bell in the technical sophistication stakes. He had hardly found anybody there who was prepared to admit that Seretse Mwamba existed, let alone tell Harry how he could contact him. Mwamba had to all intents and purposes disappeared into the secret recesses of the dark continent. He had his hands on Harry's $300 million. He didn't have to talk to him as well.

That left Eleanor. She was his only chance and it was a slim one. For four days he had tried in vain to reach her, repelled constantly by a solid wall of anonymous New England accents. It was Friday and Harry's nerves were in pieces. He dialled the New York number once again.

'I'm very sorry, Mr Fox, but Mrs Montgomery can't come to the telephone at the moment. She said to say that this has been a bad week for her. Perhaps you should try again on Monday.' The assistant sounded pleased at this. The clear implication was that Monday, too, would be a disastrous day for the contacting of Eleanor Montgomery.

'Christ,' said Harry to the empty room as he rang off. She was giving him the brush off. He knew the form. Had Parmere got to her already? Or Cabot Lodge? The bitch. He'd lent her a billion dollars and saved her millions and she wouldn't talk to him on the telephone.

Harry sat down and poured himself a substantial Jack Daniels. He must stay calm. For the hundredth time he weighed the options. There were several possibilities. First, the story was totally untrue, an unfounded rumour dreamed up to worry De Beers, possibly by the Russians themselves. That was distinctly unlikely. Had Parmere made it up to irritate Harry, to pay him back for some forgotten insult? That was out of the question. Not at all Parmere's style. He tended to deal up front, thought Harry, massaging still-stiff fingers. The second possibility was that the story was true in every respect, that the sword of Damocles was indeed hovering over the diamond price. In that case if he did nothing he would be ruined and lucky to escape with his life. The third possibility lay somewhere between the first two. The Russians had considered the option, but were as yet uncertain whether or not to put it into operation. Perhaps they had actually discarded it or were in the process of so doing. Whichever way he looked at it Harry could not get away from the fact that he just had to know what had been decided. Either he had nothing to worry about and could continue to build on his past success, or he was facing disaster.

So it was down to Eleanor. She did not like him. That had always been clear, but it hadn't mattered before. He had been in a position to give her something she wanted. Now it was the other way around. Even if she knew of the Russian intentions, why should she tell him? She would be putting her relationship with Cabot Lodge on the line to do so and for what? For his thanks? Forget it. But he had to try, had to see her. Obviously the telephone was a dead-end street. He would have to go to Aspen at the week-end. Knock on the door. Ring the bell. Trick or treat? His heart sank at the thought, but it hadn't far to sink. It had been bumping along on the bottom ever since Miles' call from Cape Town.

# IX

The English butler stood in the doorway of the Montgomery home in Aspen and looked Harry up and down. With the finely developed skill of his species he all at once made a diagnosis of Harry's personality, a judgement upon it, and at the same time communicated his verdict in a single, all-embracing facial expression of global disdain and disapproval, even withering scorn. Harry was clearly something that the cat had brought in and he peered over Harry's shoulder to see if any other detritus had arrived at the same time, a dead bird perhaps, the remains of some other less easily identified beast flattened on the road?

What he said was: 'Is Mrs Montgomery expecting you?'

Combined with the look on his face it sounded like: 'Poor Mrs Montgomery will need intensive care if she is to be confronted by anybody as ghastly as you.'

'Not exactly, but it is extraordinarily urgent that I see her without delay. My name is Harry Fox.' The butler's formality was contagious.

'I'll see if she's in' meant 'I'll be back in a second to tell you she's out'.

Harry was not invited in. Did they think he would steal the silver? Piss on the carpet? Stink the place out? As he stood on the doorstep like some unwelcome carol singer Harry vowed that if this all came out OK he would make some significant changes in his approach to life. He would return to type, hire some muscle, get back into the old ways. He had looked down his nose at Castelli, scorned him for not moving with the times, but he had been wrong. Castelli never stood on doorsteps, got shat on by butlers. He made people sweat a lot, bleed a little. There was much to be said for that method of dealing with life. For many years it had served Harry well. And this social climbing meant that ninety-nine per cent of the time you had your mouth full of piles and your face full of shoe leather. These people just *knew* where you came from, so you might as well take advantage of those origins and the strengths that they provided. The only thing that anybody respected at the end of the day was power and Mao Tse-Tung had known where that ultimately resided – in the barrel of a gun.

The butler was back. His previous manner, his own spontaneous artistic creation, had clearly been reinforced by the Montgomery seal of approval because his distaste was now quite definitely more pronounced. 'Step this way please, *sir!*' The last word, positively dripping with sarcasm, was offered as a hilarious joke, a wild parody.

Like a small, grubby schoolboy on his way to the headmaster's study, Harry followed the haughty butler across the Persian carpets of the cavernous hall. He was ushered into a large study where Eleanor sat behind an oak desk in conference with a serious-looking, business-suited assistant. She stood up as he entered the room.

'What a surprise, Mr Fox.' Stalactites and stalagmites appeared to fill the room, so cold was his reception.

'I am afraid you have found me desperately busy and I can only spare you a few minutes. This is Mr Newton, one of my legal counsel.' So what do you want, Harry Fox, friend of the Mob? thought Eleanor. Whatever it is you're not going to get it from me. She noticed immediately that the self-confidence that had always characterized him was remarkable in its absence.

Harry did not actually stutter, but the overall effect of his words conveyed the impression of a mild speech impediment.

'I very much needed to speak to you on what really, what is in fact a matter of quite considerable, is actually of very great importance to me.'

Eleanor smiled at his obvious discomfort. So you lent me drug money did you, you fearful little creep, she thought, letting the disapproval shine through in her eyes.

Harry stumbled on. 'It would mean a lot to me if we could talk in confidence.' He looked helplessly at the faceless lawyer.

'Oh, I have no secrets from Mr Newton. In fact I'd prefer him to be here.'

There was no mistaking what that meant. Harry tried to hold on to himself. If he had to tell many more people about the Russians and their manoeuvres he would end up doing the job for them, starting a rumour that would sink the price without their having to lift a finger. He steeled himself as he explained his predicament.

'And so, you see, it would be of very great benefit to me to know if the rumour is true, and also the timing of the Russian operation. It occurred to me that you might know something yourself, or would be able to discover something from Mr Cabot Lodge.'

Throughout Harry's tense monologue Eleanor had sat still, looking him up and down, a satirical smile on her face. Cat and mouse time. She was going to play with him, he saw, with a sinking feeling in his stomach. Eleanor's long elegant fingers toyed with the Santos ballpoint.

'How *fascinating*,' she said at last. 'Well, well, well. Isn't that a remarkable story, Mr Newton?' Mr Newton was not about to disagree, looked as if he was congenitally incapable of so doing.

Eleanor thought hard. That was one state secret Charles had not passed on to her. Good for him. No wonder he had been so adamant about rubies and emeralds for the engagement ring. A man who had a healthy respect for the conservation of wealth when no discredit was attached to it would make a good husband. So it looked as if Harry Fox was about to be taken to the cleaners on the Umpalan loan. In the ordinary way she would have cared about that, even perhaps offered to help out, but she remembered President Wayne's remarks. Justice were investigating this man. He was a hoodlum, a cheap crook, and he had conned her. He deserved everything that he would get.

'But if all this is true, Mr Fox, it would appear that your goose is well and truly cooked anyway,' said Eleanor. 'If, as you say, the loan principal has already been transferred to Umpala.' Her whole demeanour suggested that this culinary achievement would be in no way unpalatable to her.

At least I'd be alive and well, living in Paraguay, and

still with the potential to get my revenge on you and your revolting bedmate, you self-satisfied cunt, he longed to say. That wouldn't do in front of the lawyer. A livid red colour had revitalized Harry's cheeks, but he managed to remain silent.

'For myself,' Eleanor continued, 'I have no knowledge at all of this ingenious Russian scheme, although from what I know of the diamond industry I should say that it has every chance of success. If I understand you correctly, however, you are also asking that I attempt to prise this information, which must certainly be a state secret, from my friend the Secretary of State and pass it on to you.'

Harry nodded bleakly. The way she had phrased that confirmed his worst suspicions. Eleanor Montgomery would not help him. It had been a long shot.

Eleanor's patronizing, mocking manner disappeared abruptly, to be replaced by cold anger. 'I find it unbelievable that you can stand here in my house and ask me to persuade my fiancé to betray his country's interests, to break his oath of office. To be frank, Mr Fox, I don't like you and I never have, but I did not suspect that you would sink to such depths. Now I suspect that you and your friends have little comprehension of how one should behave in a civilized world. I must ask you to leave this house at once. Do not attempt to speak to me or to any members of my family ever again. In future talk to my lawyers.' With a nod she indicated Newton.

And then, suddenly and paradoxically, Harry felt better. It was all over: the charades, the politeness, the genteel jockeying for position, the wanking about. Out in the open at last. Now it was the naked struggle for survival, the streets of New York once again, the fists, the guns, the terror. He would hurt Eleanor Montgomery for what she had just done to him. She would pay in blood and tears for her insufferable arrogance. He, Harry Fox, promised her that.

Mr Newton stood up to see him out but Harry was already at the door, a new spring in his step, purpose in his movements once again, murder in his soul. By the time he had reached the front door the idea had come to him, struck him like a thunderbolt from on high. Nourished by hate and fed by venom, it grew as he climbed into the waiting car. On the way to Aspen airport he refined the scheme, tested it in his mind on the Rocky Mountain Airways flight to Denver. By the time he was back in Miami he had developed it into a foolproof plan that would achieve all his objectives at once. He would revenge himself on Eleanor, Cabot Lodge and Parmere and, at the same time, secure the information that he craved.

He would teach them all a thing or two about horror.

# Chapter 10

## I

Little Susie lay crumpled at the bottom of Castelli's
football-field-sized bed – a sad rag doll, beaten and bowed.
Deathly white against the jet-black sheets, she no longer
looked like jail bait. Indeed poor Susie would not have
been a success as bait of any kind. No longer succulent
enough. Her tiny frame was meanly covered now with
flaccid, unhealthy-looking skin. No longer did the sun
shine on Susie, either metaphorically or in reality. Nero
Castelli liked her to while away her time in shaded rooms
– his own equivalent of the Arab veil. If she was getting it
from the great Nero Castelli then she should not be exposed
to the lascivious glances and thoughts of lesser mortals.
For Susie this was as severe a nutritional handicap as if she
had been forbidden food and water. Now she was indeed
a drooping plant, fading, off-colour. If she had leaves they
would be falling. All along her arms was the evidence of
her habit, scars, thrombosed and occluded veins, track
marks, the legacy of inexpert needlework as she had
hurried to force the heroin into her bloodstream. Both
arms had long since ceased to be a reliable point of entry
to her vascular system and already the tiny tell-tale pin-
pricks were beginning to appear on the backs of her feet.

The six months were nearly up and both Castelli and
Fox had been right. There would be no queues to have her
back. Susie was fourteen and her future looked black. But
she didn't care about the future – was interested only in
the immediate present, for the truth was that she was short
of smack, all strung out, on the edge of withdrawal. This
was one of Castelli's little games. He actually liked to watch
the pain, the debasement and the degradation, the humili-

ation as she begged him for the drug, the almost manic enthusiasm with which she indulged in his sexual fantasies when she knew the prize would be a substantial fix.

Street-wise, she had a shrewd suspicion that Castelli was about to move her on and she was enough of a realist to know that Harry Fox would not have her back. Further than that she hadn't gone. The burning question was how to score from Castelli now, this minute. She sniffed hard and held on to her stomach. The cramps would be starting anytime. Her eyes watered and her head ached as the waves of nausea began to wash over her.

'For God's sake, Castelli, I've got to have some stuff. I feel terrible. What do you want me to do?' There was a whining quality to her plea.

Today Castelli didn't want her to do very much. Had he been a truthful man he might have replied, 'I just want to see you suffer.' But Castelli possessed no virtues, especially not that of honesty.

Susie crawled up the bed to where Castelli lay, like some latter-day version of a desert caliph, munching grapes and watching a football game on the larger-than-life Mitsubishi TV projection screen. The black silk dressing gown with its gold Chinese lettering was open, and his monstrous phallus, resembling some exotic African club, a dark and sinister weapon of aggression, lay somnolent on his stomach. Susie grabbed at it with both hands in quiet desperation. So weak had she become, so thin and wasted, she looked as if her single hand wasn't strong enough even to lift Castelli's massive penis. He watched her out of the corner of one eye as he continued to cram the large Muscat grapes into his mouth. Like a sleeping snake awakening slowly to the chanter's flute his prick began to move in response to Susie's manipulation. Susie's mind was working hardly at all but she knew that if she could make him come then she would get her fix. Her hands snatched and rubbed at his prick, pulled at his testicles. There was no denying that she had lost her touch. For all the pleasure she was giving she might just as well have been wearing boxing gloves. That was what Castelli thought anyway,

275

because, reaching forward, he hit her suddenly and without warning, a vicious back-hand blow across the face. Susie's weakened body was in no state to take such treatment and she was unbalanced anyway. She toppled sideways off the bed, ending up in a crumpled heap on the floor, crying gently, her face buried in the deep pile of the carpet.

'That was it,' thought Castelli. 'The scrap heap for Susie.'

The telephone rang by the side of his bed. Damn. He had been about to teach Susie one of his 'lessons'.

'Nero? This is Harry Fox.'

'Yeah, Harry. I'm a bit busy right now.'

'Listen Nero, we're in big trouble – the biggest. We've got to meet immediately.'

'What do you mean – trouble?'

'I can't talk on the phone, but the Umpalan thing has come undone.'

'Christ!' Castelli went white. $25 million of his own cash, $250 million of the Mob's. 'That can't go wrong. You guaranteed it,' he protested, his heart thumping in his chest.

'There might be a way out – if we work together and hang in there tough.'

'Where do we meet?' asked Castelli. He felt sick.

'Somewhere private. I've got a plan, but it's vital that people don't think we're working as a team.'

'Remember the old meeting place,' said Castelli, 'the one we used when we were setting up Union?'

'Meet you there in half an hour,' said Harry as he rang off.

Castelli looked at the telephone as if it was an instrument of God's divine retribution and then, screaming blasphemies at the top of his voice, he hurled it with all his might at the television screen.

Through the pain and humiliation, Susie, still lying on the floor, took in the situation. Something had gone badly wrong, something involving Harry Fox, that necessitated a secret meeting place. Was this her chance to get even and kill two birds with one stone? She would keep her ears open and remember everything. She might be half dead, but perhaps she could take them with her.

# II

Caroline flicked on the switch of the sauna. That was what she needed – the complete relaxation that the intense heat would provide. The motor trailers hadn't quite run to that. Perhaps next year . . . It would take about twenty minutes to hit the temperature she liked best. She walked out of the shower area across the oak floor of the deserted gymnasium, past the pool, and pressed her nose against the picture window to watch the sun set over the town of Aspen. God, it was good to be home.

Her procession through Europe had indeed been a triumphant one. Like the conquering legions of ancient Rome she had scattered the skiing barbarians before her. Her eagles hovered over the abandoned camp fires. Only the Russian Nadezhda, fighting a brave rearguard action, had been able to keep within sight of her. Caroline had won everything there was to win, and the unfortunate sporting press had long since despaired of finding new adjectives to describe her brilliance. At both Bad Gastein in Austria and Grindelwald in Switzerland, the toughest courses on the tour, her margins of victory had expanded to previously unheard-of proportions. She had the maximum possible number of points and, in the absence of serious accident, was now beyond reach. She had only to finish the competition to win all four cups – the grand slam that she wanted so much. The Russian had stuck limpet-like to Caroline. With monotonous regularity the scoreboard read:

Montgomery Caroline USA 1
Petrakeyva Nadezdha USSR 2

but Caroline's lead was always embarrassingly substantial. The persistence and determination of the Communist skier meant, however, that Caroline could never afford to relax, to slacken her efforts or reduce concentration. If she were to break a leg, for instance, the Russian would, on present form, win solidly throughout January and February and end up as champion. That suited Caroline fine. She had no intentions of backing off even when her points score put her ultimately beyond reach. There was the US team to be considered. Caroline intended them to win the championship and that meant heavy scoring on her part until the bitter end.

But now, at last, she had a breathing space, two blissful weeks away from the competition – until the meat-grinder started again on January 6th, when the circus was coming to her own home town, Aspen, Colorado. Marvin Davis' Aspen Skiing Corporation was already preparing for it in an orgy of massive spending. It would be a skiing carnival, a joyful celebration of the local girl's glorious victories, the favourite daughter who had learned her skiing on the Aspen slopes and had ventured forth to humble the world. There would be cook-outs and rock bands, torchlight processions and beacons on the mountains, country music and clogging, fireworks and free-style skiing. Already the hotels for miles around were booked to the hilt, waiting for the deluge, as all around America the skiing buffs packed up their woodies, paid their bills and locked their houses and prepared to descend on the Rocky Mountains of Colorado for the greatest jamboree in the history of American skiing. Everybody wanted to be able to say that they had seen the great Caroline Montgomery destroying the Europeans on the mountains of her childhood. President Wayne himself, it was rumoured, would be there for the downhill race.

For the moment though, Eleanor being still in New York, Caroline was alone. She had flown in from Munich, using a fictitious name to avoid the rapacious press, a day earlier than had been planned, leaving Ing and the others to return a day later. Caroline needed the time to be by herself to digest the experiences of the last few weeks and to prepare herself mentally for Miles' arrival in two days' time. It had been nearly six months since he had held her in his arms and kissed her goodbye at the airport in Seville. The day after tomorrow he would fly in from Florida to be with her once again. The thrill of excitement shot through her at the thought. Miles was no longer working for the Union Bank, but he had stayed on in Florida, fishing and skin diving with his friend Roy Felty, waiting for Caroline to return to America for the Christmas break. She longed to see him. The long wait had sharpened rather than diminished her desire for him. Absence had, as it was supposed to do, strengthened the fondness of her heart.

Caroline pulled off the Sperry Topsiders, which she wore with no socks and, as she headed towards the sauna, the big turtle-necked sweater joined them on the floor. The two perfect, conical breasts pushed straight forward – the pink nipples forming a sharp, almost upturned tip to the cone. In many ways they resembled the breasts of a fifteen-year-old, their size alone indicating that they belonged to an older girl. Picking up a copy of *Ski* magazine and passing the door of the equipment room, she walked towards the sauna. As she did so she heard the noise. Caroline stopped, and holding her head on one side, listened carefully. Silence. It had been a single, sharp sound. A ski boot falling from a bench? The wood of the sauna cracking as the heat increased? Certainly there was nobody around. Peters, the butler, was in the main house. Otherwise, it being evening, the small army of cleaning ladies that came during the day would have left for home. What Caroline did not, could not, know, as she climbed out of the skin-tight jeans, pulled off the white cotton briefs and opened the door of the sauna, was that Peters was already quite dead, lying on the floor of the hall in an ever-widening pool of his own blood, his throat slit from ear to ear, the ash white of his face a dramatic contrast to the dark red halo that surrounded it. Peters had opened his last door.

The all-embracing heat welcomed Caroline, caressing

279

her naked body. She closed her eyes and let the muscles go, one by one. Peace at last. For five wonderful minutes she lay motionless – in limbo – her mind in neutral, thoughts slowed, her brain concentrating only on the out-flow of tension as her body loosened up. She opened her eyes, noticing the beads of sweat that were already begin-ning to appear on her breasts and upper arms and among the blonde pubic hairs. Soon she would be soaking wet as the water poured out of her. She sat up and flipped a copper ladle full of green pine essence onto the hot coals, sensing the immediate increase in temperature as the liquid vapourized to steam. She lay down once again, and, letting her legs fall apart, she thought of Miles. In forty-eight hours they would be together, making love with all the incredible intensity of their long-thwarted passion. That was why she had wanted this time alone. Time to ready herself for some mystic sweet communion, or some more pagan rite. She drew her knees together, squeezing them tight as she allowed her mind the unaccustomed luxury of fantasy.

This time there was no mistaking the noise. Somebody, something was moving about in the equipment room. If it were not for the churchyard quiet of the sauna and Caroline's finely developed senses, she would not have heard it. As quietly as she could, she opened the door of the sauna, the cold air a welcome relief from the potent heat. Her bare feet made no sound on the tiled floor as she listened outside the equipment room door. Nothing. She opened the door and stepped into the room. At once the well-known smells assailed her – wax, leather, oil and plastic. Through the gloom she could make out the shelves of ski boots, the racks of skis. She was not particularly frightened or nervous. Those emotions, on the whole, had always managed to pass her by, but she shivered involun-tarily with the cold, the heat of the sauna already forgotten, like the warmth of a summer's day in the depth of winter.

She reached out for the lights, but her hand never got to the switch. Instead she found it enclosed in that of a large, unknown man who loomed up out of the darkness like an iceberg, unexpected and unannounced, appearing suddenly from the swirling mists. Simultaneously she was attacked from behind. A strong arm reached between her legs and gripped her crotch, lifting her upwards and forwards, while another snaked around her neck. Before she could shout or struggle she was airborne, immobilized, her left arm twisted behind her back, her neck in a vice-like grip, alien fingers buried deep in her pubic hairs. She opened her mouth to shout out and as she did so a wet ether-soaked rag closed over it. In the few seconds before she lost consciousness Caroline felt, with unutterable horror, a rough finger slide into her vagina.

The three men felt her go limp.

'Hit the lights, Enrico,' said a commanding voice, the English good despite the heavy Spanish accent. 'So far so good.'

The men blinked as the lights came on, their eyes acclimatizing slowly, as they surveyed the figure of the unconscious Caroline. The ether pad was still clamped tightly to her face by a swarthy Colombian, who appeared to be an equal combination of fat and muscle, a menacing version of Michelin man.

'For Christ's sake, don't suffocate her, Paco. Let some air in with the ether.'

'She sura looka good,' said Enrico, an unpleasant weasel-like Hispanic, wiry and mean-looking with a pock-marked face. Enrico was no stranger to naked girls, many an unsatisfying afternoon having been spent slavering in the front rows of Miami burlesque shows. Beautiful naked girls, however, were no part of his experience at all. The outline of his prick in the dirty, tight, blue jeans registered his prurient interest.

'I goin' to enjoy this beet, José.'

'OK. Get on with it – make it look good,' said José impatiently.

José and Enrico pulled one of the heavy leather-topped lockers from its position against the wall and together they lifted the insensible Caroline, face upwards, onto its top, her limp head hanging over one end, legs dangling over the other.

'You know what to do,' said José.

Licking his lips and swallowing hard, Paco, the fat Colombian, released the anaesthetic pad. Caroline, still deeply asleep, breathed heavily. With his other hand Paco fumbled at his zip and in seconds his stiff, short stubby penis was in his hand. He pinched Caroline's nose shut and, as her mouth opened in a reflex action to continue breathing, he pushed his prick inside, letting out a little sigh of gratification as he did so. Simultaneously Enrico dropped his trousers and pulled down his grubby Y-fronts, so that both hung obscenely around his knees. He crouched down and moved towards the rear end of the bench, his long, pointed, sallow penis jutting forward expectantly. With both hands beneath Caroline's hard buttocks he lifted her towards him and with a sudden darting motion he buried his prick deep within her.

The brilliant flash was followed by the whirr of the polaroid. José watched the film as it developed before his very eyes. It had to be a good reproduction. He would shoot a whole film, he thought, as his eyes feasted on the macabre spectacle. One or two of the pictures would undoubtedly find their way into his own personal collection. Filthy pictures, indeed. The delay suited both Paco and Enrico. Paco would himself have preferred an awakened Caroline, attempting to scream for mercy as he violated her, but for Enrico this was by far the best way. Usually women criticized his performance. On this occasion there could be no complaints at all. By the time of the sixth photograph he was ready and with a high-pitched whinneying yell he shot his load into the unknowing Caroline, polluting her body with his filth.

'That's it. Let's get moving.'

The three men wrapped the sleeping Caroline in a blanket and bundled her outside to the waiting car. It would be a long journey.

They left two pieces of evidence of their unwelcome

282

visit. Pinned to the forehead of the unlucky butler was a colour polaroid of Caroline's sexual humiliation.

# III

Miles was taking it very easily indeed. Roy and he were anchored off the reef enjoying a morning's snorkelling. He had been in the water for two hours, exercising and watching the colourful fish that made skin diving in the Florida Keys some of the best in the world. The twenty-one-foot Robalo with its twin Mercury '175' engines bobbed gently in the swell and the sun beat down on Miles' dark body as he lay prostrate on the foredeck. One hundred feet from the boat Roy Felty's snorkel spouted water as he returned from a dive. This would be Miles' last day in Florida. Tomorrow he would be in Aspen with the woman he loved. A new life would be starting – one that promised everything. For the moment he was content to enjoy the sun and the ocean. Through the headphones of the Toshiba portable stereo system with its radio attachment came the sounds of the local country music station, WCBT.

'Seems like yesterday, but it was long ago . . . The secrets that we shared, the mountains that we moved, caught like a wild fire out of control 'til there was nothing left to burn and nothing left to prove.'

Miles was far away, walking once again in the olive groves, standing with Caroline in the chapel of San José, sitting at the refectory table watching the candlelight illuminate her beauty.

'That was Bob Seger and the Silver Bullet band, with their hit, "Against the Wind" – now stand by for an important news flash.' The DJ's voice came through.

'Station break,' thought Miles idly.

'Police in Aspen, Colorado, have announced that Ameri-

283

can skiing champion, Caroline Montgomery, of the chemical family, was last night forcibly abducted from her Aspen home. During the intrusion a member of the household staff was violently slain. It is not as yet known if Caroline Montgomery has been harmed, but police believe that she has been kidnapped and expect a ransom note soon. Ms Montgomery has recently returned from the World Cup skiing competitions in Europe where her phenomenal successes had all but assured her of the World Championship. Now both the championship and possibly her life are in jeopardy. We will keep you informed concerning any new developments.'

Miles was on his feet, screaming at Roy. He flipped the ignition switch and the twin Mercurys roared to life. A sick fear and a mighty rage welled up inside him as the boat bore down on Roy.

Roy Felty's head broke the surface and he pulled off his mask, his eyes questioning at Miles' sudden approach.

'Caroline's been kidnapped,' he yelled. 'I've got to get to a telephone. Jump in.'

Flat out, the Robalo demolished the three miles to Key Largo.

'Who would *do* that?' asked Roy.

'I suppose it must be the money,' said Miles, trying to keep his voice even. 'They killed someone, probably Peters, the butler – so she's in danger if she's not dead already.' His mind was totally disembodied, the emotion draining from him as he metamorphosed into the man of action who had been given a purpose. He would have to save her. To do that he needed information. To obtain it he needed a telephone. The nearest one they could think of was the pay phone outside the Pilot House Restaurant on Fisherman's Cove. You could moor a boat right next to it.

Miles called the Aspen number collect and was soon talking to a sobbing Eleanor. She gave him the facts, but she didn't mention the polaroid. Eleanor knew that Miles loved Caroline, knew too that she planned to marry him.

She couldn't tell him that, could anyway hardly allow herself to believe in its dreadful existence.

'Have you any clue who they are – what they want?' asked Miles, his voice shaking with the strain.

'None yet. The police say we shall know soon. They killed poor Peters.' Eleanor began to cry again. 'How could anybody do such a thing?' she sobbed. 'Oh God it's so dreadful – poor Caroline. What have they *done* to her?'

'Where are you going to be?' asked Miles.

Eleanor tried to pull herself together. 'Charles is with me now. We flew in at lunchtime and we're going back to New York this evening to set up an operations centre in the Montgomery office. The CIA director and the FBI people will all be meeting there. I want you to be with us all. Can you get here as soon as possible?'

'I'll be there in four hours,' said Miles. 'Eleanor, listen, get the banks together and collect a big pile of cash – used notes. If it's money that they want we'd better be ready.'

'Oh, Miles,' said Eleanor despairingly, 'already it's getting out of control. The kidnappers left a note saying not to contact the police or they'd kill her, but by the time I learned of it it was all over America. One of the cleaners found Peters and of course she went berserk.'

'Don't worry,' said Miles, in a forlorn effort to calm Eleanor. 'They must want something. They won't kill her before they get it.' That was not very tactful, but it was probably true.

'Have the Aspen police got any leads?'

'They're pretty sure she's been flown out of the state. They found a stolen car abandoned at a small airstrip a hundred miles from Aspen.'

Miles' stomach was in a tight ball, his fists clenched, as he forced himself to think clearly, to accumulate information.

'She wasn't due back till today. What was she doing in Aspen last night?' he asked.

'She flew in early. She said she wanted to have time to herself to get ready to see you.'

Eleanor was near to collapse. Miles heard Charles Cabot Lodge's voice comforting her in the background.

'Eleanor, try to be brave. I'm leaving this minute,' said Miles as he hung up, tears of helpless rage in his eyes.

Roy Felty's Stingray Corvette consumed the Florida Turnpike at well over one hundred miles per hour on the way to Miami airport, and minutes after their arrival the hastily chartered Lear jet was filing its flight plan and readying itself for take-off.

As Felty bear-hugged him goodbye on the tarmac he said, 'Miles, when you catch up with these guys let me in on the action, won't you?'

Miles knew exactly what he meant. The Great American Way, the majesty of the law, the supremacy of the courts, would not be Miles Parmere's way, and it was not Roy Felty's way either. Theirs would be the justice of the old frontier, with a few modern refinements.

# IV

Harry burst into the study of Castelli's mock-Tudor Coral Gables home like a rocket burning off from the Cape Kennedy launch pad. He was in a frenzied rage, a homicidal maniac loosed from the padded cell.

'They fucked it all,' he screamed. 'Those fucking cunts of yours threw it all away. Those bloody wops killed the butler. God! God! Can't your people do anything right? I told you to have his teeth loosened a bit and they only go and cut his head off. Christ!'

If Castelli was as worried as Harry he was working at not showing it. 'So they waste the butler,' he said coolly. 'José said he gave them lip.'

'Gave them lip?' Harry was incredulous. 'Who cares? He gave *me* lip, but I didn't pull his balls off. When I see José he's going to find out what it's like to be really insulted.'

'Oh shut up, Harry,' said Castelli, tiring of the histrionics. 'This has been your mess from the beginning.'

There was, indubitably, truth in that, Harry was prepared to admit, calming down a bit. It could not be denied, too, that there was a certain satisfaction to be gleaned from the contemplation of Peters' bleeding corpse. That was one mess the supercilious butler would not have to clean up. Otherwise the kidnap had been an unmitigated disaster. Harry had planned it so that nothing would leak to the press, to the FBI or the police, calculating that Eleanor would deal with Castelli's and his emissary both speedily and secretly. The sexual shenanigans that he had ordered would, he had calculated, concentrate her mind wonderfully. She would do anything to get Caroline back from the sexual quagmire into which she had apparently been plunged. Of course all negotiations would have been done through an intermediary, one of Castelli's faceless foreigners, and the ticket for Caroline's release would not have been a hard one to produce. Eleanor would use her leverage with Cabot Lodge to discover exactly what the Russians were up to and within twenty-four hours he would know and Caroline would be returned, blissfully unaware of the more unpalatable aspects of her ordeal. Harry would then be in a position to make his decisions.

Of course both Eleanor and Cabot Lodge would know that he was implicated, that he was the man with the motive, but as all the arrangements would have been handled through Castelli's shadowy organization it would be impossible to prove. His alibis were cast iron. He had arranged well-attended business meetings during the entire period of the kidnapping. And if Eleanor and Cabot Lodge attempted to force an investigation of his role in the affair they would have to spend the rest of their lives looking over their shoulders, worrying about not only theirs, but Caroline's, continued good health. Of course, his days of influence in New York and Washington, such as they were, would be at an end but they were hardly money in the bank anyway if his recent reception from both the Secretary of State and Eleanor Montgomery were anything to go by.

It had been, in conception, an elegant plan, thought Harry. It would have achieved his objective of obtaining the vital information and causing maximum heartache in the process. He had pictured the agonized discussions as to whether or not Caroline should be told about the polaroids. And there was Parmere, too. Whether he found out or not about Caroline's degradation Harry Fox would be able to savour his revenge as long as he lived.

But now of course it was a whole new ball game. There was a corpse. Murder One. What did they do in Colorado? Death by injection? Gas chamber? Electric chair? Life in prison, perhaps, for the man who screwed up the career of America's and Colorado's best-loved athlete? Prison in Colorado, where they liked to ski. He wouldn't last five minutes.

They had botched it up. You couldn't push a dead butler under the carpet. This was real life, not some Agatha Christie whodunnit. So much for secrecy. Now it was FBI time, CBS time, even BB fucking C time. Christ! Every Fed in the country, every cop, every sports fan, every amateur detective from eight to eighty would be out looking for Caroline. Army, Navy and Air Force, too, from President Wayne's initial reaction. Already the media interest was phenomenal and the White House had come out with a presidential statement in which Wayne 'prayed that the evil perpetrators of this unspeakable crime should be brought swiftly to justice'.

There was, however, one good thing about the whole business. At this precise moment in time nobody had any possible reason to believe that either he or Castelli had anything to do with Caroline's abduction. One popular view, already gaining wide credence among the more gullible of the conspiracy theorists, was that the Russians themselves were behind the kidnapping, incensed by Caroline's success in the World Cup. 'Reds under the beds' as a philosophy had made something of a come-back under the no-nonsense conservatism of the Wayne administration.

So at least he was not suspected. It would have to remain

that way. That in turn meant that he couldn't approach Eleanor in any way over the matter of the Russian diamond sales. It was far too late for that.

'Is she on Soldier Key yet?' said Harry at last.

Castelli nodded, a faint smile on his face.

'And José, Paco, Enrico – they're there too, where they can't make any problems?'

'Yeah,' said Castelli, beaming broadly now.

Harry suddenly had the feeling that he was digging a pit for himself, falling into a trap. Castelli had been leading him on.

Castelli flicked his bullet-like head towards the corner.

And then Harry saw her. Little Susie – like a spectre at the feast, pale and shaking – was sitting, all but invisible, legs curled up beneath her, in a high-backed chair.

'Hello, Harry,' she said.

An icy finger poked at Harry's heart. He saw immediately that Castelli had destroyed her health and her mind, but there was something else. She had overheard every word of their conversation. She would have to be killed. There was no other way. And Castelli had watched it happen – let Harry shoot off his mouth knowing that he was signing Susie's death warrant as he did so. Castelli had manipulated him into extinguishing the one creature on earth that had given him genuine pleasure, who had actually seemed to care for him. Castelli had taken her from him, tired of her, and now it would be his, Harry's, job to destroy her.

Leering, Castelli turned to Susie. 'Run upstairs and pack, Susie,' he said nastily. 'I think "Uncle" Harry wants to take you home.'

'You piece of shit, Nero,' said Fox after the door had closed behind Susie. 'You could have stopped that.'

Still, this wasn't the time to fall out with Nero Castelli. They must stay as closely united as coupling dogs. Divided they would be knee high in it.

'Listen,' said Castelli, 'we've got the girl locked up on Soldier Key with ten of my Colombians looking after her. OK, so they screwed up topping the butler. You're the ideas man. What do we do now?' Castelli was back on the sarcasm trip.

Harry stood still, deep in thought. 'If you were a respectable kidnapper and you'd just grabbed hold of the daughter of the richest woman in America, what would you do?' he said at last.

Castelli smiled his appreciation. 'That's right. She has to be worth a lot of cash. $100 million easy.'

'And the rest,' said Harry.

'That would go a long way in South America. And if we went in for $300 million we could get the Mob off our backs if the diamond deal goes sour,' said Castelli hopefully. 'If we do it properly and cover our tracks we might be able to hang on here in America, with the Mob out of the equation.' Castelli wasn't really convincing himself.

'No way,' said Harry. 'That's too much and we couldn't take the risk of being able to keep the lid on it. Once we'd blown the girl away – and we'd have to do that – the solids would really hit the fan. There would be vast rewards, all the power of the government behind the search, and the public, too, for that matter. It would be Linbergh mark two. No, it would have to be "goodbye, America", if we take the money option and then do her in.'

'Yeah,' said Castelli. 'We can't really release her – not after the polaroid – and the whole thing going public.'

'OK, so we go for cash: $150 million in used banknotes. And we'd better get the escape line organized, too.'

For several hours the two men made their plans. Both Harry and Castelli would leave more or less immediately for Soldier Key, where Caroline was being held. Castelli's fast ocean-going yacht would be moored nearby and at the slightest sign of trouble they could cover the four miles to the international waters of the Gulf Stream in minutes. They would have ten bodyguards there, too, as well as the crew of Castelli's boat. There could be no safer place in America. In fifteen minutes they could be lost in the Caribbean, in a few hours across the Gulf of Mexico to South America. If the Montgomerys paid up they would not find 'friends' hard to make. So, who wanted to be David Rockefeller anyway, thought Harry. Maybe it was all going to be all right after all.

Unknown to either man, however, there was already a fly in the ointment, a spanner in the works. Susie had left the room and closed the door, but she had not gone upstairs to pack. Instead she had done exactly what any self-respecting child would have done in the circumstances. She had played Keyhole Kate. Wise in the ways of the world she had taken in the basic message. The bottom line was that Susie was a dead duck. She made her decision very quickly indeed. The old soldier's fate would not be Susie's. She would go out kamikaze-style. She stood up quickly and ran to the bedroom. Usually Susie was watched all day, but the bodyguards had thought she was with Castelli. Now she reached behind the heavy mahogany chest of drawers, her fingers soon finding the little 'Snoopy' address book in which she kept her telephone numbers – numbers that in happier times had been her passport to both pleasure and income. So they'd kidnapped Caroline Montgomery and intended to kill her, were holding her on Soldier Key. She pushed her match-like finger into the 'P' slot. Parmere, Miles. The Ocean Reef telephone number was next to it. She dialled the number. Miles would know what to do. He wasn't afraid of Castelli, or anyone. The story of his treatment of the two gangsters in Palm Beach had already reached folklore proportions in the twilight world of Miami's criminal classes. Susie's heart sank as she heard the recorded announcement.

'This is Lord Parmere speaking. I am not here at this minute and this is a recorded announcement. However, if you leave a message after you hear the bleep with your name and telephone number, I will contact you as soon as possible.'

Fuck. Still she would leave a message. He would get it eventually. Perhaps it would not be too late.

She spoke urgently into the telephone. 'Miles, this is Susie, remember? Harry Fox's Susie. We met in Palm Beach. I can't talk long. I'm in danger. Harry Fox and

Nero Castelli have got Caroline Montgomery. They're holding her on an island called Soldier Key. They are going to ask for $150 million ransom, but they intend to kill her anyway. There's also something about Russian diamonds – and killing the butler made a difference.'

She put the telephone down. Would Miles believe her? Had she given him enough information? Susie sat down on the bed. How long had she got? Minutes? Hours? She couldn't get out of the house. There were bodyguards all over the grounds, electric fences, Dobermanns. All the guns were locked up. She stood up, a look almost of serenity on her face. Fourteen seemed young to die, but she would leave her mark. She tiptoed down the stairs and let herself into the garage through the side door that attached it to the house. The two gallon cans of gasoline were so heavy that she nearly dropped them on the stairs, but she made it back to the bedroom. Next she went to the bathroom cabinet where Castelli kept the heroin. In the normal way she would not have risked the terrible beating that was her reward for stealing it. This time there would be no retribution. Working quickly she filled the syringe with a mammoth 'fix', several times the normal dose. From the drawer she took a box of matches.

Methodically she undid the stoppers on the cans of petrol and poured the gas all over the room, covering herself from head to toe at the same time. She sluiced the curtains, opened the door and poured the high octane liquid down the stairs. Then, like some child sacrifice to a god of war, she took up a position, cross-legged, on the big bed. She found a good vein, one that she had been saving, and bound the long stocking that she kept specifically for that purpose tightly above it, cutting off venous return to the heart. The vein stood out, blue and clear from the white of the surrounding skin. Deftly she pushed the needle in and drew back on the plunger, watching the dark red blood curl like smoke into the clear liquid of the syringe. She loosened the tourniquet and with a deep sigh of relief thrust the bolus dose of heroin into her bloodstream. The warm feeling of peace hit her instantaneously, but she retained enough motive force to complete the second, and ultimate, part of her plan. As the syringe sagged, empty against her arm, the needle still embedded in the vein, Susie lit the match.

In the study below Fox and Castelli heard the roar of the flames and smelt the fire at the same time. They had time to get out onto the lawn, but only just. Within half an hour Castelli's home, his pride and his joy – the subject once of a four-page spread in *Architectural Digest* – was reduced to a smoking ruin. The Matisses and the Picassos, the fake Degas, the genuine Canaletto and the disputed Franz Hals went with it.

'It looks as if little Susie did our dirty work for us,' said Harry, as tears of frustration and anger poured down Castelli's cheeks.

## V

While Nero Castelli's house burned to the ground, Miles Parmere sat, head buried in his hands, in the study of Eleanor's penthouse apartment in the Solo Building in New York. Charles Cabot Lodge was pouring him a large, dark beaker of Scotch. The two men were alone. On the glass table in front of Miles sat the tiny square of coloured celluloid.

'We thought you ought to know, Miles. We can't hold anything back from each other while there's still a chance of finding her alive.'

Inside Miles the anger gushed like a fountain of boiling blood. The room swam before his eyes and his body went hot and cold as he gave himself over to the emotion of hate. Icicles pricked at his skin and frozen hands clutched at his heart and then the temperature seemed to change again. A burning desire for revenge shot through him, scorching, searing his soul, consuming his mind. His hand crashed down on the table and a terrible cry exploded from his lips. There was no form to the sound he uttered, but there was no escaping the hurt, the anguish and the rage that had fathered it; the frustration and helplessness that had given it birth. It sent cold shivers down the spines of those gathered in the large drawing room next door. Eleanor, Skip, Ing, Nigel, Peter Walters, the FBI director, Colonel Leigh, the controller of the SWAT teams, and Ralston, the assistant director of the CIA, all lapsed into a nervous silence.

Miles drank hard and long on the amber liquid and as he did so he made a holy vow. Whether or not Caroline was rescued he would bring violent death to the perpetrators of this crime. Nobody who was in any way connected with it would survive the fearsome retribution that his wrath would bring to them. They would be expunged from the face of the earth, blotted out. Where possible their deaths would be cruel, painful, terrifying. They would be recycled, their foul flesh turned into daisies, bacteria, into the protein of fishes. Not one of them would live to speak of their act, to profit from their iniquity. All of them would be tried and found wanting in the private court of his mighty vengeance. If the work of destruction took him a lifetime, then so be it. He would seek them out, hunt them down, track them to their lairs in the farthermost corners of the globe and as they defecated, or made love, ate their food or prayed to their gods he would visit them and they would know as they saw his face that their lives were finished.

For twenty minutes he fought to regain his control and at the end of that time he was ready to face the others. He walked into the next room, calm once again.

The introductions were made by Eleanor, and Miles made lightning appraisals, as he himself was analysed by the others. Ingemar, solid as a rock, big and strong, and Caroline's friend and mentor. His firm handshake and honest eyes told Miles he would be a valuable ally. Skip, danger and hurt in equal measures reflected in his face, the veteran with the Air Medal who could fly a helicopter through the eye of a needle, who had saved Caroline's life before. He, too, would be a useful friend. Nigel, close to tears, willing and loyal, but perhaps lacking the hardness, the coolness, that Miles was looking for. And then there were the professionals – competent, concerned, but fundamentally politicians, theorists, word specialists, desk jockeys. As Miles had expected they were making all the running.

'I was just saying, Lord Parmere, that of course the first thing is to find Caroline. Now we have to face the possibility that the kidnappers have been frightened off by the publicity and have either killed her or released her. The second possibility rather remote, I'm afraid. Most likely, however, they will still try with a ransom note of some sort. So I am afraid that at this point it is mostly a waiting game.'

Since Lindbergh, kidnapping in the USA had been made a federal crime and Cabot Lodge had made sure that this was being dealt with at the highest possible level. Walker, the FBI director, who had just spoken, seemed sensible and realistic if a little tactless and uninspiring.

'In the meantime the search in the field goes on at maximum intensity. We have no evidence as to identity apart from the Latin appearance of the men in the photograph, headless though they are. Forensic analysis of the inside of the stolen car supports the evidence that they are indeed Hispanics. My gut instinct says Florida and California are the most likely states in which she is being held. We're concentrating the search there. One of our psychologists has suggested that the very extreme provocation offered by the polaroid might indicate a group of people who might have a very special grudge against Caroline or the Montgomerys, or perhaps the class that you represent. Another has suggested the possibility of a purely sexual motive – you know – a group of mentally unbalanced fans . . .' Walker's voice petered out. Nobody wanted to hear *that*, although, thought Miles, he was correct to explore every angle, however potentially painful.

'Of course we'll know much more when and if the

ransom note arrives,' he added by way of changing the subject.

'What's policy if there is a ransom note?' asked Miles.

'We pay it and then try to trace it. Of course we'll need evidence that she's alive – that might provide something to go on. The name of the game is to get a fix on her.' Walters' choice of phrase was not a particularly happy one.

'And if you get a fix?' asked Miles.

'Well, it's been our experience that in the majority of these cases the victim is killed after the payment and successful collection of the ransom. At that point, if we know where she is, we go in with the SWAT teams and all necessary back-up.'

That was exactly what Miles had *not* wanted to hear.

Colonel Leigh, a hatchet-faced, leathery old soldier, who had clearly pulled off a trick or two in his younger days, now spoke. 'Our boys are trained to shoot very straight – experts in this sort of thing – and we have access to Army, Navy and Air Force equipment and personnel. We go in with everything we've got. The chances would be fairly high we'd get her out in one piece.'

Skip cut in. 'I don't think that's a good idea,' he said. 'Americans just aren't good at that sort of thing. It's like Vietnam all over again – the same mistake. You can't just go in there with everything you've got, tons of equipment – all gung-ho and do-or-die. Everyone will get blown up, including Caroline.'

'Now listen here, young man,' said the Colonel. 'I don't know what rank you held in the Forces, but I really don't think you have the experience to talk about these things. Leave it to the experts.'

'No, Skip's quite right,' said Miles forcefully. 'If this were Israel – fine. They know how to do this sort of thing. It's all to do with teamwork, split-second timing and surprise – that's the most vital thing of all. Look at the chaos in the Iran "rescue" and compare it to Entebbe. You've got to be cool and calm, go in with a small, highly trained force, keeping a very low profile and hitting them when they least expect it. The more equipment and personnel, the less surprise and the more things there are to go wrong. I'm afraid your boys have been trained for a different war. They're the greatest soldiers in the world for a set-piece infantry or tank battle, but guerrilla fighting is not their bag – I suppose because it's fundamentally sneaky and undemocratic.'

Ralston, the CIA man, came in on the side of the Colonel. 'I must disagree strongly with that assessment,' he said. 'I must remind you that this entire operation is now under the statutory control of the FBI, who have standardized their procedure after the consideration of a large body of experience in these matters.'

'Oh God,' thought Miles, 'if the kidnappers don't kill Caroline these cunts are going to do it for them.'

For a couple of hours the conversation dragged on, but in the absence of any new information no important conclusions could be reached.

Through most of the discussion Eleanor remained silent, often sobbing quietly, Cabot Lodge's hand on her shoulder. Now she spoke. Still Chairman of the Board. 'It's ten o'clock and I think we should all try to get some sleep. We can do nothing until we hear from the kidnappers and the telephone lines are manned twenty-four hours a day. Let's all arrange to meet back here at eight o'clock tomorrow morning to re-assess the position.'

The meeting broke up.

Miles was staying in one of the guest rooms of the apartment. Skip, Nigel and Ingemar were in a suite at the Plaza across the road. Miles was able to have a brief word with the three men before they left, but the bond that already existed between them in the form of the absent Caroline was so strong that there was hardly any need for conversation. They would do anything to get her back, everything to obliterate her abductors.

Miles lay on the bed, impotent and alone. The dreadful photograph was indelibly printed on his mind, but there were other even more terrible speculations. Would sexual humiliation merge into sexual torture? Worse? He had to do something, but what? Caroline had disappeared without trace. She could be anywhere in America. Or South America.

Absentmindedly he dialled the Ocean Reef number and waited for his recorded announcement to end before rewinding the messages with the remote control bleeper. And there it was. Susie's frail voice was speaking to him. Her sole legacy, her last will and testament, but one whose effects would be every bit as devastating as she would have wished. Six times Miles rewound the message, his heart lightening with excitement, his mind working flat out as he carefully transcribed Susie's words. Castelli, Fox, Russian diamonds, the dead butler, a $150 million ransom demand, Soldier Key. It hung together. There were loose ends, but Miles could begin to see how it might add up. It had to be for real. There was a motive at last, apart from the cash. Castelli and Fox had revenged themselves on everyone, himself included. Susie couldn't have known that it was the butler who had been killed. The press had only mentioned the death of a 'member of the household staff'. And Soldier Key. Roy Felty's words came back to him – 'In fact there's a rumour he keeps a bunch of them in a sort of murderer's doss house on a small island he owns just north of Key Largo – a place called Soldier Key.' That was it. The pieces of the jigsaw were in place. A ransom note for $150 million, not a penny more nor a penny less, would be the ultimate confirmation.

Miles jumped from the bed and stood for a minute or two lost in thought as the plan began to form. His initial reaction had been to rush next door and tell Eleanor and Cabot Lodge, to set the wheels in motion for the FBI rescue operation, but now he saw clearly what he must do.

He walked to the telephone and dialled the Florida number. Roy Felty's voice answered.

'Roy? Miles. Listen, remember what you said about helping out? Well, I think we're in business. Can you make the Hatteras available for the next few days? Also get hold of a helicopter. Rent something fast and with an open passenger door. I can't tell you more on the telephone, but

I'll be with you tomorrow morning, hopefully with two friends. And Roy, how well do you know Soldier Key?'

'Pretty well. There's good snorkelling off the island. I've anchored off there half a dozen times.'

'Great! Dig out the marine charts on that whole area. Oh, and Roy – one more thing – remember that arsenal of yours? I think this is the time for one of its regular overhauls.'

'I think I hear what you're saying Miles,' said Roy, excitement in his voice. 'Do you have a chopper pilot?'

'I will have,' said Miles, 'in ten minutes flat.'

Miles made his second call.

Skip answered the telephone. He had only just got in.

'Skip. It's Miles Parmere. Look, it's incredibly urgent. Can you and Ing meet me in the bar immediately? Make some excuse to Nigel, but don't bring him along. OK?'

Skip and Ing had agreed immediately that the rescue could not be left to the FBI and when Miles had outlined his plan and told them about Roy Felty and his private arsenal, any lingering doubts were banished. But there were other reasons for their enthusiastic responses. Miles had seen the look in the eyes of Skip and Ing many times before. The look of men who had seen their best friends blown to smithereens, or crippled for life. Included in that peculiar and distinctive facial expression was the awareness that they had at hand the means and opportunity for revenge. The urbane sophistication of the Plaza bar was indeed an unusual environment for the emotions that shone from the faces of the three men at the corner table, but it did little to dilute their force. The waiter whose job it was to serve them had encountered a strange unwillingness on his own part to approach the table, and was not at all sure of its origin. It was as if an aura of deadly menace hovered around the trio, almost a smell of death and destruction, strong forces of violence and devastation. The waiter made a mental note to go easy on the coke. This was clearly the beginning of a paranoid reaction.

Early next morning the final link in the chain was

completed and Caroline's whereabouts absolutely confirmed. A ransom note demanding exactly $150 million in used banknotes had been received, together with complicated delivery instructions. Little Susie had got it right.

In standard moves, much like the opening of a world-class chess game, the negotiating machinery had been put into operation. Time would be required to raise the money, the kidnappers were told, evidence of Caroline's continued survival would have to be provided.

But Miles, Ing and Skip, telling no one of their intentions or destination, had already left New York bound for Florida. At Miami airport they were met by a bright-eyed and eager Roy Felty. Famine and pestilence were not on the agenda, but as the rented Fleetwood purred down US1 to Key Largo, the four men resembled nothing so much as the Four Horsemen of the Apocalypse. The three Vietnam veterans and the former skiing champion would re-create a South-east Asian hell on earth for the forces of the ungodly.

# Chapter 11

## I

Caroline woke up very slowly indeed. Movement of her head was painful and caused a cold, clammy nausea and an uncontrollable desire to vomit. For a minute or two she succumbed, heaving and retching, her powerful abdominal muscles in spasm as she voided the meagre contents of her stomach onto the earthen floor of her cell. Green bile, foul tasting, burned her throat until, at last, the awful sickness passed. Caroline was sitting on the floor in what she realized, with disgust, was a pool of her own waste. Her watch had gone and she had no idea of where she was or of what had happened to her. Carefully she searched for bearings, sought to make sense of her experiences, as the memories flooded back. She had been in the Aspen house, having a sauna, and had gone to investigate a noise. She remembered entering the locker room and the sudden smell of ether, and then nothing. She tried harder. Could she remember snatches of Spanish accents, the sensation of movement, a plane, a boat? She couldn't be sure. One thing was totally clear. She had been kidnapped and was now being held prisoner, but where, by whom, why? It was evening and very hot in the small airless room. It was December so that meant a Sun-Belt state, and she thought she remembered a boat. Could it be an island off Florida? California? Spanish accents would do for either.

The cell was small, six feet square she reckoned, and the tiny window was up by the ceiling, impossible to reach. The door with its wire-mesh observation window certainly looked solid. She looked around for tools or weapons of any kind. Nothing. There was no furniture, no mattress, just a small plastic container full of warm water. That was at least something, she thought, drinking from it greedily.

Caroline considered her predicament. Presumably she had been kidnapped for money. Her family could and would pay, but that did not mean that she would necessarily be released. She had a better than even chance of being murdered. The sickness burst over her once again as another awful realization struck her. Even if she survived it might be weeks, months before she was released. That meant goodbye to the World Championship. A very few days in her present circumstances would destroy the benefits of a year's training anyway. Then there was the question of what she could expect in the way of treatment from her kidnappers. She was totally naked. That gave little encouragement that they would treat her well. Covered in excrement and vomit she undoubtedly was, but she remained a superb and tantalizing specimen to anyone less than fastidious about personal hygiene.

The black cloud of despair descended on Caroline as she reflected on her rapid transition from the heights of happiness and success to the depths of misery and mortal danger. Very quietly she began to cry, great tears of fear and anger pouring down her cheeks. It was lucky that she was in blissful ignorance of her ordeal at the hands of Paco and Enrico, but Caroline did not feel fortunate. She thought of her mother, frantic by now with worry and grief, and of Miles, who had been on the point of flying to meet her. And Caroline thought of her dead father. Would he be watching over her? What would he have wanted her to do?

And then, as if answered immediately by a heavenly voice, she knew exactly what she would do. She would do in fact what she had striven so earnestly to do all her life. Caroline would win, or die in the attempt. She would not only survive she would triumph. There was no other way. She marshalled her thoughts. She had to prevent these people from killing her or raping her. She had to be released as quickly as possible and in the interim she had to keep fit. If she got out of this soon enough, and in one piece, she didn't intend to let the World Cup go by default to the Russian. She had about twelve days until Aspen.

She'd better start sussing out the opposition. Anyway she should eat. Caroline hammered on the door with her fists and shouted out. Within minutes the weasel face of Enrico was pressed against the thick glass square set in the door. Several times during the course of the day he had given vent to his voyeuristic longings, feasting his eyes on the comatose Caroline.

There were ten Colombians in all on Soldier Key, under the command of José. It was a shifting and shiftless population, there being a rapid turnover as contract killers were imported for a few weeks, turned loose in Miami to do their worst, before being shipped back again to be lost for ever in the sprawling anonymous cities of South America. Enrico, Paco and José, however, were more or less permanent residents, employed on a long-term basis by Castelli. As such their influence and authority was disproportionately large on the island and the other free-lance gunmen tended to avoid them. Instructions regarding Caroline had been strict. Nobody was to talk to her and at no time when she was being fed should there be less than two men in her cell. She was to be kept without clothes, blankets or any implement with which she might harm herself. Castelli did not know her at all.

So far these instructions had been kept to the letter because the word was that both Castelli and Fox would be arriving on the island early next morning on Castelli's fast Baglietto, *The Hedonist*. It was a brave man who would disobey the express instructions of Nero Castelli. Enrico was not brave, but he was intensely sexually frustrated. He had an itch that he could not scratch and it was driving him to distraction, his natural cowardice at war with his naked desire. He could not get it out of his mind that he, Enrico, had actually penetrated this beautiful creature, this famous athlete, and he had, for once, not been found wanting. He even had a polaroid picture to prove it. He was far from being an intelligent man, and had managed to avoid confronting the inescapable truth that Caroline had hardly been a willing, or even a knowing, recipient of his lust. In short he harboured some scarcely perceived desire that she might intimate to him that her experience with him had been not unpleasant, even enjoyable – that he was a *macho hombré*, who knew how to please a girl. Even the tired and ancient prostitutes on whom he spent the largest part of his not inconsiderable earnings never failed to comment adversely on his sexual performance. It was indeed a rare phenomenon for him to complete the sexual act uncriticized. Now he leered at Caroline, and, fingering the stiletto in his pocket, he resolved to disobey Castelli and investigate at closer quarters the object of his desire.

Caroline stood up as he came into the cell. She did not attempt to cover herself. There seemed to be no point. The gesture would end by being more provocative, by drawing attention to her nakedness, than if she brazened it out.

Enrico's hungry eyes roamed over her. 'So you wake up at last,' he said, not unkindly.

'Where am I? Why am I being held here?' she asked.

Enrico laughed. It was not a pretty sight. 'No questions.' His eyes fastened on to her breasts.

Caroline noticed the beginnings of his erection. Oh God, he was going to rape her.

'You look pretty good,' said Enrico, licking his lips. 'You very beautiful woman – eh?'

Caroline was undoubtedly beautiful, but she was covered in filth, and at this precise moment in time would not have wanted to be covered in anything else. However, from the look in Enrico's eye Caroline could see that he was undeterred, perhaps in some perverse way even stimulated, by her appearance. She thought fast. She had lost count of the number of articles that she had read on the subject of rape. She racked her brains to remember the recommended course of behaviour. As far as she could recall, there were two basic schools of thought on the subject, as is so often the case, both diametrically opposed, and both to some extent supported by the 'evidence'.

There were some who suggested that the prime consideration was the avoidance of physical injury, this school doubtless failing to accept the proverbial truth that sexual violation was a fate to which death was preferable. This body of opinion advocated falling in with the rapist's requests – grinning and bearing it in effect – even pretending to enjoy it. The disadvantage of this approach was that it did little if anything to discourage the rape itself except in the small proportion of cases in which feminine disgust, fear and disinclination to submit constituted the major part of the rapist's pleasure. In *that* case it might easily cause the very violence that the victim's behaviour had been designed to prevent.

An equally vociferous group advocated immediate aggressive action as the best method of discouraging the attacker. The 'kick 'em in the balls' school were, on the whole, thought Caroline, made of sterner stuff, prepared to fight and risk injury to avoid bodily pollution. In the ordinary run of events she would have tended to side with them. However, she was in no position to make an effective getaway, while cries for help would almost certainly be counter-productive.

'Thanks for the compliment,' she said at last, managing a sickly smile.

This rather threw Enrico. Caroline with a tongue in her head was a very different proposition from the supine, insensible form he had violated in Colorado. That exercise had been not far removed from the perversion of necrophilia, for which Enrico had always had a certain fascination.

'You and me,' he said with rather less certainty, 'we make it pretty good.'

Caroline had no idea at all what he meant by that. Presumably he was not too good on his tenses. He was making an unwelcome prediction. She was on to his sudden nervousness immediately. At the same time she thought that she noticed that his erection had decreased in size. Stay with a winning streak. Perhaps she would be able to treat his penis as a barometer, using it as an indicator as to what behaviour would turn him off. A woman in this situation had to use every bit of information she could.

'Perhaps if you got me some water I could clean myself up a bit and we could talk – kinda get to know each other a bit.'

God, nobody could fall for this, thought Caroline.

Enrico's erection was now near to being a thing of the past.

A long conversation while they 'got to know each other' was the very last thing he wanted. Nobody who had ever got to know him in the past had liked what they'd found out. All Enrico wanted Caroline to do was to tell him that he had been a great lover, Rudolph frigging Valentino, Don fucking Juan. After all he'd stuck it in her. It wasn't much to ask.

Once again his tongue darted over dry, cracked lips. She needed some prompting. She'd better watch out this one, better not make fun of him. He was beginning to get angry with her. He didn't know why but his erection had gone. It was her fault. She was making him feel small. He felt like hurting her. He put one hand in his trouser pocket and felt the cool steel blade. He would stick something in her.

'You know when we grab you in that house in Colorado I give you good strong fucking – you remember that?' A decidedly nasty tone had crept into his voice.

Caroline felt faint. Oh Christ. Had this worm been inside her? She felt her stomach heave, but in the nick of time she caught hold of herself. Her reply had to be right. She had noticed the change in him. She was in terrible danger. What should she say? It was like a game show – in which box was the $20,000, in which the booby prize? If she had pants on Caroline would have been flying by the seat of them. She relied in the end on blind instinct. Somehow she knew what he wanted to hear.

'So it was you. I had this wonderful dream that I was being made by this incredible man.' Caroline would not have been a serious contender for the Oscar nomination, but she managed to convey some small intimation that in her sexual experience Enrico had been unusual, unique.

It was enough, more than enough. She had pressed the right button. Great waves of gratitude poured out from Enrico. He had received a compliment at last, a mighty infusion to prop up his crumbling confidence in his manhood. Caroline watched the danger recede, the cloud of potential violence melt away.

'I give it pretty good, eh?' said Enrico, feeling better than he had in years.

From then on the sailing had been plain. In a few short minutes, they had an unwritten, almost unspoken contract. Enrico would not touch her. In return she would intimate to the others that she was making it with him, that he was a great lover, a man who knew how to sock it to a woman. In exchange, for the time she was on the island Enrico would protect her. She would pose as being his 'girl'. And so Caroline got some water and some ice, soap and a big bowl of chili, a packet of biscuits. So far so good.

As soon as she had eaten she set to work. Isometric exercises. She visualized the pages of the Canadian Air Force handbook, and worked through it by muscle groups. For aerobic exercise there would be jumping up and down and from side to side.

If she could get enough water and calories she could keep herself physically fit. In her experience that meant that to some extent the mind could be left to look after itself. *Mens sana in corpore sano*. She would concentrate hard, disciplining her mind and body at every second. She was very good at it indeed.

Enrico swaggered out to the pool where half a dozen men were lounging about. There wasn't much to do on Soldier Key except swim and drink. On the whole the latter was more popular, the pool being used for cooling down purposes only. A large trestle table stood next to the pool laden with soft drinks, tequila, and jugs of pineapple and tomato juice. In the shade of a Tiki hut the ice machine hummed twenty-four hours a day so that the Colombians could keep themselves in a state of semi-permanent anaesthesia, minds and senses dulled by the alcohol. The other substances in which they trafficked and for which they killed so effortlessly were completely disallowed for anyone in Castelli's employ. It was the kiss of death to be caught using heroin, although a blind eye was usually turned to an odd snort of coke.

'So that gringo girl, she come to appreciate what I provide,' Enrico lied boastfully, pushing out his chest as far as it would go.

The others stared at him with lack of interest and disbelief. However, he had publicly staked his claim, and although he was a small man his reputation with a stiletto was formidable. Apart from the three 'regulars', Paco, Enrico and José, nobody wanted to know very much about the girl being kept locked in the cell at the back of the house. It was not unusual for people to be kept there. Often they would scream a bit at night. In general, however, the itinerant population of Soldier Key felt that the less they knew about such things the better. Certainly they realized that it was part of their function to protect the house and island and they were never far from their guns, which sat on tables around the pool, hung in holsters from the backs of chairs. By no stretch of the imagination, however, could they be described as being on maximum alert or even combat readiness. To them it was more R and R with a touch of non-specific sentry duty thrown in.

In case his previous message had not filtered through, Enrico reiterated it. 'From now on I take responsibility for looking after the girl,' he added defiantly.

'So long as you answer to Castelli when he comes tomorrow,' said José.

'No problem,' said Enrico.

# II

The four men sat by the barbecue in Tugboat Annie's open-air bar in Fisherman's Cove, Key Largo. The weathered, bleached table with its roof of latticed palm fronds recalled some hostelry on a Robinson Crusoe island rather than one on mainland America. It was about an hour before dusk, but still warm although the sun, spent and weary now, was preparing for its night's rest. Across the causeway the sleek Hatteras was berthed between two ocean dive boats, scarcely moving on the glassy water. On the flying bridge one of the two boatmen that Roy employed polished industriously at the instrument panel as a giant pelican flew overhead. The tranquillity of the scene was not outwardly disturbed by the conspiratorial mutterings of the quartet, now the bar's only customers. The subject matter of the conversation was, however, far from peaceful. They were discussing nothing less than total war and how best to wage it. There was beer on the table, but nobody was drinking.

'Can you handle a Bell 147?' asked Roy. 'It was all I could get at short notice, and on a "bare boat" basis. What did you fly in 'Nam?' He spoke briskly, professional to professional.

'I can fly anything,' said Skip. It was neither a boast nor a reprimand and was not taken as either. It was a simple, accurate statement of indubitable, uncontrovertible fact. 'In 'Nam I flew mainly Huey Cobras,' he added.

'Miniguns?' asked Roy.

'I used to carry one Minigun and a 40mm grenade launcher, both in remote control turrets, plus four stores pylons for 76 rockets – 2.75 calibre. I guess the rented Bell doesn't run to that sort of firepower.'

They all smiled, glad of the opportunity.

The Minigun was one of the most fearsome weapons to be used in Vietnam. Capable of firing six thousand rounds a minute they would automatically track from side to side on a ten-degree pivot. In many ways it hardly resembled a gun at all, more a harbinger of death. Helicopter gunships and converted transports carrying Miniguns were often referred to as Puff the Magic Dragon.

'I saw a training film once,' said Miles. 'A chopper with a Minigun would make one pass over a football field, fifty yards by one hundred. They'd let a rabbit out in the middle of the field so that it could run about. On each pass the rabbit died.'

'We've got an M60,' said Roy.

Skip whistled his appreciation.

'It's a standard infantry general purpose machine gun – you know without the twin grips and the pintle mount of the helicopter conversion.'

'No problem,' said Skip. 'We can rig up the bipod mount on the passenger seat – maybe strap on a side-mounted sling, too. Will you be door gunner?'

Roy nodded.

'You were in the SEALS weren't you?' said Skip, genuine respect in his voice. SEAL stood for Sea, Air, Land guerrilla warfare, the dirty tricks department of the US Navy – more or less the equivalent of the Special Forces. They were sometimes known as the Black Berets, although their intense individuality and unconventionality meant that they seldom wore any uniform or distinctive clothing of any kind. The Navy connection in theory restricted their operations to within ten miles of any waterway, but in Vietnam, criss-crossed by canals, that in effect included most of the country. Roy had spent two tours mostly in the Mekong Delta region – a large portion of his time up to his neck in water. He preferred that. The water slowed down the bullets and you could piss as you walked along. Like Miles, Roy had fought the war like the VC, often on patrol for a week at a time. There was always a heavy-equipment man on his seven-strong patrols, carrying a loaded M60. He knew the weapon backwards, could change its barrel in record time, strip it with his eyes closed.

'Yes, sir,' Roy replied to Skip's question. 'And you?'

'7 Squadron, 17th Air Cavalry.'

They exchanged long glances, sizing each other up. Soon they would be going into action together. Although only a one-off operation, it brought the memories flooding back to both of them. It was going to happen all over again. But this time there was a difference, a clear purpose, an evil enemy, a life to be saved – and not just any life. The hormones were on the move once more.

Miles' finger jabbed at Nautical Chart 11451, which lay on the table in front of them. He opened up the 'Cruising Guide to the Florida Keys', with its aerial photograph of Soldier Key. 'Of course it would be good to fly a recce mission, but surprise is our most valuable weapon.'

They all nodded their agreement – Ing feeling totally lost in this military situation, but well aware that matters were being handled in an expert manner.

'Now Roy, you say that the house is L-shaped with the pool in the angle of the L – actually you can just see that from the photograph. So if you and Skip come in with the chopper from the east, out of the sun, and head towards the pool, in the morning, say at eleven o'clock, they're bound to come out of the house to investigate if they're not poolside already. You waste everybody you see and keep spraying the house with the M60. Ing and I will drop off from the Hatteras late tonight and paddle the last three kilometres in the Zodiac so as not to alert anyone. We'll spend the rest of the night in the mangroves at the south end of the island and then travel north just before dawn to take up position at the back of the house to wait for the start of your air assault. We synchronize for eleven o'clock precisely.'

'In the confusion of the helicopter attack we'll get into the house and secure Caroline. So, say, three and a half minutes from the first shot you land the chopper and start a ground attack from the far side of the swimming pool. We have surprise, firepower and, I suspect, rather more experience than the opposition. They have greater numbers and a more precise knowledge of their terrain. That's our biggest disadvantage. And we don't know exactly where Caroline is. Hopefully when the shooting starts the Colom-

bians will be too busy trying to stay alive to hurt Caroline.'
The tone of Miles' voice suggested that remaining alive
would be an unrealized ambition on the part of the
Colombians.

'So we moor the Hatteras approximately here, in nine
feet of water,' said Roy, 'leaving the boatmen on board.
That's good. There are two submerged wrecks in the way
of the conventional approach to Soldier Key, through the
so-called "safety valve". I wouldn't fancy trying that at
night.'

'We'll fix up the M60 in the chopper tonight and load it
up generally. Three cans of 7.62mm – that's 4,500 rounds,
the Light Anti-Tank Weapon and two M16 rifles.' Logistics. Miles' military training was second nature to him.

Roy chipped in. 'Yeah, and I'll take the grenades, too –
incendiaries, frags, 40mm, the lot. They might be useful
for mopping up operations.' Roy Felty was excited. He
had acquired a certain partiality to the smell of napalm in
the morning. He had one further embellishment to suggest.
'Oh, and while you guys were getting yourselves down
here, apart from going over the equipment I found some
time to mix up a Fu-Gas.'

'Christ, Roy!' said Miles.

'What's that?' asked Ing.

'Well,' said Roy, a gourmet cook now, describing a
favourite recipe, 'you take a fifty-five gallon drum of
gasoline and pour liquid soap into it, making a kind of
napalm. Then you take a Thermit incendiary grenade, a
mixture of powdered aluminium and metal oxide, and tape
it onto the front of the drum. A stick of dynamite goes
underneath the drum. You put a number 2 cap on the
Thermit and a 4 cap on the dynamite. When they blow the
dynamite pushes the napalm into the air and the Thermit
ignites it. Everything within a two hundred yard radius is
burned to a cinder. You haven't lived till you've seen it –
and a lot of people have died a split second after they did.'

'That'd be useful for covering tracks, destroying the
evidence,' said Miles, thoughtfully. 'OK, so tonight you
take the chopper up to the Ocean Reef. We can arrange for

you to spend the night there in my house. Soldier Key is only a few miles north of there. Let's synchronize watches now, not that timing will be much of a problem, because we'll be in position behind the house not later than eight o'clock and we'll be able to hear you coming anyway. Any questions?'

There were no problems. Everybody knew exactly what to do. Each had his own fantasy of what would happen if he got close to one of Caroline's kidnappers. No one would have been prepared to voice them.

Miles looked round the table. He couldn't ask for a better, more highly trained and expert assault team. And they all had a motive. If they did not succeed then nobody else could. 'Right,' he said, 'Ing and I will try to sleep for a few hours and aim to be in the Zodiac by about three o'clock and on the island well before dawn. During the assault we'll wear red arm-bands for recognition. Otherwise we'll use standard US Forces hand signals for communication if you are still airborne.'

There was nothing more to say.

Skip and Roy stood up to go. Now they would transport the weapons, already stacked in boxes in the stern of the Hatteras, to the Bell helicopter at Key Largo airport to load up for the short flight to Ocean Reef. All four men shook hands and wished each other good luck.

One thing was for sure. There would be dead people in the morning.


While the Hatteras left its berth and cruised north towards Soldier Key, Miles and Ing tried to sleep. Neither was entirely successful. Miles could not banish from his mind the ghastly visual evidence of Caroline's horrible ordeal, the fear of what she might have experienced since – and, always, the anger flooded in knotting his muscles, grinding his teeth, setting his whole body on edge until the thought of his revenge went some way towards alleviating the cold rage that periodically gripped him. Ing, too, lived with his dark thoughts, as he tossed and turned on the bunk bed. Caroline had become his life, and he would not let anybody take his life from him a second time. Already he had centred his mind on the man who, he felt, was ultimately responsible. This was Nero Castelli's island, Castelli's gunmen, Castelli's revolting plot. He, Ingemar Jorgensen, had a plan for Castelli, a very specific plan. It would involve Castelli's violent death, and it would not be a pleasant one.

Both men were relieved when the boatman turned on the lights and told them that they were within half an hour of the drop-off zone.

Miles looked at his watch: 2.30 am. Skip and Roy would be struggling to get an hour or two's sleep at the Ocean Reef house, the helicopter, fuelled and equipped, standing ready at the private airstrip.

Sitting on the edge of the bed, Miles quickly stripped and reassembled the AK47 assault rifle, more out of habit than necessity. He secured the moving parts with black insulating tape, winding it round the barrel to prevent any chance of reflection.

Ing watched him, reassured by Miles' efficiency and coolness. If they all survived this Miles Parmere would make Caroline a good husband. Ingemar never imagined he would meet the man about whom he could say that.

'Now, Ing, we've got to find some artillery for you. Have you had any experience of guns?'

'I did National Service in Sweden with the Mountain Troops. I've never used an M16, but I've kept my hand in with a pistol.' Tears filled his eyes momentarily as he thought of the competitions with the Secret Service, of Caroline's determination to win and of how she had made him apply for a gun licence so that they could all practice, unknown to the opposition. Those days seemed light years away now but their legacy, his own firearms skills, persisted.

From the Roy Felty private arsenal Miles selected two .45 Colts, the seven-shot semi-automatic standard US Army sidearm.

'Watch out for the recoil. At close quarters these leave

a big hole. It won't matter much where you hit the target.'
He showed Ing the three safety devices.

It was time to get dressed. Roy had thought of that too.

Miles selected a 'Nam leaf camouflage tee-shirt, matching trousers, lightweight canvas jungle boots and a similarly camouflaged recon. vest with front zipper, cut off at the arms. He filled some of the many pockets with spare magazines for the AK47. To the green webbed belt he attached the Italian diving knife in its black plastic sheath. Black axle grease on the face and neck. Apart from camouflage, it would help ward off the mosquitoes during the hour or so before dawn in the mangroves. Carefully Miles supervised Ingemar's preparation. At last they were ready. It was three o'clock.

Slipping quietly over the side into the small black rubber Zodiac they took a final compass bearing on Soldier Key before pushing off from the side of the Hatteras and paddling away into the blackness.


# III


The noise was like that of a distant lawnmower. One by one, the men gathered around the pool of Soldier Key became vaguely aware of it.

It was a peaceful scene. About eight men in all, instantly recognizable as of South American origin, were taking the mid-morning sun, indulging in a liquid poolside breakfast. Already the long trestle table was laden with the day's supply of refreshments. There were phalanxes of heavy glasses and big jugs of tomato juice, fruit, bread and cheese. Three of the Colombians clustered around it, having risen from their beds only minutes before. Three more men had already braved the pool and stood talking to each other in Spanish in the shallow end, leaning against the pool wall, large tumblers of Bloody Marys in their hands. Two more, one of whom was fat Paco, lay basking, stretched out on sun beds, reading, or rather looking at the pictures of comic books. .375 Magnum revolvers in leather holsters were hooked over the upright sections of their chairs.

Two hundred yards from Soldier Key the Castelli yacht, *The Hedonist*, bobbed serenely on the gentle swell. It had arrived that morning from Miami and Castelli himself was already ashore taking a mid-morning cup of coffee with José and Enrico in the dining room of the house. Harry Fox had stayed on board the boat, unwilling to mix too freely with Castelli's 'soldiers' or get too close to the Montgomery girl. To all intents and purposes he was now on the run, although his increasingly large catalogue of crimes had not actually been discovered yet. The trip to Soldier Key was the first step in his flight from the world he knew, but as yet he had not acclimatized to his new role as a fugitive, and for the moment he preferred to be by himself. He was breaking his fast on the polished teak table of the after sun deck of the Baglietto – grapefruit and black coffee. From this vantage point he had a clear view of the island and its big house, although the pool, on the eastern side of the building, was obscured from his view.

Caroline, in her cell, had not slept well. Hot and sweaty, she had, however, continued to drive herself on and now she sat, cross-legged and still naked, on the earth floor, attempting to remember the names of every single one of the children who had shared the lessons of her childhood in the private schoolroom of the Aspen house. That completed she started on their addresses, parents' names, favourite foods. With phenomenal concentration she dragged back the fractured memories and pieced together the jigsaw to complete the picture. It was a surprisingly satisfying activity. Of all the people on Soldier Key, Caroline Montgomery was the most engrossed, the last to realize that something very terrible was about to happen. It was eleven o'clock precisely.

The noise of the engine could now be seen to be coming from the small fly-like object that bore down on Soldier Key. One by one the poolsiders turned to focus upon it, lack of interest the dominant emotion. In the dining room Castelli and José heard it and José got up from the table and moved towards the open window to investigate. The two men were alone, Enrico having been dispatched to the kitchen to bring more coffee. Apart from Caroline, lost in thought in her trance-like state, Harry Fox, who was sheltered to some extent from the sound waves by the land mass of Soldier Key, alone did not realize that the island was being approached by a helicopter.

From the open window José peered upwards into the sun, shielding his eyes with his hands. He turned and spoke over his shoulder. 'There's a helicopter coming straight over the island,' he said.

'Sightseers. No sweat,' said Castelli reassuringly. It was no big deal. All over southern Florida bored holiday-makers, searching for something to do apart from sun-bathe, were taking advantage of the helicopter rides that were offered everywhere at $150 for fifteen minutes. Property speculators, too, favoured this method of seeking out suitable new investments, or of checking up on existing ones.

Around the pool one or two men reached for their sun-glasses, the more closely to inspect the intruder.

Wap-wap-wap. The helicopter was coming in fast in a looping, spiralling approach, a hungry mosquito heading for exposed skin, an angry hornet seeking retribution for disturbance of its nest. In the trees, yards from the back door of the house, Miles Parmere thumbed off the safety on the AK47, while next to him Ingemar performed the same operation on the twin Colt .45s. The soldier in Miles checked his watch. Everything was going according to plan. Soon the holocaust. Once again he scanned the exposed space between their hiding place and the door that they would use as their point of entry to the house. Muscles tensed, he braced himself for action.

Peering through the Porsche sun-glasses, Skip took in the rapidly approaching scene, his heart leaping for joy as the panorama unfolded. They were all out in the open, sitting ducks. It would be a turkey shoot. They couldn't have hoped for better. And then, after the split-second's exhilaration, he was the cold professional once more. He did not have to shout to Roy – would not anyway have been heard above the roar of the rotors. He would bank sharply and fly across the pool at right angles giving Roy a clear enfilading fire across the whole area. On the second run they would hit them with the grenades.

Skip sent the Bell into a tight, curling descent and levelled off before turning into the bank, the force of the turn pressing Roy against the passenger seat. The edge of the swimming pool area floated into the rear site of the machine gun. Roy Felty gently squeezed the trigger.

The roar of the M60 and the crash of the heavy wall of bullets against the stucco surround of the pool was the only announcement to the Colombians of their imminent journey to a different sphere of existence. At the deep end the water began to boil like a Californian jacuzzi and a wave of steaming bubbles raced in milliseconds across the surface of the pool towards the three men who were still standing in the shallow end. Their glasses arched through the air, spraying a cloud of red juice above their heads. There it merged imperceptibly with another red liquid, the life-blood of the three Colombians. The M60 burst had been aimed at the surface of the water as the helicopter flew past two feet from the ground. It was the exact level at which the belly buttons of the three men had once been. It would have been true to say that the second before there had been three separate entities in the pool. Now it would be more accurate to say that there were six. They had been cut in half. Like the sea around a sinking troopship in the midst of a shark-feeding frenzy, the water of the pool turned a dark crimson as it received the instant transfusion of the best part of twenty-seven pints of human blood, the total plasma volume of three fully grown men.

Nor was the discomfort confined to the swimming pool. A residue of bullets had struck the far side of the pool surround. The lowness of the helicopter's pass meant that the 7.62 mm bullets hit the hard surface at a glancing angle. The four men who had been attempting to ease the pangs of their early morning hunger now had a different and more pressing problem. Like a giant scythe wielded by the grim reaper, the bullets took all three men just beneath the knees and they went down like hamstrung cows, sinking to the ground as if praying in church. It was prayers, too, that sprang immediately to their lips. Prayers of an insistent kind – to mothers, to gods, to anyone that would listen. Those prayers would remain unanswered. Like drowning wasps that will sting indiscriminately, the four men clutched and scratched at each other, fighting to find shelter as if from the noon-day sun braved only by mad dogs and Englishmen.

Out of the eight men only two remained whole in body. The two on the sun beds were protected from immediate destruction by their inertia, the murderous hail of slipping, sliding lead passing beneath their sun chairs. With the quick reactions of their profession they went for their guns. Skip saw the move and immediately anticipated it. The chopper came out of its turn and began to climb once more. At about twenty metres, just out of danger from the hit-men's guns, he held the helicopter steady, hovering hawk-like above them. In Roy Felty's lap the two fragmentation grenades sat like huge bugs, pins already pulled, spoons depressed. Paco looked up and loosed off a couple of quick shots, calculating immediately that the target was out of range. In utter desperation he looked around him, taking in the carnage, the blood, and the fearful cries of the wounded. He made his decision and, gearing up his huge frame, he began to run. It was a wise decision. His colleague showed less prescience. The two black parcels of death floated down towards the pool – one landing amid the seething mass of incapacitated Colombians which heaved and twisted around the base of the trestle table, the other at the lone gunman's feet. In the same way that the water had boiled under the onslaught of the M60's barrage, the flesh, blood, bones, and brains of the four Colombians began to bubble as the fragments of black steel propelled them into eternity. Wipe out.

Paco, his short knees pumping up to his chest, was

already moving very fast indeed for a fat, muscle-bound man, but his speed increased as small bits of steel whirred overhead from the terrible blast that he had so narrowly escaped. There was one hundred yards to go across wide open space to the shelter of the trees, and his heart banged in his chest as he raced for his life.

Lazily, the chopper peeled off from its stationary position, sinking gently to within a foot of the ground. Skip 'flared' the helicopter and brought it down on the grass. Above the roar of the still-circulating rotors he screamed at Roy, 'It's the fat one!' They all knew the significance of that.

Roy Felty jumped from the open passenger exit, the M16 with the grenade launcher attachment in his hand. He knelt down quickly, took aim, and pressed the trigger. Paco had twenty yards to go to the relative safety of the trees. He was going to be all right. He could hide. So near but yet so far. The grenade hit him a stunning blow on the right shoulder, pitching him forward, off balance. As he fell he twisted around through 180 degrees, propelled by the impact of the grenade. For a brief moment he lay flat on his back staring at the sky – almost his last view of the world. It was so peaceful, he reflected, lying there, not having to run. If it wasn't for the pain in his shoulder . . . Paco tried to sit up, momentarily disoriented, his thoughts disorganized. As he did so his eyes flashed one last message to his fevered brain, his last mental act. Lying between his legs, almost wedged between the copious flesh of his thighs, for all the world like a third, diseased testicle, lay the black, serrated 40 mm grenade. And then Paco ceased to exist, wiped unceremoniously from the face of the earth. First to go, atomized, vapourized, reduced to miniscule chains of amino-acids, the building blocks of its protein, was that sad appendage whose sordid exploits had generated so much sorrow and hurt. The mills of God, grinding as ever at their slow pace, had ground, not for the first or last time, exceeding small. Paco had starred in his last polaroid.

*

As the crash of machine-gun fire announced the start of the assault, Miles Parmere launched himself from the trees towards the back door of the house. Ingemar was in hot pursuit. In a second, crouching low, they were across the open space. Miles did not try to break down the door, nor did he rush into the room. If there was anybody inside they would be facing the other way, having turned to investigate the gunfire. Surprise as always was the most valuable weapon of all. The AK47 cocked and at the ready, held in the crook of his left elbow, right finger on the trigger, he bent and with his left hand simply opened the door. He stepped quickly and quietly into the room. It was the kitchen and Enrico, a pot of steaming black coffee in his right hand, stood rooted to the spot. As predicted, his back was towards Miles, as he attempted to make sense of the sounds of total war which had erupted from the front of the house. Miles crossed the room noiselessly and as he did so he transferred the assault rifle to his left hand. With his right, he reached for the Grisbi knife.

Enrico's mind was just about to come off the back burner. The house was being attacked. He should get hold of a weapon. That was as far as his mental processes had got when he was grabbed around the waist from behind. The rifle's snout nuzzled in beneath his jaw, the body of the gun clamped tight against his midriff. On the right side of his neck he felt a sudden, pricking pain as the pin-sharp point of the diving knife hovered over his right carotid artery, already breaking the skin. Enrico went cold and clammy with shock as his peripheral circulation shut down in reflex action, constricting the capillaries and turning him a deathly white.

'Where's the girl?' asked Miles.

No sound came from Enrico's open mouth as he stood stock still in an effort to delay, if not to avert, his fate.

'The girl!' demanded Miles, making a quick sawing motion with the knife – enough to send warm blood running down Enrico's neck.

The voice was a croak as the words rasped from Enrico. 'Last room. End of corridor.'

'Right or left?'

'Right.'

Enrico's mind fought for the brilliant intervention, the remark that might save him from too early an experience of Purgatory. He would have only one chance. 'I saved her from the others,' he offered at last.

'I shall remain eternally grateful,' said Miles Parmere.

He had a funny way of showing it. For a split second the rifle and the encircling arm were removed, but the light that Enrico saw so briefly at the end of the tunnel was the light of the oncoming train.

Miles put his left hand, still holding the rifle in the small of the Colombian's back and pushed with all his might. Never for one instant did the Italian knife move from its position. Enrico dived forward and, as he did so, the razor-sharp blade plunged through the right lobe of his thyroid gland, slicing through the neck muscles, before cutting into the carotid artery like a sabre-thrust into wet blanc-mange. Enrico's arms flung forwards sending a thick stream of black coffee onto the wall where it was joined a split second later by arterial blood pumping straight from the heart at 120 mm of mercury pressure.

Miles stepped quickly over the squirting corpse, speaking quietly over his shoulder to Ing. 'Ing, go to the end of the corridor – last door on the right. Make contact with Caroline. For God's sake, don't let her out. Kill anyone who comes into the corridor.'

Ing vaulted over the dead Enrico, both Colts in his hands. Miles opened the kitchen door leading out into the corridor. From the front of the house he heard the crash of the fragmentation grenades. The diversion was working well. Ing sprinted off to the right and knelt on the floor by the last door.

'Caroline. Caroline. It's Ing. Miles is here. We've come to get you out.'

'Christ, Ing, what's happening?'

Miles tried two doors, but the rooms were empty. The third was the dining room.

Castelli was crouching in the corner. José, a snub-nosed Beretta in his hand, was kneeling by the window. He snarled back over his shoulder, 'They've sent in the fucking Marines.'

They were the last words he said.

Miles fired three shots from the waist. The first exploded against José's shoulder blade. The second shot passed through the upper lobe of the right lung, blowing a hole as big as a tea plate in the area of his right chest where it made its exit. The third bullet entered the right lower side of the skull base where it reorganized the cerebellum and the brain stem. 'Long time since I've seen brains,' thought Miles.

And then there was Castelli.

The muzzle of the AK47 swung slowly towards him, like a tank turret searching for a new target. It centred slap bang in the middle of his stomach. Castelli could almost feel the bullet although the gun had not yet been fired at him. His bowels turned to liquid. Murder was on the face of Miles Parmere. It was plain to see. If anyone doubted his purpose there was José's broken body to prove them wrong.

'How are you going to die, Castelli?' asked Miles.

Castelli lost control of his anal sphincter. Staring at death he shat himself.

'Anybody else in the house?' asked Miles through clenched teeth.

'No,' said Castelli with the truth of the man for whom all lies would now be superfluous. Enrico would have already met José's fate.

Miles called out over his shoulder. 'Ingemar, in here, quickly.'

Ingemar's thick frame loomed up in the doorway.

'Is Caroline OK?'

'Yes.'

Miles hadn't time to feel the relief. That would come later. There were still things to attend to. A final shattering crash from outside marked the demise of Paco. It was followed by a total silence, the lull after the storm.

'I don't think you have met Nero Castelli,' said Miles with the formality of an equerry introducing a provincial mayor to royalty at a Buckingham Palace garden party.

Ingemar Jorgensen stood still and pulsed with his hatred. He had promised himself this moment and now it had arrived. He aimed a .45 directly between Castelli's eyes.

'Crawl over here, Castelli,' he growled.

Castelli crawled. As he did so he thought of past occasions when *he* had made men crawl. In an instant he became a believer. Maybe he could work something out with the Good Lord. Do a deal. The men he had killed and tortured had been honest mistakes; the girls he'd beaten and turned into addicts – a case of poor judgement; and Susie who'd gone out like a Buddhist monk? He hadn't really meant her any harm. In future . . . but there would be no future. No future at all. Castelli was painfully aware that the case he had just laid before the Lord was not exactly a cast-iron one. It looked as if it would be thrown out of court.

He knelt at Ingemar's feet and looked up at him. A faithful dog? A penitent supplicant? Even in this unaccustomed role Castelli still radiated pure evil.

Ingemar stepped forward and in a sudden movement clamped Castelli's neck between his massive thighs. Gritting his teeth to maximize the effort he began to close the two faces of the vice. Castelli was a Brazil nut, caught fair and square in the arms of a silver nutcracker. He fought for breath, his fingers clawing desperately at Ingemar's powerful legs. Stars exploded before his eyes as the venous return from his head was cut off and the pressure in his skull began to rise. The room swam before him, Parmere's face becoming indistinct and blurred. He opened his mouth and tried to scream as Ingemar tightened further the rippling, straining muscles of his upper legs. Castelli's staring eyes began to protrude like those of a fish and his face went a dark crimson and then ultimately blue as its oxygen was used up. And then, deep inside his head, it all went 'pop', and, like a pricked balloon, his whole body went soft and limp.

As Ingemar released the pressure Castelli toppled forwards onto the carpet – stone dead.

Ingemar turned to look at Miles. No words passed. Caroline had been revenged.

Miles looked at his watch. It was two and a half minutes past eleven o'clock.

Roy Felty called out from the front of the house. 'Miles. All secure out here. Are you OK?'

'We've got Caroline. She's fine. Opposition neutralized in here.' Seldom had a situation been so understated. José, Enrico and Castelli had been very comprehensively neutralized indeed.

'That yacht of Castelli's is trying to pull up anchor,' Roy shouted. 'We can take it out with the LAW.'

Harry Fox. Miles had forgotten him. His job was not over yet.

'I'm coming out,' he yelled. 'Ing, you and Skip knock that door down and get Caroline out.'

He raced from the house, passing at a run through the carnage of the war zone. Christ, this was the real thing. The swimming pool area looked like a Jack the Ripper convention, the dissecting room of some deranged anatomist.

Two hundred and fifty yards from the house the Castelli yacht was humming with activity. On the after-deck he could make out the figure of a frantically gesticulating Harry Fox and across the water his anguished commands could be heard clearly. 'Get that fucking anchor up, you turds,' he screamed.

The engines revved mightily and the water churned as the powerful propellers began to rotate.

Harry Fox. The man who'd thought the whole thing up.

Roy ran easily beside Miles, the anti-tank rocket launcher dangling by his side. 'Christ,' he shouted as they ran, 'we really wasted the bastards.'

'One more to go,' Miles grunted.

Side by side they knelt on the little sandy beach. Roy

was dying to use the weapon, but Miles was firm. 'Vengeance is Mine saith the Lord,' he said.

Roy wondered if he had intended the pun.

Miles steadied himself. Quickly he removed the safety pins, and opened the end covers. He telescoped the inner tube outwards, thereby cocking the firing mechanism. Now he leant forward, the launcher held over his right shoulder, right hand on the top and side of the weapon, finger on the firing button. He steadied it with his left hand under the muzzle, and peered through the sight.

Harry Fox stood in the stern, both hands on the rails, staring out at Soldier Key, able only to imagine the devastation that had just descended on it from the skies. He had got to get into international waters. There he'd have a chance. In a few minutes he could be there. What were those two people doing on the beach?

Miles aimed for the side of the boat, about three feet below the place where Harry stood. The engines would be there – and the fuel tanks.

'Goodbye, Harry Fox,' he said as he pressed the firing button.

With a muzzle velocity of 476 feet per second the missile streaked towards the yacht and the flash at the point of firing was the last thing that Harry saw on this earth. The HEAT rocket exploded in the gas tanks of the Baglietto and the bits of Harry Fox were deep fried before they hit the ocean.

The Bell helicopter was five miles from Soldier Key, heading back to the landing strip at Ocean Reef. Caroline and Miles were strapped tightly into the passenger seat, Caroline swathed in blankets. She nestled in his arms and he kissed her gently. The roar of the engine made conversation impossible. There would be time for that later. Now they had to get back, to contact Eleanor, to let her know that Caroline was safe.

The muffled thunder of the Fu-gas explosion carried above the noise of the rotors and, looking back, they saw the orange cloud rise into the sky above Soldier Key. There would be little evidence of the raid. Miles looked down at Caroline's face. What was she thinking? And then in a flash he knew exactly the answer to his unspoken question. She was thinking of January 6th and Aspen. Miles smiled wryly, but he wouldn't have wanted it any other way.

# IV

A transcendental silence had descended, dramatic in its contrast to the noise that had everywhere existed a few moments before. Fear, excitement, dread, hope, were all contained within it, and other, less worthy, emotions, too. Everything seemed to be suspended in time, the motion picture stopped short at a single frame, while in some ghostly projection room an unseen technician worked frantically to repair the fault, to get things moving once again.

Miles, Eleanor and Charles Cabot Lodge stood together, huddled close for moral support. Would this be where it all came undone? A few hundred yards above them, to the right, a converted landcruiser had been modified into a platform, on which, now, the President of the United States and the First Lady stood, peering intently through binoculars, surrounded by secret servicemen and local dignitaries.

All night long in the overcrowded town the discussions and arguments had raged as rumour had worn the mask of fact and truth had known the reception accorded to fanciful exaggeration. Could Caroline Montgomery win? Could she rise above the tragedy of her kidnapping to make the grand slam, overcome the handicap that would have provided the most valid and respected excuse for failure. Soon, within seconds, they would know. It was miraculous that she was racing at all. The media account of the kidnapping and its bloody conclusion had been, to say the least, incomplete. There was the dreadful carnage at the place called Soldier Key, details of which were already seeping out. It apparently resembled a Vietnam battlefield, the trees burned and defoliated, the house a shell, human tissues in such profusion that it appeared many had met their fate. The official line was that this had been an episode in a gangland drug war, a larger-than-life, up-dated version of the St Valentine's Day massacre. There were few in south Florida who doubted this or mourned their loss.

The cover-up had been personally sanctioned by the President on the grounds of national security, and the Coast Guard and the local county police had been persuaded not to press their investigations too diligently. Wayne, nervous lest the progress in the Middle East talks should be jeopardized by leakage of the Russian's diamond plan, was determined that the real reason for the kidnapping should remain secret. Emotionally, too, he approved of the rough-and-ready justice and the cold efficiency of the free-enterprise rescue operation. It would have made the kind of film that he very much liked to watch. Then, of course, there was Caroline, the daughter of his friends. She wanted to marry the English buccaneer who had butchered her captors. It would hardly have done to have him sitting in the Florida state electric chair for successfully doing a job that the FBI would almost certainly have bungled. Nor had Wayne been spared the polaroid. Eleanor had calculated that if there was going to be a secret and total amnesty then that might be a deciding factor. It had not been, but it had made a big difference to Wayne's personal attitude towards Miles. He had not been acting as a callous mercenary, a man who enjoyed inflicting death and destruction, but as an agonized fiancé, who had chosen to act rather than to cry. And then there had been the skiing. Wayne wanted Caroline to win, to beat the Russian, and he had come to Aspen today to watch her do it.

Eleanor slipped her hand into Miles'. She had been distraught when, in the middle of the kidnap negotiations, he had suddenly disappeared with no statement of his intentions or plans. She felt guilty now that she had doubted his resolve, his ability to hang around in the

328

kitchen when the heat began to rise. It was unusual for Eleanor to be wrong about somebody, but now she was prepared to admit openly that she had been wrong about Miles Parmere. If only Bill could have met him. She knew, too, although Miles did not, that there were plans afoot with regard to his future employment. Charles Cabot Lodge and the President had been working for some time on a joint scheme with the British to set up a highly secret anti-terrorist organization, one that would carry the war to the opposition, to the Libyans, to the enemies of democracy wherever they existed. They needed a top liaison man who could integrate British and American operatives and coordinate policy. Miles, a former major in the British army, about to marry a famous American, seemed to both President and Secretary of State an ideal man for the job. After all he had just demonstrated his talents – his organizational ability, willingness to act independently and to accept, even demand, responsibility.

Miles held Eleanor's hand tightly as they both bombarded the Almighty with their prayers.

'If this comes out all right,' said Miles, 'I thought we might announce our engagement at the celebration party. If you approve, that is.'

Eleanor approved and turned to say so when the roar of the crowd announced Caroline's high speed exit from the starting gate.

Caroline had thought that Val d'Isère had been the one that mattered – that if she could win convincingly there the opposition would lose their resolve to compete with her. Well, now they had got it back. There were few if any of her competitors who had rejoiced at her kidnapping, but gift horses were not to be looked in the mouth and most felt that her terrible experience would have taken the edge off her skiing. Certainly Nadezhda's confidence seemed greatly to have increased and she was already leading the Aspen downhill competition by a substantial margin. No longer was Caroline considered an automatic winner. If, as seemed possible, she had been psyched out by her ordeal she could still beat herself. The eyes of the other girls could not hide these thoughts from Caroline and, in the psychological warfare which was such an integral part of World Cup skiing, not a few of them made no effort to conceal their changed view of her.

None of them could have understood the way her mind worked. Caroline positively thrived on challenge and difficulty, used it to push herself further, had found her way to turn adversity to advantage. Today she would go faster than ever before. She would prove them wrong. It was the added incentive she needed.

As she came out of the gate she was already working on getting the vital psychological balance right. An ounce of emotion, two ounces of cool calculation, season with technique, a pinch of anger, a touch of pride, blend with the years of training, serve on the plate of experience. It was a recipe for winning – and for getting down the hill just that bit faster to Miles.

The red, white and blue of the US ski team colours merged into one, becoming indistinguishable to the spectators as Caroline flashed past them at seventy miles per hour. It was immediately apparent that she was skiing with a new brutality and power and there was something almost cruel about the way she attacked the mountain. At this speed she would either win by a mile or end up badly injured. Which would it be? The home crowd screamed their approval and from thousands of voices came the raucous chant of CAROLINE, C . . . A . . . R . . . O . . . L . . . I . . . N . . . E.

Remember to ride a flat ski. Gliding now, no edges till the turn. Watch that bump coming. Keep the mountain smooth. Pre-jump, good! Upper body forward. Back almost parallel to the slope. Hold the line into the turn. Weight the outside ski for the curve.

Caroline knew she was going fast, very fast indeed. There was only one thing that could make her go faster and it was something that she was still learning how to control. Ing and she called it 'synthesis', when the mind stopped working on manual and went over to remote control, when all the energies fused together in the ultimate purpose. Caroline searched for the button, a blind person fumbling for the light, and then suddenly her finger was on the switch. The metaphysical mood enveloped her. Synergy. She came out of the second steep section of the run and the crowd began to vibrate with pent-up excitement. The network newsmen began to babble their commentaries.

'Amazing speed . . . never before achieved in women's skiing . . . faster than most of the men . . . she must fall . . . inspired skiing . . . after her ordeal . . . words fail . . .'

It seemed that almost before she had left she had arrived, wrapped in Miles' arms, way past the finish line.

The time was announced and both Caroline and Miles turned to look at the digital clock.

'Christ!' they both said in unison.

## V

They had to fight their way up to the mountainside house. The President was already there to greet them. For once words failed the wise old politician, as he hugged Caroline and massaged Miles' shoulder.

'You make me proud to be American,' he managed at last and Miles could have sworn that there was a tear in his eye.

Caroline's eyes shone. She had got it all now. Fought for it and won it. The competition was far from over, but there was not a skier on the circuit who had not that afternoon conceded defeat. Now she and Miles would announce their engagement.

They went inside to an enthusiastic welcome from the fifty or so guests who had been invited to the after-race party. Ing, Skip, Roy and Nigel, like small children at a wedding, bubbled their excitement, mobbing Caroline and

331

lifting her into the air. It was their victory celebration as well.

Tray after tray of Pol Roger Rosé Champagne made the rounds and the energy and enthusiasm crackled around the room like electricity. It was a sporting triumph for Aspen and America as well as a personal one for Caroline.

Eleanor shouted for silence. 'Mr President, Mrs Wayne, friends. I have a short announcment to make. Miles Parmere and Caroline have asked me to say that from this moment on they are officially engaged to be married.'

Once again pandemonium broke loose as Caroline and Miles were besieged by well-wishers offering their congratulations.

A few minutes later President Wayne called Eleanor aside. 'I've heard the word that there's an important news headline tonight. Should be coming on just about now. I think we ought to see it. Might be of interest to the happy couple.'

With difficulty Miles and Caroline were extracted from the seething crowd and they all went into the large study where the television was kept. The NBC nightly news was starting.

'In a surprise development today the Russians announced their intention of selling their entire stockpile of diamonds on the open market. Sales are to start immediately. This move is seen by our diplomatic correspondent as an indirect attack on the South African economy. The announcement this afternoon has led to panic selling of diamonds throughout the world, but, in the absence of buyers it has not been possible for sellers to obtain a price for their stones. A spokesman for De Beers, who were thought to exert a monopoly on the sale of diamonds and who had previously handled all sales by the Russians, said that this was a cynical and unfair attempt by the Russians to destabilize the market and advised people to hold on to their diamonds. However, he also stated that De Beers would not be prepared to buy up the Russian stones and would be in effect unable to support the diamond price. Until some stability returns to world markets it appears for the moment that gem stone diamonds have become literally worthless.'

'Well, that lets us off the hook, Charles,' said the President. 'I am afraid it's decreased your net worth a bit, Eleanor,' he added sheepishly.

Eleanor Montgomery didn't have a care in the world. 'I've always maintained that diamonds are for wearing, not buying and selling,' she said cheerfully. 'Think of all those gorgeous Russian stones I'll be able to pick up for small change. And look what a perspicacious husband I shall have,' she added, flashing her ruby and emerald engagement ring.

Cabot Lodge blushed deeply. Could that be construed as profiting from inside information?

'There you are, mother. I always disapproved of your spending all that money on diamonds,' Caroline laughed. 'Now you see, *I* haven't lost anything at all.'

Eleanor laughed louder. 'Caroline, remember when we were in London and that nice Mr Brown brought over the Cartier diamonds. Remember the one you liked, the big pink one?'

Caroline nodded.

'Well, I bought it for you that afternoon. It cost me $350,000.'

Caroline Montgomery was one of the very few people in the world who could find the loss of that sort of money absolutely hilarious. She roared her appreciation.

Miles fished in his pocket, eventually producing a grubby $5 note. 'I'll tell you what,' he joked. 'I'll buy it from you. Make an excellent engagement ring.'

# BIG APPLE

## *Pat Booth*

Anne Carrington – beautiful, intelligent, successful: a top psychiatrist with an exclusive New York practice.

Adam Phipps – poor little rich boy with the looks of a god, the morals of a sewer rat . . . and a computer programme that could crack Wall Street.

Mariel O'Sullivan – angel-faced bad time girl determined to make Adam her meal-ticket, if she can keep him in the gutter long enough.

This explosive trio scorch a trail of passion and depravity across New York and Europe, until Adam's financial dealings trigger off a deadly intrigue that threatens Anne's career – and Adam's life.

Spanning the glittering world of international high-life and the shadowy underworld of bizarre and jaded sex. BIG APPLE is a searing novel of ambition, greed and lust.

**Other bestselling Warner titles available by mail:**

| | | |
|---|---|---|
| ☐ Marry Me | Pat Booth | £5.99 |
| ☐ The Big Apple | Pat Booth | £5.99 |
| ☐ Temptation | Pat Booth | £5.99 |
| ☐ The Lovemakers | Judith Gould | £6.99 |
| ☐ The Texas Years | Judith Gould | £6.99 |
| ☐ Dazzle | Judith Gould | £6.99 |

*The prices shown above are correct at time of going to press. However, the publishers reserve the right to increase prices on covers from those previously advertised without prior notice.*

**WARNER BOOKS**
Cash Sales Department, P.O. Box 11, Falmouth, Cornwall, TR10 9EN
Tel: +44 (0) 1326 569777, Fax: +44 (0) 1326 569555
Email: books@barni.avel.co.uk

**POST AND PACKING:**
Payments can be made as follows: cheque, postal order (payable to Warner Books) or by credit cards. Do not send cash or currency.

| | |
|---|---|
| All U.K. Orders | **FREE OF CHARGE** |
| E.E.C. & Overseas | 25% of order value |

Name (Block Letters) _____

Address _____

_____

Post/zip code: _____

☐ Please keep me in touch with future Warner publications

☐ I enclose my remittance £ _____

☐ I wish to pay by Visa/Access/Mastercard/Eurocard

Card Expiry Date

☐☐☐☐☐☐☐☐☐☐☐☐☐☐☐☐☐☐   _____